Disaster
at
Stalingrad

Dedication

For my friend Thomas Bilbao, without whose enthusiasm, good will,
and original thinking this book could never have been written, and
to whose incisive insights on the Second World War I am deeply indebted.

Disaster
at
Stalingrad

Peter G. Tsouras

Foreword by
Ralph Peters

Frontline Books
London

Published in 2013
and reprinted in this format in 2019 by Frontline Books,
an imprint of Pen & Sword Books Ltd,
47 Church Street, Barnsley, S. Yorkshire, S70 2AS

www.frontline-books.com

Copyright © Peter Tsouras, 2013, 2019

The right of Peter Tsouras to be identified as the author of this work
has been asserted by him in accordance with the

Copyright, Designs and Patents Act 1988.

ISBN: 978 1 52676 073 9

CIP data records for this title are available from the British Library

Printed and bound by TJ International Ltd, Padstow, Cornwall

Typeset by Donald Sommerville

Pen & Sword Books Ltd incorporates the imprints of Pen & Sword
Archaeology, Atlas, Aviation, Battleground, Discovery,
Family History, History, Maritime, Military, Naval, Politics,
Social History, Transport, True Crime, Claymore Press,
Frontline Books, Praetorian Press,
Seaforth Publishing and White Owl

For a complete list of Pen and Sword titles please contact

PEN & SWORD LTD
47 Church Street, Barnsley, South Yorkshire, S70 2AS, England
E-mail: enquiries@pen-and-sword.co.uk
Or
PEN AND SWORD BOOKS
1950 Lawrence Rd, Havertown, PA 19083, USA
E-mail: Uspen-and-sword@casematepublishers.com

Contents

Plates

Unless noted otherwise, all items are from the author's collection.

Plate 1: Keitel, Brauchitsch, Hitler and Halder (*Bundesarchiv 146-1971-070-61*); Joseph Stalin; Roosevelt, Churchill and their chiefs of staff.

Plate 2: T-34 tank with German markings (*Bundesarchiv 101III-Hoffmann-023-11*); Soviet tank production.

Plate 3: Manstein (*Bundesarchiv 183-H01757*); Paulus (*Bundesarchiv 183-B24575*); Seydlitz-Kurbach; Raus; Heydrich; Canaris (*Bundesarchiv 146-1979-013-43*).

Plate 4: Zhukov; Chuikov; Soviet tanks destroyed in battle.

Plate 5: British 'Arms for Russia' poster.

Plate 6: *Tirpitz* in Altenfjord; US Navy drawing of *Tirpitz*; recognition chart of *Admiral Hipper*.

Plate 7: HMS *London* and USS *Wichita*; HMS *King George V.*

Plate 8: USS *George Washington* (*US Naval History and Heritage Command*); HMS *London*; USS *Tuscalsoosa* (*US Naval History and Heritage Command*); USS *Wichita* under fire (*US Naval History and Heritage Command*).

Plate 9: Hawker Sea Hurricane; Fairey Albacore; Douglas TBD; Vought SB2U Vindicator.

Plate 10: Junkers Ju 88 (*Bundesarchiv 101I-421-2069-14*); SS *John Witherspoon*; Convoy PQ-17.

Plate 11: Adolf Galland (*Bundesarchiv 146-2006-0123/Hoffmann, Heinrich/CC-BY-SA*); Josef 'Pips' Priller; Lt. David McCampbell.

Plate 12: USS *Wichita* and *Wasp* in Scapa Flow (*US Naval History and Heritage Command*); *Spitfires* aboard *Wasp* during the Malta operation (*US Naval History and Heritage Command*); USS *Wasp* mortally wounded.

Plate 13: Tresckow (*Bundesarchiv 46-1976-130-53*); Stauffenberg; Rudel; Stuka over Stalingrad (*Bundesarchiv 183-J20510*).

Maps

A Matter of Mastery

I have all but given up reading alternative history. Too many works in the genre are implausible, historically superficial, emotionally naïve, uninformed as to technical expertise and, not least, written in so slovenly a manner that any remaining faith one has in our education systems, whether in the United States or the United Kingdom, collapses like a pup tent in a hurricane. The waste of paper (or electrons, for that matter) in the production of plainly bad books is sufficiently dismaying to turn an oil-company executive into a tree-hugging environmentalist.

But there is one brilliant exception to the sorry state of alternative history: the works of Peter G. Tsouras. His re-imaginings of history always delight, consistently inform, boldly challenge and wonderfully reward discriminating readers (a dying breed, alas . . .). Why are this old soldier's narratives so much richer – and so much more fun to read – than the efforts of his would-be peers? To formulate a useful answer, turn to the 'Five Pillars of Alternative History', the fundamental requirements for such a book to be worth the cost in money, time and intellectual engagement.

Let's take these one by one:

A compelling, convincing vision. If an alternative-history narrative does not grip us with logic – the recognition that this could have happened – the entire structure falls flat. It's not enough to tell a story the author thinks is 'really cool', while ignoring or remaining ignorant of the complex web of facts that render his or her version impossible. (I have never had any patience with what I call the 'spaceships-at-Pearl-Harbor' school of alternative history.) We have to be captured by the recognition that, yes, but for a few matters of happenstance, the author's vision might have come to pass, changing history.

This is one regard in which Peter G. Tsouras excels. Whether writing about the American Civil War or the Second World War, his plots are built on taut logic and a vision so convincingly grounded that the reader's response is, 'Yes, yes! Absolutely!'

The point of quality alternative history isn't to push the envelope into the realm of the absurd, but to delve into the precision machinery of history and make small adjustments to the gears that produce major, inevitably different outputs. Indeed, the worst judgement a reader can pass on a work of alternative history is to reach a point in the book at which he or she slams it shut and declares, 'Naw, that never could have happened.'

So . . . a crucial quality in this author's works (and I have read every one of them, avidly) is baseline believability. The logic of the plots is always finely tooled; nor does Tsouras leave loose ends. His vision is always as comprehensive as it is precise in detail. The book you are about to read is a perfect example of the richness of this accomplished author's grounded-in-fact imagination. Taking his alternative road to Stalingrad, I was, as an old Russia hand, utterly convinced.

Historical and technical knowledge. Two aspects of this author's background give him an enormous advantage over other practitioners in the genre. He is a sophisticated historian with a wide range of period interests (I can't help but hope that this proud Greek-American will, one day, write an alternative version of the Trojan War and its after-effects); and he has had a long, successful career as a US Army officer, as well as concurrent responsibilities from the tactical to the strategic level of our intelligence system. He knows what happened, down to the 'sub-atomic' details, but his insider experience also lets him grasp why things happened and how slight alterations in events or personal relations might have led to very different outcomes. He knows what soldiers can do and won't do; and he knows not only what political leaders are supposed to do, but what they actually end up doing. He's the kind of in-depth historian and experienced soldier who fully understands that, after all of the order-of-battle tables are tallied, the weather and terrain have been analyzed, and the various options studied, a decisive battle may be lost because a key commander had indigestion.

This particular book could not have been written by someone who did not understand historical realities as diverse as the Allied supply route through Iran; ship tonnages on the Murmansk run; Wehrmacht equipment refurbishment policies; the personalities of Soviet and German generals; or opposing sniper techniques. One pleasant surprise for me, by the way, was how thoroughly this soldier understands the environment of mid-twentieth-century naval warfare – his depictions of fleet actions are simply terrific.

Grasp of character. The film may have been fun, but, no, Abraham Lincoln didn't have the temperament or martial-arts skills to be a Hollywood vampire hunter. Alternative history doesn't work if the author doesn't understand the actual personalities of the figures he enlivens on the page – or human complexity in general. One routine problem with alternative-history novels is that they are populated by stick figures, not flesh-and-blood men and women with credible desires, fears, faults and idiosyncrasies. Hitler and Stalin are classic examples. These two men, grotesque and cruel as they may have been, were also human beings with biological imperatives and emotional needs (however twisted). In too many novels or films, Hitler simply rants and Stalin icily orders executions, popping up in plots as cartoons of themselves. In contrast, Tsouras understands that the decisions such men make and the actions they take must be grounded in their actual psychology and mundane circumstances. Of course, the same law applies to less exalted characters, as well.

In developing an alternative-history scenario, an author is free to imagine the behaviour and inner life of a character, as long as his or her projections are based upon the known facts about that individual (this applies to 'straight' historical fiction, as well). When Tsouras re-imagines history, the great names come to life – and make credible decisions based on the different developments confronting them. In his plots there are not only no factual loose ends, but no emotional ones, either. That reflects a detailed study of the historical figures, but also a life of careful observation of his fellow human beings.

Writing ability. Different forms of writing demand different prose techniques. In alternative histories, the focus should be on events and characters presented in transparent prose that never calls attention to itself. The writing should be so clean and clear that it disappears, leaving only the author's vision. But clean, clear writing is very hard. There is always the temptation to turn a clever phrase, or to add another adjective or adverb, or (a common sin) to laundry-list facts that, while showing off the author's research, bore the reader to blood-tears and push him or her out of the plot. Tsouras has been writing professionally for decades, and the practice shows. Even when he addresses infernally complex situations or arcane technical details, the writing is a spotless window that lures the reader to look deeper inside. Tsouras's prose isn't glamorous or extravagant or, for that matter, snappy. It's disciplined and appropriate.

Storytelling ability. Writing ability and storytelling ability are often confused with one another, but, while related, they involve separate talents and skill-sets. In my own writing career, I've encountered many a would-be novelist who, because they wrote competent non-fiction, assumed that they could easily write fiction. But writing a military report, or a business proposal, or journalism or a historical treatise does not automatically equip a writer for the vastly more demanding matter of creating life on the page and making the reader constantly repeat the timeless question, 'What happens next?' The non-fiction writer reports or makes a pitch. He or she may analyze, criticize, proselytize, pontificate or predict, but the effort is always about providing information (true or willfully distorted) to a reader for a practical purpose. The novelist/storyteller, by contrast, is a literary Dr Frankenstein, struggling bravely to create not only a living being, but an entire living world. He or she chooses, from an infinite number of possibilities, the unique combination of body parts that will spring to life for the reader. The non-fiction writer declares, 'It's a fact.' The novelist cries 'It's alive!'

I realize that my point here runs counter to what many well-educated adults imagine, but, having written a wide variety of non-fiction and fiction over more than three decades, I can attest that writing competent (if not artful) non-fiction can be taught to most intelligent people, but creating fiction requires innate talent (that has to be developed with patience and resolve). Prose writing involves a skill-set that can be acquired through hard work; storytelling is refined magic. Tsouras has both the professional writing skills and the gift of narrative magic that let him deliver addictive, rewarding alternative-history treasures. Stir in his deep historical and technical knowledge, his human understanding, and his wonderfully quirky, thoroughly convincing vision of what might have been, and the reader with this volume in hand is in for a rare treat: a book of the first quality, and a hell of a reimagining of the hell that was Stalingrad.

Ralph Peters

(Author of *Endless War* and *Cain at Gettysburg*)

'The Dancing Floor of War'

———•———

There is no doubt that Stalingrad was the decisive battle in the war against Germany. Up to Stalingrad, the flood tide of German victories seemed unstoppable. After Stalingrad it was a remorseless ebb tide for the Wehrmacht that only ended in the ruins of Berlin and a bullet in the brain of Adolf Hitler.

Upon what did this turning point in history pivot? Soviet propaganda emphasized the resolve of the Russian fighting man, Stalin's decisive 'not one step back' order, and the immense output of Soviet war industries heroically relocated to the Urals. All of this was true, but it was not the whole story. What is missing in that is the keystone in the arch of victory.

That keystone was logistics. It is that which feeds, clothes, equips and sustains the fighting man. It begins in the wheat fields, mines and steel mills, continues to factories that produce uniforms, tanks and shells, and its end is when the cook dumps a meal into a mess tin, or a quartermaster issues a new rifle, ammunition or uniform. Disrupt any part of this process, and you disrupt the ability of the armies to fight. Frederick the Great's dictum 'Without supplies, no army is brave' was as true in 1942 as when the Prussian king said it two centuries before.

It is little known that, as the German 1942 summer campaign roared to life, the logistics lifeline of the Red Army, Soviet war industries and the population in general was badly frayed and near to snapping. Most of Soviet war industry had either been lost to the Germans or had been evacuated to the Urals where it was being reassembled. In a miracle of improvisation, many of these factories were put back into operation in a very short time, but it still was not enough. Vital materials such as aluminium and copper were in short supply, the aluminium necessary for tank and aircraft engines, and the copper for myriad uses, especially brass for cartridges and shells. The Soviet Union by then had also lost its richest agricultural lands and a huge part of its population. What remained was reduced to a diet that teetered between constant hunger and malnutrition. Soviet prewar stocks of motor vehicles, especially trucks, had been reduced by more than half, and new production was meagre.

Given these disabilities, how did the Red Army humble Hitler's ambitions at Stalingrad? What was their margin of victory? Though subsequent Soviet historians were loath to admit it, that margin was the massive aid provided by Great Britain and the United States. Edward R. Stettinius, the man responsible for coordinating the provision of war supplies to America's allies, stated, 'Enough supplies did get to Russia . . . to be of real value in the summer fighting of 1942.'[1] The US Army Center for Military History was clear that 'In committing munitions and equipment to the titanic defence of Stalingrad, the USSR knew that material losses could be mitigated in ever mounting quantities by future lend-lease receipts.'[2] Even a major participant in the battle and future leader of the Soviet Union, Nikita S. Khrushchev stated, 'if we had to cope with Germany one to one we would not have been able to cope because we lost so much of our industry'.[3] This author was told by a senior Russian military historian at a July 1992 seminar on the Second World War at the Russian Military History Institute that foreign aid, even in November 1941, exceeded Soviet production, so much damage had the Germans already inflicted by then.

At that time, most aid received by the Soviets was from Britain, provided at great cost to the British war effort and the British people who went short in innumerable ways to support their allies. American aid had just begun and was in the form of raw materials. It was to grow exponentially until, by the time of Stalingrad, American trucks and jeeps, canned food, and dried eggs and milk were ubiquitous to the average Red Army man, one of whom commented that it was only because of Lend-Lease that the troops were able to get more than one meal a day. British and American tanks and planes were making up about 15 per cent of the total Soviet inventories, a not inconsiderable margin. More importantly and out of the sight of the soldier, the factories were relying on Canadian and American aluminium to build four out of every ten tank and aircraft engines. In effect, foreign aid made it possible for the Soviets to complete 40 per cent of these weapon systems. Essentially, for every thousand tanks or planes the Soviets produced by the time of Stalingrad, 150 were made in Britain or the United States, and another 340 were built with Canadian and American aluminium. Without that aid, the Soviets would only have been able to deliver 510 tanks or planes per the thousand they actually did. Supporting this are Stalin's repeated requests for priority materials, with aluminium and concentrated foods such as meat and fats at the top of the lists.

None of this denigrates the bravery or heroism of the Red Army soldier or the sacrifice of the civilian population. It does emphasize, however, that bravery and heroism are far more effective with a tank and a full belly than without them.

Thus this alternative history will take that path not taken, the one of sacks of wheat, tons of aluminium, great convoys stuffed with trucks, explosives, tanks, and thousands of the other countless elements of war that made their way from the fields and factories of Great Britain, Canada and the United States across oceans, mountains and deserts to reach the Soviet Union. Then will the drama of battle be played out.

The weight of woes was not all on the Soviet side of the scale. German resources were inadequate for the campaign that eventually unfolded. Hitler's stated objectives for the 1942 summer offensive were to destroy the bulk of the remaining Soviet field armies east of the Don and to overrun the Caucasus and Transcaucasus regions of the Soviet Union to acquire the economic resources Germany lacked, primarily oil. These objectives were to be undertaken consecutively. However, when Hitler decided to accomplish them concurrently, he badly overstretched German resources in all categories, condemning his armies to be neither strong enough in the attack on Stalingrad nor in the lunge into the Caucasus.

Hitler further compounded these errors by becoming obsessed with taking the city of Stalingrad and condemned his 6th Army to be burned out in what was essentially Verdun on the Volga. Ironically the original planning did not emphasize any importance attached to the city itself other than as a location towards which 6th Army would be directed. The city fighting devoured men the way German mobile operations did not. The Germans called it the 'Rats' War', *Der Rattenkrieg*, so vicious and remorseless it was. Homer, perhaps the most profound observer of men in war, captured the imagery and essence of that battle in lines written some 3,000 years before.

> Both armies battled it out along the river banks –
> They raked each other with hurtling bronze-tipped spears.
> And Strife and Havoc plunged in the fight, and violent Death –
> Now seizing a man alive with fresh wounds, now one unhurt,
> Now hauling a dead man through the slaughter by the heels,
> The cloak on her back stained red with human blood.
> So they clashed and fought like living, breathing men
> Grappling each other's corpses, dragging off the dead.[4]

Hitler again compounded the problems burdening his forces by his chronic inability to accumulate a reserve without immediately expending it. So, as 6th Army screamed for reinforcements, there were no available operational reserves on the Eastern Front. At the same time the Soviets were accumulating huge reserves. Herein is an insight into the nature of German and Soviet command. Hitler's growing insistence that he make all important decisions, which rapidly devolved into reserving his permission to move even single divisions, hobbled his outstanding stable of generals. As Hitler curtailed the initiative allowed his generals, Stalin increased the command scope of his own team of talented officers. He also showed a much more balanced and shrewd strategic grasp, and listened to and often followed the advice of his leading commanders.

What masked Hitler's imposed burdens on his forces were their outstanding combat capabilities. German training and tactical and operational expertise were clearly superior to those of the Soviets. Air–ground coordination was a particularly lethal tactical combination.

What resulted was that German resources dwindled as their forces continued to struggle beyond their culminating point. Soviet resources at the same time continued to grow, fed by a careful accumulation of reserves and the resources in material and supplies provided by their own relocated war industries and the arrival of increasingly large amounts of foreign aid, chiefly through the Arctic Convoys and through the Persian Corridor, with the transpacific route through Vladivostok beginning to come on line. Germany was inexorably losing the war of material. Ironically, it was not their inevitable defeat that strikes one but how close they actually came to winning, as Charles de Gaulle once observed.

In 1944, General Charles de Gaulle visited Stalingrad and walked past the still-uncleared wreckage. Later, at a reception in Moscow, a correspondent asked him his impressions of the scene. '*Ah, Stalingrad, c'est tout de même un peuple formidable, un très grand peuple,*' the Free French leader said. The correspondent agreed. '*Ah, oui, les Russes . . .*' De Gaulle interrupted impatiently, '*Mais non, je ne parle pas des Russes; je parle des Allemands. Tout de même, avoir poussé jusque'à lá.*' ('That they should have come so far.').[5]

'That they should have come so far' offers a tantalizing hint at how close the issue actually was. What would it have taken, within the realm of rational options, for the game to have gone to the Germans is a question that always hangs in the air, with its answer just out of reach.

The decision nodes, where events hung in the balance, are like the railway switching yards of history. The smallest change can send a train laden with the might of armies in a totally different direction. The changes then start branching exponentially.

The great Theban general, Epaminondas called the great plain of Boeotia 'the dancing floor of war', a primal description of a blood-soaked ground that fully applied to that other blood-soaked ground between the Don and the Volga. The task of alternative history is to change the tune on that dancing floor, to see what unexpected fate the new beat and step will bring forth.

Notes

As we march down one of history's roads not taken and into an alternative history of events, that history requires references in the form of endnotes to reflect its own literature – the memoirs, histories and other accounts that it would have generated. These have been added to the real references. The use of these alternative reality notes, of course, poses a risk to the unwary reader who may make strenuous efforts to acquire a new and fascinating source. To avoid frustrating, futile searches, the alternative notes are indicated with an asterisk (*) before the number.

Chapter 1

Führer Directive 41

The Wolfsschanze, Führer Headquarters, Rastenburg, East Prussia, 4 April 1942

As Hitler read through the Oberkommando der Wehrmacht (OKW – Headquarters of the Armed Forces) Operations Staff briefing for Operation Blau (Blue), the plan for the 1942 summer campaign, the angrier he got. The Wehrmacht's Operations chief, Colonel General Alfred Jodl, had become attuned by now to Hitler's body language and braced himself.

'This is not what I want!' Hitler said. He fumed at the plan and its General-Staff trained officers, so steeped in the traditions from Scharnhorst to Schlieffen, the very system that Hitler had concluded was manifestly inferior to the intuitive judgement of his genius. Behind that contempt was the rage that so many of these generals, as well as the senior commanders at the front, had obeyed his orders grudgingly and with the most obvious of reservations. 'No! No! No! I will have no more of these vague, elastically framed tasks!'

By that he meant the mission orders on the *Auftragstaktik* principle that granted the commander in the field great leeway and initiative in exactly how he executed those orders. Freedom of action was the last thing he wanted to give Field Marshal Fedor von Bock, commander of Army Group South. The last time he had done that for his senior officers was in Operation Barbarossa, the invasion of the Soviet Union the previous June. And what had they done with that freedom of action? They had failed to take Leningrad and Moscow and were stunned by the Russians' winter counteroffensive. Their precious General Staff methods failed them when the Russians came howling through the snow to throw them back in panic, that brother to blood-stained rout. The whole army would have come apart at the seams if he, Adolf Hitler, who had held no more than a corporal's rank in the Great War, had not issued his stand fast and fight it out order. He had saved the army through this act of sheer will.

Now they were back to their old tricks. Freedom of action be damned. It was only their way of giving themselves the leeway to fail and then blame it on him. His attitude to the professional army was becoming indistinguishable from what he had once told an acquaintance was the way to deal with the opposite sex. 'When you go to a woman, take a whip.' Now he would hold the whip over the Army's generals.

'I want no generalities, Jodl. Do you hear me? I want this plan in exacting detail.' Jodl attempted to explain that senior commanders were traditionally given the initiative to plan their own methods. The look on his Führer's face made Jodl instinctively take a step backwards.

Hitler snatched the plan out of Jodl's hands and said, 'I will deal with the matter myself,' and stormed off, leaving the man shaken.[1]

The conception of Operation Blau was Hitler's. It was his child, and he now had to take it severely in hand after it had been spoiled into sickliness by the Army and Wehrmacht Operations staffs. He would make a man of it. It had the audacity and ambitious sweep of Barbarossa, but this time he would control it and force it to victory. He went to the map of the Soviet Union and swept his fingers across its south. Here, he said to himself, between the Donets and the Don, we will engage and destroy the bulk of the remaining Soviet field forces.

And all this was to be only the opening move to quench Germany's insatiable thirst for oil. Hitler had been driven in so many of his schemes by an obsession with economic resources, and oil was above all his focus. Oil was vital not only for the Wehrmacht but for the very existence of modern Germany, and Germany had no oil. Its synthetic oil production could not come close to meeting demand, and Romanian oil could not either. The only remaining source within Hitler's grasp was in the vast mountainous region of the Soviet Caucasus and Transcaucasus between the Black and Caspian Seas.

The two oilfields at Maikop in the Kuban east of the Black Sea and Grozny, capital of the Chechens, in the mountains produced about 10 per cent of all Soviet oil. South of the mountains in the Transcaucasus, however, lay the richest oilfields of all around the capital of Soviet Azerbaijan at Baku on the Caspian Sea. These fields produced 80 per cent of Stalin's oil, about 24 million tons by 1942.[2] Transcaucasia, which included the Soviet republics of Georgia, Armenia and Azerbaijan, was also the location of the richest manganese mines in the world, supplying the Soviet Union with 1.5 million tons annually, half of its needs.

The struggle between the Donets and Don was meant only to clear the way for the simultaneous thrust across the Caucasus to the oilfields of Baku on the coast of the Caspian and farther north to Astrakhan at the mouth of the Volga. Oil was what Germany and the Soviet Union both needed. With this stroke he would take it and at the same time deprive the enemy of it. As a bonus, the route for Allied supplies to the Russians from Persia would be severed at the moment when it seemed to be reaching the tonnage of aid sent by the Arctic convoys.

His imagination took flight as he dictated to his secretary ten single-spaced pages of minute directions for the upcoming offensive. As he finished he could see Stalin being dragged in a cage through the Brandenburg Gate to celebrate his triumph.

The Kremlin, Office of the General Secretary of the Communist Party of the USSR, 7 April 1942

Stalin had unconsciously divined Hitler's plan for the summer offensive. All you had to do was look at the map. The wide open steppe that stretched from the Donets to the Volga and beyond fairly beckoned to a mechanized invader. Yes, it would be a drive to the south that the Germans would try, then across the mountains of the Caucasus. This region was rich in economic targets, and he knew of Hitler's obsession with such booty. But then he made a further divination that obscured the spot-on accuracy of the first. He believed that, before heading south, Hitler would drive on Moscow for the decisive battle to take the ancient Russian capital. Only then, Stalin concluded, would he turn to the Caucasus. He did not know that, two days before, Hitler had issued Führer Directive No. 41, that ordered just such an attack to the south as the primary German effort for 1942.

The directive was based on the conclusion that the 'enemy in his anxiety to exploit what seemed like initial successes has spent during the winter the bulk of his reserves earmarked for future operations.'[3] The Stavka, or command element of the armed forces of the Soviet Union,[4] had indeed accumulated eleven new reserve armies as a strategic reserve. Georgi Zhukov, the most brilliant and successful of Stalin's generals, urged him to concentrate that force to destroy the German Army Group Centre. Instead, Stalin distributed them across five fronts for the defence of Moscow.[5] The Germans had done their best to make Stalin's wish father to that thought. They had conducted numerous reconnaissance missions over Moscow and left detailed city maps to be captured by Soviet patrols. It was all Stalin needed to continue to deceive himself. It was a remarkable achievement in self-deception in the face of the accurate intelligence to the contrary from a number of highly placed Soviet agents of proven veracity.

Hitler's directive instead stated that the centre of the front was to be held on the defensive 'while all available forces are concentrated for the main operation in the southern sector, with the objective of annihilating the enemy on the Don and subsequently gaining the oilfields of the Caucasian region and the crossing of the Caucasus itself.'[6] Hitler's emphasis at this point was clearly on securing the oil of the Caucasus. He said plainly, 'If we don't secure Maikop and Grozny, then I must put an end to the war.' The city of Stalingrad on the Volga did not loom at all in the scale of things for Hitler. Its only importance was as a war armaments centre and Volga crossing, both of which would be lost to the Soviets if the city were simply bypassed.[7]

The Wolfsschanze, 13 April 1942

'Yes!' said Hitler has he took off his spectacles. 'This is just the sort of analysis I need.' He then read it out loud to the officers assembled at the Führer Naval Conference.

> In their endeavour to support Soviet Russia, Great Britain and the United States will make every effort during the coming weeks and months to increase shipment of equipment, materiel, and troops to Russia as much as possible. In particular the supplies reaching Russia on the Basra–Iran route will go to the Russian Caucasus and southern fronts. All British or American war materiel which reaches Russia by way of the Near East and the Caucasus is extremely disadvantageous to our land offensive. Every ton of supplies which the enemy manages to get through to the Near East means a continuous reinforcement of the enemy war potential, makes our own operations in the Caucasus more difficult, and strengthens the British position in the Near East and Egypt.[8]

Hitler's summation was simple, 'This reads like an annex to my Directive 41. I congratulate the naval staff. Its conclusions fully support that directive.'[9]

He had every reason to give praise. By midsummer of 1941, it had become apparent to both Moscow and London that the Germans were thrusting towards the Caucasus. The British and Russians jointly occupied Iran in August, ousted the pro-Axis shah, and began to prepare the ports, oilfields, railways and roads to receive supplies and equipment. After Pearl Harbor large numbers of American troops began arriving to serve in auxiliary capacities for the British as American ships began to reach Persian Gulf ports. From January to April 45,000 tons of cargo originating from the USA and Canada had been transferred to the Soviets. Britain contributed another 2,500 tons. In May alone the tonnage was expected to double, almost equalling the tonnage sent by one Arctic convoy. The first American Douglas A-20 Havoc light bomber was flown into Persia in February. By April another 38 had arrived with monthly deliveries of about a hundred a month scheduled. The Americans built a truck assembly plant which began work in April and was scheduled to assemble almost 400 that month and over a thousand a month thereafter.[10] The Persian Corridor was beginning to swell with cargoes headed for the Soviet Union just as Hitler had determined that that door to the Caucasus must be slammed shut.

German Embassy, Ankara, 15 April 1942

Franz von Papen, the German ambassador to the Republic of Turkey, had every reason to feel satisfied. General Emir Erkilet had just told him that 'participation in the war against Russia would be very popular in the Army and in many sectors of the population'.[11] The pro-German element in the Turkish

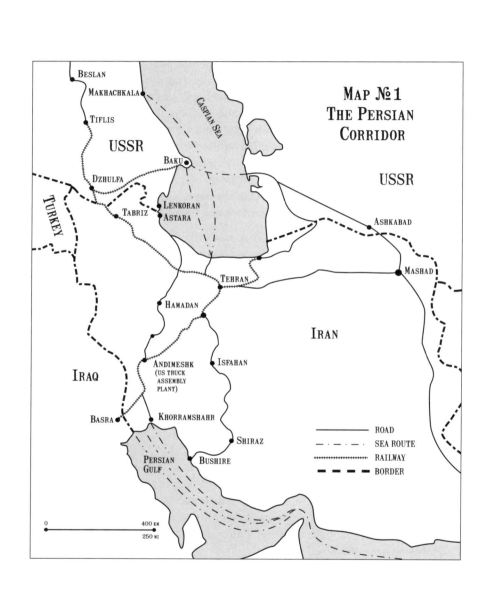

MAP №1
THE PERSIAN
CORRIDOR

BESLAN
MAKHACHKALA
TIFLIS
CASPIAN SEA
USSR
BAKU
DZHULFA
TURKEY
TABRIZ
LENKORAN
ASTARA
USSR
ASHKABAD
TEHRAN
MASHAD
HAMADAN
IRAN
ANDIMESHK
(US TRUCK
ASSEMBLY
PLANT)
ISFAHAN
IRAQ
BASRA
KHORRAMSHAHR
SHIRAZ
PERSIAN
GULF
BUSHIRE

———— ROAD
—·—·— SEA ROUTE
++++++ RAILWAY
▬ ▬ ▬ BORDER

0   400 KM
250 MI

Army was becoming more assertive, with encouragement coming from Berlin. Germany had been plying the Turks with reasons to enter the war on its side for over a year. Noted military historian John Gill observed,

> In an especially well-received measure, the Führer wrote a personal letter to Turkish President Ismet Inönü recalling the comradeship of the First World War, the common interest in reducing British influence in the Mediterranean and the shared concerns about the USSR. These efforts culminated in a treaty of friendship signed by the unsuspecting Turks on 18 June 1941, only four days before the invasion of the Soviet Union.[12]

The poorly equipped Turkish Army became the recipient of huge amounts of captured French and Soviet equipment, especially artillery and machine guns. German training teams were actively at work with the Turks to bring their army out of its World War I mindset into something vaguely resembling readiness for modern war. If the Turks were to join the Axis, they had to be prepared to contribute effectively.

Papen had assured the Turkish leadership that Turkey would have 'a leading place in the Axis new order', and that Germany would ensure that important 'territorial rectifications' would be made in Thrace, the Dodecanese Islands, northern Syria and Iraq all the way down to Mosul, and even in the Crimea. Especially attractive was the promise of Turkish territorial expansion into parts of the Caucasus inhabited by ethnic Turks, the Azeris, and even into Central Asia with its Turkic Uzbeks, Turkmen, Kazakhs and Kyrghiz. This had great appeal to the Pan-Turanism of important elements in Turkish society.[13]

Probably the most important encouragement was a remarkable gesture by Hitler to transfer all of the Muslim prisoners captured from the Red Army, most of whom were of Turkic origin, to Turkey for 'internment'. These numbered over a quarter million of the over three million Soviet POWs taken in the great encirclement battles of 1941. The gesture by Hitler had come about because of the visit to the Eastern Front at the height of the German rampage in 1941 by a group of senior Turkish officers arranged by Colonel Ali Fuat Erden. They were aware of the death by starvation that awaited Soviet POWs and pleaded with Hitler to spare their fellow Turkic Muslims.[14]

Hitler had been impressed by the opportunities. He had looked upon the Turks positively as former allies from the First War but had come to see them in another light after the recent visit of an Arab delegation. The Arabs had told him that the Germans really should be Muslims because it fitted their nature better. He had not known much of Islam before this encounter but was now intrigued by it. He pondered the history of Europe and concluded that the defeat of the Arab invasion at Poitiers (Tours) in AD 732 had been a great lost opportunity for the Germans.

Had Charles Martel not been victorious at Poitiers – already, you see, the world had fallen into the hands of the Jews, so gutless a thing was Christianity! – then we should in all probability have been converted to Mohammedanism, that cult which glorifies heroism and which opens the seventh Heaven to the bold warrior alone. Then the Germanic races would have conquered the world. Christianity alone prevented them from doing that.[15]

In his recorded dinner conversations he would constantly insult Christianity as making the Germans too weak and compassionate, but praise Islam as the only religion he could respect. Come the final victory there would be an end to the churches in Germany:

. . . all the confessions [denominations] are the same. Whichever one you choose, it will not have a future. [Italian] Fascism may in the name of God, make its peace with the Church. I will do that, too. Why not! It won't stop me eradicating Christianity from Germany root and branch. You are either a Christian or a German. You can't be both.[16]

If Hitler looked upon the Soviet Muslims as useful auxiliaries in his war against Bolshevism, he would have nothing to do with anti-Soviet East Slavs – Russians, Ukrainians and Belorussians. Although he had millions of them in POW camps, very many of whom would have been glad to join the war against communism, he abhorred the idea of putting weapons in their hands. It was a justifiable conclusion given what he intended to do to them after his victory – those who survived were to be reduced to illiterate serfs of the *Herrenvolk*.

The German Army was far more practical and appreciated the possibilities these POWs presented. They had a leader ready-made in the captured Soviet general and war hero, Andrey Andreyevich Vlasov. He had been captured after his 2nd Shock Army had been cut off and destroyed in the fighting for Leningrad in early 1942. He surprised his captors by declaring that Stalin was the greatest enemy of the Russian people and stated his willingness to form an army to fight the communists. Hitler would only go so far as to allow the creation of a Russian Liberation Army, simply as a propaganda ploy. Vlasov would receive no troops to command, although a million Soviet citizens were taking up arms fighting for the Germans, but these were German Army con-trolled personnel. For Vlasov, a Russian patriot, there was only the bitter frustration of a priceless opportunity thrown away.[17]

Hitler's priorities were elsewhere. Thus, by early 1942, the last of the surviving Soviet Turkic and other Muslim POWs had been released into the custody of the Republic of Turkey. Goebbels brilliantly used this Nazi 'humanitarian gesture' to drive home pro-German sentiment in the Muslim world. It also had the effect of demoralizing the remaining Turkic troops in the Red Army and required the most brutal repression by the NKVD, which further alienated that part of the Soviet population.[18]

The Germans expected that, if Turkey entered the war, it would put pressure on the British in Syria, Iraq, and Persia but put its main effort into an invasion of the Caucasus. The Germans as well asked for U-boat access to the Black Sea and for sole access to Turkish chromite ore, vital to German war industry.

Now if only the Turks would go along. The problem was that the Turkish leadership was split. The Army was increasingly for war; the President was unsure, and Prime Minister Sükrü Saracoglu favoured the West. All this time, the British had not been idle and were doing their best to keep Turkey neutral. In the face of this balance, 'Hitler ordered preparation of a plan to rearrange the constellation of political power in Ankara to suit Berlin's purposes better.'[19]

Stavka, Moscow, 25 April 1942

The logisticians on the Soviet General Staff were the most frightened of men. The reports they had to present to Stalin would have stunned a man with a lesser will or a more forgiving approach to failure than the *Vozhd*.[20] Not that Stalin did not worry. He too was frightened, but he was patient and steady. He had panicked in the opening days of the German invasion when the shock had sent him to cower at his *dacha* outside Moscow for two weeks. When a delegation from the Politburo arrived, he thought they had come to arrest him. Instead they begged him to take the state in hand again. Since then his grip had not so much as quivered.

He did not shoot the logisticians as he had the military intelligence officers who had tried to warn him of the German invasion. He had learned not to dispose of everyone who brought bad news. That only resulted in more bad news arriving in the form of nasty surprises. But their reports would have snapped the nerve of a lesser man.

The Soviets had barely survived 1941. Losses had been beyond enormous. The battles for Moscow alone had cost 2.5 million irrecoverable losses, a figure that would long remain a state secret, and at the same time millions of men of military age were now under German control.[21] Huge areas of the most productive parts of the western Soviet Union had been overrun by the Germans. Of those thousands of factories that had been evacuated to the Urals, many were still in the process of reconstitution. Soviet war production was in a potentially deadly trough.

Soviet territorial, population, agricultural and industrial losses had been staggering. Every index of production showed a collapse after 1940.

Soviet 1942 raw materials production compared to that of 1940

Iron	32 per cent
Steel	44 per cent
Iron ore	33 per cent
Coal	46 per cent
Oil	71 per cent

Key elements of industrial production had also collapsed compared to 1940. Of the 145,000 trucks supporting industry, barely 35,000 were still operational. Of the 58,400 metal-working lathes working in 1940, only 22,900 remained. Electric power had been reduced from 48 to 29 billion KwH. Ferrous sheet metal production, of which modern mechanized warfare devoured vast quantities, fell from 13.1 million tons to 4.5 million.

Agriculture was in even worse condition. Of the 150 million hectares of sown area in 1940, barely 67 million remained in Soviet hands. The cattle herd had fallen from 55 to 28 million. Horses were still essential for agriculture and for the Army to pull its artillery and wagons, and of the 21 million available in 1940, only 8 million remained. These losses led to a collapse of food production.

Soviet 1942 foodstuffs production compared to that of 1940

Meat	38 per cent
Milk	47 per cent
Grains	31 per cent
Potatoes	31 per cent
Sugar	52 per cent
Vegetable oils	32 per cent
Eggs	37 per cent

Unconsciously, not a few Soviet senior officers thanked God for the aid pouring in from the Western Allies. The British had made extraordinary efforts after the invasion of the Soviet Union. Churchill had said in the House of Commons that if Hitler had invaded hell he would find something favourable to say of the devil. Churchill loathed the Soviet Union as the totalitarian thug that it was, having attempted to strangle it in its cradle after the Bolshevik Revolution. Yet he recognized that the enemy of his enemy was for the moment his friend, and that Germany could not be defeated without the Russians. Otherwise the long night would close on Western civilization. Strategic necessity is rarely pretty.

This aid was sent by Arctic convoys at a time when British resources were being stretched to the limit after they had been driven from the continent at Dunkirk and in Greece. It was sent even though it meant starving the desperate struggle in the Western Desert that defended Egypt and the Suez Canal, the lifeline to the British Empire in India and beyond. Tanks that could have given short shrift to Rommel were winched off British ships at Murmansk and Archangelsk. The British people had almost no replacement clothing because of the vast amounts sent to Russia. By November 1941 locomotives by the hundreds and railcars by the thousands had been shipped to strengthen the Iranian State Railway as an additional route for aid to the Soviet Union. By that month, by Russian admission, British and American aid was exceeding Soviet production.[22] Even though the loss of Malaya in early 1942 cut off the

British supply of rubber, they shared their own precious reserve with the Soviets.

Despite this outpouring of aid, which left the British with a desperately slim inventory of their own, Stalin demanded more and more. He wanted 30,000 tons of aluminium immediately for the engines for Soviet tank and aircraft factories. He wanted a monthly quota of 500 tanks and 400 aircraft and belittled the equipment that was sent at such cost. Churchill firmly rebuffed these outlandish demands and stated to Stalin that any precipitate action would lead to disasters that would help only Hitler. Nevertheless, he did arrange for 5,000 tons of aluminium to be shipped from Canada with another 2,000 tons to follow each month.[23]

The British deliveries came from their own production and from their allocation of Lend-Lease aid from the United States. In late September 1941 the Anglo-American Supply Commission travelled to Moscow and was treated coldly. In consequence, Churchill asked President Franklin Roosevelt to increase aid to the Soviets. Roosevelt promised that from July 1942 until January 1943 the United States would deliver to Britain and the Soviet Union 1,200 tanks a month, rising to 2,000 a month thereafter. He promised aircraft deliveries of 3,600 a month as well.[24]

From October 1941 to 30 June 1942, the Soviets had received most of the promised 1.5 million tons of aid. Over 83 per cent of it came across the Atlantic to the Arctic ports of Murmansk and Archangelsk. The rest came first by ship and then overland through the Persian Corridor into Soviet Azerbaijan, and by a third route across the Pacific in Soviet ships from American ports, undisturbed by the Japanese who wished to stay out of the war with the Soviet Union.[25] Most of the Soviet ships were in fact chartered American ships conveniently reflagged with the hammer and sickle.[26]

Soviet losses in the first year of the war had been so severe that Allied aid was vital. In 1941–2, Allied-provided (mostly British) tanks amounted to 15 per cent of the total Soviet tank force. The first Lend-Lease cargoes arrived at Russian northern ports in November 1941 carrying 59 Curtiss fighter planes, 70 M3 light tanks, 1,000 trucks, and 2,000 tons of barbed wire. Convoy PQ-16, which sailed in May 1942, delivered 321 tanks and 2,500 trucks in addition to huge amounts of general cargo. Most of the military equipment was employed in the areas closest to the ports – around Leningrad and Moscow – in order to minimize the already grinding strain on Soviet railways.

American-provided supplies and war materials far exceeded the tonnage of actual weapons. Already, American trucks and jeeps were becoming ubiquitous, coming in a stream that filled a vital gap left by Soviet losses and anaemic production.

It was precisely in these areas of sustenance and transport that Lend-Lease was so vital to the Soviet war effort. If soldiers are malnourished or cannot be moved expeditiously about the front, the importance of tank and other weapons production pales.

The Soviets had indeed made heroic efforts to maintain production, but 1941 had been devastating. Not only were large industrial areas lost, but 1,500 factories had been moved to the Urals ahead of the Germans and were out of production for many months. By early 1942 production had resumed on a large scale.

Whole new populations were drafted to replace lost industrial workers as factories ran around the clock. Women, 'fighters in overalls', shouldered much of this work. The Soviet bureaucracy was as indifferent to their welfare and safety as the generals were to their soldiers' wellbeing. Yet out of this supreme achievement came 11,000 tanks in the first six months of the year.[27] This concentration on weapons production came at a great price. The Soviets simply did not have the resources to build a balanced force.

Sustaining production and the forces in the field, however, was the vital Allied contribution to the Soviet war effort – specialty steels and other metals such as aluminium (without which the engines for Soviet tanks and aircraft could not have been made), machine tools, munitions, and the explosive components of munitions. The American chemical industry was able to produce almost immediately a huge volume of explosives that the Soviets simply could not have replaced. These were the calories of war.

Huge amounts of field telephone wire, radios, radar sets and other communications equipment were filling a void. The Soviets had a phobia about communicating by radio and preferred wherever possible to use telephone wire, which they could not have done without American aid. American Ford, Willys and Studebaker trucks and jeeps were making up the grave shortfall in Soviet production of these vehicles.

As important was the growing amount of food for a country whose most productive agricultural areas were now producing food for the Germans. American dehydrated eggs were soon known as Roosevelt's eggs, a play on the word Russian word *yaitsa* which means both eggs and testicles. Canned spam and other meat called *tushonka*, stewed pork in gelatin, were becoming common along with beans, dried peas, butter, vegetable fat, oil and margarine, canned or dried milk, grits and coffee.[28] Not a few amazed German soldiers would be lectured by their officers when they would capture a Studebaker truck filled with American canned food that the Americans would someday pay for all this.

The Americans, had they known, should have worried. Stalin was playing a deep strategic game. In December, when the Germans were within miles of the Kremlin, he had sternly reminded the panicking General Staff that the Germans were only a temporary enemy. The main enemy, the *glavny vrag*, was the United States. Lenin had so identified the Americans as the most dangerous of communism's enemies, as did Hitler. It was this ideological legacy of the founder of Soviet power that legitimized Stalin in the eyes of the party and people, and the part about enemies he took with deadly seriousness.

That did not keep him from bargaining for every ton of wheat, fats, aviation fuel or aluminium, every bullet, truck or plane he could squeeze from the Americans. The myriad influential Americans sympathetic to the Soviet Union would pressure their government into pouring forth the materials of war.

They did not work alone. Inside the US Government, agents of the NKVD, Soviet military intelligence (GRU) and members of the Communist Party of the United States (CPUS) worked directly on orders from Moscow. Roosevelt's chief advisor, Harry Hopkins, who played a critical role in the Lend-Lease talks, was a Soviet agent. Most important of them was Dexter White, Assistant Secretary of the Treasury, who had got himself appointed to oversee all Lend-Lease shipments to his master in the Kremlin. White ensured that the US armed forces were not allowed to make any inquiries on the operational use or performance of any of the equipment sent to the Soviets. The Soviets refused to allow the Americans to send observers and technicians to the Eastern Front.[29]

The Soviets were all too often non-cooperative or even hostile to Britons and Americans working in the Soviet Union on Lend-Lease aid; some of them were arrested to disappear into the Soviet *gulag*. Those naval and merchant marine personnel who arrived in Soviet northern ports discovered that they were not out of danger once they had docked. The main port of Murmansk was regularly bombed by the Luftwaffe from bases in Northern Norway. Then they were shocked by what they experienced at the hands of their allies. They often found the Russians charming but terrified of being seen to fraternize with Westerners by the NKVD. Added to that was the abject poverty seen in the ports, the zombie-like slave labour from the *gulag* and German POWs used to unload ships, the brutal medical care, 'the numerous petty formalities, the passes and visas, the plethora of guards and the prohibition of movement', all of which strained the morale of everyone involved. It certainly killed any flirtation with communism in many of them.[30]

Chapter 2

A Timely Death

In the air over the Tirolian Alps, 23 April 1942

Grossadmiral Erich Raeder had much to think about in his long flight from Rome to Berlin that morning.[1] He was not distracted by the beauty of the mountains before him or the Isonzo River, a silver trickle between the peaks, a vertical battlefield where hundreds of thousands of Italians had been slaughtered in eleven battles against the Austrians in the Great War.

For Raeder, who had commanded the Kriegsmarine since 1928, the problem uppermost in his mind was Hitler's dilettante approach to naval warfare.[2] The man was as clueless as Napoleon had been about naval power, and it was naval power that kept Britain in the war. The emperor had commented ruefully, 'Wherever wood can swim, there I am sure to find this flag of England,'[3] a sentiment Hitler by this time no doubt shared. And as with Napoleon it was likely to be his undoing.

When the war started the Kriegsmarine could array against the might of the Royal Navy only 11 cruisers or larger ships, 21 destroyers, and 57 U-boats. The Navy did not even have its own aviation arm. It had to depend on Göring's Luftwaffe. The overbearing Reichsmarschall had jealously declared, 'Everything that flies belongs to me.'[4] Not surprisingly, Göring allocated barely 5 per cent of the Luftwaffe's aircraft to support the Navy despite its complex requirements. Raeder had counselled Hitler against going to war with Great Britain until the German naval building programme was completed in 1945. Otherwise, he had bluntly told Hitler, the Kriegsmarine's only option in a naval war with the Royal Navy was to die gloriously.

Raeder just shook his head at how easily Hitler was influenced by men like Hermann Göring, who never lost an opportunity to disparage the Navy in favour of his precious Luftwaffe. Before the war, Hitler had taken a great interest in naval matters and a great pride in the heavy ships slipping off the German shipyard ways. As the war had sunk in the mire of Russia, his enthusiasm had become merely sympathy for the Navy's problems that yielded not a Reichsmark of further resources. Now his meetings with Raeder were more likely to provoke a denunciation of the Navy as being a relentless futility since the war with Denmark in 1864 with the shining exception of the U-boats. He had threatened to scrap all the heavy surface ships. Raeder had responded in a memorandum that stated bluntly, 'England, whose whole warfare stands or falls with its control of its sea communications, will consider it as good as won if Germany scraps its ships.'[5]

Where to begin, he thought? The Führer takes no serious interest in the Mediterranean, that which the British themselves call 'the sea of decision'. Take the Suez Canal and you mortally wound the British, more even than by taking London. He had urged Hitler to send Rommel to North Africa to march on Suez shortly after the fall of France but had been ignored. In the end, Hitler had sent this remarkable general there, but only to stop the Italians being flung out of North Africa on their ear. Yet, the Canal was still within Germany's grasp as Rommel made himself a legend handing the British one defeat after another. The problem was Malta, though, that island in the centre of the sea from which the British savaged Rommel's seaborne logistics. Raeder had begged Hitler to take it, but after the heavy losses in the airborne and seaborne invasion of Crete the year before, he was loath to risk it. Consultations with the Italian naval staff over just such an operation were what had taken him to Rome. The Italians were not enthusiastic. He was not surprised. They did not like to get hurt, and the war for them so far had entailed nothing but hurt and humiliation. They would follow only if Germany led. And Hitler was not so inclined.

Even more distressing was Hitler's failure to understand the concept of a balanced fleet. He was all enthusiasm for the U-boats that were savaging the Allied merchant fleets under the command of the remarkably able Admiral Karl Dönitz, but he had nothing but contempt for the surface fleet. He remembered Germany's huge investment in its First War navy which fought only one major battle and then rusted away to mutiny in 1918.

Earlier in the war, *Graf Spee* and *Bismarck* had savaged enemy shipping only to be hunted down and sunk. Now that Hitler had got himself stuck in a war with the Soviet Union, he had even less interest. If anything, the demands of the Eastern Front were voracious competitors for the same industrial production and fuel. The loss of those ships had made Hitler shy of risking the remaining heavy ships to the point they were under so many restrictions that decisive engagement of the enemy was largely avoided. Raeder did not want to lose them either, but was willing to take more risks, especially in the North Atlantic, to achieve decisive result.

Only the U-boats found favour in Hitler's eyes. That was due to Dönitz, whom Raeder had appointed Commander of Submarines in 1935. Almost alone among senior naval officers he had advocated a relentless attack on the soft shipping of the enemy and had revived the wolfpack tactics of the First War, vastly improving their capabilities with stronger, more hardy boats and advanced communications, especially the unbreakable naval Enigma cipher. Although Germany had begun the war with fewer than sixty boats, their success triggered a vast expansion of construction so that now they roamed the seas as the terror of the Allies, and like their wolfish namesake, pulling down one victim after another.

Hitler may not have appreciated the surface navy much, but he was not about to let its ships rust away. His fears of an Allied invasion of Norway prompted him to state at the Führer naval conference of December 1941 that, 'The German fleet must . . . use all its forces for the defence of Norway. It would be expedient to transfer all battleships there for this purpose. The latter could be used for attacking convoys in the north, for instance.' Not surprisingly, Hitler stated at the Führer naval conference of 13 February 1942, 'Time and again Churchill speaks of shipping tonnage as his greatest worry.' Slowly his concern for an Allied invasion was replaced with the necessity to disrupt the Allied convoys to Russia. By this time most of the Navy's capital ships had been concentrated there. The next month he issued orders that more submarines and aircraft were to be stationed in Norway to destroy the convoys.[6] He had fixated on an Allied invasion of Norway which the British had cleverly encouraged. That led him to declare, 'Every ship not stationed in Norway is in the wrong place.' He was right but for the wrong reason.[7]

Raeder realized that he was not going to be chief of the German Navy much longer. Sooner or later he would have to offer Hitler his resignation. Who would he recommend as his successor? His preference was for Admiral Rolf Carls, Commander Naval Group North, a man with the breadth of understanding to command the Navy. Second was Karl Dönitz. He worried about Dönitz on two counts. The man had concentrated so much on submarine warfare that Raeder felt he would let the surface fleet wither away. Also troubling was Dönitz's enthusiastic support of National Socialism and his near worship of Hitler. He was far more political than Raeder believed proper. He had said publicly 'in comparison to Hitler we are all pip-squeaks. Anyone who believes he can do better than the Führer is stupid.'[8] So enthusiastic was he that he was referred to as Hitler Youth Dönitz.

If Dönitz's political enthusiasm unsettled Raeder's concept of a non-political, professional naval officer, his attitude towards the Jews appalled him. Raeder was firmly in the Christian tradition of the German Navy and fought relentlessly to protect the Navy from Nazi neo-paganism. As a Christian gentleman and naval officer, he had also gone toe to toe with Hitler himself to defend Jewish naval officers and those with partial Jewish blood and even obtained their reinstatement in the Navy.[9]

Against these black marks was the undeniable fact that Dönitz was a brilliant officer and was commanding the Navy's only successful operation. Still . . . for the Navy's sake, and perhaps its soul, it would have to be Carls who would succeed him.

Raeder was jolted out of his concentration as the starboard engine flamed. Then the plane went into a steep dive.

Ramushevo, on the edge of the Demyansk Pocket, 25 April 1942

Ramushevo burned on both banks of the mile-wide Lovat River. On the east bank the reinforced Panzerjäger battalion of the 3rd SS Division *Totenkopf* had broken through the last of the encircling Soviet units that had hemmed in an entire German corps in the Demyansk Pocket. On the west bank, the Jäger divisions of General Walther von Seydlitz-Kurzbach had hammered through five Soviet defence lines to relieve the pocket. Now only the river separated them. It would not be long before German pioneers put a pontoon bridge across.[10]

On the east bank, the SS were mopping up the last of the Russians still holding out in the ruins. No prisoners. Tough did not do them justice. They were hard as Krupp steel with a ruthlessness not seen since the Mongols. When the division was formed in 1939, its enlisted ranks were filled with concentration camp guards. Now 80 per cent of them were killed, wounded or missing, but the Soviets had paid many times over.

Krupp steel aside, their losses would have been 100 per cent if had not been for the new automatic rifles that many of them had been issued as a test. This was the Maschinenkarabiner 1942 (MKb 42, quickly dubbed by the troops as the Stürmgewehr – assault rifle). The new weapon effectively outranged the Soviet submachine gun, but at the same time was far more deadly in close combat than the German bolt-action rifle. It also filled the role of a light machine gun and was reliable in the worst cold of the Russian winter. Armed with this weapon, the SS simply shot their way through every Soviet unit in their path.

It would have done them no good if Seydlitz's Silesian and Würtemberger Jäger had not fought their way through to the river. These were elite light infantry, and they had broken through Soviet defence after defence in a month's vicious fighting over ground that froze, thawed, and froze again as the Russian winter fought with spring. Seydlitz's tactical handling of the relief had been brilliant, and his physical courage exemplary. He was the scion of a great military family whose famous ancestor was Frederick the Great's superb cavalry general and often second-in-command. At the battle of Zorndorf against the Russians in 1758, the king had issued an ill-informed order to Seydlitz, who commanded the other flank of the Prussian Army. He replied, 'Tell the king that after the battle my head is at his disposal, but meantime I hope he will permit me to exercise it in his service!'[11] His descendant was no less determined to use his own judgement.

His ancestor had also been famously known for charging full tilt between the descending blades of two windmills. Seydlitz had inherited that trait as well.

Nanking, China, Headquarters, Soviet Advisory Group, 25 April 1942

General Vasili Ivanovich Chuikov was chafing at his inaction. The war was almost a year old, and he had seen none of it. At the beginning of May he was finally due to return from the Soviet military mission in China. He had requested immediate assignment to the front. 'I wanted to get to know the nature of modern warfare as quickly as possible, to understand the reasons for our defeats and to try to find out where the German Army's tactical strength lay and what new military techniques it was using.'[12]

While in China he and the other officers chafed to get back to the Motherland in its peril as the news of one disaster after another was announced. Chuikov was born a peasant, had thrown in his lot with the Bolsheviks in 1917, and risen through rough talent. A distinguished record put him on the road to success and two tours in China as an advisor to the Nationalist Army followed. He had commanded an army in the invasion of eastern Poland in 1939 and another in the war against Finland in 1940 when failure was clinging to everyone else. He learned a great lesson, concluding that an orthodox military approach would not work in an unorthodox situation. He had been bold enough to write up a summary of why Finnish tactics had been so effective and recommended countermeasures.[13]

He had done so well that Stalin had sent him to China as part of the military mission to advise Chiang Kai-shek and personally briefed him as a mark of his favour. That favour was prized as much as his disfavour was deadly. Four years before Stalin had slaughtered his senior officer corps in fear of a coup led by the brilliant Marshal of the Soviet Union Mikhail Tukhachevsky, the creator of Soviet mechanization in warfare and the concept of deep battle. Luckily for Chuikov, he had not been a part of the great man's clique and survived when all around him were being shot or sent to the camps.

Troop train of the 6th Panzer Division, 25 April 1942

The men slept in the lullaby rocking of the train as it sped across the Ukraine, Poland, the Reich, and then into France. La Belle France. From the frozen hell of Russia the men would detrain into a dream world of a French spring. From frozen ground to soft beds, from frozen rations to warm bread, from Russians who were trying to kill them all the time, to French women who were willing to please a man, almost all the time. The 6th Panzer Division had been sent to France to re-equip and rebuild as a reward for its fine fighting record, an investment in future glory.

Hardly a man would argue that the division's survival and success was due to its commander, General Erhard Raus. Not only had he beaten the Russians at every turn, but he had repeatedly rescued his men who had been cut off by the enemy. They had affectionately coined the slogan, '*Raus zieht heraus!*'

('Raus gets you out!'). Raus was an Austrian with a talent for armoured warfare that some men had compared to that of Rommel. Both had gone through the hard school of the Gebirgsjäger, or mountain troops, in the First World War and won their laurels. Both were also exacting trainers of men and had inculcated the Gebirgsjäger creed of aggressive initiative and high training to their men. The test had been battle. For Rommel it had been the sand of Africa. For Raus it had been the snow of Russia.

Raus could not afford to sleep. Already in his mind's eye, he was seeing the transformation of his worn-out division into a resharpened sword. A thousand and one things needed to be done. The absorption of thousands of replacements, reception of hundreds of new fighting vehicles and heavy weapons, then training, training, training, and again training. He had made them lethal, and now they were to rest, rebuild. Already he was planning on making them even more lethal.

Borisov, Headquarters, Army Group Centre, 25 April 1942

The commander of Army Group Centre, Field Marshal Günther von Kluge, counted himself lucky to have an operations officer with the brilliance of Colonel Henning von Tresckow. He had been one of the main architects, along with General Erich von Manstein, of the plan for the attack through the Ardennes in the 1940 campaign in the West that had destroyed France.

Tresckow was from an ancient Prussian military family and in June 1918 he had become the youngest lieutenant in the Imperial German Army at the age of seventeen. In the last few months of that war he won the Iron Cross First Class for his outstanding physical feats and the moral courage to take independent action. His superior at the time remarked, "You, Tresckow, will either become chief of the General Staff or die on the scaffold as a rebel.'[14]

What few knew in 1942 was that Tresckow was a determined member of the plot to remove Hitler. A committed Lutheran Christian himself, he once said, 'I cannot understand how people can still call themselves Christians and not be furious adversaries of Hitler's regime.'[15] As early as 1938 he had said, 'Both duty and honour demand from us that we should do our best to bring about the downfall of Hitler and National Socialism in order to save Germany and Europe from barbarism.' In the 1941 campaign in Russia he had been sickened and appalled by the treatment of Russian POWs, the infamous Commissar Order, and the murder of Jewish men, women and children by the Einsatzgruppen as well as personal observation of the massacre of Jews at Borisov. His appeal to the then army group commander to take direct action had fallen on deaf ears.

Almost single-handedly he began to organize a plot to kill Hitler. He had made contact with like-minded men in Berlin and elsewhere, some of whom had already tried to kill Hitler, but the man had the devil's own luck. At the same time he recruited into key positions in Army Group Centre a number of sympathetic officers.

He was immediately impressed with a visitor from Oberkommando des Heeres (OKH, Army High Command), the young Major Claus Graf von Stauffenberg who had already made a name for himself as the star of the General Staff. Born to an aristocratic Catholic family from southern Germany, Stauffenberg was descended from one of Germany's greatest heroes, Field Marshal August Graf von Gneisenau, the soldier who had defied Napoleon's legions at the moment of Prussia's overthrow in 1806 and who in 1815 had rallied the beaten Prussian Army to fall on the French Emperor's flank at Waterloo. The young Stauffenberg had grown up in a spirit of pious Catholicism, aristocratic traditions of service to the state, a classical education, and the aura of romantic poetry. One biographer described the 37-year-old count:

> Stauffenberg's reputation as a brilliant General Staff officer continued to grow. Everyone wanted to know him, even older officers, generals reporting from the front, and the Chief of the General Staff himself sought his advice. His habit of interrupting an evening's work to recite a poem by Stefan George contributed to his aura of distinctiveness and intellectuality.

It was at this meeting that Tresckow concluded that his visitor was a 'non-Nazi, and indeed saw Hitler and National Socialism as a danger'. The mass murder of the Jews had shocked him to the core of his being.[16]

He would have been even more impressed if he had known that Stauffenberg kept a large portrait of Hitler behind his desk so that visitors could see that the man was mad. In discussing that madness, he had stated flatly to another officer, 'There is only one solution. It is to kill him.' At that time, though, he still thought that sort of thing would have to be accomplished by someone of more exalted rank.

Berlin, 24 April 1942

Carl Friedrich Goerdeler had been immensely relieved to draw Tresckow into the Berlin-centred move against Hitler. A World War I veteran, former mayor of Leipzig, and a conservative monarchist, he had had a distinguished career in government and economics. He had also become one of the chief organizers of the anti-Hitler plotters and had been designated by the group to assume the office of chancellor after Hitler's removal. He had travelled overseas extensively, warning everyone he could of the dangers of Hitler, including Churchill. He had passed on to the British government his opinion that 'the Führer had "decided to destroy the Jews, Christianity, Capitalism"'.[17]

A number of the anti-Hitler plotters were monarchists like Goerdeler. The problem for them was not the restoration of the monarchy but upon whom to place the imperial crown. The old Kaiser had died in exile in the Netherlands. Crown Prince Wilhelm, his oldest son, was passed over. He had too much baggage. He had been too enthusiastic an early supporter of Hitler, although he distanced himself after the Night of the Long Knives. His oldest son and heir, Wilhelm, had been killed in France in 1940 while serving in the German Army. His younger son, Ludwig (Louis) Ferdinand (1907–94), unlike all his male ancestors, had not received a military education and was widely travelled, having lived in the United States for a while, becoming a friend to Henry Ford and an acquaintance of President Roosevelt. Returning to Germany, he became an avowed anti-Nazi.

Goerdeler concluded that, after the chaos of National Socialism, the German people would look back to the Second Reich as a time of stability and prosperity and associate that with the monarchy. For the prince's sake, he would do nothing to draw him into the plot. Ludwig would remain on the shelf as a possibility.[18]

The North Atlantic, 25 April 1942

For the U-boat crew somewhere in the North Atlantic, their kill of an American merchant ship off Iceland had been ecstatic. The captain had ordered a round of schnapps to each man since it was their boat's first sinking. The boat was one of the hundreds produced by German yards and now infesting the waters between Britain and North America. Many ranged ever farther, to the Mediterranean, the South Atlantic, and beyond to the Indian Ocean. A few even reached Japan to carry vital high-value war supplies to their ally.

Yet, while the taste of the liquor was still in the mouths of this crew, the sound of the dying ship as it broke up and sank stopped every man in his celebration. The groans and shrieks of rending metal were all too human as they echoed through the water and the U-boat's hull. It was like a wounded man in no-man's-land screaming out his death agonies, something all too common to their brothers fighting in Russia. Like the German infantry, the *Landser*, they would get used to it.

For the Allies the war had reached a crisis. In the first months of 1942, the Germans had sunk an average of over 500,000 tons of shipping each month. Imports into Britain fell by 18 per cent compared to 1941.[19] At the same time, both Britain and the United States were giving priority to shipments of war materials to the Soviet Union. The strain on resources was simply not sustainable.

Two events in the murky world of cipher decoding had thrown the Allies into their precarious position. The German Navy's B-Dienst (Beobachtungsdienst, Surveillance Service), and the xB-Dienst (Decryption Service), which had already broken the main British naval cipher by 1935, had broken Allied Naval Cipher No. 3 in February. This was the system by which the British,

Canadians and Americans coordinated their efforts in the Atlantic. The U-boat killings soared. Now the Germans could see into the Allies' convoy communications, while the Allies were suddenly blinded. The British had largely broken the German Enigma cipher system by early 1942 and even the more complex German naval version.[20] Then the German Navy cipher department added another layer of complexity to its Enigma machine by adding a fourth wheel that baffled the British codebreakers at their Bletchley Park centre. Shipping losses soared.[21]

Office of the Chief of Naval Operations, Washington, DC, 25 April 1942

Admiral Ernest King was in a foul mood, a normal setting for the man. His own daughter joked, 'He is the most even-tempered person in the United States Navy. He is always in a rage.' This angry temperament made him the most disliked senior officer of the war, but he concentrated his loathing especially against the British ally of the United States. General Ismay, Churchill's military chief of staff, described him as 'tough as nails and carried himself as stiffly as a poker. He was blunt and stand-offish, almost to the point of rudeness. At the start, he was intolerant and suspicious of all things British, especially the Royal Navy; but he was almost equally intolerant and suspicious of the American Army.'

His Anglophobia was so pronounced that he had ignored British suggestions after Pearl Harbor to black out American coastal cities and run merchant shipping in more easily protected convoys. The result had been a staggering loss of 2,000,000 tons of shipping in the months after Pearl Harbor.

Now the British were trying to organize the first major British–American naval effort of the war, the escort of a large convoy to Russia to be provided in part by an American battleship and heavy cruisers. King had finally agreed to this against his every Anglophobic instinct, and he knew no good would come of placing American ships under the Royal Navy's command.

He especially did not like the British First Sea Lord, Admiral Sir Dudley Pound, who had the reputation of being something of a back-seat driver. It did not help when Pound remarked to King in May that 'These Russian convoys are becoming a regular millstone round our necks.'[22] That attitude was already causing friction with the commander of the Home Fleet, Admiral Sir John 'Jack' Tovey. Unlike King, Pound's staff found their boss easy to work with, despite his habit of dozing off at meetings. He was suffering from a degenerative hip condition which robbed him of sleep. Infinitely more serious was the brain tumour that the Royal Navy's examining physician did not report.

So King gritted his teeth as the USS *Washington*, one of the Navy's two new North Carolina Class battleships, sailed as flagship of Task Force 39 (TF.39) along with the heavy cruisers *Wichita* and *Tuscaloosa*, the aircraft carrier

Wasp, and four destroyers, in support of the Arctic convoys to Russia. The *Washington* was one of the most formidable battleships in the world at 36,000 tons and armed with nine 16-inch guns. It would join Tovey's force of the battleship *Duke of York* (38,000 tons and ten 14-inch guns), heavy cruisers *Cumberland*, *London*, and *Norfolk*, light cruiser *Nigeria*, aircraft carrier *Victorious*, and five destroyers.

Trondheim, Norway, 25 April 1942

The reason that King had to force himself to send TF.39 and its heavy ships to escort the Russia-bound convoys lay under camouflage nets in the fjord at Trondheim. These ships were what Admiral Raeder would have called a fleet in being, that ever-present threat that forced the British to keep a strong home fleet.

The menace anchored at Trondheim was the 43,000-ton battleship *Tirpitz*, sister ship to the lost *Bismarck*, and armed with nine 15-inch guns. Laid down in 1936 and commissioned in February 1941, it was the first battleship with a welded hull and armour. With it were the heavy cruisers *Hipper*, *Lützow* and *Admiral Scheer*, each with six 11-inch guns. A half-dozen destroyers balanced out this force. Combined with some of Admiral Dönitz's submarines and attack aircraft from Göring's Luftwaffe, these ships loomed as a constant threat to any convoy that dared make the long voyage to Russia.

As soon as *Tirpitz* had been sent to Trondheim in January, Churchill had made clear the import of its presence. He demanded:

> the destruction or even crippling of this huge ship . . . The entire naval situation throughout the world would be altered . . . The whole strategy of the war turns at this period on this ship which is holding four times the number of British capital ships paralysed, to say nothing of the two new American battleships retained in the Atlantic. I regard this matter as of the highest urgency.[23]

Another German task force anchored even farther north at the port of Narvik. The twin battlecruisers *Scharnhorst* and *Gneisenau* (nine 11-inch guns) and heavy cruiser *Prinz Eugen* (eight 8-inch guns), and four destroyers. *Scharnhorst* and *Gneisenau* were battleships in everything – tonnage and armour – but their guns. Production problems led to the postponement of their fitting out with 15-inch guns. These ships had been stationed in France, but the Royal Air Force (RAF) had too great an interest in bombing them. At the same time Hitler wanted them stationed in Norway to prevent any Allied landings. In a bold dash codenamed Operation Cerberus they had slipped through the English Channel unharmed.[24] The British codebreakers at Bletchley Park were still struggling to overcome the latest security upgrade of Enigma and so were unable to warn the Royal Navy of the German plan.

Originally Raeder wanted the two battlecruisers refitted with 15-inch guns, but Hitler would not approve the resources required. Instead of a stay in German yards then, they were sent to Narvik in Norway, to join Destroyer Flotilla 8 and U-boat Flotilla 11, to complicate British efforts to escort convoys to Russia.[25] The crews were none too happy about that. France had been the cushiest posting in the entire Wehrmacht, with good food, pleasant weather and friendly French women. In Narvik they were discovering what the crews of the capital ships and submarines at Trondheim already knew. The food was awful, the weather foul and the Norwegian women hated them.

Prague, Headquarters of the Reich Protector, 25 April 1942

Reinhard Heydrich savoured the man's death. After all, it was Raeder who had driven him out of a promising career in the Navy over a trifling affair with a woman in 1931. That strait-laced prig had drummed him out of the Navy for dumping one woman for another. That was just what was wrong with the old Germany, too many ideas whose time had passed. Heydrich had given himself to the new Germany that swept away the past and organized itself around the shining ideal of the *Volk*, the master race, whose advantage was the only real morality.

He paused only long enough in feeding his hatred to consider that he actually owed the late Grossadmiral Raeder a thank you. If he had not been set adrift from the Navy, he would never have found the brilliant calling that was truly his. He was Reich Protector of Bohemia and Moravia, the choicest bits of the old Czechoslovakia. They called him the Blond Beast for the way he had crushed resistance in the protectorate and vastly increased war production. He fed the Czechs on plentiful carrots so their factories would continue to produce the torrent of high-quality weapons the Reich needed in its death struggle with the Bolshevik monster. When that task was completed, he had plans to 'Germanize the Czech vermin', but only after a rigorous racial classification of the population. He insisted that 'making this Czech garbage into Germans must give way to methods based on racist thought'. That meant that up to two-thirds of the Czechs would eventually be deported to Russia or exterminated.[26]

This assignment had been a reward for his excellent organizational work as the chief of the Sicherheitsdienst or Security Service of the SS. He had become the right-hand man of the head of the SS himself, Reichsführer Heinrich Himmler, to whom he was personally devoted for their shared vision, and was rewarded with the highest SS rank of Obergruppenführer. It was he, after all who had forged the documents that had fooled Stalin into believing his officer corps was plotting against him and caused him to murder 35,000 of them. It was he of whom the Führer himself had stated that, had he a son, it would be someone like Heydrich. Perhaps it was that Hitler saw the same ruthlessness in Heydrich that he found in himself, and for both of them this focused on the Jews. It was Heydrich who had organized the concentration camps and began the first large-scale killing of Jews, beginning with the invasion of Poland and the Soviet Union where his Einsatzgruppen killed by the hundreds of thousands. When that proved too slow, he had headed up a conference in the Berlin suburb of Wannsee in January 1942 to plan the organized extermination of all eleven million of Europe's Jews.

He had more than enough malice left over never to overlook the opportunity to injure the Navy, repeatedly backing Himmler and Göring, in their power-play attacks. So no one was more surprised than Heydrich when he received a call from Admiral Karl Dönitz, Raeder's successor, asking him to lunch. He was even more surprised at the naval honour guard that awaited him at Navy headquarters and the appearance of Dönitz himself as his car drove up. As their hands fell from their mutual salutes, Dönitz reached out to shake Heydrich's hand. He was shocked to feel how soft and moist it was. He almost recoiled but mastered himself to grip it strongly. At lunch they were joined by a number of officers, all of whom had been Heydrich's friends before his dismissal from the Navy.

It was clear that Dönitz was courting him. The man positively purred. Heydrich had nothing against him; Dönitz had had no part in the court of inquiry or taken a stand against him. In fact, Dönitz was a good Nazi Party man, an officer in Hitler's favour not only for his savaging of Allied shipping but for his political enthusiasm. He was that combination almost all his other flag officers were not – efficient and National Socialist.

After coffee the rest of the officers excused themselves. Brandy was poured, and Dönitz got to the point – slowly.

> *Herr Obergruppenführer*, it was the Navy's loss that you were denied further service. But you have still been of great service. The Czech factories that you have taken in hand are providing vital components to the Navy. You can say that every Allied ship that slips under the water has been given a helping hand by you.

Heydrich's cold face did not betray his annoyance. He thought that if he had known they were filling Navy orders, he would have put a stop to it. Just another way to torment Raeder. He was a man who enjoyed eating his revenge cold. But that dish was about empty. Raeder was dead, so what was the point? Perhaps there was advantage here. Dönitz was clearly there cap in hand.

'It is time to let bygones be bygones. The Navy needs your help,' said Dönitz. Ah, there it is, thought Heydrich. His blue eyes narrowed, and the faintest flicker of a smile broke his face.

Chapter 3

The Second Wannsee Conference

Headquarters, 1st Reserve Army, Moscow Region, 5 May 1942

The army staff learned quickly that their new acting commanding officer had more than just a sharp tongue. He was known to grab a man by the collar and shake him till his teeth rattled. Vasili Chuikov was a man to be reckoned with as he transformed this collection of reservists and cadre into a fighting formation. They would be needed soon, he knew, in the fighting that would erupt in the spring and flame all summer.

Chuikov dashed from his headquarters shouting for his driver. 'Come on, Grinev, we're going for the jugular!' He had decided to relieve one of his division commanders, and the drama would rebound through the whole army as an object lesson in what Chuikov demanded from his subordinates. Grinev was waiting and leapt to the door of his Lend-Lease jeep for the boss. In seconds they were splattering mud on anyone close to the road. Time getting around was to be kept to a minimum, and Grinev was only too happy to comply as he shot down the road. He loved this American vehicle, so sturdy and reliable, and had become expert in manoeuvring down what the Russians shamelessly called roads.

Chuikov had not noticed that this time Grinev was drunk as the jeep gathered alarming speed. 'Grinev, don't drive so fast,' Chuikov shouted. The jeep just kept going faster until it came to a bend in the road. Grinev lost control, and the jeep overturned. Chuikov awoke in hospital. The doctor told him he had injured his spine and that he had to stay on his back. He would write, 'For a few days I lay on a special bed, strapped down by the shoulders and legs, being given traction treatment. However, healthy and hardy by nature, I was on my feet again in a week, though I walked with a stick.'[1]

The Crimean Front, 8 May 1942

Sappers and infantry of the Bavarian 132nd Infantry Division climbed silently into their assault boats on the beach east of Feodosiya on the southern flank of the Kerch Peninsula. It was the late evening of 7 May. They silently paddled down the coast in the dark until the German artillery exploded with a stunning barrage against the Soviet defenders of Kerch. Only then did the Bavarians turn on their motors whose noise was masked by the thunder of the guns. They entered the great water-filled antitank ditch that ran along the front right down to the sea. The Soviet infantry in their fighting holes did not have a chance as the Germans leapt from their boats, gunning them down.

Führer Directive 41 had set the opening act of the drive to the south as the destruction of the Soviet front on the Kerch Peninsula and the capture of the great naval base and fortress at Sevastopol. Manstein's 11th Army pried open the Soviet defences and collapsed their defence. After that it was a rout. At a cost of only 7,500 casualties, Manstein had destroyed three Soviet armies and taken 170,000 prisoners. Hitler was more than pleased. This most talented general had cleared the southern flank for his drive to the Caucasus. Now he could concentrate on reducing the great naval fortress of Sevastopol.[2]

Kharkov, 8 May 1942

Walther von Seydlitz arrived in the city with the memory of the last kiss from his wife as he left her in Königsberg after a few days of hurried leave. The commander of Army Group South, Field Marshal Fedor von Bock, eagerly welcomed the hero of the Demyansk Pocket to his command. The strong LI Corps of six divisions was his reward. Two of them were Austrian, one of which was the 44th Infantry Division, successor to the lineage and traditions of the famous *Hoch- und Deutschmeister* Regiment of the old Imperial Austrian Army.[3] He would serve under General der Panzertruppen Friedrich Paulus who had been in command of the 6th Army since January.

Paulus greeted him cordially; he had been complimented by Hitler with the assignment of an officer of Seydlitz's reputation and favour. Seydlitz, on the other hand, was uneasy. Paulus's reputation in the Army was that of a plodder, a colourless General Staff officer, a protégé of the Chief of the Army General Staff, Franz Halder. He had been selected by Hitler for command because of his compliant diligence. Seydlitz would have been even more uneasy had he read the man's efficiency report from his staff tour:

> A typical officer of the old school. Tall, and in outward appearance particularly well-groomed. Modest, perhaps, too modest, amiable, and with extremely courteous manners and a good comrade, anxious not to offend anyone. Exceptionally talented and interested in military matters, and a meticulous desk worker, with a passion for war games and

formulating plans on the map-board or sand-table. At this, he displays considerable talent, considering every decision at length and with careful deliberation before giving the appropriate orders.[4]

Paulus apparently had turned inside out the famous dictum of Field Marshal Helmuth von Moltke that a staff officer should appear less than he was, in other words hide his light under a bushel. With Paulus what you saw was what you got. 'The quintessential staff officer had become a major field commander, a position to which he was strongly suited by education and intelligence but not, perhaps by temperament.'[5]

Paulus had had little command experience before taking over 6th Army. He had seen action in 1914 but then spent the rest of the war as a staff officer. He had commanded a company in the Reichswehr and a battalion briefly, but his life became that of the staff. He served as chief of staff to a motorized corps in 1938 under Guderian, who described him as 'brilliantly clever, conscientious, hard working, original and talented', but already had doubts about his 'decisiveness, toughness and lack of command experience'[6] Bock might have echoed these observations because in the crisis of a major Soviet attack, he felt Paulus had been far too slow in counterattacking.

Then there was the gossip that Paulus was too much under the influence of his sharp-tongued chief of staff, Colonel Arthur Schmidt. That could be a problem, Seydlitz reflected. He too had a sharp tongue and was not afraid to use it. Tilting at windmills was a family tradition.

Before Seydlitz could join his command he took the opportunity to tour Kharkov. The city had fallen so quickly that its factories had been captured intact. The Germans had converted the huge tractor plant into a tank repair and refurbishment facility, not only to mend German equipment but to put captured Soviet tanks, specifically the T-34 and KV-1, in condition. He spent a whole day as the guest of the plant director on a special tour. He was amazed to see the factory yard filled with Soviet tanks freshly painted in German colours and marked with the German black cross outlined in white.[7]

Barvenkovo Salient, 12 May 1942

Working on the premise that it was not enough to strike while the iron was hot, but that one had to strike first to make the iron hot, Hitler determined to clean up a very dangerous salient in Army Group South's front. That was the Barvenkovo Salient just south of the great industrial city of Kharkov. Sixth Army would attack from the north while 1st Panzer and 17th Armies would strike from the south pinching off the salient. The attack was scheduled for 18 May. The Soviets beat them to the punch.

Marshal of the Soviet Union Semyon Timoshenko brought to Stalin the plan to strike out of the salient and encircle the enemy's 6th Army with two fronts. He struck on 12 May, pressing 6th Army back as Paulus committed reserve after reserve. But the Germans were much more adept. In a masterful turnabout Bock counterattacked with 1st Panzer Army snapping off the spearhead Soviet armies. Bock's troops eventually linked up with Seydlitz's *Hoch- und Deutsch-meister* Division. Timoshenko was not done, though. The trapped armies turned about and threw themselves at the blocking German divisions. A German division commander described what came next:

> The Russian columns struck the German lines in the light of thousands of white flares. Orders were bellowed by officers as commissars fired up the battalions. The Red Army soldier stormed forward with arms linked. Their hoarse shouts of '*Urrah*' resounded terribly through the night.
> The first waves fell. Then the earth-brown columns turned away to the north.
> But there too they ran into the barricades manned by the mountain infantry. They now reeled back and charged into the German front without regard to losses. They slew and stabbed everything in their path, advanced another few hundred metres and then collapsed in the flanking German machine-gun fire. Those who were not dead staggered, crawled or stumbled back to the ravines of the Bereka.[8]

For three nights they came before they broke. By 22 May, Timoshenko had lost two full armies and seen two more savagely mauled at cost of almost a quarter of a million men in prisoners alone against 29,000 German casualties. Hitler showered Friedrich Paulus with honours, and the press eagerly focused on his humble origins. From this moment Paulus seems to have developed a case of hero worship for his Führer. Congratulations poured in to the embarrassment of the self-effacing Paulus. One of them was in a letter from Major Stauffenberg, who had stood by his side through part of the battle. He wrote,

> How refreshing it is to get away from this atmosphere to surroundings where men give of their best without a thought, and give their lives too, without murmur of complaint, while the leaders and those who should set an example quarrel and quibble about their own prestige, or haven't the courage to speak their minds on a question which affects the lives of thousands of their fellow men.[9]

Hitler was now pouring reinforcements into Army Group South. Ten panzer and seven panzergrenadier divisions were transferred from Army Groups Centre and North as well as large numbers of infantry by reducing the establishment of most of their infantry divisions from nine to six infantry battalions. Army Group South swelled from 20 to 68 divisions and almost 1,500 tanks.[10]

Hitler was preparing Thor's Hammer itself to wield against the Soviets. In addition to the German reinforcements, he ordered that all their allies should concentrate their contingents to cover the long front that would be opened between the Donets and Don Rivers. So hundreds of thousands of Italians, Hungarians, Slovaks and Romanians gathered for the great offensive. The most powerful force was the Italian 8th Army of ten divisions including three *Alpini* or mountain divisions, elite units of the Italian Army.

Oberkommando der Marine (OKM), Berlin, 15 May 1942

'*Wie dumm von mir!*' ('How stupid of me!') Dönitz exclaimed as he read the report forwarded from the German intelligence network in Switzerland. He was staggered, but now all the coincidences, the lost submarines and the Allied interception of various rendezvous between U-boats and oilers and supply ships, and the destruction of so many weather ships, all came together. He handed the report to the chief of his Operations staff whose eyes grew wide as he read the summary.

> Over the last few months, Germany's naval ciphers, which are used to give operational orders to the U-boats, have been successfully broken. All orders are being read currently. The source is a Swiss American in an important secretarial position in the US Navy Department.

This was Bletchley Park's worst nightmare, that sharing with the notoriously lax Americans would compromise their work.

The operations officer in turn handed the report to the chief of the Naval Communications Department. The man's face went into shock and then righted itself. He stated with vehemence, 'Continuous current reading of our radio traffic is out of the question.'

Dönitz's reply could have been carved from ice, 'You will notice that the agent has been verified. Read it aloud so everyone can hear.' With clenched teeth, the signals officer read that the agent 'was related to our Military Attaché, and often travelled to London with the US Navy delegation, so he should be well informed'.

The man looked up. '*Herr Admiral*, this cannot be true. The system is just too complicated to break, with almost an infinite number of settings on the machine. We have even had the codebooks printed in water-soluble ink on pink paper to make them easy to destroy to prevent capture.'

Dönitz remained the only calm man in the room. 'I call your attention to the obvious answer to all these bewildering coincidences in the loss of so many boats.' He read on,

> 'The British Naval Intelligence Office are giving a lot of help to the Royal Navy in the fight against the U-boats. A special office has specialized in dealing with codebreaking since war broke out. For several months it has been very successful. They can now read German Admiralty orders to the U-boat commanders. This is a great help when it comes to hunting for U-boats.'

I would say that last sentence is an understatement. In light of this, *meine Herren*, it would seem reasonable to assume that this is exactly what has happened. The enemy has taken possession of the keys and reads the orders currently for the U-boat rendezvous.[11]

He looked at the staff. 'Change the damned codes.'

Then he turned to his aide and said, 'Get me Heydrich on a secure line at once.'

Heydrich was in the air from Prague within the hour after receiving Dönitz's call. The admiral was waiting for him as his car sped to the naval headquarters at two in the morning. Dönitz whisked him to his office and showed him the reports. Even Heydrich's impassive expression was broken as he read on.

'You know, Dönitz, we can turn this to our advantage. I destroyed the best of Stalin's senior officers with just such an opportunity to deceive the enemy.' He leaned back in his chair. 'You know, that if the enemy has broken the naval Enigma code, they surely have broken the less complex Luftwaffe and Army Enigmas. Oh, how *dicke* [fat] Hermann will squirm.'

The irony was that Heydrich was only half right. Indeed, the British had broken Enigma and were reading the Luftwaffe and Army's traffic, but the addition of a further rotor to the naval Enigma machines had slammed the door shut for the British codebreakers at Bletchley Park. Since February they had been unable to read any naval Enigma messages.

It did not occur to Dönitz that all the coincidental losses he cited had occurred before the upgrade of naval Enigma only two months before. For Heydrich, though, the thought of what this knowledge could do to his enemies within the Reich leadership was like a sweet taste on his tongue. Dönitz was struck by how vulpine the man looked at that moment; his normally ice blue eyes burned like those of a carnivore closing in for a kill.

Arctic Convoy PQ-16, 25 May 1942

The pilots of Kampfgeschwader 30 (KG30 – Bomber Group 30) exulted in another victory. Below them the SS *Empire Elgar* staggered under the hits by their Ju 88 dive-bombers. It went down quickly, the British Valentine tanks filling its hold breaking loose and crashing into the bulkheads.

For the first time, the Germans had made a concerted effort to stop an Arctic convoy. The death of the *Empire Elgar* was one of nine out of thirty-five ships lost to aircraft, U-boats, and mines. The Ju 88 crews boasted six of the kills. None of the losses, however, compared to the destruction of the *Empire Elgar* in importance. This ship was a 2,847grt heavy lift vessel. It had been launched early in the year and completed in April at West Hartlepool in the United Kingdom. This was its first voyage. It was a very special ship, equipped with powerful derricks to unload heavy cargo, such as tanks, locomotives and aircraft, from other ships. It was intended to stay in the Russian northern ports where its derricks would be vital in unloading operations. The Russians had nothing like it in the way of heavy unloading derricks. Without it, getting cargoes ashore would be a time-consuming effort when every day counted in getting supplies and equipment to the hard-pressed Soviet forces.

North Atlantic, 25 May 1942

The crew of *U-103* were preparing the nine pennants, each signifying a sunk ship, to fly on their return to Lorient. The men were in the best of moods. They had had a gloriously successful voyage in the Caribbean, and they were heading home to the comforts of soft French billets.

It was then that their captain was shocked out of his good mood when his signals officer handed him the latest Enigma decryption from OKM. The man was ashen-faced even under the normal pallor of a submariner denied sunlight. Schultze read, sucked in his breath, and muttered, '*Lieber Gott!*' Then to the signals officer, 'Müller, ask that the message be confirmed.'

'I have, *Herr Kapitän.* It is confirmed.'

Schultze called over his executive officer and showed him the message. The younger man almost whispered the word 'Loki'. The captain turned back to the signals officer. 'You know what we must do with all outgoing transmissions now.'

The captain went to his cabin to think. Loki. The codename had been given to the captain, his executive officer and signals officer only orally. It was never to be printed or written down. It was the fail-safe code from OKM telling every U-boat that Enigma had been compromised, that the enemy was reading their mail. He had not thought much about the possibility so adamantly sure was the Navy that Enigma was unbreakable. Then he laughed to himself. The full import of the codename truly struck home. Loki in Norse and Germanic mythology was the trickster god brimming with deceit and betrayal.

The Wolfsschanze, Rastenburg, East Prussia, 25 May 1942

Dönitz and Heydrich had jointly requested this meeting with Hitler at his headquarters in the pine forests of East Prussia. Dönitz thought it was fitting that he was accompanied into Hitler's wolf's lair by a human wolf.

Neither was surprised when Hitler flew into a towering rage. It was as if his own child had been struck down. He raved that the plans for the entire 1942 campaign which would win the war had now been dashed. Dönitz had never seen him in such a fury. But when that rage subsided, he seemed to reach out to Heydrich for some consolation in a way Dönitz had never seen him act towards anyone else.

Dönitz was surprised then at how Hitler acted the role of proud father. He was even more impressed at how Heydrich played his part for all it was worth. He knew how to manage Hitler. He knew that you either had to bring good news, or if forced to bring bad news to sweeten it with solutions. Preferably you brought both.

In this case the sweetener to the bad news was that it was Heydrich's own Sicherheitsdienst that had discovered the compromise of Enigma. By implication it was more than just patting himself on the back but an assertion that Hitler's own SS had succeeded where the Luftwaffe and Army had let him down, and since Hitler was the personification of the German people they had by extension let the Reich down. It allowed Hitler to play the aggrieved father figure to every common German soldier who had died unnecessarily because of the failure of the generals.

True to his agreement with Dönitz, Heydrich cast his protection over the Navy, pointing out without any real evidence that had the other services implemented the advanced security fixes to their Enigmas that the Navy had, there would have been no compromises. The failure had been with their simpler systems. They had been broken, which gave the British the key to the more secure naval Enigma. Heydrich should have been a lawyer hypnotizing a jury he was so skilful at weaving truth, innuendo and outright fabrication into a story Hitler wanted to believe.

Dönitz shrewdly let Heydrich do all the talking. He was further amazed at the man's ruthless backstabbing of Göring, the great rival to his own boss, Himmler. He was playing a deadly hand, undermining Göring. Having heard of Hitler's comment about Heydrich being the ideal of the son he never had, the SS man obviously had the son's role of heir apparent in mind.[12]

Finally Hitler asked the obvious question. 'How fast can we change the codes?'

Heydrich was ready with the answer.

> Immediately, *mein Führer*. We have The Lorenz SZ40 Schlüsselzusatz [cipher attachment] for the standard Lorenz teleprinters. It is far more complex than even the Enigma machines. They are already being installed to communicate between OKW and its major commands and should be operational any day now. This was planned some time ago.
>
> But we lose a priceless opportunity to turn the tables on our enemies if we suddenly stop using Enigma. Yes, we can change the codes, but we must continue to use Enigma and feed the enemy false information to manipulate him into putting his head into a noose. You remember it was your approval of our plan to trick Stalin into purging his generals that paid such dividends. I ask you now to listen to the Grossadmiral describe the noose he has in mind.

Hitler leaned over to give Dönitz his complete attention.

56–58 Am Großen Wannsee, Berlin, 26 May 1942

Heydrich convened a meeting of the Wehrmacht and services chiefs of communication and intelligence as well as the finest minds in German cryptology. The lovely villa, set in a leafy Berlin suburb, was the perfect out of the way setting for a conference. He had used it in January for another conference on the Jewish question. He expected this conference to go as well.

He surveyed the room with a stare that most men could not meet. He needed to exert a moral ascendancy over the lot of them. He began. '*Meine Herren*, we are here to discuss the extent of the Enigma compromise and the outline of Operation Waterloo. The Führer has entrusted me and the Sicherheitsdienst with complete authority in this matter.' Not a peep from the faces at the table.

'You will see in Grossadmiral Dönitz's report the distressing number of coincidences that have occurred involving the loss of U-boats and other ships.' He looked at the Luftwaffe's communications chief and went on,

> The Luftwaffe has its own record of coincidences as you can see in the Reichsmarschall's report, the most damaging of which have been the evasion of our fighters by Bomber Command's raids. Then there is the steady loss of transport aircraft shuttling troops and vital cargo to Rommel's army in Africa. You will also note that the Italians, who use the much simpler commercial version of Enigma as their naval code machine, have suffered very heavy naval losses, for example at the battle of Cape Matapan and in their shipping convoys to North Africa, where in each case the enemy seems miraculously to appear.

He looked now directly at the chief of Fremde Heere Ost (FHO, Foreign Armies East), the Wehrmacht's chief of intelligence for the Eastern Front, Colonel Reinhard Gehlen. Heydrich knew that Gehlen was in the midst of a major reorganization of the FHO to which he had just succeeded as chief having been its deputy for most of the last year. He was drawing in a stream of very talented men – linguists, geographers, anthropologists, lawyers and able junior officers. Here obviously was a serious man. Fortunately, he did not know how serious. Gehlen was a member of the group planning to assassinate Hitler. '*Herr Oberst*, we have not heard from OKH on this matter.'

Gehlen stood:

> *Herr Obergruppenführer*, the *Amis* [Western Allies] and the Soviets may be allies, but a deep gulf of suspicion divides them. All of these instances of compromised intelligence, these coincidences of losses, involve only operations conducted by the British and Americans. We see no such pattern with the Soviets. If, and I say if only conditionally, the *Amis* were providing the Russians with critical intelligence derived from Enigma, they certainly have made no use of it.

> We have scoured our records of Enigma messages sent by OKW and the Army and have found a number of instances where, had the Russians known of the intelligence contained in them, compromise would have provided them splendid opportunities to disrupt our operations seriously. In no instance do we see them doing so. It is our conclusion that the *Amis* are not sharing operational or strategic intelligence based on any compromise of Enigma with the Russians.

Gehlen, of course, was not aware that Stalin had refused to believe the major piece of decrypted intelligence – the plan for the German attack on the Soviet Union – when the British sent it to him. The British had provided the intelligence but not the source of that intelligence. After that they had offered nothing derived from listening in on Enigma. Heydrich looked at him coldly, 'You are sure of this, *Herr Oberst*?'

> I repeat, *Herr Obergruppenführer*, there is no intelligence reporting that even hints that the Russians know Enigma has been compromised or have received intelligence derived from that compromise. This is backed by the fact that there is no correlation between highly revealing operational information being transmitted and the Soviets suddenly taking advantage of it.

Heydrich rejoiced, not that anyone at the table would have noticed.

The Wolfsschanze, Rastenburg, East Prussia, 27 May 1942

Heydrich had planned to return to Prague the day after the conference, but yesterday's revelation by Gehlen changed his mind. The first thing the next morning, Heydrich flew to Hitler's headquarters with Gehlen in tow. He let the intelligence officer brief Hitler then took the credit for sorting out the mess and establishing the fact that the British were not passing any intercepted information to the Soviets. Hitler burst out laughing. 'You see the humour, don't you, *meine Herren*? The British are keeping the secret of our summer offensive better than we have!'

He looked more relaxed now than anyone had seen him for months. The crushing Soviet counterattack before Moscow last December, the near collapse of the front, and then the constant crises through the winter had worn him down. Now he leaned back in his stuffed chair and gloated.

> You see, this mess has confirmed a great strategic truth that I have spoken of before. The British and the Bolsheviks are natural enemies. Otherwise the British would have fallen all over themselves to give the Russians all the information they could. They want to help them only so far, and even that far is because that gangster Churchill has kept them in this war that is not in the interest of the British Empire.

Heydrich and Gehlen settled in for another one of Hitler's monologues:

You see, when we had them on their backs after Dunkirk, I offered them peace. I ask you, has a victor ever been more generous all through history? The English are our cousins. Only fellow Aryans could have created something as powerful as the British Empire. War with Britain I maintained was racial fratricide. And had anyone but Churchill been in power, they would have seen the reason of it all and accepted my offer to guarantee the integrity of the British Empire. And there would have been British troops fighting in Russia alongside their race brothers against the Bolshevik scum.

Had their King Edward still been on the throne, we would have had that accommodation. He was a man of vision and a secret friend to us. His wife, that American woman, introduced him to our friends in Britain. Did you know, Gehlen, that in 1940 while serving as a British liaison with the French, he was actually working for us, delivering their plans? Had Churchill been thrown out, the king was willing to resume the throne under the guidance of a Reichsprotektor. Churchill must have got wind of something or why else would he have exiled him to be governor of Bermuda. They will not let Edward back into their damned island.[13]

The first war where *Englander* fought *Deutscher* was an obscenity. I know. I fought them. Hard as nails. Stout Aryan fighting men. You know, in the thirties before we came to power, I met one of their parliamentary leaders, a young man named Harold Macmillan. We discovered that we had been directly opposite each other in France. I sketched the map of the area and he agreed I was spot on. I related to him how stupid it was for us to have fought each other and told him of just such an example why it was so. At the end of 1914, when both sides started digging in, one of our West Saxon regiments was directly across from a British regiment from Wessex. We tried to tell them that it was absurd for the same tribesmen, West Saxons all, to be fighting each other. Even then the English were set on being unreasonable. But I tell you that, once I have sorted out Stalin, the English will come hat in hand to us and throw Churchill to the wolves.

At last he paused and put away his memories. Gehlen noticed that two hours had passed. Hitler stood up to indicate that their meeting was over. He extended his hand to the SS man. 'Your timing was perfect, Heydrich. I am leaving on 1 June to establish my headquarters in Ukraine with Army Group South.' As the two left, Hitler said to him, 'You have done such a good job with the Czechs, I had thought to appoint you to get the French in hand, but now after this Enigma business, I think I have something even more important in mind for you.' He almost added to the end of the sentence the words 'my son'.

Heydrich flew back to Berlin with Dönitz a well satisfied man. He would spend the night in the capital completely unaware of how satisfied he should have been. Had he remained in Prague, he most likely would have been dead. Two soldiers from the Czech army in exile in Britain were waiting to kill him. The British had sent them because Heydrich had been far too successful in exploiting Czech industry to support the German war effort. It should have been easy. Heydrich took the same route like clockwork every day. Only, that day, he had been at the Wolfsschanze. They would not get a second chance. In the coming days Heydrich would not often be in Prague, and the two Czechs were quickly betrayed.

Mountains of southern Chechnya, 30 May 1942

Khasan and Hussein Israilov watched the white parachutes descending through the moonlight into the mountain valley. Shadowy figures emerged from the woods to run over to the men who were just landing. Before long the visitors were standing in front of the brothers. 'Welcome to Chechnya,' Khasan said as he offered his hand and introduced himself and his brother. His visitors were two officers of the German Abwehr, the Wehrmacht's military intelligence arm. They had an interesting proposal.

The Chechens were of great interest to the Abwehr. They were a possible open sore for the Soviets, and an abscess in the Caucasus would be of great help in upcoming operations. The Chechens were a particularly virulent pathogen. They were a warrior people with a broad cruel streak and had been converted to Islam in the seventeenth century. They had tormented the Georgians to the south and the Russians to the north before Tsar Nicholas I decided to crush them. It took thirty years against a determined resistance led by the legendary Shamil finally to succeed at the cost of thousands of lives and only by chopping down all the forests of Chechnya to deprive the insurgents of cover.

The Abwehr had discovered that Khasan had begun an insurgency to free his people from the grip of Soviet power. The example of the drubbing the Finns had given the Red Army early in the Winter War of 1939–40 had inspired him:

> ... to become the leader of a war of liberation of my own people ...
> The valiant Finns are now proving that the Great Enslaver Empire is powerless against a small but freedom-loving people. In the Caucasus you will find your second Finland, and after us will follow other oppressed peoples.[14]

The war of liberation had begun in February 1942. Khasan had 5,000 men under his command and had extended operations even into neighbouring Dagestan. News of his insurrection had caused the immediate desertion of almost 70,000 Chechens in the Red Army.

The Abwehr's interest in Chechnya coincided nicely with the fact that near the capital of Grozny was one of the major oilfields of the Soviet Union. Israilov was no fool; the German interest was transparent, but he made it clear to the Abwehr agents that he did not intend to exchange one master for another. The Germans assured him he had nothing to worry about.

Chapter 4

Race to the Don

Headquarters, Army Group South, Poltava, Ukraine, 2 June 1942

Hitler was in the best of moods at the conference with his generals. Within a few weeks they had given him two great victories at Kerch and on the Donets that had netted over 400,000 prisoners and huge amounts of booty. He eagerly greeted his senior commanders in Army Group South: army group commander Fedor von Bock, Paulus (6th Army), Colonel General Ewald von Kleist (1st Panzer Army), Colonel General Hermann Hoth (4th Panzer Army), Manstein (11th Army), and Colonel General Richard Ruoff (17th Army).

In all of their discussions, he kept the focus on the objective of the Caucasus and its vital oilfields. The city of Stalingrad was hardly mentioned at all. Paulus's and Hoth's armies plus the allied contingents were to drive from the Don to the Volga. It would be on these wide open steppes that the great battles of encirclement would be conducted as they had been in 1941, destroying the last of the Stavka reserves. Despite this intended crushing of Soviet armies, the operation's essential mission was to guard the flank of the 1st Panzer and 17th Armies before they plunged into the Caucasus. These operations were to be consecutive rather than concurrent. Hitler spoke of bringing Manstein's 11th Army north as soon as it captured Sevastopol. The start date for Operation Blue was set for 28 June.

At that point Manstein thought it the right time to make a suggestion:

> *Mein Führer*, the drive into the Caucasus will put a premium on mountain troops. I fear our own Gebirgsjäger will not be enough for such endless mountains. The Romanian Mountain Corps in my army have given a good account of themselves. They would be very useful in the Caucasus and reduce the strain on our men as would the Italian Alpini Corps.

Hitler had been so pleased with Manstein's victory at Kerch that he waved his approval. He was in such a good frame of mind that he went on to share his vision with Manstein.

> I have dreamed such dreams, Manstein. I have seen our panzers pouring down through the Caucasus into ancient Persia to pass by the tomb of

Cyrus the Great and the ruins of Persepolis where Alexander consigned Persian glory to the flames. I have seen them reach the Persian Gulf and then strike eastward across Afghanistan to India itself to seize as war booty for the Reich the jewel in the British crown.[1]

Manstein was not the sort to suffer fools gladly, but he was disciplined enough to know when to hold his tongue. India, indeed. In his mind he ran over the logistics required. If Hitler ever got the German Army to India it would be only in midst of an opiate dream.[2]

Trondheim, Norway, 2 June 1942

As his aircraft was preparing to return him to Berlin, Dönitz kept thinking how impressed he had been with Admiral Otto Schniewind's argument. The acting commander of the 1st Battlegroup, *Tirpitz* and *Hipper*, had put before the head of the Kriegsmarine a daring and aggressive plan on his visit to Trondheim two days ago.

I propose nothing less than a major fleet action, *Herr Grossadmiral*. We have in Norway now seven major ships, and we have been reinforced with more destroyers and E-boats. I don't believe the Allies will invade Norway. Rather they will do all in their power to help the Russians now that the spring offensive has begun. My objective is the total destruction of their next convoy, this PQ-17.

Dönitz was more than a little surprised. Schniewind's superiors had been far more hesitant to commit to such a major action. It took courage to go against them as well as urging a fleet action on the chief of the Kriegsmarine, a submariner to the core. However, as devoted to the U-boat mission as he was, Dönitz was anything but parochial. In fact, Schniewind and he were not far apart.

'Schniewind, hear me out. I have been working along just such lines.' It was Schniewind's turn to be surprised.

Already the orders are being prepared to transfer three U-boat flotillas from France to Norway to reinforce our effort against the convoys. That should more than double the number of boats available to cooperate in this attack. I have the Führer's blessing to move strongly against the convoys. He has agreed to order the Luftwaffe to be more forthcoming in its support as well.

With that he struck the table with his fist:

We must strike with every asset we have. We must deliver such a decisive and crushing blow that they will never dare send another convoy to Russia.

Brest, 5 June 1942

A sour rumour was running through the U-boat crews in the eight U-boat flotillas based in French ports that half of them would be transferred to Norway to join the three already there.[3] The crews were not happy. It was harrowing enough to serve in a U-boat without having to look forward to returning to a frozen, unfriendly Norwegian port. Every man had a French girlfriend or was a welcomed patron at the local brothels now that there was no other traffic moving through the ports. The U-boat men did a collective shudder as the rumour swept through their boats.

Order followed on rumour, and for once the two said much the same thing. It was Norway alright for the 1st, 7th, and 10th Flotillas. The boats in port were to move immediately; those at sea were to move shortly after they returned to port and the men had had their well-deserved R&R. They were urged to make the most of it.

Along the Donets River, 10 June 1942

In the early morning hours of the 10th assault boats carrying elements of 6th Army's 297th Infantry Division crossed the 60 yards of the Donets and secured the east bank. Pioneers quickly threw over a pontoon bridge. Upriver an intact bridge was seized by *coup de main* from its surprised Soviet guards. By morning 6th Army was pouring across the river to its start line for the coming offensive. Hitler had been concerned about 6th Army's bridgeheads over the Donets all day, and his level of anxiety had been only barely relieved by reports of their success.

The Berghof, Berchtesgaden, 15 June 1942

Hitler was happy to have his short break at his mountain retreat interrupted by Dönitz. He was eager to see how he had fashioned his noose. The admiral reported to him in the great hall with its massive plate-glass windows that gave the Führer an appropriate Wagnerian background. He was unsettled to see Göring there as well:

> His podgy face, many chins, corpulent belly and splendid uniforms (cut from the finest materials to his own design), combined with the perfume he used, gave the impression of a degenerate Eastern potentate rather than the leader of the Luftwaffe and Hitler's successor designate.[4]

Hitler cordially extended his hand to the admiral. He was comfortable with Dönitz who, unlike the stiff and traditional Raeder, was a true National Socialist. Göring was equally cordial, though Dönitz realized what duplicity could lurk behind *dicke* Hermann's eyes.[5]

Dönitz deftly laid out the plans for Operation Rösselsprung (Knight's Move). The full strength of the Kriegsmarine – surface ships and submarines – supported by the Luftwaffe, would strike at Convoy PQ-17 and utterly destroy it.

The operation would begin by the deployment of several submarine flotillas to locate, shadow and harry the convoy. The chosen battleground would be east of Bear Island. As soon as air reconnaissance had located the convoy, Naval Group North in Kiel would issue the order for the surface battlegroups to put to sea. They would steam at maximum speed and converge about 100 miles northwest of North Cape about halfway to Bear Island. Luftflotte 5 was to conduct simultaneous reconnaissance sweeps 200 miles out to sea in a wide arc as well as fly fighter escort for the battle groups. Once contact was made with the convoy, the battle groups would destroy its cruiser escort. Thereafter, the merchant ships would be at their mercy either to be sunk or escorted back to Norwegian ports as German prizes. Tankers were high on the list of ships to be captured.

Dönitz emphasized that contact with a surface force of equal or superior size was to be completely avoided. The fleet would rely on the Luftwaffe to give warning of the approach of any such force. U-boats would deploy to attack any such force.[6]

Göring was the first to speak, almost eagerly. 'I shall guarantee you that Luftflotte 5 will conduct reconnaissance to 500 kilometres [approx. 300 miles].' Hitler nodded his approval. Dönitz glanced between them and caught the subtle body language. So the Führer did have his little talk with Göring. Heydrich had told him how much the Reichsmarschall had been embarrassed by the revelation that the British had been reading the Luftwaffe's mail. Well, it was to the Kriegsmarine's advantage that he now wanted to over-compensate.[7]

Now Hitler spoke:

> Yes, yes, Dönitz. I agree that contact with large British naval forces is to be absolutely avoided. But do not forget the aircraft carriers. They are a great threat to your ships. I tell you that the aircraft carriers must be located before the attack and they must be rendered harmless by our aircraft beforehand.[8]

Dönitz was prepared for this:

> *Mein Führer*, rest assured we have given much thought to keeping the British focused elsewhere. Before the operation we shall let the British learn that Battlegroup 3 is preparing to foray into the Atlantic through the Denmark Strait.[9]

The Admiralty, London, 18 June 1942

The message from the British naval attaché in Stockholm, Henry Denham, hit the Admiralty like a bombshell. He warned that the Germans were preparing a major fleet action to destroy PQ-17. All seven major German ships, two light cruisers, three destroyers, several E-boat squadrons, six U-boat flotillas and a strongly reinforced Luftwaffe contingent would take part. It was clearly an all-out effort.

What made the report so convincing was that Denham classified it A3, one of the highest grades, which meant the source was absolutely reliable and the information most probably true. That source was an officer in the Royal Swedish Navy who had given the same reliable information when *Bismarck* sortied in 1941. What Denham did not know was that the Swedes had tapped the landlines that the Germans ran to Norway.[10]

This information forced a reappraisal of the defence of the convoy. Admiral Pound believed the risk to the convoy too great to proceed. Churchill at a conference with his senior naval commanders demanded that the convoy proceed despite the risk. 'Risk', he said, 'is in the blood of the Royal Navy. What better way to finish off the Germans than with a decisive battle. Their fleet in being keeps far too many ships in home waters, ships that could better be used elsewhere, especially in the Mediterranean and Pacific.'

Churchill was not aware of the tension between Pound and Tovey. They had been discussing the tactics to be used in defending the convoy. Tovey put the proverbial skunk up on the table.

'If the *Tirpitz* catches up with it under favourable conditions, the convoy is sure to be destroyed. I want permission to turn the convoy around if *Tirpitz* makes a show of it so that the Home Fleet can protect it.' He had in mind also that the Home Fleet, except in emergency, was forbidden to get within range of the Luftwaffe. Nor was it able to escort the convoy all the way to Russia.

'No, absolutely not,' Pound said. 'I intend, instead, to scatter the convoy should the *Tirpitz* be on the prowl.'

Tovey was aghast. 'But that would be sheer, bloody murder.' But the First Sea Lord was adamant.

At the conference Pound was clearly not happy at the Prime Minister's insistence on a decisive battle. But Churchill looked at Tovey, whose command of the Home Fleet would be tested. Churchill could sense that he had a fighting man there. 'Bring me a clean kill. Not another Jutland. Put them all on the bottom.'[11]

'But, Prime Minister,' Pound said, 'it is our policy that our capital ships should not approach within range of the enemy's aircraft.'

Churchill flicked the ash off his cigar, glared at Pound, and said, 'We have an aircraft carrier that can protect the Home Fleet. How does the First Sea Lord contemplate coming to grips with the German Navy otherwise?'

Pound attempted to argue that the risk was too great. He pointed out that HMS *Victorious* was the only aircraft carrier left to the Home Fleet and that at least two would be needed in any case. He then threw down his trump card: the naval Ultra was still blind. If anything would have given Churchill pause it was that, but clearly he had had enough. 'Nelson would not have weighed and measured risk like a Levantine merchant haggling over six ounces of cinnamon. The policy is changed. The Home Fleet will engage and destroy the enemy.' Pound's days were numbered.

San Diego Naval Base, 19 June 1942

The figurative bomb that had exploded in the Admiralty sent splinters all the way to the USS *Wasp* which had just arrived on the West Coast. Immediately after the conference, Churchill had called President Roosevelt to beg for the return of the USS *Wasp*. That aircraft carrier had originally accompanied the USS *Washington* to Britain and then did vital service in defending the convoys to Malta. He had been much taken with the gallant action of that ship, and its escort of a second convoy, so that he had radioed its captain to say, 'Many thanks to you all for the timely help. Who said a *Wasp* couldn't sting twice?'

Admiral King's reaction was hurricane force. The battles of the Coral Sea and Midway had reduced the US Navy to only three carriers in the Pacific. The President had to take the full power of King's wrath and threat to resign. Even FDR's fabled charm wilted in the face of the admiral's fury. Yet Roosevelt was a war president little short of Lincoln's ability. The strategic scales were finely balanced. On the one hand King was absolutely correct that the Navy desperately needed the *Wasp* in the Pacific. On the other there was the urgent appeal of America's hardpressed cousin to ensure the safety of the convoy that would keep Russia in the war.

Roosevelt knew the risk the Navy took. He had loved the service ever since his days as Assistant Secretary of the Navy in the First World War. Certainly more than the Army, the Navy had the affection of his heart. Chief of Staff of the Army General George C. Marshall on one occasion had to appeal to the President not to use the term 'we' when referring to the Navy and 'them' when referring to the Army. Yes, he loved the Navy. He also knew the Navy and he knew its valour was more adamant than the armour plate of its battleships. He finally made the decision. The *Wasp* would return to the Atlantic.

King's revenge was petty. *Wasp* was about to exchange its old Vought SB2U Vindicator dive-bombers for new Douglas SBD-3 Dauntlesses and replace its torpedo-bombers with Grumman TBF-1 Avengers. He decided that if he could not keep the carrier in the Pacific, he could at least keep the newer aircraft. He ordered the *Wasp* to proceed directly to Britain with its original compliment of Vindicators.[12]

Upon reflection, King thought that there was some slight satisfaction to be found in seeing *Wasp* snatched back by the Royal Navy. *Wasp* had been designed simply because the United States had another 15,000 tons authorized for building aircraft carriers after the *Enterprise* and *Yorktown* were built, by the Washington Treaty of 1922 on limiting the size and number of warships in the major navies. It had only three-quarters the tonnage of those two carriers and half that of HMS *Victorious*. It was underpowered and had almost no armour or protection from torpedoes. And, like all American carriers, it had a wooden teak deck, unlike British carriers which had armoured decks.

At least, King thought, Roosevelt had not been hornswoggled by Churchill into giving up one of the bigger carriers. If that had happened, his troubles would have been over, for the following towering rage would have stroked him out.

Along the Donets east of Kharkov, 19 June 1942

Major Joachim Reichel, Operations Officer of 23rd Panzer Division, was headed for XVII Corps forward command post to look over the division's march area. He was not aware that the pilot of his Storch light observation plane had wandered over the front lines until a rifle bullet punched through the plane's fuel tank. The plane landed near the Russian lines. They had barely landed and got out of the plane when an enemy patrol arrived. Reichel and the pilot were shot on the spot. The patrol leader was then horrified to find that Reichel's uniform bore the red trouser stripes of a General Staff officer. He realized that he had just killed the most prized of all prisoners; strict orders had been issued to all Soviet units that such prisoners were to be kept alive and well treated. To hide the evidence of his blunder, the patrol leader had the men stripped of their uniforms and hastily buried.

He had the good sense though to retrieve the map board and documents that Reichel had been carrying. When they were read by Timoshenko at his Southwest Front headquarters, he immediately had them flown directly to Moscow by special courier aircraft. They were the initial plans for Operation Blue. That night they were in Stalin's hands. He dismissed them immediately as a deception. He pounded the table at his generals and insisted that Moscow was the target.

Hitler, on the other hand, took the loss far more seriously. He became incoherent with rage and ordered the court-martial of the major's division and corps commanders. The offensive of 68 German and 30 allied divisions had been profoundly endangered. At the urging of Bock and Paulus, he agreed to maintain the schedule for the offensive. It was simply too late to change. On the 22nd 6th Army had seized another bridgehead over the Donets at Kupyansk. Things were now going to happen automatically.

Hvalfjord, Iceland, 27 June 1942

Convoy PQ-17 departed the Icelandic port with 37 ships for the Soviet ports of Murmansk and Archangelsk. The holds of its ships were stuffed with 156,000 tons of cargo designed to keep the Soviets fighting – almost 600 tanks, 300 bombers, and 5,000 trucks, in addition to general cargo that included specialized vehicles, radar sets, steel plate, ammunition, and foodstuffs. A Soviet tanker was filled with linseed oil. The military equipment alone was enough to equip several fronts and an air army. It was the largest convoy yet. Twenty ships were American, twelve British, two Soviet, one Dutch, one Norwegian, and one Panamanian.[13]

Sailing with the convoy was its close escort of six destroyers, four corvettes, three minesweepers, two antiaircraft ships, and four trawlers under the command of Commander J. E. Broome, RN, to provide antisubmarine and anti-air protection. Two submarines shadowed the convoy should it be threatened by German surface ships.

The 1st Cruiser Covering Force was also ordered to rendezvous with the convoy on 2 July and remain with it until the 4th or 'as circumstances dictate'.[14] Four cruisers, HMS *Norfolk* and *London* and USS *Wichita* and *Tuscaloosa*, and three destroyers were commanded by Rear Admiral L. H. K. Hamilton, RN. The admiral was more than pleased to have the two American cruisers with his covering force. Each had nine 8-inch guns compared to eight for his two Royal Navy cruisers. Also, the American ships were newer, with much thicker armour on belt, turret and deck. He knew how thin-skinned his own ships were in comparison. He was worried about HMS *London* in which he carried his flag. The ship had already been repaired once for significant stress damage that had led to hull cracks and popped rivets.

A third layer of defence was added by the distant covering force of the battleships HMS *Duke of York* and *King George V* and USS *Washington*, heavy cruisers HMS *Cumberland*, *Kent*, and *Nigeria*, aircraft carriers HMS *Victorious* and USS *Wasp*, and fourteen destroyers. The American ships had been re-designated TF.99, commanded by Rear Admiral R. C. Giffen, USN, who had his flag aboard *Washington*. Tovey was prepared to sortie with the only two Royal Navy battleships left in the Home Fleet. The only other battleship was HMS *Nelson* which had just completed repairs in May but was scheduled to return to the Mediterranean as a vital escort to the Malta convoys.

The fact that the United States had been in the war barely six months presented another problem with the crews of some of its merchant ships. Suddenly confronted with a global naval war and its supply demands, America's pool of experienced seamen was inadequate and had to be filled out with what were perhaps unkindly referred to as 'mercenaries and an international mob of cutthroat nomads'. Thus it was fortuitous that each merchant ship was also provided with naval guncrews to man its antiaircraft defences.

One ship in particular was a problem child. The SS *Troubadour*, a 22-year-old, British-built, 5,808-ton steamer that now flew the Panamanian flag. As soon as America entered the war, 'its seventeen-nation crew of ex-convicts and the rakings of the US deportation camps', promptly scuttled it. One month before at New York its ammunition magazine had been deliberately flooded.[15]

The British had their own problems despite the hard school of the first two years of the war. The rule was that a seaman's wages were stopped when his ship was sunk, a morale builder if there ever was one. Qualified seamen were in such short supply that the government began conscripting men for the Merchant Navy. Retired men in their seventies were called back, and teenagers too young for the Royal Navy found work at sea. At one point, the British would become so desperate as to recruit inmates from Glasgow's notorious Barlinnie Prison to act as firemen for a £100 bonus. 'The men broached a consignment of rum intended for the Russian-based minesweeper flotilla and [the report continued with typical British understatement] a disturbance ensued.' Clearly the convoy would have more to worry about than the Germans and the Arctic.[16]

Voronezh, 28 June 1942

This large city, only 280 miles south of Moscow, was both a major armaments centre and the junction linking vital north–south rail lines that ran between Moscow and the Volga basin and the river routes that linked Moscow with the Black and Caspian Seas. At the confluence of the Voronezh and Don rivers, Voronezh commanded numerous river crossings over the Don as well. Stalin fully expected 4th Panzer and 2nd Armies to attack from the area of Kursk north towards Orel and Moscow. On the morning of the 28th, those two German armies instead attacked towards Voronezh, 120 miles distant.

Stalin still clung to the notion of Moscow as the German objective; only now he believed the attack would be from the direction of Voronezh! However much the Germans worried that Major Reichel's misfortune had let the cat out of the bag, they could not have asked for a more dangerously misleading appreciation of their intentions. For the Germans, however, possession of Voronezh was to guard the northern flank of Army Group South's offensive. After it was quickly taken, 4th Panzer Army would rush down the west bank of the Don cutting off Timoshenko's Southwest Front. It would be another great encirclement as in 1941, but this one would break the back of the Red Army.

The spear tip of the German attack was the new 24th Panzer Division created from the conversion of German cavalry units. It struck like a thunderbolt with the VIII Fliegerkorps providing direct support. The panzers overran several Soviet rifle divisions then bounced the first barrier, the Tim River, driving over the bridges as men tore away the burning demolition fuzes.

Almost the first man over the bridge was the division commander, ahead even of his panzer regiment. That evening the panzers raced into the village of Yefrosinovka. The German commander could only exclaim, 'What's going on here?' He saw 'a forest of signs at the entrance of the village, radio trucks, staff horses, trucks'. They had found by chance the headquarters of the Soviet 40th Army. Most of the headquarters personnel barely escaped, but they had lost their equipment, and now 40th Army was leaderless.[17]

As 4th Panzer Army reached the halfway point to Voronezh, 6th Army launched its attack northeast from Volchansk with General der Panzertruppen Leo Freiherr Geyr von Schweppenburg's XL Panzer Corps, the other arm of the great encirclement of a great part of Timoshenko's Southwest Front that Hitler had been so confident of. His orders were to link up with 4th Panzer Army's XLVIII Panzerkorps under General Kempf. Everyone expected that another huge haul of prisoners would result, as it had time and time again since the Germans first crossed the Soviet border on 22 June 1941.

Soviet Azerbaijan, 30 June 1942

Over 2,000 trucks had rolled out of the American-built truck assembly plant at Andimeshk that month and crossed the Persian border by rail into Soviet Azerbaijan where they were reloaded into Soviet boxcars. Three more assembly plants were under construction. Some 120 A-20 Havoc bombers had been flown in and transferred to Soviet aircrews. Overall, 92,000 tons of Allied cargoes had been sent to the Soviets that month by this route. That was 47 per cent of all aid. In contrast, the deliveries to the Soviet Far East across the Pacific amounted to only 15.6 per cent of all aid. If anything happened to the Arctic route, it seemed that the Persian Corridor could more than pick up the slack. Clearly, the OKM staff had been prescient in its predictions of the danger presented by the Persian Corridor.[18]

Kirkenes, Norway, 30 June 1942

Göring had been as good as his word. He had heavily reinforced Colonel General Hans Stumpff's Luftflotte 5, which already had concentrated 264 aircraft in northern Norway. Barely a week ago 115 Focke-Wulf Fw 190 fighters of Jagdgeschwader 26 (JG 26 – Fighter Group 26) arrived from France only days behind the hurried arrival of their ground crews. The airfields around Bardufoss and Banak were fully able to accommodate them.

The Fw 190 outclassed even the latest British Spitfires and added a fighter element that was directly meant to counter Hitler's fear of the enemy's aircraft carriers. Göring had focused on the Führer's anxiety in this matter and gave him his word that the Luftwaffe would take care of the aircraft carriers. In addition to the Fw 190s, Stumpff's force included 74 reconnaissance aircraft, mostly from KG 40 based in Trondheim, 103 Junkers Ju 88 bombers, 30

Junkers Ju 87 Stuka dive-bombers of Stukageschwader 30 (StG 30), and 42 Heinkel He 111 torpedo-bombers of KG 26. The Navy had another 15 Heinkel He 115 torpedo-bombers on floats, almost the only combat aircraft Göring had allowed it to possess. The only aircraft that probably could not be used to strike at the convoy at distances of 150 miles or more was the Stuka with its limited range of 310 miles. The other bomber aircraft all had ranges exceeding 1,200 miles.

With JG 26 came General der Jagdflieger Adolf Galland. Göring had sent him to coordinate Luftwaffe operations. It was a shrewd choice. The 26th had been the command in which he had so distinguished himself that Göring had appointed him as inspector-general of all the Luftwaffe's fighters, essentially a staff job since the Jagdgeschwadern were not under his operational command. He had led the pilots of the 26th in the Battles of France and Britain, achieving ninety-six kills in air-to-air combat. For that and his leadership of JG 26 he was awarded the Diamonds to his Knight's Cross with Oak Leaves and Swords.[19]

Rösselsprung would not be the first time he had worked with the Kriegsmarine. Shortly after his promotion he had prepared and executed the German air superiority plan (Operation Donnerkeil) for the Kriegsmarine's Operation Cerberus, from his headquarters at Jever. The Navy had been very appreciative; not a single ship suffered damage from air attack, and Luftflotte 3 shot down forty-three British planes.[20] Galland's presence would do much to facilitate cooperation between the Kriegsmarine and Luftwaffe in the coming operation.

Chapter 5

The Battle of Bear Island

Hvalfjord, Iceland, 1 July 1942

At two in the morning the cruiser covering force put to sea to shadow PQ-17. In command was Rear Admiral Louis 'Turtle' Hamilton, of whom it was said that he was a 'bachelor wedded to the White Ensign, courteous, unflappable and popular'. He was also an aggressive commander who believed along with Churchill that the best place for the German surface fleet was on the bottom. That was about all he agreed on with Churchill, castigating him for his failure to use the RAF to help clear the sea of Kriegsmarine vessels rather than bombing Germany.[1] He had been heartened to know that the USS *Wasp* would add its airpower to that of HMS *Victorious* in this operation.

He had been more than pleased at the enthusiasm and cooperation of his two American cruiser captains. His orders were not to engage any force heavier than his. Unfortunately that order was a conundrum of sorts. Of the seven major German ships that were expected to challenge the convoys, according to the report from Sweden, only two, *Hipper* and *Prinz Eugen*, matched his own 8-inch guns. The problem was that both ships were part of task forces that included ships with heavier guns. In effect, his orders were not to fight anything larger than a destroyer. He would see about that.

'Anything larger' was to be handled by the Home Fleet covering force following at a distance of 200 miles.

In issuing his operations order, Hamilton directed that, 'The primary object is to get PQ-17 to Russia, but an object only slightly subsidiary is to provide an opportunity for the enemy's heavy ships to be brought to action by our battlefleet and cruiser covering force.' He also clearly stated that, 'It is not my intention to engage any enemy unit which includes *Tirpitz*, which must be shadowed at long range and led to a position at which interception can be achieved by the Commander-in-Chief.'[2] Now, only if the Germans would co-operate, he could pull off the classic role of the cruiser and pull *Tirpitz* towards its destruction at the hands of the battleships. Any other group of German ships he would not hesitate to fight it out with.

Reporting aboard *Wichita* was Admiral Giffen's flag lieutenant 'for temporary additional duty', whose job it was to write an 'hour by hour chronicle' of the voyage. Lieutenant Douglas Fairbanks, Jr., USNR, was an intelligent and perceptive man, and his chronicle would do much to untangle the events that were to come.[3]

That night Fairbanks recorded the address of the executive officer in the hangar deck aft on the coming operation to the entire crew who listened with 'solemn, tense faces'. Later that evening Captain H. W. Hill gathered his officers in the wardroom and in an impersonal command tone reminded them of the importance of the convoy to the war effort, that it was worth $700,000,000, and that there was intelligence that there was likely to be a knock-down, drag-out naval battle to protect it. Now that they had this warning, they were to do their utmost. Discipline had to be perfect. Fairbanks then recorded that Hill 'leaned on the table and smiled: "Do you realize, I've been in the Navy since before many of you were born?" His eyes glistened visibly as he went on, "All my life I've been studying, training, and waiting for this one moment – and now it's come!" He sighed, wagged his head, and with a wave added, "Good luck to you all!"'[4]

Both sides were rolling for the whole pot; every available heavy ship had put to sea. The Germans were determined to destroy the convoy. The Allies were equally determined to defend the convoy and fight it out with the Germans. The British particularly were haunted by the lost opportunity in the great naval battle of the First World War at Jutland in 1916 when the German High Seas Fleet was allowed to escape and serve as a threatening fleet in being for the rest of the war. For too long the German surface fleet centred on the *Tirpitz* had filled the same role as its ancestor.

The determination to prevail is vital in any military or naval contest, but there were concrete obstacles in its way. The closer the Allied forces approached Norway, the closer they came to the reach of Luftflotte 5's aircraft. For the two Allied carriers to support the big ships, they in turn had to come within range of the same German aircraft and that included JG 26's Fw 190s, at that time the finest fighters in the world.

And therein lay a problem. The Vindicator dive-bombers aboard *Wasp* were already obsolete before the war. Their crews disparagingly referred to them as Vibrators or Wind-indictors. The Royal Navy had taken over a French order for Vindicators and renamed the aircraft the Chesapeake and had to up-gun and up-armour the aircraft. Aircrews referred to it as the Cheesecake. They were withdrawn from British service in late 1941. The *Wasp*'s fighter squadron was equipped with Grumman F4F Wildcats. Its torpedo-bombers were the Devastator TBD-1, nicknamed the Torpecker by its crews. It was slow and scarcely manoeuvrable, with light defensive weaponry and poor armour relative to the weapons of the time; its speed on a glide-bombing approach was a mere 200mph, making it easy prey for fighters and defensive guns alike. The aerial torpedo could not even be released at speeds above 115mph. Torpedo delivery requires a long, straight-line attack run, making the aircraft vulnerable, and the slow speed of the aircraft made them easy targets for fighters and antiaircraft guns.[5] *Wasp*'s air wing counted 75 aircraft – 27 F4F fighters, 33 Vindicators, and 15 Devastators.

The Royal Navy's Fleet Air Arm was equipped with Fairey Albacore biplanes capable of level, dive- and torpedo-bombing roles but whose maximum speed was barely 140mph. They were already relics. Fighters were Sea Hurricanes of 885 Squadron, which were easily worn out in the stress of carrier operations. *Victorious*'s air component consisted of Albacore Squadrons 817 and 832 and Sea Hurricane Squadron 885, for a total of 42 aircraft.[6]

Kirkenes, Norway, 1 July 1942

The signalmen of the Luftwaffe's 5th Signals Regiment thought they had been assigned to the back of beyond in the frozen Norwegian north where their primary mission was to intercept Allied and Russian aircraft radio communications. As unappreciated as they may have felt in such an isolated posting, they were worth their weight in gold. Their equally priceless counterparts in the Navy's B-Dienst had laid bare enough Allied signals to give the Germans an enormous advantage. They were aided by a strong agent network in Iceland and enough local sympathizers to give them advance warning of every convoy sailing. The Germans knew exactly when PQ-17 and Hamilton's cruisers had left Iceland.[7]

Because of their warnings, the German 1st Battlegroup had departed from Trondheim early to avoid British air reconnaissance. *Tirpitz* and *Hipper* had arrived in Narvik to join the other two battlegroups under battlegroup commander Admiral Schniewind. His flag flew from mighty *Tirpitz*. The combined fleet would move farther north the next day to Altenfjord. From there they would be able to throw themselves across the path of the convoy in the quickest time as it passed between Bear Island and the southern tip of Spitzbergen. The absence from Trondheim of the German battleship was itself of great intelligence value to the Allies. The ogre was loose upon the seas, just as the intelligence from Sweden had predicted.

The Home Fleet was cruising northeast of Iceland when the report was received that the *Tirpitz* was loose. Admiral Tovey was more than concerned for, if *Tirpitz* and *Hipper* were gone, that meant they had either moved up the coast to join the other German heavy ships or that they had struck directly northwest to intercept the convoy. If the former were true, the original operational plan would hold. If it were the latter, his battleships and carriers would have to race to intercept them for the Germans had at least one day's

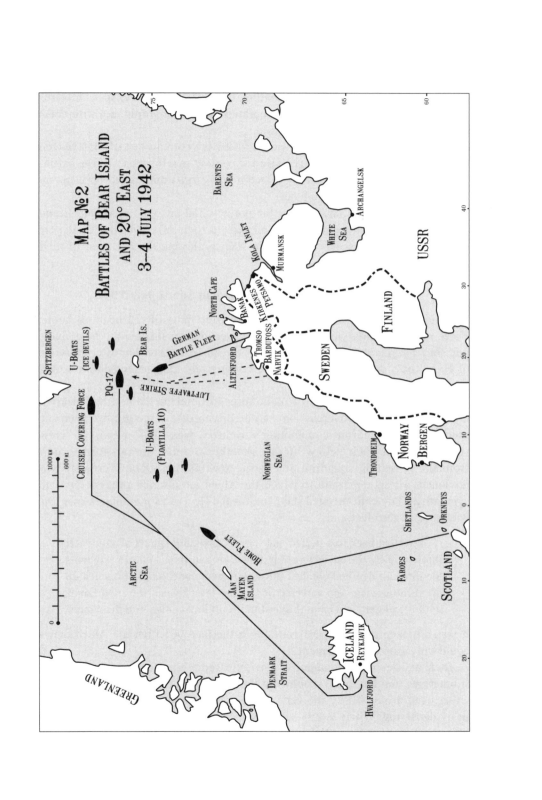

MAP № 2
BATTLES OF BEAR ISLAND
AND 20° EAST
3–4 JULY 1942

SPITZBERGEN

U-BOATS
(ICE DEVILS)

BEAR IS.

GERMAN
BATTLE FLEET

NORTH CAPE

BARENTS
SEA

ARCHANGELSK

KOLA INLET

MURMANSK

WHITE
SEA

BANAK

KIRKENES
PETSAMO

TROMSO
BARDUFOSS
NARVIK

ALTENFJORD

LUFTWAFFE STRIKE

PQ-17

CRUISER COVERING FORCE

U-BOATS
(FLOATILLA 10)

NORWEGIAN
SEA

FINLAND

USSR

SWEDEN

TRONDHEIM

NORWAY
BERGEN

SHETLANDS

ORKNEYS

FAROES

SCOTLAND

HOME FLEET

JAN
MAYEN
ISLAND

ARCTIC
SEA

1000 KM

600 MI

GREENLAND

DENMARK
STRAIT

ICELAND
REYKJAVIK

HVALFJORD

75

70

65

60

40

30

20

10

0

10

20

head start and less distance to go. At least the lack of signals from the convoy escorts and Hamilton's cruisers indicated that the enemy had not made contact. In the absence of any further information, he turned his force to speed towards where the enemy might be. He desperately hoped he would not find them already savaging the sheep in the fold.

To his immense relief a scout plane found the convoy just off Jan Mayen Island. At the same time, observers on the convoy saw the masts of the battleships, and for a while the convoy feared it was *Tirpitz* until a trawler properly identified them as the Home Fleet.

At noon that same day, just as the convoy had passed Jan Mayen Island heading northeast, the convoy escorts sighted their first U-boats. They were driven off, but the escorts broke radio silence alerting the B-Dienst to their location.[8]

73° North, 3° East in the Norwegian Sea, 2 July 1942

Early in the afternoon, PQ-17 passed its counterpart QP-13 heading home. There were now three German reconnaissance aircraft shadowing the convoy, and they hung stubbornly on the rim of the horizon. Late that afternoon one of Hamilton's destroyers reached the convoy and came alongside a tanker to refuel.

Suddenly eleven He 115 floatplane torpedo-bombers made a half-hearted attack under the low overcast only to be driven off by the gunfire from the escorts. The squadron commander's Heinkel was shot down, its crew scrambling into their yellow liferaft. Another German aircraft turned back from the retreating squadron and raced towards the bobbing crew. It was obviously a rescue mission to which the Allied antiaircraft gunners gave no sympathy. They concentrated their fire on the He 115 as it skimmed over the wavetops at zero feet and:

> . . . throttled back to a perfect halt amidst the giant spouts of salt water thrown up by the shells crashing down around them. Within moments the three airmen had climbed into the rescue plane; its pilot opened up the throttle wide, and careered across the sea between the shell bursts until it had gathered enough speed to lift off and vanish into the clouds.

It was a brazen deed of great courage in the face of which the Allied crews could only gape in amazement.[9]

Their amazement was about to turn into something far less edifying. The submarines that had been shadowing them had been trying to attack but had either been driven off by the very active escorts or found themselves socked in by dense fog. When *U-255* surfaced it found the convoy had disappeared into the fog. *U-456* trailed after by following the convoy's oil slick. The U-boats were now reinforced with another six which all took up position as a screen across the convoy's path. That same day Dönitz issued the order for the fleet to attack the convoy the next day.

Altenfjord, Norway, 3 July 1942

In the early morning hours, the German fleet slipped out of Altenfjord screened by a dozen destroyers and two E-boats. *Hipper* led the way with Admiral Carls flying his flag from it. The day was bright in the perpetual light of the Arctic summer. The fiord was tricky to navigate, full of hidden rocks, but Admiral Carls had ordered his commanders to defer to their Norwegian pilots as they wended their way to the open sea. As it was, *Lützow* nearly smashed into a ledge of jagged rocks barely under the surface. They sailed directly north towards Bear Island and the convoy, which was reported to be heading east to pass 30 miles north of it. Bear Island, a rocky and uninhabited 70 square mile Norwegian possession, was 240 miles from Altenfjord. It would be the fulcrum of the coming clash.

For two days now German reconnaissance aircraft had been skimming around the convoy radioing its location as it moved steadily east at 8 knots. Its escorts darted around the convoy's edge driving off the U-boats in a game of cat and mouse in which neither side had scored a kill, though it was not for lack of trying. A number of torpedoes were only stopped by the concentrated fire of the escorts and the guncrews on the merchant ships, blowing them out of the water sometimes at the very last minute. The mood was tense among the convoy and escort crews, but their morale had been boosted by their success. It would never be higher.

Broome received a signal from the commander of the submarine HMS *P.614*[10] which stated that 'if heavy enemy surface units attacked, he intended to remain on the surface, receiving the reply from Broome, "So do I."'[11]

On the bridge of *Tirpitz* Schniewind looked up to follow the noise of engines. Overhead a formation of twenty-three He 111 torpedo-bombers from KG 26 at Bardufoss was flying towards the convoy led by the Geschwader's acting commander Hauptmann Eicke. The admiral did not see another thirty Ju 88 dive-bombers of KG 30 that were flying ahead of the torpedo-bombers. Eleven of the Kriegsmarine's He 115 torpedo-bombers had also set out to attack the convoy. At the bases from which all these aircraft had just departed another mixed strike force was preparing to launch on order after the first had struck and was on the way home. The mission of the strike forces was to sink as many ships as possible and so disorganize the convoy that it would fall easy prey to the surface ships and the gathering wolf pack of U-boats codenamed Ice Devil.

A Gruppe from JG 26 would join the fleet as it approached Bear Island to fly top cover, an ever mindful reminder of the Führer's admonition to watch out for the carriers. With a round-trip range of 500 miles, the Fw 190s could just reach Bear Island and have a little precious loiter time. This would require the other two Gruppen of JG 26 to relieve each other in rotation. A patrol pattern SSW of Bear Island would also likely serve to intercept any Allied carrier aircraft.

Gruppenkommandeur Major Josef 'Pips' Priller's III./JG 26 of thirty Fw 190s would have the honour of the first rotation. Priller was a killer in the sky with seventy kills to his credit, most of them against the RAF, having shot down more Spitfires than any other German ace.[12] He was a stocky, little man, jovial by nature, well-liked by his men, and with a penchant for talking back to his superiors. His three squadron commanders were the best in the Luftwaffe.

They need not have worried at that time about the carriers. The Home Fleet with HMS *Victorious* and USS *Wasp* had not even passed Jan Mayen Island, 600 miles (1,000km) west of Altenfjord and almost as far to Bear Island, and was unaware of the location of the German ships, only that the *Tirpitz* and *Hipper* were missing from Trondheim. Fog along the Norwegian coast had prevented RAF reconnaissance of the naval bases at Narvik and farther north. It had also blanketed the convoy route intermittently. Tovey and Hamilton both knew that the German surface fleet had orders to be at sea, and signals intelligence indicated that German communications were spiking. It was not much to go on, but Tovey made some shrewd guesses based upon what he knew of the Germans and the location of the convoy. Within half an hour the Home Fleet had changed course and was steaming for Bear Island at 28 knots. From the decks of his two carriers, reconnaissance aircraft took off to scour the sea between the Home Fleet and Bear Island.

If Tovey was far away, Hamilton and his cruisers were paralleling the convoy only 40 miles to the north. So far as he knew, the German reconnaissance planes did not know where he was.

74° North, 5° East, Norwegian Sea, 3 July 1942

Major Erich Bloedorn, commanding KG 30's Ju 88 dive-bombers, caught the convoy in its eight-column formation just west of Bear Island just as it was turning northeast to go around the island. Bloedorn could not help but shout to himself, '*Ausgezeichnet!* [Excellent!]'

The Ju 88 dive-bombers climbed high in order to gain the altitude from which they could come screaming down on the enemy to drop their bombs. This would distract the enemy guncrews from the attacks made by the He 111 torpedo-bombers as they came skimming right over the waves. They would come in from the southern flank of the convoy and from the rear at an oblique angle. The He 115s were to attack the head of the convoy, also from an oblique angle, at the same time.

But plans have a way of going awry in wartime, especially in matters of coordination. Despite Hitler's orders for the Kriegsmarine and Luftwaffe to cooperate in this operation, old animosities still lingered, animosities that had become habits. So the strike of the He 115s came in too early and did not wait for Bloedorn's dive-bombers to start the show and draw British and American eyes upward.

Instead, they were drawn to the water as the lumbering He 115s came in for the attack. They were spotted quickly by one of the antisubmarine trawlers of the escort. Within minutes Broome signalled the escorts, 'to close the convoy at best speed to give antiaircraft support'. Air attack warnings sounded and the guncrews on the merchant vessels flew to their guns. The escorts swiftly drew in from their normal 3,000 yards perimeter to 1,000 yards. So well-drilled was the escort force that the torpedo-bombers could not find a way through the streams of lead to attack any of the merchant ships. The antiaircraft ships *Palomares* and *Pozarica* were particularly effective in sending up such a hail of fire that the Heinkel crews dared not drive home their attacks. Chastened, they pulled away in defeat, jettisoned their remaining torpedoes and flew off, to the relief of the escorts.

Bloedorn's initial elation had lasted only seconds until he realized that the convoy was already in action against a torpedo-bomber attack. 'Who the hell can that be?' he muttered. Whoever it was had just ruined his plan of attack. He thought quickly and decided simply to revise the attack sequence. He radioed the He 111 torpedo force to wait as he led his dive-bombers up to attack altitude.

The Ju 88 was a formidable aircraft able to deliver a pinpoint attack with a 2,000kg bomb big enough to smash any merchant or escort vessel. Bloedorn's planes fell on the convoy seemingly out of nowhere. Each of his squadrons struck as prearranged on the flanks or centre of the formation. Bloedorn led the attack into the centre of the convoy, down, down, down, with a big ship in his crosshairs, then released the bomb and hauled the control column back hard to pull his aircraft up and out of the way. He had not seen a single puff of antiaircraft fire, but now he felt the blast wave roll past his plane from the bomb he had just dropped. He looked back to see a cloud of black smoke rising from the centre of the ship. He would learn later that it was the Soviet ship *Donbass* that he had struck, one of the larger ships in the convoy at almost 8,000 tons. Its cargo of ammunition started exploding, and then with a thunderclap that pulsed over the sea and ships around, it blew to pieces.

From the bridge of the *Keppel*, Broome could see that at least four more of his ships had been hit and were burning. The British oiler, the 8,400-ton *Aldersdale*, had not been touched. Luck had nothing to do with it. The German Navy had hopes to capture oilers and live off their heavy oil which was in such short supply. Oilers were not to be attacked.

The Ju 88s regrouped to the south. Bloedorn was amazed that there appeared to be no losses. He led his planes back to the convoy to simulate another run as the air around them filled with black puffs of smoke and tracer.

Good, he thought, keep watching us. The half dozen Ju 88s that had not released their bombs now hurtled down in a screaming high dive. One exploded in an orange burst and another trailed smoke and then broke apart.

But already the He 111s had begun to make their runs. The Allied lookouts were still scanning the sky when the torpedoes began to splash into the water. Signalman Taylor aboard the *Palomares* saw a Heinkel approach, drop its fish, and climb quickly. A few of the ship's Oerlikons and pom-poms opened fire to no avail. Captain Jauncey was in the process of throwing the helm over when the torpedo struck. The ship shuddered with the explosion in the engine room. The seawater rushing in flooded the boilers. The *Palomares* was dead in the water and listing when another torpedo surged by to hit the American Liberty ship *Christopher Newport*, destroying its engine room. The rescue ship *Zamalek* quickly steamed over to take off survivors. *Zamalek*'s flinty Welsh captain was surprised as the Liberty ship's mostly black crew cheerfully boarded his vessel in their best shoregoing clothes.[13]

The *Christopher Newport* drifted abandoned now as other ships swerved to avoid it. Elsewhere another torpedo 'skimmed the stern of *Aldersdale* to hit the Russian tanker *Azerbaijan* which disappeared behind a huge sheet of flame'. Amazingly, *Azerbaijan* emerged at 9 knots still going. Its largely female crew had stood by their ship. The day had started out hard on the Russians.[14]

The Americans and British were not denied their share of the *Furor Teutonicus*. Leutnant Hennemann, a squadron leader, was just about to become legend. This daring young officer had already received a letter of commendation from Göring for destroying 50,000 tons of Allied shipping. Now he came in just over the water in an interval between the ship columns, dropped a bomb on a ship 'then banked across the bow of the *Pozarica* with all the panache of a medieval Landsknecht, apparently contemptuous of the shell bursts of the ack-ack ship's pom-poms'. His aircraft now burning from a number of hits, Hennemann flew so low that ship's gunners fired level, many of their rounds striking other ships. He released his torpedoes which bounced over the water then submerged to hit the British *Navarino*. Hennemann's plane crashed into the water just ahead of Broome's *Keppel*. The polyglot crew of the passing Panamanian *El Capitán* could see the crew writhing in the flames. The seamen cursed them and cheered in a brutal lack of chivalry. Only later would the survivors of the British and American ships who had also observed the hero's death uniformly praise the courage of Hennemann and his crew. Hennemann was posthumously awarded the Knights Cross.[15]

Behind them another torpedo struck the American *William Hooper*, blowing its boiler clear out of the ship to hit the water with an enormous splash. Astern many of the crew of the *Navarino* had fallen into the water from capsized lifeboats. As the *Bellingham* ploughed right through the struggling seamen, one of them raised a fist and shouted defiantly, 'On to Moscow . . . See you in Russia!'[16]

On the approaches to Bear Island, 3 July 1942

Broome had broken radio silence as soon as the air attack began, alerting both Tovey and Hamilton. At the same time, Bloedorn had radioed the fleet that his attack was beginning. That also triggered the dispatch of the second strike group from its airbases in Norway. Now all three surface groups were converging, unknown to each other, on the stricken convoy off Bear Island.

Broome was immensely relieved two hours later to see the arrival of Hamilton's cruisers. Eight of his ships had either been badly damaged or sunk. The additional protection of the cruisers would be a great help should the enemy attack again. Both Broome and Hamilton launched their scout planes to patrol to the south and southeast of the convoy. Tovey's scout planes by now had also come within range. They broke radio silence to report that the entire German surface force was heading straight for Bear Island. The report stunned the command group on the bridge of the *Duke of York*. Tovey realized that the Germans would strike the convoy a good four hours before he would get there. He radioed Hamilton this news and ordered him to screen the convoy until the Home Fleet arrived. Hamilton had just given the same order having received the same warning from his own scout plane. Hamilton would have his cruiser screening mission, just as he had anticipated. He then told Broome to keep his ships moving east to put as much distance between them and the oncoming German ships. He detached submarines *P.614* and *P.615* to his own cruiser force. If their original mission was to defend the convoy against German capital ships, they would have the best chance of that by operating with his cruisers.[17]

As word spread of the approaching German fleet, near panic set in among many of the merchant crews. On the *Troubador* the crew mutinied and overwhelmed the naval armed guards. At gunpoint they forced the captain to alter course – due south towards the German ships.[18]

The convoy escorts were still close in, in case of another air attack. For proper antisubmarine protection, they should have been several thousand yards farther out from the convoy. That was just the opening that the Ice Devil pack needed. A dozen U-boats moved to attack. First to be sunk were the disabled ships left in the convoy's wake. The *William Hooper* disintegrated, sending a fiery shock wave over the sea as its 10,000 tons of ammunition exploded. The first of the steaming ships to be struck was the ungallant *El Capitán*. It fell out of line and began to sink by the stern. That exposed *Pozarica*, which took two torpedoes, stopped dead in the water and began to list. Broome quickly ordered his escorts farther out to drive off the U-boats. As he watched his ships swinging towards their new positions, his own ship shuddered with one torpedo hit then another. The *Keppel* sank so quickly hardly a man survived. The convoy was now without a commander.[19]

Ten miles southwest of Bear Island, 3 July 1942

Hamilton's reconnaissance floatplane never saw the Fw 190 that shot it down. The admiral only knew that it had stopped transmitting. Tovey's scouts suffered the same fate, all but one, and it was able to radio its sighting of the German fleet as still on course to Bear Island.

The next Hamilton knew of the Germans was when his own destroyers sighted their counterparts screening Carls's fleet. The destroyers reported the Germans as coming in three columns, each in line ahead, with *Tirpitz* in the centre column. Hamilton's plan was to protect the convoy by pulling the Germans to the northwest away from Bear Island.

The destroyers began the show. Hamilton's ships shot forward to pierce the German screen and launch their torpedoes at the German capital ships. The German destroyer captains were just as aggressive, launching their own attacks on the British to throw off their torpedo strikes. Carls had the advantage now that Hamilton was blinded from the air. Luftwaffe reconnaissance aircraft reported that the convoy was steaming north of Bear Island while the cruiser force was southwest. He told off his port column, 2nd Battlegroup's *Lützow* and *Scheer*, to engage the Allied cruisers while he went after the convoy with the 1st and 3rd Battlegroups.

From the bridge of HMS *London* it was clear to Hamilton what the enemy was doing. Carls had thrown a spanner into his plan to pull the German fleet northwest away from the convoy. Hamilton now knew that Tovey was approaching quickly with the Home Fleet, but it would be a good four hours before he could arrive. Hamilton had no choice but to attack with such force as to compel the rest of the German ships to engage. If he had followed his orders and not engaged, he would never have lived down the shame of leaving the convoy to the mercy of the German surface ships.

First though he had to get through *Lützow* and *Scheer*, and that problem was emphasized as strikes from their 11-inch guns began to splash around his cruisers. They outranged his 8-inch guns by several thousand yards. Although he had four ships to these two, his would have to cross this beaten zone in which the German guns could hammer them before they could reply.

The Wolfsschanze, East Prussia, 3 July 1942

Clouds of mosquitoes hung about the woods throughout which the buildings and huts of the Wolfsschanze were scattered. As Göring got out of the staff car that had brought him from the airstrip, a cloud of the tiny tormentors, attracted by his heavy cologne, fell upon him with more fury than his own Luftwaffe over Rotterdam or London. He fled inside Hitler's headquarters waving his baton as if it would drive the mosquitoes away. Göring joined Hitler and soon puffed himself up as the reports came in of the Luftwaffe's success in striking the convoy. He reminded Hitler that another strike force was now in the air and a third waiting to follow. Göring could see that Hitler was also pleased, but he was pacing back and forth nervously. 'All well and good, Göring, but what about the enemy aircraft carriers?'

He was prescient. While Hamilton charged, dive- and torpedo-bombers from *Victorious* and *Wasp* were taking off for a strike at the Germans. They formed up and headed out in separate formations so as to come in from different directions.

Dönitz had also taken his Führer's anxiety on board. He had directed that U-boat Flotilla 10 screen Carls's ships far to the west. One of these boats reported large air formations heading northeast. The flotilla commander ordered his boats to head in the direction from which the planes had come.

Three miles northeast of Bear Island, Barents Sea, 3 July 1942

The convoy was leaderless when the second Luftwaffe strike force attacked. There had hardly been time for command to pass to the next senior officer, captain of the British destroyer escort *Offa*, as the dive- and torpedo-bombers swooped in. With *Palomares* and *Pozarica* gone, a huge hole had been left in the air defences of the convoy, which the Germans were quick to exploit as the convoy's formation began to break down.

There were victims enough for both aircraft and U-boats though the submariners were all too often angered when a carefully lined up target was taken out by the Luftwaffe. One such was the 5,400-ton American *Pan Atlantic*, with its cargo of tanks, steel, nickel, aluminium, foodstuffs, two oil stills, and a great deal of cordite, which was about to take a pair of torpedoes from Kapitänleutnant Bohmann's *U-88* when a Ju 88 swooped down and hit it with two bombs. They struck the cordite hold blowing the bow off the ship. Water rushed in through the gaping hole, and down it went its stern hanging in the air, its propeller still turning as it disappeared beneath the waves. The 7,200-ton *John Witherspoon*, loaded with tanks and ammunition, next took a spread of four torpedoes from *U-255*. A 200-yard cloud of smoke rose from the ship as it seemed to drift away. The crew were barely able to escape in lifeboats before the *John Witherspoon* broke in half and sank.[20]

By now the convoy had completely come apart with merchant ships running their engines to speeds the builders had never contemplated just to flee from the slaughter. The British *Earlston* fled north with its cargo of explosives and crated aluminium. Several Ju 88s followed and dropped their bombs but missed. A third put its bomb close enough to the target's port side to rupture the hull and the engine-room steam fittings, shifting the engines from their mounts and bringing the ship to a halt. The crew abandoned ship as it settled. Just then *U-334* surfaced and put a torpedo into it. The German captain watched as:

> . . . a pillar of smoke about 200 feet high billowed up, preceded by a blinding blue flash. The heavy naval steam launch which had been

trapped in a cradle on top of No. 2 hatch was picked up bodily by the explosion and hurled a quarter of a mile across the sea. The ship broke in two, and the bows sank almost at once. The air was filled with the terrible sound of the heavy cargo – Churchill tanks, antiaircraft guns, and trucks – rearing loose in the holds, and the groaning of the ship's members under the unintended strain.[21]

The messages were crowding in to the communications sections of the Kriegsmarine and Luftwaffe staffs in Berlin and at the Wolfsschanze. From *U-703* came: 'Pinpoint AC.3568. 5,476-ton *River Afton* sunk. Cargo aircraft and tanks. Three torpedoes.' Hitler was grinning as his aide read off every kill. Göring's smile faded when it was a Navy kill. It reappeared whenever a Luftwaffe kill report came in. He jumped up and clapped his chubby hands when the report of the sinking of three more ships by Ju 88s came in.

'SS *Pankraft* blazing.' A flight of Ju 88s attacked from 4,000 feet and left the ship a mass of flames. The 5,600-ton freighter carried a cargo of TNT and 5,000 tons of crated aircraft parts, with bombers lashed to the deck The crew abandoned ship, the captain and the chief officer the first into a lifeboat. The second officer stayed with the ship to ensure the evacuation of the rest of the crew. He was killed as the last man off the ship as a Ju 88 flew by and strafed him. When the fire reached the TNT cargo, the *Pankraft* blew up.

An American merchantman, the *Daniel Morgan*, carrying a cargo of food and leather, was destroyed by a combination of air and submarine attacks. Its hull was split open by Ju 88 attacks and it was finally sent to the bottom with four of its crew by the torpedoes of *U-88*. *U-703* had fired four torpedoes at the British *Empire Byron* and missed but finally hit with a fifth fish which sent the cargo of army trucks on deck flying through the air. *Empire Byron* sank stern first, taking eighteen of its crew down too.[22]

The Germans did not quite have everything their own way. The American *Peter Kerr* fleeing eastward threw up such an effective wall of antiaircraft fire that repeated attacks by seven He 115s were beaten off and two of them shot down. A Royal Navy corvette depth-charged *U-457* as it was lining up a shot on the burning Dutch *Paulus Potter*. Far more embarrassing for the Germans was the attack of an unidentified Ju 88 on a German U-boat riding on the surface. An investigation would later be launched, but for want of a culprit it had to be dropped. Apparently no crew admitted to the error.

Seven miles southwest of Bear Island, 3 July 1942

Hamilton was happily ignorant of the disaster that had fallen on the convoy as he attacked the German fleet. Perhaps if had known what little help he could have offered, he would have cancelled his attack and pulled back to screen for Tovey's Home Fleet. The point was moot. The enemy was there, and he had to gain time for the battleships to arrive. He thought of Nelson's instruction to his captains before Trafalgar. 'Our country will, I believe, sooner forgive an officer for attacking an enemy than for letting it alone.'[23]

The cost of that decision came home when shells from the 11-inch guns of the *Lützow* straddled the *London*. He would not be within range for another ten minutes. The next German salvo struck a few yards to port sending huge geysers of red water from the sighting dye to drench the ship. Hamilton could see the water spouts from *Scheer*'s salvoes perilously close to the nearby *Norfolk*. The Americans, he could see, were keeping up smartly. Although the German guns were heavier, their two cruisers had only twelve of them. His own four cruisers disposed of thirty-four 8-inch guns. His ships would actually be delivering a much greater weight of metal than the Germans when they closed the distance. He was counting on that as well as the fact that the big-gunned German cruisers were weakly armoured compared to the American cruisers.[24]

His three destroyers had raced ahead to throw themselves at the enemy, veering only to launch spreads of torpedoes. The two Germans had to steer nimbly to dodge them, throwing off their gunfire. Still the cruisers had not yet closed the range. Their guncrews sweated under their hoods counting their own heartbeats as they strained for the moment when they could feed their guns.

The Germans were too good not to get the range. They turned hard to port crossing Hamilton's 'T', presenting all their gun turrets to only the forward turrets of Hamilton's cruisers. He saw *Wichita* stagger from a direct hit by two shells, but it kept on going despite the flames licking from its superstructure. Aboard the American ship, damage control parties were fighting the blaze. The damage could have been worse. One of the enemy shells had struck the 6-inch armour belt and failed to penetrate but some hull plates had been sprung.[25]

The grim look on Hamilton's bridge turned bright when an observer pointed to a torpedo hit on *Lützow*. The German ship slowed and fell out of line, though its fire did not slacken. Seemingly in revenge for that injury, one of its secondary-gun shells smashed into the destroyer USS *Rowan*, followed by another two until the smaller ship was a shattered, burning hulk.

By this time, Hamilton had turned his ships to port to parallel the Germans; they were finally in range. He had directed the Americans to take on *Lützow* while the British cruisers dealt with *Scheer*. The guns on all his ships seemed to go off at once so eager had the guncrews been. Thirty-four 8-inch shells converged on the two German ships. Most missed but two struck the *Lützow* just above the damage done by the British torpedo, penetrated the thin 3-inch armour belt:

> [and] exploded inside a magazine containing cans of oil, smoke dispensers, incendiary bombs, aircraft bombs for the cruiser's recon-naissance floatplanes and depth charges. The bulkheads on that deck were blown out and the burning oil developed into an intense fire.

The shells had also cut the electricity supply needed to work the ship's main guns. The turrets were now stuck in their last firing position.[26]

Scheer's gunners were also eagerly working their guns and poured shells into *Norfolk*, but amazingly most simply went through and through its thin armour without exploding, but one tore into the aft turret just as the powder bags were coming up the ammunition hoist. The explosion blew the turret out of its well and over the side. *Norfolk* staggered out of line and fell behind as its crew fought the fires set by the giant puncture wounds to their ship. *London* pressed on, duelling with *Scheer*, neither landing a crippling punch.

London's chief engineer came to the bridge and reported to Hamilton that he was worried because the hull plates had been loosened and rivets popped from the stress of action. 'I'm worried, sir, that we are taking on too much water.' Just then one of the ratings shouted to look up. Flying over them in the direction that *Tirpitz* had taken were the torpedo- and dive-bombers of the *Victorious* and *Wasp*.[27]

Five miles northeast of Bear Island, 3 July 1942

Carls and his command staff aboard *Hipper* stood transfixed by the shattered detritus of the convoy – burning and sinking ships that had been left behind in the wake of the fleeing survivors that were still being harried by the Luftwaffe and U-boats. Debris, lifeboats, burning oil drifted between the dying ships. Already the admiral's force had taken a prize, the SS *Troubador* sailing towards them as they sailed around Bear Island, flying every white bedsheet on the ship instead of its colours. A destroyer had stopped it and put a prize crew aboard, and now it steamed back towards Narvik.

The rest of the Allied vessels were within his grasp. His ships could take prizes where aircraft and submarines could not. At that moment he was reminded by the Luftwaffe liaison officer that Priller's planes were about to reach the limit of their fuel and had to turn back. Carls was not overly concerned at this point, sure that his force was beyond reach of any carrier-based aircraft. Priller's group had already turned back before it reached the point of no return. The admiral was almost immediately corrected by the arrival of a message from *Scheer* that a large flight of enemy aircraft were heading in his direction.

Priller's only reaction as his radio crackled with the news was to tap his fuel gauge and laugh, 'At last, something worth killing!' as he turned his group back to intercept the enemy. He was calculating how many minutes of fuel his planes would have – ten at the most, ten minutes of combat time, to destroy or drive away whatever was making for the ships and then race back to the Norwegian airfields, gliding the last on fumes, no doubt. Right now they had to climb in order to drop down on the enemy like so many falcons among pigeons.

He followed a bearing based on *Scheer*'s signal, and within two minutes located the incoming flight. Chugging along incredibly slowly were 28

Albacores and 14 Sea Hurricanes with the latter flying cover above the torpedo-bombers. It was going to be very one-sided, Priller thought. The Fw 190 had long since outclassed the Hurricane, and the Albacore was just so much flying poultry, a biplane in 1942! Priller led the attack, leaping down upon them from 2,500 feet and coming up behind the last aircraft in the formation. Like all successful pilots he knew that the secret of success was to get as close to the enemy as possible, virtually ramming distance. He almost flew into the Hurricane before firing and saw large pieces of it fly off as it shuddered and started to burn. Priller pulled up and over the dying plane and right up to another, fired and saw the pilot's canopy shatter before the aircraft spiralled down. He was now coming through the Albacores, who were still unaware of the Germans. Death was upon them.

He pulled up and climbed again to rejoin the fight. The British formation was scattered everywhere by now with Fw 190s chasing the Albacores and duelling with the Hurricanes. It did not last long. He had to call off his pilots lest they use too much fuel for the return to base. That was the only thing that saved the handful of British planes, three Hurricanes and five Albacores. HMS *Victorious* was now an almost useless ship with the sad remnants of its three squadrons fleeing home.

Priller's group flew away elated at their glorious last-minute victory. They had no idea that the first strike group from the *Wasp* was approaching Bear Island on a different course than the ill-fated British. Priller did pass II./JG 26 commanded by Hauptmann Connie Meyer on its way to fly cover for the surface ships. Galland's little brother, Wilhelm-Ferdinand commanded one of its Staffeln and was an ace twice over. Priller was surprised to hear another Galland voice over the radio. 'You just can't help yourself, hey, Pips, can you?' It was Adolf Galland congratulating him on his victory. Priller was not surprised that his old boss was back in the air. Sitting at Kirkenes must have been an agony for him.

Priller keyed in the radio, 'Well, if it isn't the General der Jagdflieger himself. I'm surprised your staff job hasn't fattened your behind too much to fit into a cockpit!'

'Ach, Pips, *du Schwein*, you haven't changed a bit, and if you keep shooting down the British like this, no one will care. I just hope you left something for poor Meyer and his boys.'

'Enough to go around, *alte Junge*, Two carriers, remember, there are two carriers out there.' He looked at his watch again and only then realized to his surprise that it was near midnight, yet the sun flooded through his cockpit canopy with an afternoon's lazy brightness.[28]

Chapter 6

The Battle of 20° East

The Wolfsschanze, East Prussia, 4 July 1942

Göring was riding high. If this had been anywhere else, he would have ordered the best champagne to celebrate the Luftwaffe's unparalleled successes in what was to be called the Battle of Bear Island. But Hitler was a puritanical tee-totaler, and you would wait a long time to see anything more interesting than a glass of water at his table.

Hitler might as well have had a bottle or two, though, so high was he on the roll of victories that were flowing into his communications centre. The convoy was all but destroyed and a large flight of planes from an aircraft carrier shot out of the sky. 'See, Göring, See! I foretold how dangerous the aircraft carriers would be. If it had not been for my admonition, they would have sunk every one of our ships!'[1]

He was rubbing his hand at the booty that Carls's ships were taking among the wreckage of the convoy. The admiral had detached the light cruiser *Nürnberg* and three destroyers to finish off what was left of the convoy escort and take the surrender of the remaining ships that could not outrun them. Incomplete reports indicated a dozen or so ships had been sunk or were sinking. A half dozen more scuttled themselves when it looked like the Germans would capture them. The rest were being rounded up and boarded by prize crews. The biggest prize was the oiler *Aldersdale*. Only one ship had put up a fight to the very end, the Soviet tanker *Azerbaijan*. It continued to attempt to outrace the German destroyer sent after it and, when overtaken, its largely female crew depressed their antiaircraft guns to fight it out. The destroyer's 12.7cm guns settled the matter quickly, and when the prize crew came on board, there was no one alive except a few very badly wounded women. Before the German sailors could inspect the ship, it shuddered from an internal explosion, its hull burst open, and a river of bright yellow linseed oil gushed into the sea.[2]

Hitler just shook his head, 'Such racial filth to use women to fight.' Göring thought to himself that it was actually an example of defiant courage at its best. This flicker of chivalry was all that was left of the gallant WWI fighter ace, now a morphine-addicted brute.

But Hitler had not lost the thread of the operation. He was speaking to Dönitz on the phone at the Admiralty in Berlin. 'What is Carls doing, now? There are still carriers out there, are there not?'

'Yes, *mein Führer*, but according to the JG 26 report, they destroyed almost all of the British planes. *Victorious* is without any aircraft. It might as well be sunk as far as this battle is concerned.'

'Well, what about the American carrier?'[3]

Five miles due east of Bear Island, 4 July 1942

Yes, what indeed about the American carrier? Carls's ships had turned about after arriving at the scene of the convoy's destruction and headed back the way they had come to rescue *Lützow* and *Scheer* in their battle with Hamilton's cruisers. He had been surprised by the air attack that Priller had just barely intercepted. The American carrier, with twice as many planes as *Victorious*, was still out there. But where? He had ordered Meyer's group to patrol in the direction that the British planes had come from on the assumption that the American planes would follow the same flight path. He was now racing in that direction in any case to come to the aid of his two hard-pressed cruisers. That would put him within cover range of Meyer's planes, but they could not linger long. He must see off the British cruisers and sail for home. By then the third group from JG 26 should be in the air to cover his ships. A lot of assumptions, he thought to himself.

Still, it was an immensely successful operation in general, though disappointing in that the one light cruiser and three destroyers he had left behind were the only part of the surface fleet that had done anything, and in the end that was nothing more than sweeping up after the Luftwaffe and the U-boats, who would be insufferable in boasting of their laurels. If anything the reputation of the surface fleet would diminish with this victory.

There was still time to pluck a few of those laurels for his big ships if he could sink those enemy cruisers.

A hundred miles to the southwest, instead, it was the U-boats that saw another chance to gather laurels. U-boat Flotilla 10 fresh from Lorient, France, was patrolling in wolf packs of six boats the approaches to Bear Island along the path most likely to be taken by the Home Fleet. Their positioning was astute, and the Home Fleet sailed right into the patrol screen of the wolf pack, consisting of *U-155*, *U-166*, *U-172*, *U-506*, *U-509*, and *U-514*. The signal of the sighting went out and included the information that one carrier's deck was full of aircraft.[4]

The Allied destroyers quickly detected the Germans and pounded on them in a furious depth-charge attack before any of them could lay a good firing plot. Antisubmarine aircraft launched from both carriers to join the hunt. The first kill went to the British. Depth charges burst open *U-506* sending the telltale huge oily bubbles, debris, and the ultimate sign of a kill – bodies – to the surface. Leaving three destroyers behind to keep the U-boats occupied, the Allied capital ships continued on at 28 knots sweeping past the slower submarines and screened by the remaining escorts still throwing depth charges. They were going somewhere fast.[5]

Ten miles due east of Bear Island, 4 July 1942

That somewhere was southeast of Bear Island across the expected path of the German ships returning to their bases in Norway. The frantic radio messages in the clear from the convoy begging for help had stopped. Tovey realized that disaster had overtaken the merchant ships. There was only one chance to retrieve something from this debacle and that was to do just what Churchill had demanded – put the Germans on the bottom.

He had hoped that the two carrier strike groups might find *Tirpitz* and the other ships and hurt them enough to give his own battleships and cruisers an advantage. But now he was getting news of the decimation of the British strike group. It was going to be up to the Americans.

Wasp's strike group had come in on a longer, different route than *Victorious*'s ill-fated planes. A few miles ahead they could see the German ships steaming south in two parallel columns. The sixteen Vindicators climbed to dive-attack altitude as the fifteen Devastators dropped to run above the water. There were only a half dozen F4F fighters because Tovey had no knowledge that the Fw 190s had joined Luftflotte 5. The naval Enigma remained unreadable, and the Luftwaffe Enigma had nothing to say about it. In any case, events were moving faster than messages could be decoded.

Carls, on the other hand, was by now completely aware that there was another swarm of planes out there. The Luftwaffe reconnaissance aircraft shadowing the convoy had been directed to cover the German ships to the west and southwest. One of them, a lumbering Focke Wulf 200 Condor reconnaissance bomber, sighted the incoming American strike force and radioed it immediately to Carls as well as the patrolling group from JG 26.

Tirpitz had been repeatedly briefed to the American crews as the prime target. Now the huge ship with its long guns was easily picked out, heading south at high speed. Heavy cruiser *Hipper* followed. The Americans attacked with torpedo-bombers first to pull German attention to the deck and then the dive-bombers. The lessons of Midway where just such an approach, albeit entirely by accident, had devastated the Japanese carrier force, had not been lost on the crews of the American carrier wings.

Carls had already pulled in his destroyer screen tight around his big ships to mass their antiaircraft fire. Every antiaircraft gun on every ship was fully manned and ready for action. Every man was at his defence against air attack or battle damage station. So it was when the Americans pounced they were met by well-aimed and concentrated fire. The slow Devastators were the first to feel it. Their limping speed attracted the fire of the escorts, and here and there they began to fly apart and crash into the water, spewing debris. The crew of the destroyer *Karl Galster* cheered as one of the Devastators skimmed right over it in flames to crash on its port side. The crew of the *Friedrich Eckoldt* were also cheering as another torpedo-bomber burst into flames several hundred yards to starboard. Their cheers turned to panic when they saw that the explosion that had killed the plane had also released its torpedo to bounce into the sea, submerge and run. There was no time to escape, and the torpedo struck *Eckoldt* amidships. Its engines crippled, it caught fire and fell away from the battle group.

Seven torpedo-bombers survived to get close enough to *Tirpitz* to drop their fish. Three were badly aimed and simply missed. *Tirpitz*'s captain pulled his ship hard to port to dodge another two which left their white wakes streaking just past the ship's turning bow. He was not fast enough to dodge a third torpedo which struck the stern.

The dive-bombers had lined up 4,000 feet above *Tirpitz* and wheeled over one by one to dive into the attack. The trick worked just as it had at Midway. No one on the ships saw them coming. The first Vindicator, piloted by the squadron commander, made a perfect hit on the deck ahead of A turret. The bomb crashed through the thin deck armour and exploded in the storage spaces below, sending a cloud of debris and flames a hundred feet into the air. The second bomb fell immediately to the port side and exploded. On any riveted ship, that would have split the armour belt and hull plates, but *Tirpitz*'s welds held.[6]

The third Vindicator pilot never got to find out if he would have hit the ship. A Fw 190 caught him with a burst of fire just as he was about to release his bomb. Dead at the controls, he fell into the sea. Meyer's group had arrived, drawn immediately to the defence of *Tirpitz* by the Condor's warning. The Americans did not have a chance. Galland did not hang back and quickly found one of the four Wildcat fighters flying in to protect the dive-bombers. He deftly got on the enemy's tail, closed up, and fired. The Wildcat flamed and went down. He looked about for another target, but the feral Fw 190s had hunted everything out the sky it seemed; only three Vindicators and two Devastators were to survive that action of the thirty-one aircraft that had begun the attack.

They too would have been shot out the sky had not Meyer's group also been short of fuel. Meyer called them back as the Americans fled southwest. As his group departed, they flew past *Tirpitz*, and each Fw 190 shook its wings in salute. Galland brought up the rear, elated with the performance of his old command, but looking down on the battleship he was unsettled to see fire burning from a gaping hole in its forward deck and oil trailing from its stern.

Five miles southwest of Bear Island, 4 July 1942

Tirpitz and its companions continued sailing to the sound of battle. Carls could see the smudge of smoke from the stricken *Lützow* and another smoke cloud beyond. The cruiser was making only 5 knots and still absorbing round after round from the two American cruisers.

Scheer's fight against the two British cruisers was going better. *Norfolk* was out of action and listing from holes smashed in its hull by the German's 11-inch shells; fires sent their smoke upwards for *Tirpitz* to observe. *Scheer* had turned all its attention now to *London*, which kept closing the distance.

Hamilton had that pugnacious English battle sense that propelled him to come to grips with the enemy. He would destroy *Scheer* if he had to ram it. Suddenly his ship was straddled by enormous geysers of water. A 15-inch salvo from *Tirpitz* 14 miles away found his range. The bridge was blown into fragments that fell like hail into the surrounding sea. Another round plunged through the deck and into the engine room smashing everything and killing everyone. Fires leapt from severed fuel lines. It would not be long before the fires reached the magazines, but there was no one left to order them flooded. The men on the bridge of the *Tirpitz* watched as they saw the strike of each round glow orange and red on its victim. There was that almost but not quite restrained pleasure of a well-struck blow. Then the magazines blew.

Wichita and *Tuscaloosa* were now alone against the entire German surface fleet. They had pounded *Lützow* into a flaming wreck that was not long for the surface, but with *Tirpitz* and *Hipper* coming down from the northeast and *Scharnhorst*, *Gneisenau* and *Prinz Eugen* coming down on a parallel course four miles away, they were about to become the meat in a German sandwich. Captain Hill's big moment had come.

As the senior of the two American cruiser captains, he ordered *Tuscaloosa* to follow and swing hard to port until they were heading straight for the Germans. A signalman rushed up to the bridge to hand him a message. It was from Tovey to HMS *London*; the communications room had deciphered it. It read: 'Proceed southeast to 72° 30′ North, 20° East. It is imperative you delay enemy as long as possible.'

Hill could only think that as long as possible was only minutes away. Splashes from *Scharnhorst*'s guns were already leaping from the water around them as the German ship ranged in on them. *Scharnhorst* and its sister *Gneisenau* were in effect battleships with 11-inch rather than 15-inch guns. While Hill had been able to pound it out with *Lützow* because of its thin armour, he would have no chance at all against their 14-inch belt and turret armour. At best he could sting them. And that's what he did by his rapid turn. He crossed the 'T' of the German Battlegroup 3 coming towards him line ahead and concentrated the fire of his two ships on *Scharnhorst*. Eighteen guns roared as their almost 400-pound projectiles converged on the German ship. Three struck. Yet, the 32,000-ton behemoth just kept coming. Its forward turrets fired, and their shells straddled *Wichita*. They had the cruiser's range; the next salvo would hit.

Hill had sent the two remaining destroyers, HMS *Somali* and USS *Wainwright*, on a desperate torpedo run at the oncoming German ships. Already *Scharnhorst* was turning its column to present its guns broadside as the destroyers closed at 32 knots, their engines straining for everything they could give. Their torpedoes splashed and ran towards the Germans as the destroyers turned away. The battleship turned quickly aside to let the torpedoes pass but in doing so was unable to train its guns for the killing salvo on *Wichita*.

But the attack sacrificed *Wainwright* which was struck repeatedly by 12.7cm shells from the German destroyers. One shell hit at the waterline, flooding forward compartments. Another cut through to an ammunition storage area and exploded starting a fire. Others burst on the starboard boat davit, the port motor whaleboat, in the galley, scullery, engine room, after crew's berthing compartment, and the forward stack. Fires raged through the sinking ship among the dead and wounded. Its own little 5-inch aft turret kept firing as long as the gun could bear. The captain, Lieutenant Commander Thomas L. Lewis, was the last man alive on the bridge as the destroyer went under.[7]

Gneisenau's guns joined the fight, then *Prinz Eugen*'s. Lieutenant Fairbanks on *Wichita*'s bridge had a ringside seat for everything that was happening, his chronicle for now forgotten. He saw *Gneisenau*'s first round hit on *Tuscaloosa* that smashed its aft battery. Then the sea around *Wichita* erupted as *Tirpitz* and *Hipper* joined in. Only the cruiser's swift manoeuvring was able to make it dodge every hit. *Tuscaloosa* was not so nimble or lucky. Two of *Tirpitz*'s 15-inch shells struck amidships and exploded. The cruiser gushed flames and black smoke, slowed and began to list. Where the shells had hit was a gaping red inferno that was spreading beneath decks. The captain ordered the magazines flooded, then 'Abandon Ship!' The lifeboats had all been shattered, but desperate men leapt into the frigid water. Others tried to help the wounded who filled the companion ways. Now shells from the other German ships struck home one after another until *Tuscaloosa* turned over and sank.

Captain Hill got the last hit in. One of *Wichita*'s shells struck *Scharnhorst*'s bridge, a perfect shot through the armoured viewing aperture, wiping out the entire command group, including Admiral Ciliax. It was the resulting confusion from the now leaderless Battlegroup 3 that allowed *Wichita* to flee at top speed southeast to rendezvous with brave *Somali*.[8]

Carls took a moment now to reassess the situation. His fleet had succeeded in its mission. At least fifteen of the Allied merchant ships had been captured and were sailing to Narvik in convoy with *Nürnberg* and three destroyers. The rest of the convoy was on the bottom or burning and about to sink. His surface fleet had destroyed three of the enemy's heavy cruisers and two destroyers compared to the loss of his own heavy cruiser *Lützow* and one destroyer, and moderate damage to *Tirpitz* and *Scharnhorst*.

He watched as *Lützow* burned and finally capsized. His destroyers had transferred the surviving crew as well as scouring the surrounding water for the crews of the sunk British and American cruisers. His staff urged him to leave the destroyers behind to do this or simply abandon the enemy survivors as the British had done to the *Bismarck*'s crew, of whom all but 114 out of 2,200 had perished. Most died of hypothermia. A U-boat and a trawler were only able to find three men still alive. The British had claimed that they had spotted a U-boat and thus could not risk their ships while stopping to pick up German survivors. That excuse had stunk to high heaven the Germans thought. Carls put a firm stop to that line of thinking. '*Meine Herren*, may I remind you that the German Kriegsmarine fights a knightly war. We will save these men, and let it be a reproach to the English.'[9]

72° 30' North, 19° 45' East, the Norwegian Sea, 4 July 1942

Just to prove that life is unfair, Carls's chivalry was going to cost him dear. After the fight with the cruisers, the time it took to rescue survivors proved costly. It was as if, by lingering at the site of his victory, he was trailing his coat past both the Royal and US Navies. It was time that Tovey used to position the Home Fleet right across Carls's way home. Tovey had calculated the most direct route from the last sighting of the German fleet as it sank Hamilton's cruisers and then marked just where he wanted to be to intersect it – right on the meridian of 20° East.

Carls's staff and the captain of the *Hipper*, Karl Topp, remonstrated with him but to no avail about the dangers of remaining in the area. Topp was outspoken, 'With respect, the enemy carriers have not been accounted for. They are still out there and able to launch more strikes.'

The admiral was a firm man but not a martinet. He did not shut down Topp with an order but chose to reply:

> Kapitän Topp, we can expect the third group from JG 26 to arrive at any time, followed by the others in rotation as soon as they are refuelled and rearmed. The closer we get to home the more time they will have in the air over us. Don't forget that U-boat Flotilla 10 is also screening to our west and would alert us if the Home Fleet approached.

He did not know that Tovey's ships had barrelled right through the U-boat screen and left enough destroyers to keep them dodging depth charges and not able to surface and signal.

Topp would not give up. 'I would feel a lot safer if we set a course for home directly.'

Carls thought the expression of a firm opinion from a subordinate was to be encouraged. He threw the man a bone. 'Just in case, then, Captain, we will send a few of our floatplanes from *Tirpitz* and *Gneisenau* to search to the west.

We will also request the Luftwaffe to hurry up its support for our return home.'
He saw that Topp still wanted to argue:

> Topp, the enemy has shot his bolt. We shall be back in port in seven
> hours. The enemy dare not approach so close to the reach of the
> Luftwaffe, especially when this fleet is still fit for battle. What can he
> do in such a short time?

He turned away and stepped out onto the weather bridge, and that was that.

Carls's message to the Luftwaffe unfortunately went through Headquarters,
Naval Group North, to commander of Naval Forces Norway to the commander
of Luftflotte 5. When it finally reached KG 26 and KG 40 at the airfields at
Bardufoss and Banak, most of the planes had been pulled into their hangars
for maintenance, and the crews were off celebrating, as only aviators can. The
maintenance crews were swarming over the aircraft separating out those with
battle damage and beginning first echelon maintenance on the rest. Only
Priller's group of JG 26 was in relatively good shape.

About three hours later, Carls was to be the recipient of too much
intelligence too late. In quick succession he received reports from U-boat
Flotilla 10, the B-Dienst, and his own floatplanes that the enemy had indeed
stolen a march on him and was cruising between him and his Norwegian bases.
The U-boats had finally broken free of the British destroyers and surfaced to
report the passage of the Home Fleet. The B-Dienst had decrypted Tovey's
message to the late Hamilton telling him to rendezvous at 72° 30′ North, 20°
East. Finally one of the floatplanes radioed the enemy presence just a few miles
to the southeast.[10]

Wasp's Wildcats had pounced on the rest of the floatplanes within range
before they could radio the presence of the Home Fleet. The American pilots
were out for blood after the loss of most of their first strike force, as were the
few surviving British air crews. There were still 23 fighters aboard *Wasp* as
well as 20 dive-bombers and 3 torpedo-bombers. The *Wasp* still had more than
one sting, as Churchill had said in May. *Victorious* had another few aircraft
left and was still game for the next round. Aboard *Wasp* was Lieutenant David
McCampbell, who was beside himself that he had not been able to accompany
the first strike on the *Tirpitz*. He was convinced that he could have accounted
for a few of those Fw 190s and got back too, not an inconsiderable concern.

The planes seemed to leap off the carrier decks to circle until they were all
in the air before heading off. Tovey was determined to fix or slow down the
Germans with this air attack while his big ships closed the distance. No one
was more surprised than Carls when the air attack alarms were sounded. He
rushed out to the weather bridge to see for himself, just in time to watch the
Vindicators diving on to the fleet. He ordered immediate evasive action and
for the destroyers to move in close to provide more antiaircraft protection for
the big ships. It became plain that *Tirpitz* was the object of the dive-bombers'

special attention. The huge ship was still nimble and threw up a leaden storm, dodging bomb after bomb and plucking a plane or two out of the air. The last pilot in the attack felt the 20mm shells stitch through his plane just as he dropped his bomb. He knew it was off target as he pulled away, the plane sluggish to the controls. He looked back and down as the 1,000lb bomb fell and fell to strike not the sea, but at the very last moment the battleship's prow. The fuze worked perfectly, and the prow disappeared in a mushroom of black smoke. When it cleared, all that was left of its elegant shape was twisted metal.

The handful of torpedo planes, three Devastators and two Albacores, also went after *Tirpitz*. The close-in destroyers shot down the low-flying biplanes, but a Devastator got through to drop its fish. It slid under the water with a splash and disappeared, its path marked only by a trail of bubbles. It struck *Tirpitz* amidships and blew through the hull into the crew spaces. Luckily they were empty. The ship rocked with the blow but did not slow down. The damage-control parties sealed off the damaged areas quickly.

The *Hipper*, consort to *Tirpitz*, received some of the attention meant for the bigger ship and took a bomb that blew a hole in its forward deck and another that knocked out its forward turret. It was all Kapitän Topp could do to keep his ship in the battle line as fires licked out of the twisted holes.

The Home Fleet was barely 30 miles away sailing at 28 knots line ahead. Aboard USS *Washington*, Vice Admiral Giffen addressed the crew. 'We go into battle on the 166th anniversary of our Declaration of Independence. We sail with a ship bearing the name of our first president. All of America sails with us today. It is up to us to show the world that we are worthy of the men of 1776 and Washington himself.'[11]

As he closed in Tovey turned the line to port to run roughly parallel to the disorganized course the Germans were on as they tried to fight off the stinging cloud of dive-bombers. At 24,000 yards, the gun captains gave the order to fire. 'The fire gong sounded its "ting ting" and the director layer, his left hand automatically spinning and elevating the hand-wheel, squeezed the trigger with his right hand, and the electric circuits from the turrets were completed.'[12] Twenty British 14-inch guns and nine American 16-inch guns thundered, long flames, the residue of their propellant charges, shooting fiery tongues from the barrels after their huge projectiles raced ahead at almost three times the speed of sound.

Tirpitz was their target. Tovey and the officers on the bridge of *Duke of York* cheered as they saw that the German ship was wreathed in splashes but marked also by orange bursts of flame where it was hit. *Tirpitz*'s well-trained damage-control parties quickly got the fire from the hit in the superstructure under control, but the aft turret had been pierced by two of the big American shells. The explosion found the powder bags for another salvo just lifted up through the magazine well. It blew the top and back off the turret; the great guns were blown loose from their mounts and crashed onto the deck. Fire danced out of the split turret as huge chunks of armour and debris fell into the ocean on either side of the ship.

Then the *Tirpitz*'s own guns spoke before the next enemy salvo could be fired, and it was *Duke of York* and *King George V*'s turn to take a very hard punch. It was a tribute to the German ship and its crew that after absorbing such punishing blows they could coolly hit back. *Washington* absorbed repeated hits from the 11-inch guns of *Scharnhorst* and *Gneisenau* which profited from the enemy's concentration on *Tirpitz*. *Washington*'s thick, tough armour was proof enough against the German shells. Aside from superstructure damage, its armour belt and turrets only showed serious gouges and scorch marks.

Into the beaten zone between the two thundering lines of ships the destroyers charged to make torpedo attacks on the enemy's ships. The sea was filled with white wakes as torpedoes were launched. When they had expended their fish, the destroyers would get in close to fight it out with their guns. The ever-observant Lieutenant Fairbanks would later record that 'they resembled nothing more than mailed knights in wild charges'. In short order the German *Z-30* was on fire and sinking while HMS *Obdurate* caught a stray torpedo and quickly went down.

German destroyers *Richard Beitzen* and *Z-24* slipped through the mêlée to launch torpedoes on *Duke of York*. The battleship tried to turn hard to port to avoid them, and one passed a hundred yards to its stern, but the other struck the stern and jammed the rudder in such a position that the ship was now locked into a wide circle. *Beitzen* swung back and circled around to come up right alongside *King George V* at less than a hundred yards on a parallel course. *Beitzen* raked the British superstructure with its fire, destroying antennas, radars and antiaircraft guns, and driving fragments through the bridge's armoured viewing slit to wound the captain and most of the officers and men with him. Following behind, the *Washington* was already hotly engaged with the two sister battlecruisers but pulled to starboard enough to depress its forward battery as low as possible. One salvo and *Beitzen* disintegrated. *Washington* just ploughed through the wreckage; it did not include a single survivor.[13]

To the rear, the three Allied cruisers pulled out of line to strike northwest and come up on the other side of the German battleline. Instead, *Scheer* and *Prinz Eugen* took the same course to head them off leaving the six battleships to themselves to pound each other to bits. At this point neither admiral was able to influence the battle. Tovey was desperately trying to find a destroyer to take him off the circling *Duke of York* while Carls found that the damage to *Hipper* had knocked out its radios. Signalling by flags was possible but difficult in all the smoke.

Allied Carrier Group, Norwegian Sea, 4 July 1942

Priller had been the first to get his group into the air. It took barely thirty minutes to fly the 150 miles to the battle. He had only to guide on the columns of smoke and the gun flashes. Behind him those of the Ju 88s and He 111s that were not too badly damaged from their attack on the convoy were rolled out, refuelled and rearmed. Enough crews were found who had not yet replaced their blood supply with alcohol to get about fifty planes into the air.

No aircraft were visible over the battle, but along their flight path there appeared the top heavy bulk of aircraft carriers and two destroyers. Priller said to himself, 'The Führer will enjoy the gun camera film I am about to shoot.' He could do little to aid battleships in battle, but he could keep the enemy from tormenting them with his carrier planes. He led his twenty Fw 190s into the attack straight out of the sun. They were in among the Sea Hurricanes and Wildcats so unexpectedly that three of them went down in the first pass. The Germans turned and hunted their targets.

Priller flamed his first Wildcat, amazed at how slow and clumsy it was, and then looked down to see the two carriers. One had at most a half dozen aircraft on its flight deck. The other must have had thirty or more. These were the Devastators and Vindicators from the first strike on the German fleet, now refuelling and rearming for a second strike. He said to his wingman over the radio, 'Follow me down!' They came up from the fantail right over *Wasp*'s flight deck strafing the packed aircraft with 20mm cannon fire. Fuelled planes and bowsers burst into flames behind them. As Priller and his wingman pulled up and around, they could see the explosions of ordnance carried by the aircraft on the flight deck. He said with a laugh to his longtime wingman, Heinz Wodarczyk, 'Shall we go again or do you think they've had enough of the glory of the German Luftwaffe?'

By the time he had gained altitude, most of the British and American fighters had been shot down or chased away – all except one. And this one had shot down two of Priller's experienced pilots, amazing in light of his aircraft. McCampbell now found himself the object of a dozen Fw 190s. His safety was in the fact that so many of them were after him that they endangered each other. He slipped down to the deck and around the *Victorious* hoping to lead any of his pursuers through the ship's antiaircraft fire. Priller now felt the challenge of the chase and followed the American down and around, ignoring the fire from the ship. His wingman was not so lucky and began to trail smoke. 'I am hit, Pips!' he shouted into this radio. That pulled Priller back to shepherd his wingman to safety. Heinz Wodarczyk and he had been together too long for Priller to abandon him.

By now Priller had lost three of his planes to air combat and another to antiaircraft fire while two more were damaged and had to be guided home. Another pilot pointed to the east where a flight of a dozen Junkers and

Heinkels was coming in. They had homed in on the fight, and so Priller made room for them as they attacked. This was their second air battle in twenty-four hours, and many of them were tired. Audacity in battle is a factor of strength, and strength comes from rest. Most of their attacks were not pressed home with the élan of their fight with the convoy. Yet the Ju 88s did make several hits on both carriers. The armoured steel deck of *Victorious* absorbed the explosions. Nothing penetrated to the hangar deck or fuel and ammunition. The *Wasp*'s teak decks were no barrier at all to the German bombs, which crashed through to explode inside the hangar deck, filled with bombs and torpedoes ready to be sent topside. The explosions ripped through the ship igniting aviation fuel in turn. Piling on misery were the torpedoes dropped by the He 111s. Two of them hit home. Within minutes the carrier was listing to port as flaming wreckage from the splintered deck fell overboard.[14]

Confident that *Wasp* would soon go under, that *Victorious* had taken repeated hits to its flight deck to make it useless, and having expended their bombs, the German fighters and bombers headed back to their Norwegian bases. Another flight of Ju 88s and He 111s passed them coming out and were told to go in the direction of the battleships.

Lieutenant McCampbell had landed on *Victorious* as soon as the German planes had flown off to be refuelled. He taxied down the deck dodging the jagged steel where the German bombs had hit, following the surviving Sea Hurricane and made it into the air. They flew after the German dive- and torpedo-bombers, heading north. The Wildcat and the Hurricane fell on the last two Heinkels in the formation. McCampbell came up close before pressing the firing button. The plane's wing tore off, and it plummeted to the sea. He saw that the Hurricane had splashed another one.[15]

By the time the two fighters reached the naval battle, McCampbell had shot down two more Heinkels and was on the tail of a Ju 88. The presence of an unknown number of Allied fighter pilots panicked the Ju 88s. They scattered, jettisoned their bombs, and headed for home. The Wildcat and the Hurricane followed. McCampbell watched one enemy catch fire and explode. He saw that the Hurricane had scored another kill. They saluted each other as they turned back to *Victorious* to rearm.[16]

Surface Engagement, Norwegian Sea, 4 July 1942

Among the capital ships the battle had broken into three parts. *King George V* and *Tirpitz* were slugging it out while *Washington* duelled with the two battle-cruisers. The cruisers were pounding each other as they moved off on a northerly course. A destroyer had finally picked up Admiral Tovey, but the action was too hot to put him on another of the big ships. Admiral Carls was still unable to communicate with his ships. Each captain just fought it out.

The two German heavy cruisers were evenly matched with the Allied cruiser force. The three British ships concentrated on *Scheer* while *Wichita* took on *Prinz Eugen*. *Scheer* was bigger-gunned and more heavily armoured than the British heavy cruisers. Its shells were more powerful and destructive than those of the British 8-inch guns; its armour belt of 3.1 inches and turrets of 5.5 inches compared lethally to *Kent*'s and *Cumberland*'s 1 inch for belt and turret. Their only advantage was that they had more than twice as many guns. In the end, *Scheer* was just plain luckier. It gutted *Cumberland* which burned and drifted away.

The big guns were gaining the upper hand in the other fights as well. *Tirpitz*'s remaining turrets were firing heavier metal than *King George V* and scoring hits at the waterline, piercing the armour belt and flooding interior compartments till the British ship slowed perceptibly. The German armour-piercing shells were better made, and their propellant more powerful. Watertight hatches failed as the big German shells gutted the British battleship. It slowed and began to settle.

Washington had battered *Scharnhorst* into a wreck at closer and closer range with its 16-inch shells. *Gneisenau* was not in much better shape with turrets out of commission and fires raging below decks. *Washington*'s own armour had been largely proof against the smaller German guns. The Kriegsmarine would rue the day it had decided to postpone the fitting out of these two battlecruisers with 15-inch guns. *Washington* moved on past them to come up on *Tirpitz* from the stern where one turret had been knocked out. The two forward American turrets pumped a rapid salvo into the German ship at short range. The *Tirpitz*'s superstructure crumpled, spewing debris in every direction into the sea, shutting down the ship's electrical system that controlled the guns. Fires were burning everywhere as the crew scrambled out of the wreckage dragging their wounded to the deck. *Washington* came up on the port quarter, firing at the unheard-of distance of half a mile. There were no misses at that range.

Tirpitz was a dying beast, crippled but dragging itself forward on engines that still ran while every other ship's function had been killed. The crew were spilling over the side as *Washington* fired again and again, tearing great jagged holes. Then *Tirpitz* perished in an explosion that broke its back and seemed to lift the ship from the centre. The German battleship broke in two and each part began to sink. *Washington* circled its fallen prey.[17]

Carls was a realist and knew that *Tirpitz* was doomed as soon as *Washington* struck that first crushing blow. He ordered *Hipper* out of the fight and signalled by flag to *Scharnhorst* and *Gneisenau* to follow. Only *Gneisenau* was able to do so. *Scharnhorst* was adrift, its captain and other senior officers dead, its engines shattered. The surviving destroyers formed a rearguard on the heavy ships. *Kent* might well have gone the same way as *Cumberland* had not Carls pulled the German cruisers after him as he withdrew at top speed back to

Norway. Light cruiser *Nigeria* had had little part in the fight among the heavies, but now would get in the last lick, following close on the retreating Germans to release a spread of torpedoes. Two struck *Prinz Eugen*, the last ship in line. The German cruiser stopped as its engines quit and the sea rushed in. In fifteen minutes it sank.[18]

That was the last engagement in the struggle that would be named the Battle of 20° East. The only task left for both sides was to get their stricken survivors back to port. The remnants of the Home Fleet lingered only to save what they could and pick up survivors. For this the destroyers did yeoman work, picking up over 3,000 men from the sea, British, American and German. The Allies could claim victory since it was the Germans who abandoned the field, but the losses on both sides were numbing. It was a victory only on a very narrow counting of the points. For the Allies, the news that they had lost the battleship *King George V*, the carrier *Wasp*, heavy cruisers *Cumberland*, *London*, *Norfolk*, and *Tuscaloosa*, and five destroyers was grim. The British Cabinet was stunned.

Kent took *Duke of York* in tow and gathered up the remnants of the Home Fleet to sail home to Scapa Flow. Tragically, on the way home they encountered the wolf pack they had barged through two days before. Lieutenant Hans-Günther Kuhlmann acquired the British battleship through the periscope of *U-166*. It was barely making 8 knots, about what a merchant ship might make. How perfect, Kuhlman thought. The escorts coursed alongside the battleships and carrier, but now there was that perfect gap. 'Torpedo los,' he said, and two torpedoes shot out of the bow tubes in a burst of bubbles. Both hit. The great ship was mortally wounded and would slowly sink. Kuhlman and the other U-boat captains forbore to attack the destroyers that came alongside the settling battleship to take off the crew. But they did circle the remaining capital ships and dart in repeatedly to attack. Here again the escorts proved their worth, dashing back and forth to depth-charge the enemy. *Victorious* had a few planes left that managed to dodge the damaged portions of the hull to take off and assist in spotting the U-boats. In the end *Duke of York* was avenged when depth charges smashed open *U-155* and *U-514*. Still, the Kriegsmarine had come out well ahead.[19]

Without a doubt the two battles – Bear Island and 20° East – had been an Allied strategic disaster of the first order. The losses suffered by the Allies were only the beginning of the dividends the operation would pay the Germans. To add insult to injury the Germans were to make enormous propaganda points by filming the arrival in German ports of the fifteen captured Allied merchant ships and their cargoes and the parading of their crews.[20]

The Wolfsschanze, East Prussia, 4 July 1942

Dönitz flew in late at night to report to Hitler. The leader of the Third Reich kept very late hours so the admiral was ushered right in to see him. Hitler was waiting for him, a report in his hand. The only other man in the room was Heydrich. The look on Hitler's face was grim. He looked up over his bifocals and said, 'The British are claiming a victory over our fleet. The BBC is saying nothing else. It is Jutland all over again, Dönitz. Our fleet sailed out and ran home after getting beaten.'

Without hesitation, Dönitz replied, 'Then may God grant the British another such victory!'

Hitler looked puzzled. Dönitz immediately pointed out that the Allies, and particularly the British, had suffered a strategic catastrophe. They had lost the entire convoy and in such a way to discredit them not only with the rest of the world but with their own people. The naval battle south of Bear Island had gutted the Home Fleet, and embarrassed the Americans with the loss of their carrier while under British command. It was sure to lead to dissent between them or an outright falling out. 'I would also wager, *mein Führer*, that it will be next to impossible for them to recruit merchant crews for another convoy. We have slammed the door to Russia shut for you.' Dönitz was happy to have this time alone with Hitler. He was fortunate that Göring had grown weary and retired or he would be greedily claiming all credit for the Luftwaffe.

While Hitler paused to consider this, Dönitz opened his valise to show Hitler the preliminary reports on the war booty on the captured ships taken from their manifests. He began reading off the lists till Hitler's eyes grew bright with greed. 'Five thousand tons of aluminium, 2,500 Studebaker trucks and a year's worth of parts, 22,000 tons of explosives, 40,000 tons of food,' and a myriad of other precious resources that would feed war's voracious appetite.

Heydrich deftly added more lustre to the Kriegsmarine's accomplishment by praising it for originating and planning this operation. How fat Göring would pout the next day as Hitler sang the Navy's praises. He added slyly, 'Do not forget, *mein Führer*, that this victory was won on the Americans' national day of independence. Salt in the wound, salt in the wound.'

By now Hitler's imagination was racing to the moon with the consequences of this victory.

> Oh, and yes, we shall use this war booty well. This Canadian and American aluminium will make German tank engines and not Russian ones. I shall give all the American trucks to Bock, and all that American food shall feed his men. I want the Americans to twist in the wind over this. Oh, Goebbels will swoon over the possibilities.[21]

Chapter 7

Counting the Victories

Stary Oskol, 1 July 1942

The encirclement had been perfectly executed. The Germans had thrust into the wide steppe between the Donets and Don after seizing crossings on the former river three weeks before. Here Hitler hoped to trap and destroy the last of Stalin's reserves.

Geyr's XL Panzer Corps arrived at Stary Oskol only to find the wide grassy and empty steppe inside their *Kessel* was empty of Soviet forces.[1] Against all expectations the enemy had flown and had even been able to carry away their heavy equipment. The Germans had grown too used to being able to encircle vast numbers of Soviet troops who had been nailed to the ground and unable to manoeuvre by Stalin's refusal to allow his commanders any tactical flexibility. This was indeed something new.

Geyr immediately reported the enemy retreat and requested permission to strike directly for the Don River and capture its crossings. Paulus refused and ordered, 'You will swing north to link up with the Fourth Panzer Army coming down from Voronezh.'[2]

Sevastopol, Crimea, 3 July 1942

The defences of the great Soviet naval base and fortress of Sevastopol had finally been cracked wide open by Manstein's 11th Army after three weeks of crushing bombardment by the greatest concentration of heavy artillery seen so far in the war. The guns and heavy mortars had smashed bunkers, cupolas and galleries one after another. The 88mm flak guns of the 18th Flak Regiment earned fame by firing their flat-trajectory high-velocity shells directly through the gunports and apertures of the Soviet defences.

The 110,000-man Soviet garrison had been decimated. Now panic flew among the survivors:

> In a barricaded gallery within the very cliffs of the bay, about 1,000 women, children, and troops were sheltering. The commissar in command refused to open the doors. Sappers got ready to blow them in. At

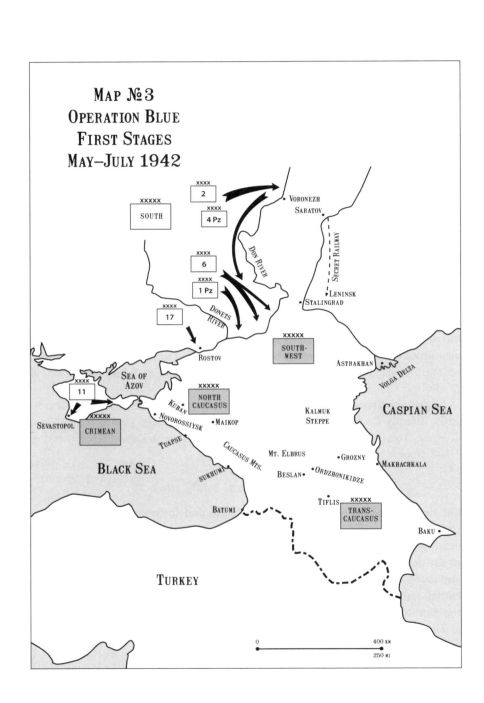

MAP №3
OPERATION BLUE
FIRST STAGES
MAY–JULY 1942

XXXX
2

XXXXX
SOUTH

XXXX
4 Pz

• VORONEZH
SARATOV •

XXXX
6

DON RIVER

XXXX
1 Pz

SECRET RAILWAY

XXXX
17

DONETS RIVER

• LENINSK
• STALINGRAD

XXXXX
SOUTH-
WEST

• ROSTOV

ASTRAKHAN •

VOLGA DELTA

XXXX
11

SEA OF
AZOV

XXXXX
NORTH
CAUCASUS

KUBAN

CASPIAN SEA

XXXXX
CRIMEAN

SEVASTOPOL •

• NOVOROSSIYSK   • MAIKOP

KALMUK
STEPPE

TUAPSE

CAUCASUS MTS.

MT. ELBRUS

• GROZNY

• MAKHACHKALA

BLACK SEA

SUKHUMI •

BESLAN • • ORDZHONIKIDZE

BATUMI •

TIFLIS •

XXXXX
TRANS-
CAUCASUS

BAKU •

TURKEY

0   400 KM

250 MI

that moment the commissar blew up the entire gallery. A dozen German sappers were killed at the same time.[3]

Manstein attributed this action to the Soviets' complete contempt for human life as he described the garrison's fight to the death. Perhaps he should have considered that it was the German record for the barbaric treatment of their prisoners that made a fight to the bitter end preferable to German captivity. It requires no wisdom at all to give an enemy such determination.

Manstein had a very useful blind eye. Not only was he indifferent to the treatment of Soviet prisoners, but he had obeyed Hitler's infamous Commissar Order to shoot all captured communist officials. He had also lent thousands of his own Army troops to help the SS Einsatzgruppen massacre Jews. Resisting these orders might endanger his goal of becoming Chief of Staff of the Army. Complying with them could only facilitate his ambition. That, and his crushing of Sevastopol, convinced Hitler and those around him that in Manstein he had found a very hard man. And to this very hard man, he would give a field marshal's baton.[4]

This was also the man who had put his career on the line in 1934 in protest over the dismissal from the Army of one of his officers who was classified as a *Mischling* because he had a Jewish grandparent. For him a German was someone who was of German culture, especially one who put his life in service of the country as a soldier.[5]

On the outskirts of Voronezh, 4 July 1942

The speed of the Blitzkrieg was taking any freedom of action out of Bock's hands as *Grossdeutschland* Motorized, 16th Motorized, and 24th Panzer Divisions all bounced bridges over the northern Don, their advance elements in between the retreating Russian columns. The speed of their advance surprised the Soviet bridge guards. At Semiluki, on the way to Voronezh, the Soviet engineers had lit normal fuzes which were burning as the Germans started to cross. Corporal Hempel of the reconnaissance battalion jumped into the water to rip out the fuzes, the last one barely 8 inches from 125 pounds of explosive.

Grossdeutschland's assault-gun units, with infantry riding on the vehicles, quickly penetrated into Voronezh as far as the railway marshalling yards but were driven back by a strong Soviet counterattack. The ease of the penetration convinced Bock that the city could be seized quickly and still allow him to swing his panzers south to trap Timoshenko's retreating forces before they could cross the Don.[6]

This was the first action of *Grossdeutschland* as a division. It had been formed as an elite infantry regiment from the *Wachtregiment/Berlin*, the Army's guard formation for the German capital, in 1939. The name, meaning Greater Germany, had been chosen because recruits came from all over the country; it was not based on a single locality like most of the rest of the infantry divisions. It had distinguished itself in France and in Russia in 1941, in the latter campaign suffering 4,070 casualties and completely turning over its strength. Reorganized as the Army's elite division in early 1942, it was decreed that:

> All new men taken into 'GD' must be young, preferably volunteers, at least 1.70 metres [5ft 7in] in height, must have perfect eyesight without glasses, and must have no criminal record. It was further required that all members come up to the 'ideal picture of the German soldier', a requirement held even more important for NCOs and especially officers. In addition, Inf. Div. (mot.) *Grossdeutschland* was to receive the latest and best equipment as soon as it was released for use by front-line units.[7]

The result was a military instrument as sharp and deadly as the spear of Achilles, as shown in the daring valour of men like Corporal Hempel.

Stavka, Moscow, 5 July 1942

Chief of the Soviet General Staff General Boris Shaposnikov picked up the phone to call Stalin. He had been the bearer of nothing but bad news since the war began, but Stalin kept him on when so many other messengers had been shot. Shaposnikov was a former tsarist officer, general staff trained, who had thrown in his lot with the Bolsheviks and in the ensuing years had never got on Stalin's bad side by posing any sort of a threat.

'Comrade Stalin, we are just getting word from the British that their convoy has been destroyed.'

Stalin cut in. 'Well, they always overreact these capitalists, so melodramatic about losses. So, how many ships did they really lose?'

'All of them, Comrade Stalin.'

There was quiet on the other end of the line for a very long time. Stalin felt just as he had when he had been told that the Germans had attacked on 22 June 1941. He could feel the same sort of paralytic shock seeping through his body, the same feeling that had cast him into such a trough of depression that he had hid in his *dacha* for the first ten days of the war. Foreign Minister Molotov had had to announce to the people the news of the invasion. Without Stalin, the communist leadership had panicked and lost its nerve. They were so frightened that they instinctively called upon the Almighty for help and begged the Russian Orthodox Patriarch of Moscow to address the nation the next day. The cleric delivered a rousing patriotic appeal to defend the Russian lands as their ancestors had done against Tatar, Pole, Swede, Frenchman and German. It was a great speech, but it was not Stalin's.

Finally Stalin spoke. 'All, you are sure, all?'

'Yes, every one. Those that were not sunk were captured by the Germans. It gets worse. The British were defeated by the German fleet in a battle in the Norwegian Sea and lost several battleships.'

Stalin fought off the tendrils of paralysis. He was the *Vozhd*; he summoned power from deep within. His mind raced to all the possible strategic and political consequences of the disaster. Would Churchill survive this catastrophe? Stalin despised him as an anticommunist to the bone, but he knew that the Englishman would fight Hitler to the death. He was not so sure of anyone who might succeed him. The NKVD[8] analysis said that none of them had the will or ability of Churchill. It would be all too easy for the British to make a separate peace if they were led to it by a well-meaning fool.

Then what about the Americans? Roosevelt had never shown the hostility to the first communist country that Churchill had and had been cooperative and helpful. How would his domestic enemies, none of whom were in the socialist camp, damage him with this defeat?

These questions all pointed to the central issue – the continuance of aid. That aid was becoming vital to the war effort. His propaganda apparatus could trumpet the heroic feats of Soviet production all it wanted, but he knew that Canadian and American aluminium was vital to the making of tank and aircraft engines, that American aviation fuel was keeping a larger and larger part of the Red Air Force in the air, that American trucks were becoming essential to create any sort of mobility in both battle and logistics.

How then was the Soviet Union to continue to receive this aid? The Persian Corridor and the Pacific route were the only substitutes, and neither was in any condition to take up the slack immediately. He would have to encourage the British and Americans to concentrate their shipments through those two routes. Persia was by far the more important. Shipments through there would go directly to most threatened part of the front, just to the north of the Caucasus, in that wide almost empty space between the Don and Volga.

He would have to order the communist parties and sympathizers in the Allied countries to support Churchill and Roosevelt and address the deepest condolences to both leaders with saccharin words of sympathy and thanks from the Soviet people. Yes, and they would give the strongest encouragement not to let this setback stop the convoys. Look at all the setbacks the Soviet Union had suffered and yet was fighting on. He would give the entire world-wide propaganda apparatus a good crank, a very good crank.

Beyond that there was the central problem of how to get by now that the materials from the Arctic route had been stopped. He stopped to consider how prescient he must have been to have ordered the 'secret railway' built, that ran from Saratov, north of Voronezh, down the east bank of the Volga to Leninsk only some dozen miles east of Stalingrad. It had been built so quickly that there had been no time to lay a track bed; the sleepers were laid directly on the ground. It was single-tracked with sidings for trains to wait as others passed. Part of the Trans-Siberian Railway had had to be dismantled to find the resources for it, but it had been done. If the Germans succeeded in taking Voronezh and its marshalling yards, he would still have an alternative route to bring Allied war materials from Persia to the threatened Moscow front.[9]

The White House, Washington, DC, 5 July 1942

Admiral King had always been careful to hide his temper from the President. But now he was in full warpaint and feathers. 'Mr President, the loss of the *Wasp* reduces our carrier strength by a full 20 per cent! We have only four carriers left, and the Essex Class won't be coming into service until late this year and next year.[10] I tell you, sir, we can no longer support both the Arctic convoys and hold the Japanese at bay, much less go over to the attack.'

He had just done what Franklin Roosevelt abhorred. He had asked the President to choose. King now envied Marshall. The general had figured out early as Chief of Staff that Roosevelt liked to employ an informal, bantering, almost jovial approach, which would allow him later to say that he had not really made a commitment. Marshall had used his stiff and formal manner to underline the finality of any decision that he asked Roosevelt to make, a decision he could not back out of later.

Now King was pressing the President in just the same manner, no more 'our' Navy wink-winks, nod-nods. But Roosevelt needed it both ways. He far more than King realized the centrality of keeping both the British and the Russians in the war. And in a way he was as much an Anglophile as King was an Anglophobe. He was a comfortable member of that transatlantic community of class, culture and belief. Churchill and he were two gentlemen who saw that Western civilization was at stake.

In a way, Roosevelt was also like Stalin in that he realized as a war leader that setbacks and cruel defeats must be endured and overcome. He was not like Stalin, though, in that he was answerable to the people, and the people were influenced by the press, and a very powerful part of the press were the Hearst papers owned by a Roosevelt-hater of the first order. He wistfully thought how nice it would be to have William Randolph Hearst shot.

But King would not let go of the issue. 'How many times must we pull the British bacon out of the fire, sir?'

Roosevelt straightened up in his wheelchair:

> Must I remind you that the British were holding off the Nazi wolf for more than two years before Hitler declared war on us. They are at the end of their resources, and I suggest you consider what strategic situation the United States would be in if the British had caved in? Gentlemen, we agreed last year that if the United States entered the war, we would have a Germany-first policy. The Germans were and remain the primary threat. We must keep our eye on the ball.

He looked at King as if to tell him to who was boss. The admiral got the hint.

> I have had the most distressing talk with Churchill. His government has been rocked to the very bottom by the twin disasters at Tobruk and with the convoy and Home Fleet. He does not think he will survive in office much longer. A motion of no confidence will be made in the House in a few days.

In the end, the chiefs agreed that aid to Britain and the Soviet Union must continue but that the Russian supplies would have to go by way of the Persian Corridor and the Pacific Route. There was no alternative, but it would take time for both those avenues to begin to funnel the volume of material that had been sent through the Arctic to Murmansk. That Roosevelt and Stalin had arrived at the same conclusion was due to the iron logic of their predicament.[11]

Bock's Headquarters, Poltava, Ukraine, 5 July 1942

Hitler was so alarmed at the failure of the encirclement and the failure of Bock to destroy significant Soviet forces on his drive to Voronezh that he flew immediately into the Army Group South headquarters. He would have gone two days earlier but for his attention to Rösselsprung. Now he was face to face with Bock, riding a wave of elation over the twin victories of Rösselsprung and Sevastopol. He told the army group commander, 'I no longer insist upon the capture of the city, Bock, I also no longer consider it [Voronezh] to be necessary and I leave it up to you to move south immediately.'[12]

Hitler was correct in his operational assessment that Voronezh was not important. Its significance lay in the fact that he and his generals believed Timoshenko's forces could be destroyed as the Germans advanced in the direction of Voronezh, just as they believed that more of Timoshenko's Southwest Front could be destroyed as the Germans moved in the direction of Stalingrad. The cities themselves were only of secondary importance as a rail junction in the case of Voronezh and a war materials manufacturing centre in the case of Stalingrad. They correctly saw that the enemy's forces were the main objectives. They were still not sure why the Soviets were escaping destruction, but Hitler thought it was that they were simply disintegrating as a fighting force. It was then only necessary to press hard on the heels of a rout. He had reminded Bock that the purpose of his drive towards Voronezh had been to destroy enemy forces and cover the army group's flank.

All very good for the Supreme War Lord. But after that conclusion he failed to act on it and deliver a decisive order to turn away from Voronezh. Instead, he left the decision to Bock. This was a profound failure of leadership. Unfortunately, the army group commander was getting pulled into a hornet's nest just then and becoming preoccupied with the tactical rather than the operational imperatives. The Soviets were now using cities as fortress centres of defence into which they sucked large numbers of ill-prepared Germans.

The House of Commons, London, 9 July 1942

'How does Winston do it?' Lord Beaverbrook, the man called the First Baron of Fleet Street and former wartime Minister of Aircraft Production and Supply, and now Lord Privy Seal, just shook his head in wonder at the performance he had just witnessed on the floor of the House from its gallery. He was the greatest newspaper man in Britain but, unlike Hearst, he was a friend of the country's war leader. 'Winston can fall into the black pit of Hades and come up with his arms full of sunshine.'

What he had just witnessed was the British Lion defending himself in terms of such power and persuasion that the vote of no confidence had failed, just barely, but by just enough to keep him safe for now as prime minister. Churchill's power of rhetoric had been vastly aided by the fact that there seemed no one able to step into his shoes. That there were no capable rivals in his Conservative Party had been made evident by the fiasco of 1940 when the Chamberlain government had collapsed, and he had been the only choice. The options had not got any better since. The problem was aggravated by the fact that in the British system war cabinets included all major parties for the sake of national unity. The alternative of the leader of the Labour Party, Clement Attlee, coming to power was too much for Conservatives, still in a majority in the House, to contemplate. He was a genuine patriot and determined supporter of the war against Hitler, but he was no war leader. Churchill had pegged him right when he had said that Attlee 'was a very modest man but that he had much to be modest about'. A man whose whole life had been set on redistributing wealth could be no war leader.

Tobruk and the battles in the Norwegian Sea had been the milestones that had nearly sunk Churchill. One more would surely take him to the bottom. But he had found one great advantage that had come out of the disasters. The German surface fleet had come out of hiding led by the great bogeyman, the *Tirpitz*. Now most of the German ships were on the bottom, and the rest too battered to be a threat to anyone. Although at great cost to the Royal Navy, prestige, morale and the American alliance, the German fleet in being had been eliminated. And with it the threat to the convoys. Theoretically, they could be resumed.

All too theoretically. The shock of the convoy's loss had been felt most keenly among the old salts of the Merchant Navy. They were making it quite clear that not a man would sign on for any ship going to Russia's Arctic ports. That, and Roosevelt's call to inform him that the United States would not support another Arctic convoy, sealed their fate. Churchill deftly plucked a silver lining from this rent garment. The Home Fleet would not have to be rebuilt to its previous size to watch a now non-existent German surface fleet. The Royal Navy's already over-stretched resources could more efficiently be allocated to those theatres upon which the survival of Britain depended, particularly the Mediterranean. Now that Rommel was at the gates of Egypt, every ship was needed to run the reinforcement convoys through to Alexandria.

Stavka, Moscow, 12 July 1942

Hitler and Stalin came to critical conclusions almost at the same time in mid-July.

Stalin finally gave up the notion that Moscow was the main German objective and began to transfer Stavka reserves south. He also listened carefully to his general staff. Another great encirclement of Soviet forces was out of the question. He listened to reason, and no one was shot. Instead, he had called Timoshenko on 12 July and said, 'I order the formation of the Stalingrad Front, and the city itself will be defended to the last man by the 62nd Army.' Stalin was desperate to delay the enemy in order to bring up reserves and to finish the city's defences.

His generals were doing their best to buy him that time by increasingly skilful delaying actions. They would hold the Germans just long enough to make them deploy, and then, before becoming decisively engaged, they would retreat.

As skilful as this may have been on some larger scale, to the troops involved it was demoralizing. In what seemed a headlong flight towards the Don a sense of hopelessness began to pervade the Red Army. A woman on the staff of one of the armies wrote,

> It was an absolutely desperate situation. The Germans were so well equipped. They had motorized divisions. We tried to fight them in the field but they spotted us from the air . . . I felt it was all so hopeless. Yes, I was a convinced communist but for the first time in my life I started praying, crying out to God to help me. I tried to remember my grand-mother's prayers.

A great Russian writer of the war, Viktor Nekrasov, recalled,

> The general mood was frightful. The Germans were deep inside Russia, descending like an avalanche on the Don – and where was our front – it did not exist at all . . . When civilians asked our retreating troops where they were going, we could not look them in the eye.[13]

Retreat they did, which is what saved so many of them, even before Stalin gave permission, retreat back to the lower Don and across to avoid the terror of encirclement.

Führer Headquarters, Vinnitsa, Ukraine, 15 July 1942

Hitler transferred his headquarters from Rastenburg to Vinnitsa in the Ukraine (codenamed Werewolf), relieved Bock, and began to assume greater control of operations. The heat greatly affected him in the special bunker that had been built for him, and he was short-tempered and even less willing to listen to his commanders than before.

What was actually a fairly well controlled Soviet retreat was in Hitler's eyes evidence of disintegration and panic, Homer's 'comrade of blood-curdling rout'.[14] It was then that he was seduced by what he saw as an abundance of riches. The drive towards Stalingrad became secondary to alluring possibilities at Rostov at the mouth of the Don, gateway to the Caucasus. He divided Army Group South into Army Groups A and B. The former under the command of Field Marshal Wilhelm List included 11th, 17th, and 1st Panzer Armies. Army Group B, under Weichs, retained 2nd, 6th, and 4th Panzer Armies. So Hitler had flung his forces at the opposite ends of the vast front from Voronezh to Rostov, leaving only 6th Army marching largely on foot in the direction of Stalingrad.

With Hitler's movement of his headquarters came his entourage of lackeys. Field Marshal von Kluge's aide, Leutnant Philipp von Boeselager, had accompanied his master to Werewolf and recorded his impressions:

> At the table were seated representatives of all the ministries. Although I was surrounded by men in various uniforms, I was one of the genuine military men present. These gaudy outfits and tinny decorations seemed to me worthy of a decadent royal court. What I heard of the conversations was so dreadfully banal that I remember it perfectly.[15]

Hosting the lunch was Reichsleiter Martin Bormann, head of the Nazi Party and the *éminence grise* of the headquarters. To Boeselager it was instantly apparent that the man was 'brutal, careless, violent, he was a man who immediately inspired fear'. Bormann was an out-and-out pagan who openly despised all things Christian. He stated, 'National Socialism and Christianity are irreconcilable.' Access to Hitler was closely held in Bormann's hands; he realized that access also put great power in those same hands. It was in his interest to make sure that Hitler had no favourites who did not have to pay obeisance to him. No chief eunuch of any Turkish sultan or Chinese emperor had a better understanding of the power that access gave. It was no wonder he was called the 'Machiavelli behind the office desk'.[16]

So disgusted was Boeselager at the conversation and its anti-Catholic vitriol that he got up abruptly and left the room for a smoke and to calm down. Bormann ordered his return and asked why he had left. The young officer said that he had accompanied the field marshal to discuss the fate of his surrounded army at Rzhev but had only heard twaddle at the headquarters. 'Take this man away,' Bormann ordered the SS guard. He was locked up, but Kluge snatched him away and hurried him to their plane. He heard him out and said, 'That's enough, that's enough. This time I was able to save you. The next time, you'll keep your mouth shut. But basically, you're absolutely right!'[17]

Stalingrad, 16 July 1942

Chuikov still walked with a cane when he entered Stalingrad Front head-quarters with his chief political officer. No one had information, but rumours flew that the Germans were approaching the great bend in the Don, only some 45 miles from Stalingrad. Earlier that month his reserve army had been renamed 64th Army and ordered to the front on the west side of the Don, but the move had been so hurried that vital elements of it were still far away in Tula. His mission was to cover the lower part of the big bend of the Don. He was not encouraged by the state of morale of the neighbouring 62nd Army on his right. He encountered a number of individual soldiers walking east who said that they were 'looking for someone on the other side of the Volga'; he also intercepted a truck filled with fleeing officers from two of its divisional staffs.[18]

> In everything I could see a lack of firm resistance at the front – a lack of tenacity in battle. It seemed as if everyone, from the army commander downwards, was always ready to make another move backwards ... When I asked where the Germans were, where their own units were, and where they were going, they could not give me a sensible reply.[19]

As he was trying to assemble his army, Chuikov found himself replaced by General V. N. Gordov. It had been a trying time for Chuikov; Gordov was doctrinaire, refused to listen to subordinates, and lived in a world of unreality. His nonsensical orders left the army reserves on the east bank of the Don.

Rostov na Donu, 23 July 1942

Like Voronezh, Rostov, near the Black Sea mouth of the Don,[20] was defended as a fortress with unbelievable bitterness by the Soviets. At the implacable heart of the defence were NKVD troops, the fanatical fighting arm of the secret police. As protectors of the regime they had been specially trained in street fighting. One German commander said,

> The struggle for the city core of Rostov was struggle without pity. The defenders refused to allow themselves to be captured, fought to the end, fired from concealment when overrun and not discovered or wounded until they were killed. German wounded had to be placed in armoured personnel carriers and guarded. If this was not done we found them later murdered or stabbed.[21]

Finally the Germans secured the city as the last of the defenders slipped across to the eastern bank of the Don. Now they had the wide river at its mouth as a final barrier against the Germans. The only way across was seemingly impossible to take, the intact bridge over the Don with its strong guard. Now 17th Army's commander turned to the Brandenburgers, the special operations regiment of the German Army, every man a volunteer.

At 02.30 on 23 July Leutnant Grabert and his company slipped quietly through the dark towards the bridge. Grabert was with the lead squad when the Soviets detected them and opened fire. He rushed forward at the head of his men and overwhelmed the guard, ran across the long span, and set up a bridgehead. For an entire day Grabert and his men held out against vicious counterattacks. When at last they were about to be overrrun, the Stukas came screaming down from the sky to blast away the enemy.

Over the bridge rumbled the tanks of LVII Panzer Corps towards the open plains of the Kuban that led to the Caucasus and beyond to the oilfields of Baku. The tanks rolled past the bodies of Leutnant Grabert and most of his men, and into the Kuban steppe. The road to the Caucasus had been blown wide open.

Werewolf, 23 July 1942

Hitler was in a row with his methodical and colourless Chief of the Army General Staff, Generaloberst Franz Halder. He was a master of military logic, which was why Hitler was in such a foul mood, that and the heat of a Ukrainian summer. 'The Russians are conducting a planned withdrawal, *mein Führer.*'

'Nonsense,' Hitler shot back, 'they're fleeing, they're finished, they're at the end after the blows we've inflicted on them in the past months.' Hitler did not know that the Stavka was committing new and inexperienced armies, such as the 62nd and 64th Armies, to the front rather than its high quality reserves.

Halder would not back down. 'We haven't caught Timoshenko's main body, *mein Führer.* Our encircling operations were failures. Timoshenko has directed the bulk of his army group ... to the east across the Don and into the Stalingrad area, other elements to the south into the Caucasus. We don't know what reserves are there.'

> Oh, you and your reserves. I tell you we didn't catch Timoshenko's fleeing rabble in the Stary Oskol area ... because Bock spent too much time at Voronezh. Then we were unable to catch the southern group, which was fleeing in panic, north of Rostov because we turned south with the mobile units too late and forced 17th Army to the east too soon. But that's not going to happen to me again.

He waved Halder aside when the general attempted to interject.

It's imperative that we disentangle the massing of our mobile units in the Rostov area and deploy 17th Army as well as the 1st and 4th Panzer Armies to quickly catch and encircle the Russians south of Rostov, in the approaches to the Caucasus. At the same time the 6th Army must deliver the death blow to the remaining Russian forces which have fled to the Volga in the Stalingrad area. On neither of these two fronts can we allow the reeling enemy to regain his composure. But the emphasis must be on Army Group A's attack against the Caucasus.[22]

Halder implored Hitler not to split his forces on such divergent missions and to maintain his own original plan that the objectives be consecutive and not concurrent. 'We must take Stalingrad before we advance into the Caucasus.' Halder was even more upset that Hitler was so convinced of the disintegration of the Red Army that he had changed his mind and decided to send Manstein's 11th Army to help take Leningrad and had directed that a number of first-class divisions be pulled out of the line. For example, he was sending the *Grossdeutschland* to France as an OKW reserve. His favourite 1st SS Division *Leibstandarte Adolf Hitler*, his own bodyguard, he was also sending to France to be converted to a panzer division as part of a new SS panzer corps.[23]

Hitler was about to lose his temper completely when his aide announced Manstein's arrival. He cooled down quickly. The victor of Sevastopol rode high in his favour, and he had summoned him for the ceremony of presenting him with his field marshal's baton. 'Welcome, welcome, *Herr Generalfeldmarschall*,' he said emphasizing the new rank. 'I want your opinion. Halder tells me that we cannot split our resources by two main efforts – the Caucasus and Stalingrad. What do you think?' Hitler was fishing for the answer he wanted to beat down Halder even more.

'*Mein Führer*, General Halder is correct in that the risk is great.' Hitler's face fell. He was not happy with that response:

But I believe that we can pad the margin of risk enough to execute two divergent objectives. Keep the 11th Army here as a reserve to be committed either to the Caucasus or Stalingrad as future needs dictate, send the Italian and Romanian mountain divisions to the Caucasus, and keep the *Grossdeutschland* and *Leibstandarte* divisions here where they will be needed to finish off the Red Army.

He could see Hitler's objection and preempted it. '*Mein Führer*, if you leave these reserves here, I promise you I will crack open Leningrad like a rotten egg after we have taken Stalingrad.' Hitler was convinced. He then cancelled 11th Army and *Grossdeutschland*'s transfer. *Leibstandarte*'s orders were not changed; he had great plans for his new SS panzer corps. Besides, it was not in him to accede completely to anyone's recommendations.[24]

On that same day he ordered Paulus to make Stalingrad his primary objective.

Big Bend of the Don, 22 July 1942

It looked as if 6th Army's momentum would overrun the Soviet forces backing into the Big Bend of the Don. They had cleared the west bank except for two large pockets, one across from the east-bank town of Kalach and the other to the north across from Akimovka. Both 62nd and 64th Armies were in the Kalach pocket. Now Hitler came to the rescue of the Red Army. Sixth Army simply stopped. It had outrun its supplies and worse because Hitler had diverted half of Army Group B's motor transport to support Army Group A's attack into the Caucasus. Sixth Army would have to rely on its 25,000 horses. Seemingly, it was 1914 again, in the age before motor transport had become ubiquitous. Worse yet:

> Sixth Army stopped dead in its tracks while swarms of vehicles and men from the 4th Panzer Army cut left to right across its line of advance on their way to join Army Group A. Enormous traffic jams developed. Tanks of one army mingled with those of the other; supply trucks got lost in a maze of contradictory signposts and directions handed out by military policemen.

As a result Paulus watched the Soviet rearguards disappear into the limitless distances of the steppe.[25]

Ironically, had 4th Panzer Army been sent directly against Stalingrad at this time, it could have easily bounced into the city, but the fleeting moment had been lost. Only after the army had extricated itself from the traffic nightmare, did Hitler once again change his mind. He detached XL Panzer Corps to Kleist's 1st Panzer Army and sent the rest of Hoth's 4th Panzer to cover 6th Army's southern flank in the drive on Stalingrad.

At this now crimped rate of supply 6th Army would not be able to wipe out the Soviet bridgeheads for another two weeks. Paulus's forces were also so spread out that a concentrated attack was not possible; he could not bring up two of his corps before the Italian 8th Army arrived to take their place.

The Soviets were perplexed at the sudden German halt. It never occurred to them that the Germans had simply run out of fuel or were confused. Nevertheless, it was a welcome breathing spell. It was more than welcome. When it came the senior staff of the 62nd Army had been standing machine pistols in hand on the bridge over the Don at Kalach threatening to shoot the panic-stricken men fleeing to the east bank. Now the rearguards reported, 'No more enemy contact.' Front commander Timoshenko asked his chief of staff, 'What does this mean? Have the Germans changed their plans?' Whatever the reason, there was an opportunity to be seized. 'If the Germans are not following up there is time to organize the defence on the western bank of the Don.'[26] He brought up the newly formed 1st and 4th Tank Armies to reinforce the bridgeheads.[27] He was going to attack, but was relieved on 23 July, and replaced by Gordov.

The new front commander was to bring those same qualities of leadership to his command of the Stalingrad Front as had made Chuikov's life so difficult.

On 24 July the Germans introduced the green 64th Army to war as they attacked through howling dust storms. They were quickly to learn that one has not known war until one has fought the Germans. Now back in command, Chuikov found the forward elements of his army driven back by Seydlitz's LI Corps with strong air support. The Germans then struck his main line of resistance, which had just been filled with units that had not had time to prepare their positions properly, were understrength and lacked their proper logistical support, much of which was still back in Tula. Still, Chuikov held off strong German attacks and was on the point of closing a gap between his divisions:

> It looked as though we would succeed after all in halting the enemy and closing the gap, but panic appeared among our troops. It broke out not at the front but in the rear. Among the medical ambulance battalions, artillery park and transport units on the right bank of the Don, someone reported that German tanks were a mile or two away. This report was certainly an act of provocation and at this time it was enough to make the rear units rush for the crossing in disorder. Though channels unknown to me the panic was communicated to the troops at the front.[28]

Chuikov sent his personal staff and his artillery commander to stop the rout at the bridge. German reconnaissance had spotted the mass of vehicles funnelling over the bridge and summoned the Stukas. With their sirens screaming they fell upon the terrified Russians and bombed and strafed them. Four of Chuikov's senior staff were among the dead. That evening the Luftwaffe came back and broke the bridge.

In a sense the Germans should have been flattered by the arrival of these new Soviet tank armies. The Soviets had simply copied the Germans in the organization of their tank forces. The irony was that they had had a very advanced organization of their tank and mechanized forces until 1938 when Stalin ordered them disbanded because they were the creations of Marshal Tukhachevsky whom Stalin had just shot at the beginning of the great purge that was to decimate the leadership of the Red Army. This military genius had put into practice what Western advocates of armoured warfare such as Basil Liddell-Hart and J. F. C. Fuller in Britain and Charles de Gaulle in France had only advocated. All this Stalin had undone. Thus, when the Germans attacked in 1941, Soviet tank forces had been penny-packeted in brigades to support infantry forces. Tukhachevsky's mailed fist had become nothing more than a feeble, open-fingered slap. The Germans were able to make a great slaughter in the first six months of the war because of this.

Amid the slaughter, though, came several nasty surprises for the Germans. They encountered heavier and better-armed tanks than anything in their army – the huge KV-1 and KV-2 heavy tanks, and the superb T-34 medium tank, all with the deadly 76mm gun. Luckily for the Germans, the destruction of the Soviet senior officer corps and the break up of the armoured formations in the 1937–8 purges made the Soviet tanks vulnerable to being destroyed piecemeal. Now the new tank armies were increasingly equipped with the T-34 which represented half of all tank production by the middle of 1942.

Other reforms of an institutional nature, based on the realization that the traditional military principles, feudal and reactionary as they might be, gave armies staying power in the field. Suddenly the Red Army began to assume all the old, long-despised trappings of military authority: sharp and rigid rank differentiation as the basis for discipline, strict observance of military etiquette, class status for officers, including special privileges and distinctive uniforms and insignia, the recognition of the Russian as opposed to the revolutionary military tradition, and the awarding of medals and decorations. Indeed, one of the urgent requests for aid to the British, who were more than a little surprised, was for a huge amount of gold braid.

London, 24 July 1942

As if the bitter cup of the convoy disaster was not enough for the British, Churchill now had a message from Stalin that added insult to injury:

> Of course, I do not think steady deliveries to northern Soviet ports are possible without risk or loss. But then no major task can be carried out in wartime without risk or losses. You know, of course, that the Soviet Union is suffering far greater losses.

Even after the loss of the convoy and the savaging of the Home Fleet, Stalin was demanding a resumption of the Arctic convoys.

> Be that as it may, I never imagined that the British Government would deny us delivery of war materials precisely now, when the Soviet Union is badly in need of them in view of the grave situation on the Soviet–German front. It should be obvious that deliveries via Persian ports can in no way make up for the loss in the event of deliveries via the northern route being discontinued.[29]

The brutal Allied losses at sea combined with the constant daylight of the Arctic summer to prevent any further convoys until the autumn when the long night would begin to limit German air attacks The problem was not the availability of ships, nor the threat from the German surface fleet, which now hardly existed. The British and American merchant crews simply refused to sign on for any Arctic convoy. When the government had threatened to impress them, they struck. Churchill's bluff had been called.

Now there were only two remaining routes for Allied aid to reach the Soviet Union: the Persian Corridor and across the Pacific to Vladivostok, the latter of which was an American problem. The British problem then was to send the cargoes that would have gone north all the way around Africa and through the Persian Gulf to Iran. Delivery time would be greatly slowed because of the immense distance involved. But it was the best Churchill and Roosevelt could do.

Big Bend of the Don, 26 July, 1942

With or without gold braid, General Gordov was preparing to attack with all his forces to cut off the German units that had broken through. The plan was good, but Gordov's execution was incompetent. Beginning on 26 July his forces attacked piecemeal over three days. With his army resupplied Paulus counterattacked with a major pincer operation against the Kalach bridgehead. The Germans sliced through both flanks of 62nd Army. The two panzer corps attacked from the north and south as the Stukas raced ahead to strike the enemy, while Seydlitz's LI Corps advanced between them. The Soviets resisted bitterly as Gordov threw his tank armies at the Germans in the hilly ground at the north end of the pocket. The battle swirled over the heat-baked steppe.

> Like destroyers and cruisers at sea, the tank units manoeuvred in the sandy ocean of the steppe, fighting for favourable firing positions, cornering the enemy, clinging to villages for a few hours or days, bursting out again, turning back, and again pursuing the enemy.[30]

Above them the Luftwaffe and Red Air Force duelled in the sky to send burning planes to crash among the tank battles or sought out each other's supply columns. But time and time again, German superiority in communications, manoeuvre and air–ground coordination made the difference. The Soviets suffered huge losses.

As the fighting raged along the Don, Chuikov was making shrewd observations of enemy capabilities, just as he had during the Finnish War. He was watching the Germans through fresh eyes for this was the first time he had seen them in action. He noted how much of the German battle drill depended on the Luftwaffe's effective close air support. He interrogated a German pilot and asked him how he thought the war would go. The man replied, 'The Luftwaffe is the big fist in battle. Both the airmen themselves and the ground forces have faith in it. If we hadn't had the Luftwaffe we would not have had such successes in the West or the East.'

He also observed that the German artillery, instead of ranging deep into the Soviet rear, methodically crushed the forward positions, a technique right out of the First War. Chuikov was also critical of the panzers whom he said did not go into combat without infantry or air support and were hesitant when they did.

One more question he asked the captured pilot. How did he think the war would go? The German shrugged and said, 'The Führer made a big mistake about Russia. He and many other Germans did not expect the Russians to have such staying power, so it's hard to say about the end of the war.'[31]

Stalin Order 227, 28 July 1942

It was evident even in Moscow that the Red Army was unravelling on the Don despite the commitment of the new tank armies. NKVD reports made it brutally clear that things were going to go smash. The Red Army was demoralized and inept. It was also eating its own seed corn. Cadet regiments had been thrown into the battle only to be wiped out. One staff officer recalled:

> They were too young, just eighteen, and without military experience. They were called to battle as ordinary soldiers, they died as ordinary soldiers; there was not time to get promoted. Their courage covering the retreat was outstanding and while they tried to stem the German on-slaught our commanders either disappeared or sat behind the front line issuing instructions which bore no relation to reality.[32]

So desperate had the situation become that Stalin issued what quickly became known as the 'Not a Step Back' (*Ni Shagu Nazad!*) Order No. 227. It was a brutal admission that the country's back was up against the wall.

> The population of our country, which relates to the Red Army with love and respect, is beginning to become disillusioned with it, is losing faith in the Red Army, and many of them curse the Red Army for giving up our people to the yoke of German oppressors while itself escaping to the east ... Every commander, Red Army man and political worker must understand that our resources are not unlimited. The territory of the Soviet state is not a desert, but people ... our fathers, mothers, wives, brothers, children. The territory the enemy has seized and is trying to seize is grain and other foodstuffs for the army and the rear, metal and fuel for industry, mills and factories supplying the army with weapons and ammunition, railways. After the loss of Ukraine, Belorussia, and the Baltics, the Donbass and other provinces we have much less territory, hence many fewer people, much less grain, metal, mills, and factories. We have lost over 70 millions of population, over 13 million tons of grain a year, and over 10 million tons of metal a year. We now have no superiority over the Germans in human reserves or in grain stocks. To retreat further means to destroy ourselves, and, along with that, to destroy our Motherland.[33]

Ankara, 30 July 1942

Hitler's plan, codenamed Operation Gertrude, to 'rearrange the constellation of political power in Ankara' had fallen into place as July wore away. It had been helped along by the fortuitous death of Prime Minister Refik Saydam on 9 July. Although this was largely a figurehead position, the pro-German faction manoeuvred to fill his office with General Erkilet, a devoted supporter of Pan-Turkism. Next Foreign Minster Saracoglu was removed because his intransigence would invite German retribution and deny Turkey its share of the 'spoils of war'. The greatest stumbling block remained the Turkish President himself. Finally, on the last day of the month, the plotters quietly removed Inönü and confined him in a coastal villa to 'recover his health'.

The next day they put their signatures to a secret treaty with the Third Reich to enter the war and attack the Soviet Union.[34] The plan, crafted jointly by the German and Turkish general staffs, to form the Muslim Red Army POWs interned in Turkey into auxiliary legions to help liberate their homelands immediately went into effect. There were enough Azeri Turks to form a small corps of several legions, and separate legions were formed of Crimean and Volga Tatars, Uzbeks, Turkmen, Kazakhs, Kirghiz, and Tajiks from Central Asia, and Chechens, Ingush, and Dagestanis from the Caucasus. It was easy to equip them from the mountains of Soviet small arms and artillery captured in the great battles of encirclement in 1941. Almost to a man, the POWs had volunteered to fight. Good treatment by the Turks had allowed them to recover their health, and the relentless pan-Turanist and pan-Islamic propaganda applied by the Turkish government had whipped them up to a fever pitch of vengeance.

Chapter 8

'Those Crazy Mountain Climbers'

Berlin, 1 August 1942

Heydrich was pleased with himself. He had used the Navy carefully to put him in charge of the cipher systems of the Wehrmacht. It had not been a next big step to induce Hitler to let him also take over military intelligence, the Abwehr. Add to that his control of the SS's Sicherheitsdienst, and all the reins of intelligence and counterintelligence were in his hands.

Admiral Wilhelm Canaris, the head of the Abwehr, had been Heydrich's commander and mentor when he was a naval cadet and junior officer. For a long time, though, Heydrich had suspected Canaris of being in contact with the British MI6. Indeed he was, for the express purpose of getting rid of Hitler, whom he despised for leading Germany to ruin. Heydrich had sniffed so close to the truth that the British had launched their failed assassination attempt against him partially to protect Canaris. Now Heydrich was in a position to do something about his suspicions. He confronted Canaris.

He was stunned when Canaris matter-of-factly admitted it. 'Of course, I am in contact with the British. That's my job, Reinhard. Better to deceive the enemy when you can actually communicate.' He then went on to describe the contacts and the deception operations each was a part of. Of course, it was all a carefully prepared cover story. He had had the wit to plan ahead for the time when it might be needed. Thus the angel of death passed over him.[1]

Heydrich's cozy arrangement with Dönitz had led to the great victories at sea. The Kriegsmarine was riding high. Now he would bring it down. To this Göring listened with great attention.

> The Navy's bolt is shot, *Herr Reichsmarschall*. Except for the U-boat service, it has nothing left to offer the war effort. Nothing, except personnel. There are almost 800,000 men in the Kriegsmarine, most of them with nothing to do since most of the capital ships were sunk or so severely damaged as not to be reparable.

Heydrich could see the greed flicker in Göring's eyes.

Heydrich's role in turning the Enigma compromise to Germany's advantage and his backing of Dönitz's attack on the convoys had elevated his reputation with Hitler beyond even his fatherly affection. Hitler would deny him nothing. So Heydrich's suggestion that half a million men be transferred from the Navy to the Luftwaffe, SS and Army was eagerly approved by Hitler. The Luftwaffe would profit most from an influx of high quality and technically adept personnel. The Army desperately needed combat replacements for the open, running sore of the Eastern Front. And, of course, the Navy was also a source of just the sort of racially pure and fit men the SS wanted.

Naval personnel were transferred as individuals, not as organized units as the Soviets were successfully doing with their naval personnel. Heydrich made sure that they would lose all connection with their former service. Dönitz threatened to resign, but swallowed his pride. The Führer knew best. It did not take him long to discover that the knife in his back had been stuck there with Heydrich's clammy hand.[2]

The Kuban, early August 1942

As 6th Army stalled on the Don Bend after its exhausting victory, Army Group A had plunged south across the 300-mile Kuban towards the Black Sea coast and the passes through the Caucasus Mountains. The Kuban stretched between the Black and Caspian Seas and was bound on the north by the Don Steppe and the south by the forbidding ranges of the Caucasus. It had been settled as a marcher land against the wild tribes of the mountains by even more ferocious Cossacks.[3] The three German armies attacked on line with 17th Army crossing the Don and striking south along the Sea of Azov to move down the Black Sea coast. The 1st Panzer Army in the centre attacked towards Maikop and Armavir and 4th Panzer Army towards Pyatigorsk. Each of these last two objectives led to a major highway through the mountains. Across their path lay two major water obstacles, the Manych and Kuban Rivers, flowing east to west. Pyatigorsk in particular led to the Georgian Military Highway along which Allied aid from Persia flowed.

It was a race. The Germans were intent on encircling the Russians. The Russians were intent on not being encircled as they conducted a fighting retreat into the ideal defensive terrain of the mountains. In their drive south the 16th Motorized and 3rd Panzer Divisions of 4th Panzer Army swept up to the 400-mile-long Manych River. It was the last great physical barrier before the mountains were reached.

It had been made an even greater barrier by the hand of man. The river was essentially a series of dams and their reservoirs, often a mile wide. It was a thorny problem for the commander of the 3rd Panzer Division, General Hermann Breith. The banks of the narrowest parts of the reservoirs were strongly held by NKVD troops. Instead of attacking there, Breith's infantry crossed in assault boats at the widest point, 2 miles across, just above a dam. The surprise was complete, and the Germans overran the dam to prevent its demolition. Within minutes the armoured columns of the division were crossing and heading south towards Asia.

Northeastern Turkey, early August 1942

The Turkish–German treaty of alliance may have been secret, but it did not take long for the British and the Soviets to discover its existence. Even if they had not, the sudden presence of hundreds of Wehrmacht officers and NCOs in Turkey, the transfer of an expeditionary corps, and the redeployment of the Turkish armies to the borders would have been a resounding tip-off.

For both of them the imminent entry of Turkey into the war might turn out to be the straw that broke the camel's back. The British had stripped just about every unit they safely could from their 10th Army guarding Syria, Iraq and Persia and sent them off to shore up 8th Army on the Egyptian border. They arrived just in time barely to stave off Rommel's attack in July. There would be precious little left to stop any Turkish thrust into 10th Army's area of operations.

The Soviets had as much if not more to fear. This new threat meant that their forces between the Caucasus and the Turkish border would have to fight front and back. Now both the oilfields at Baku and the Persian Corridor route of supply from the Allies were in danger. With the greatest reluctance, Stalin released a few more armies from Stavka reserve to bolster the defences of the Transcaucasus Front that defended the Soviet republics of Georgia, Armenia and Turkic Azerbaijan.

Things looked far more difficult from the perspective of the German advisory group in Ankara. Although captured French and Soviet weapons stocks had done much to modernize the Turkish Army as far as artillery and automatic weapons went, its logistics were, to put it kindly, primitive, consisting largely of pack animals in caravan trains and a very limited number of motor vehicles. Signals and communication remained grossly inadequate. The Turkish Air Force was simply in no condition to go up against the Russians. Göring was prevailed upon to scrape up a few Luftwaffe fighter units, pulling them from Norway now that the Allies had put a temporary halt to their convoys.

That meant that the German expeditionary corps, XLIV Corps (97th and 101st Jäger Divisions), commanded by General der Artillerie Maximilian de Angelis, would be operating on a shoestring. These divisions, however, had been organized and trained to operate under difficult conditions. They were taken from Army Group A. Field Marshal List had raised a bloody fit over the loss of these two specialized divisions at the end of July. He was more than mollified by their replacement with the even more specialized LV Mountain Corps (3rd and 5th Gebirgsjäger Divisions) which were being wasted as normal infantry in Army Group North around Leningrad. Now List would have four of the German Army's seven mountain divisions; the rest remained locked in battle in the desolate reaches of Lappland. At the last minute Hitler confirmed the transfer of the three excellent mountain divisions of the Italian Alpini Corps.[4]

Stalingrad, 1 August 1942

Chuikov handed over command of 64th Army to a replacement on 30 July. He had been relieved by the front commander, who summoned him to his headquarters in the city. Gordov told him, 'The enemy has been pinned down in our defence positions, and he can now be wiped out with a single blow.' Chuikov was astounded that the front commander could say such a thing after the drubbing the Germans had given them. Chuikov would write later, 'I came to the conclusion that the Front Commander did not know the situation at the front. He took wishful thinking for reality, and did not realize that a new threat, a large-scale attack, was imminent.' Gordov angrily dismissed his concerns and told him to write a report on his actions as army commander.

Wishful thinking was also afflicting the commander of the remnants of 62nd Army, who reported that his army was 'firmly holding its defensive positions' and, with 1st Tank and 21st Armies, 'is completing the encirclement of the enemy'. It reminded Chuikov of the anecdote about the man who caught a bear. '"Bring it over here," someone said, "I can't," he replied. "It won't let me."'[5]

Two days later Chuikov was ordered by the Front Military Council personally to examine the situation south of Stalingrad and take whatever measures necessary. He found chaos. Divisions were retreating ahead of the oncoming Germans who had crossed the Don farther south. They had taken heavy losses. He took them under his command and ordered them to set up defensive lines north of the Aksay River.

Another division was arriving at two railway stations in the area. The Luftwaffe, as ever informed of ripe prey by its reconnaissance, attacked both stations just as the troops were unloading. Chuikov was walking to the buildings where his communications had been set up at the Chilekov Station when he saw three flights of aircraft coming towards him. 'Suddenly there was the roar of explosions . . . I could see the carriages and the station buildings on fire, with raging flames rapidly leaping from one building to another.' Chuikov thought to himself if only air cover had been provided to the stations, all this loss could have been avoided.[6]

He was out of touch with 64th Army headquarters for long periods inspecting, reorganizing, threatening, bringing hope to beaten men and getting soaked in frequent downpours. On one occasion his sudden arrival at a unit nearly cost him his life. He was wearing a British aid raincoat which a sentry recognized as foreign. And foreign to this man meant German. Chuikov missed death only by the barest of margins as he blurted out the response to the sentry's challenge.

The Luftwaffe continued to torment any Soviet unit on the road. It so savagely strafed and bombed his 29th Rifle Division marching to set up positions along the Aksay River that it suffered more casualties than in the fighting west of the Don. Nevertheless, Chuikov was confirmed in command of these forces, the Southern Group, which he had already positioned along the Aksay.

On the 5th, the Germans attacked and drove a wedge over the river. Chuikov observed that they used the same battle drill as in the fighting west of the Don, 'air attack, then artillery, then infantry, then tanks. They did not know any other order in which to attack.' Chuikov determined to defeat this battle drill by an artillery strike on their assembly areas followed by an infantry attack. He fretted about taking these odds and ends of units into even a simple offensive operation. He had no tanks and no air support either, nor antitank weapons. He had to hit before the Germans could ferry their tanks across the river. He struck at daybreak. The artillery thundered down on the unsuspecting Germans who broke and fled back across the river. Their tanks never crossed, and he did not even have to employ his infantry.[7]

For the next ten days, the Germans again and again tried to cross the river in force. Chuikov threw them back each time, each time varying his tactics. He would counterattack at night or at dawn when the Luftwaffe could not be in the sky. His artillery ranged into the depth of the German positions disrupting their attempts to concentrate. Chuikov and his scratch force had shown that the Germans could be beaten.

Stalingrad, 4 August 1942

Colonel General Andrei Yeremenko's leg still had not recovered from the last of the three wounds he had suffered so far in the war. He was thankful that he was flying in one of these comfortable American Dakota transport aircraft rather than taking an overland route to Stalingrad. The *Vozhd* had just appointed him to command both fronts defending Stalingrad. The plane landed at the small airport on the outskirts of the city. Waiting for him was People's Commissar Nikita S. Khrushchev.

Yeremenko braced himself. The Ukrainian commissar was a Politburo member and close to Stalin. Cold and ruthless as his master, he had executed the created famine in 1931–2 that starved to death up to ten million of his fellow Ukrainians on Stalin's orders. He had also supervised the building of the Moscow subway in which thousands died. Dread preceded him, and fear followed in his wake. Yeremenko in contrast was an affable man who always had time for his subordinates. Somehow they would have to get along. On one thing they were in complete agreement. Stalin's 'Not one step back' order would be ruthlessly enforced.

Even the rear was in panic. The port city of Astrakhan on the estuary of the Volga where it entered into the Caspian Sea was in fear after a German air raid. Astrakhan was a vital rail and water communications hub that fed supplies and reinforcements to Stalingrad. It was filled with terrified refugees and crated machinery from evacuated plants. Now huge, greasy clouds of black smoke poured from the burning oil storage tanks the Germans had hit.[8]

The Big Bend of the Don, 7 August 1942

By 7 August the spearheads of the 16th and 24th Panzer Divisions had met on the Don across the river from Kalach. Sixth Army had cut off the forward elements of 62nd and 1st Tank Armies – nine rifle divisions, two motorized and seven tank brigades. It took the Germans another four days to mop up the pockets, bagging 50,000 prisoners, 1,000 armoured vehicles, and 750 guns. Of the 13,000 men the 181st Rifle Division had begun the fight with, barely a hundred were able to escape across the Don. This was just the sort of encirclement that the Germans had been seeking but had so far eluded them. It took another four days to round up all the cut-off Soviet forces. It was almost like beating game as they set fire to the brush to drive them out of hiding. Paulus's chief engineer, after meeting with his commander, said that 'The Army was full of hope ... my eyes met those of Paulus, questioning, almost unbelieving ... were the Russians finally at the end of their tether?'[9]

There were still more Russians to deal with on the west bank of the Don. Next Paulus attacked the smaller of the two bridgeheads to the north, but the Soviet armies there were able to avoid encirclement and withdrew across the Don. The fighting had not gone all one way. The Germans had taken heavy losses, the harbinger of more to come. One soldier wrote home, 'Many, many crosses and graves, fresh from yesterday.' Paulus's infantry had marched, fought and bled for the last month. They were exhausted, and there was still farther to go. One pioneer observed hopefully, 'The only consolation is that we will be able to have peace and quiet in Stalingrad, where we'll move into winter quarters, and then, just think of it, there'll be a chance for leave.'[10]

Maikop, 9 August 1942

Major Adrian von Fölkersam was one of those daring men attracted to special operations. The Brandenburg Regiment drew such men like a magnet, and among that elite Fölkersam was one of the best. He was the grandson of a Russian admiral and spoke the language fluently. Now he and the detachment of sixty men he called 'the Wild Bunch', Russian-speaking Balts and Germans, were miles behind the lines in the town of Maikop with its surrounding oil wells and refineries. The problem was that the Soviets still held the town and did not seem in any hurry to leave.

The Wild Bunch had arrived in Maikop in a very ordinary way; they drove in dressed in NKVD uniforms. Fölkersam called on the commanding general and introduced himself as Major Turchin from the Stalingrad Front. The general seemed pleased to see someone who had been close to the action and assigned them good quarters in the town. For the next few days the Brandenburgers wandered about coolly, finding out where everything of importance was.

On the evening of 8 August they could hear the rumble of guns to the north. Army Group A was driving south. A Russian officer told Fölkersam that the Germans were only ten miles away. That night he called his men together and issued them their final instructions. He wanted chaos and confusion among the enemy.

In the morning Leutnant Franz Koudele walked into the main military telephone communications office and announced to the officer in charge that Maikop was being abandoned. The officer was not inclined to argue with an NKVD officer and promptly fled with his men. Koudele now found himself connected to every Soviet command in the Caucasus and flooded with messages demanding to know what was going on to the north. 'We cannot connect you, sir,' Koudele replied with just the proper tone of anxiety in his voice. 'Maikop has been abandoned.'[11]

The panic at the telephone office spread, abetted by the rest of the Brandenburgers, and triggered a Soviet stampede out of town, the general near the front. At the oilfields, Fölkersam's men stopped the Soviet engineers from destroying the facilities on the authority of the general who had already fled. The engineers then joined the exodus.

That same day 13th Panzer Division of 1st Panzer Army overran the Maikop oilfields and was greeted by Fölkersam who, in a way, gave them the keys to the city. Somewhere behind the advancing columns were 10,000 oil industry workers ready to keep the fields running for Germany.[12]

Krasnodar, Kuban River, 13 August 1942

The Romanian 3rd Army made good progress working along the coast of the Sea of Azov while 17th Army's V Corps was locked in bitter fighting to take Krasnodar on the Kuban River. The fighting for this former capital of the Don Cossacks had been bitter. The Germans had reached it on the 10th and met determined Soviet resistance in the orchards and suburbs. There were huge oil refineries around the city of 200,000 people. They went up in flames as the Soviets destroyed everything of value to the Germans while evacuating as much of the population and useful material as possible. They had to hold the bridge over the Kuban in the city centre.

The next day 1st Battalion, 421st Infantry Regiment, had fought its way within 50 yards of the bridge unbeknownst to the Soviets. They watched the tightly packed flow of personnel and equipment crossing the bridge. It looked as if once again the Germans would be able to pull off another daring *coup de main* and seize the crossing. A company commander leapt to his feet pointing his pistol. He took three steps forward and was immediately shot through the head. His men charged. This time the Soviet engineer officer in charge of the bridge was alert. The racing Germans were only 20 yards from the bridge when he blew it.

> At half a dozen separate points the bridge went up with a roar like thunder, complete with the Russian columns on it. Among the smoke and dust, men and horses, wheels and weapons, could be seen sailing through the air. Horse-drawn vehicles, the horses bolting, raced over the collapsing balustrades, hurtling into the river and disappearing under the water.

Without the bridge, it took the Germans until the night of the 13th and 14th to find a way across the river and resume their advance.[13]

Mount Elbrus, 13 August 1942

The men of the 5th SS Division *Wiking* at first saw what they thought was a great white cloud sitting in the distance. As they got closer the towering twin summits of Mt Elbrus became clear. Its west peak was the highest point in Europe at 18,510ft. Its permanent icecap fed twenty-two glaciers.

Most of the men of the *Wiking* Division were volunteers from northern Europe who had joined the Germans to help wage their anti-Bolshevik struggle. Of its three motorized regiments, *Germania* was recruited from ethnic Germans, *Westland* from Dutch and Flemish volunteers, and *Nordland* from Danes, Norwegians, and Swedes. With them was the Slovak Fast Division (1st Slovak [Mobile] Infantry Division), together forming LVII Panzer Corps.

Behind them came XLIX Mountain Corps with the 1st and 4th Gebirgsjäger Divisions and the three Italian Alpini divisions. Their objective was the Klukhor Pass with the glaciers of Mt Elbrus hanging above. Through the pass ran the Sukhumi Military Highway to the port of Sukhumi on the Black Sea coast, which was the southernmost of the Soviet Black Sea Fleet's remaining three major naval bases.

After the loss of its main base at Sevastopol, the fleet had occupied bases at Novorossiysk, Tuapse, and Sukhumi along the narrow coastal strip below the mountains. Each was also defended by an army, and each was now a target. V Corps was heading to Novorossiysk, the Romanian Mountain Corps was attacking through the foothills of the Caucasus to Tuapse, and XLIX and the Alpini Corps were to open the way to Sukhumi for the Vikings of the SS and the Slovaks. From Sukhumi it was only a hundred miles to the Turkish border at Batumi.

Initially List had planned for LVII Panzer Corps to be the main force in the drive on Tuapse. However, he concluded that it would be wasted there. The Romanians would be enough to fix Soviet forces in that direction. It was not necessary to attack all three Soviet naval bases in strength. His mountain corps would punch through the mountain passes that would give the Germans access to the thin coastal strip and roads to Sukhumi. Take Sukhumi, and the other two bases would be cut off – another great battle of encirclement. Unfortunately, the Gebirgsjäger and Alpini would be spent in simply fighting through the mountains. That's where LVII Panzer Corps came in as the exploitation force.

While the mountain troops were breaking through the high passes, 1st Panzer Army was to 'advance parallel to the eastern foothills of the Caucasus Mountains to seize Nal'chik and Mozdok, cross the Terek River, and capture Grozny, the coast of the Caspian Sea near Makhachkala, and ultimately Baku'.[14] To help his panzers get through the mountains of southern Chechnya, List assigned to 1st Panzer Army the new LV Mountain Corps.

Already Stalin was pouring reinforcements into the North Caucasus Front commanded by his old crony from the Civil War, Marshal of the Soviet Union Semyon Budenny. They were desperately needed; the front was burnt out and in a shambles. In a report of 13 August to the Stavka, Budenny wrote that of his seven armies four were no longer combat effective, three of them down to fewer than 7,000 bayonets each. Rifle divisions were reduced to 300 to 1,200 bayonets. He complained that the reasons for failing to defend the Kuban were:

> the complete absence of tanks and motorized units . . . the weakness of
> aviation, the extreme exhaustion and paucity of the infantry, the absence
> of reserves, and the weak command and control of the forces and com-
> munication with them on the part of the weak newly formed front staff.

He concluded by saying that 'The Front's chief mission is to defend the axes to Tuapse and Novorossiysk resolutely. Therefore, it is necessary to resolve [this mission] by means of a solid defence of the mountain defiles that protect Tuapse and Novorossiysk.'[15] Nowhere did he mention Sukhumi.

Adding to Budenny's miseries, Lavrenti Beria descended on the region. The ghoulish head of the NKVD came to spread terror among the native peoples of the Caucasus. The Imperial yoke had been bad enough, but they had writhed under the crueller yoke of Soviet Power. For good reason, Stalin doubted their loyalty, and he sent Beria to use the only tool he knew – terror. Stalin, the Georgian, had no love for these peoples, many of whom were Muslim, especially the Chechens who had raided down into Georgia for centuries before the Russians finally subdued them. Of course Beria's cruelties accomplished just the opposite of what he had intended. Everywhere the arrival of the Germans was met with rejoicing, gifts of food and cattle, and volunteers, many, many volunteers.

Beria's ruthlessness had been a pillar of Stalin's rule as the war threw defeat after defeat at the Red Army. Stalin trusted no one, but Beria's usefulness had given him a certain protection from Stalin's paranoia. That did not keep Stalin from keeping a dossier on Beria as a serial rapist and paedophile. You never knew when that might prove useful.[16]

These were heady days for the Germans; Hitler's fantastical dreams infected the men of Army Group A as they rolled over the Kuban. The engineers were calculating how much bridging equipment they would need to cross the Nile, and 'whenever a trooper was asked, "Where's our next stop?" he would frivolously reply, "Ibn Saud's palace".' The mountain troops joked as they marched over the hot, flat steppe, 'Down the Caucasus, round the corner, slice the British through the rear, and say to Rommel, "Hello, general, here we are!"'[17]

Kharkov, 14 August 1942

Tank crews from *Grossdeutschland* Division took possession of 150 Soviet T-34 medium tanks at the Kharkov Tractor Repair Plant and loaded them onto flat cars. Their destination was the siding at a large former Soviet training centre outside of Rostov.

A week before Hitler had gone back on his decision not to transfer the division to France and convert it to a panzer division. He would send it to France after all. Again Manstein had had to plead with him not to do so and suggested an imaginative alternative. *Grossdeutschland* could be converted in a much shorter time if it were done in theatre and with the Soviet tanks being repaired in Kharkov. At first Hitler was dead set against it. '*Das ist wanzig, Manstein, heller wanzig* [This is madness, Manstein, sheer madness]! To reequip the iconic division of the German Army with the creations of these *Untermenschen* is completely unacceptable.'

Manstein was all honey and light:

> *Mein Führer*, I appeal to you as a frontline soldier of the First War. Who else but the man who has to fight the battles can see what weapons he needs. You yourself have told us how the men in the trenches understood the war better than the General Staff. I have here a message from the commander of *Grossdeutschland* requesting these tanks.

'No, Manstein, no. It is unacceptable.'

The field marshal had detected a lessening of his Führer's anger. The appeal to him as a frontline soldier had some effect. Hitler had never hesitated to bring down the General Staff a peg or two by saying that he alone had been in the trenches the way most of them never had been. Only he understood what the average soldier, the *Landser*, was going through. Now for the clincher. 'You know, *mein Führer*, it would be a delicious irony to use these tanks as nails in the coffin of the Bolsheviks.' He got his way. To make up the earlier loss of *Leibstandarte*, Hitler agreed to transfer Raus's 6th Panzer Division from France to be reequipped with Soviet tanks. They could turn over their complement of new German equipment to *Leibstandarte*.

As long as the Soviet tanks had not been burnt out or the turret ring damaged, they could be repaired. At the Kharkov plant the tanks had not only been repaired but improved. Each one had been outfitted with a radio as all German tanks were. Instead of just a crank to turn the turret, an electrical system was installed to make engaging a target faster. The German tankers loved the T-34; it was easier to maintain, more heavily armoured and better armed with its high-velocity 76mm gun than even the best of the German tanks, the Mark IV.[18]

Kluhkor Pass, 16 August 1942

The Gebirgsjäger were eager to pass through the *Wiking* and Slovak divisions to begin the ascent into the mountains after a long, hot march through the Kuban. The Alpini were no less eager. Their corps commander had moved from unit to unit addressing them:

> *Ragazzi* [My boys], the eagles of our ancestors look proudly down upon you. You have marched farther than any legion of *la città eterna*. Now the great mountains of the Caucasus tower over us. You will conquer them! Roma will give you a triumph such as Caesar would have envied. *Viva l'Italia! Viva l'Alpini!*

The elite troops of the Italian Army were excellent. The mass of the Italian Army, however, suffered from the deep incompetence of the officer corps compounded by the corruption and unrealities of the Fascist regime.[19]

The German and Italian objectives were the high mountain passes, the most important of which was the 9,230-foot Klukhor Pass and the beginning of the Sukhumi Military Highway. Defending a 275-mile stretch of mountains and passes was the 46th Army. It had largely neglected the defence of the passes, never believing the Germans would attempt to break through such forbidding terrain. At most the passes were defended by companies or battalions. The company at the mouth of the Klukhor Pass had no idea of the troops they were up against. The 1st Gebirgsjäger Division fixed the enemy's attention to their front with a demonstration, climbed the flanking mountain, and fell upon their rear, collapsing the defence by the evening of the 17th. They were followed by the Austrians and Bavarians of the 4th Gebirgsjäger Division, and together they pushed on to overwhelm the strong Soviet defence of the pass exit.[20]

Planning Germany's attack on the USSR in 1941. From left, Field Marshal Keitel, Chief of Staff of OKW, Field Marshal von Brauchitsch, C-in-C of the Army, Hitler, Gen. Halder, Chief of Staff of the Army.

Marshal of the Soviet Union and brutal dictator, Joseph Stalin, was as murderous as Hitler but a far more rational war leader.

The men trying to keep the Soviet Union in the war through military aid: President Roosevelt and Prime Minister Churchill (*seated*). Behind them stand (*from left*) Adm. King, Gen. Marshall, Gen. Dill, Adm. Leahy, and Adm. Pound.

Soviet T-34 tank refurbished and improved at the Kharkov Tractor Factory for use by the Germans.

Soviet military production was severely disrupted by the German invasion which forced the relocation of thousands of factories to the Urals and elsewhere. The tank factory at Chelyabinsk was so large it became known as Tankograd.

Field Marshal Erich von Manstein, conqueror of the Crimea, the only man Hitler could call on to retrieve the situation at Stalingrad.

Col. Gen. Friedrich Paulus, commander of the 6th Army, a competent general until the situation required him to think for himself.

Col. Gen. Walter von Seydlitz-Kurbach, hero of the Demyansk Pocket, commander of LI Corps and later of 6th Army, a man of decisive initiative.

Maj. Gen. Erhard Raus, Austrian commander of 6th Panzer Division, beloved by his men for being able to get them out of any scrape.

Reinhard Heydrich, the second man in the SS, organizer of the Final Solution, and self-styled heir to Adolf Hitler.

Admiral Wilhelm Canaris, chief of the Abwehr, German military intelligence, and early mentor of Heydrich in the Navy.

General Georgi Zhukov, Stalin's best general, who had saved Leningrad and Moscow. Could he now save Stalingrad?

Maj. Gen. Vasili Chuikov, the fiercely tenacious commander of the 62nd Army in the defence of Stalingrad.

ARMS FOR RUSSIA . . . A great convoy of British ships escorted by Soviet fighter planes sails into Murmansk harbour with vital supplies for the Red Army.

Above: British poster emphasizing the importance of the Arctic convoys in keeping the Soviet Union in the war. Red Air Force support was much exaggerated.

Left: Some of the hundreds of Soviet tanks destroyed in the fighting in the great bend of the Don.

The nightmare of the British and the heart of the German fleet in being, the battleship *Admiral Tirpitz*, in Altenfjord, Norway (*above*); and in a US Navy recognition drawing (*left*).

The heavy cruiser *Admiral Hipper*, seen here in a US Navy recognition chart, was the flagship of the greatest fleet action in German naval history.

Soviet tanks and infantry in the encirclement of 6th Army.

One of many T-34s destroyed in the *Totenritt bei Leninsk* that cleared the way for the fall of Stalingrad.

The destruction of the Stalingrad Front by the German 11th Army.

The fighting in Stalingrad was so close and bitter that the German soldiers called it *Der Rattenkrieg*.

Warrant Officer Vassili Zaitsev with his Mosin-Nagant sniper's rifle.

Oberjäger Heinz Pohl with his Kar 98k rifle. He took on the cover name of Major König to deceive the Soviets in the fighting in Stalingrad. He and Zaitsev combined to change the course of history.

'Manstein is Coming!' The LX Panzer Corps' *Grossdeutschland* and 6th Panzer Divisions broke through, keeping Manstein's promise to relieve the surrounded German armies.

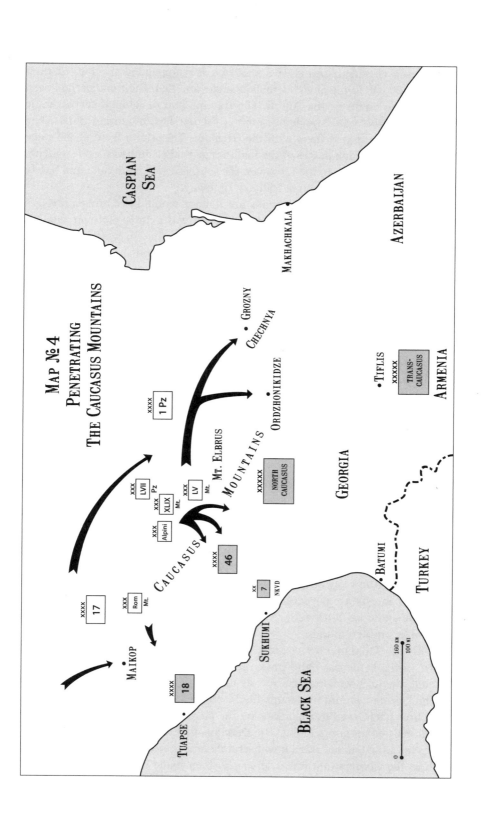

It was a close-run thing. The attackers had expended the last of their ammunition just as the Soviet defenders broke and fled. Their margin had been filled by the mules of the Alpini. The Italians had developed special mule supply units that could navigate some of the harshest mountain trails. They had generously shared them with the Germans. The Alpini were at the same time clearing the high passes of the main range to the southwest and suddenly found themselves also in the forests on the southern side, with Sukhumi barely 12 miles away on the Ossetian Military Highway.[21]

Mules or not, neither the Germans nor Italians would have broken through the increasing Soviet resistance had not the Luftwaffe flown close air support. Flying through mountain valleys is tricky in peacetime. In wartime it adds a whole new dimension to risk. One man who positively relished the intensified risk was Major Hans-Ulrich Rudel who had used every bit of influence and pull to bring his new squadron of Stukas to the fight. Rudel was the ideal new German – devoted to National Socialism and Hitler and as lethal as the plague. For him:

> Fighting in the narrow valleys is a thrilling experience. It is easier after we have been into every valley a few times and know which valleys have exits, and behind which mountain it is possible to get out into open country. This is all guesswork in bad weather and with low lying clouds. When we make low level attacks on some valley road occasionally the defence fires down at us from above because the mountains on either side of us are also occupied by the Ivans.[22]

Particularly dangerous to the troops fighting their way down the rear slopes of the mountains was an armoured train whose artillery raked the Germans. Every time Rudel's Stukas attempted to take it out, timely warnings of their approach caused it to flee for safety into a mountain tunnel. The train always won the cat and mouse game with the Stukas until the day Rudel changed the rules. While the train was hiding in its lair, Rudel's Stukas hit the tunnel mouth with special bombs that collapsed the entrance, sealing the train inside.

Rudel tried to answer every call for close air support, but 'battles in the mountain forests are particularly difficult; it is fighting blindfold'. Yet time and time again his Stukas delivered steel on the target, earning the praise of the troops on the ground.

With the Klukhor now cleared, the *Wiking* and Slovak divisions flowed down through the pass and onto the Sukhumi Military Highway as it led through the lush semi-tropical forests towards Sukhumi, only 25 miles away.

The German mountain troops could not resist the opportunity to climb Mt Elbrus itself, even as the attack on the passes began. The Italians heard of it and insisted on going along. The Germans had wanted the glory for themselves until the Italians asked how useful the mules were. A group of men from each of the German and Italian divisions then made the ascent and planted their division flags and the swastika and royal Italian flag on its summit. It made an enormous propaganda splash, but Hitler launched into one of his tirades at what he thought was a wasteful stunt. His architect, Albert Speer was there:

> I often saw Hitler furious but seldom did his anger erupt from him as it did when this report came in. For hours he raged as if his entire plan of the campaign had been ruined by this bit of sport. Days later he went on railing to all and sundry about 'those crazy mountain climbers' who 'belong before a court-martial'. They were pursuing their idiotic hobbies in the midst of a war, he exclaimed indignantly, occupying an idiotic peak even though he had commanded that all efforts must be concentrated upon Sukhumi.[23]

He need not have worried. Sukhumi was well in hand.

Chapter 9

The Terror Raid

Big Bend of the Don, 21 August 1942

The 62nd Army had been consumed in the fighting west of the river. All of its divisions had been destroyed, and only remnants and its headquarters had escaped over the river. The forces left to 1st Tank Army were transferred to the 62nd, and the tank army disappeared. It also picked up one division from 64th Army, most of which had been able to escape over the Don thanks to Chuikov's leadership.[1]

In wiping out the Kalach pocket, the Germans had not been able to bounce across the river immediately because 6th Army by this time was both exhausted and its combat power badly depleted. There were only 163 tanks left in the army's panzer corps. Despite the Soviet losses in the bridgehead, the Germans had been badly wounded as well. The combat power of a number of the infantry divisions had fallen dangerously, with severe losses since the offensive had begun. Many were reduced to companies of forty to fifty men, even before they had crossed the Don.[2]

It was not until 16 August that the main bridge over the Don at Kalach was seized in a daring attack by Leutnant Kleinjohan and men of the 16th Pioneer Battalion. Incredibly the Soviets had not destroyed the bridge after the remnants of the Kalach pocket had fled across it. The western bank of the Don was much higher than the eastern and gave the Germans a splendid view of the hasty defences the Soviets were throwing up. Five days later, at dawn, the infantry of Seydlitz's LI Corps marched across the bridge and straight into combat against a violent Soviet defence.

Seydlitz's infantry widened the bridgehead to a depth of over a mile and width of 3 miles. The next night XIV Panzer Corps assembled on the west bank and watched as burning vehicles lit the way for an endless Soviet air attack on the bridge. This failed, and with first light on 23 August, 16th Panzer Division began to cross. It assumed a wedge formation as it passed through the German lines to burst through the Soviet defences and head northeast to its objective of the Volga.

By afternoon, with dust trails billowing behind them, they could see the silhouette of Stalingrad to their right. Every tank commander stood in his turret to watch. As they passed the northern suburbs a mass of antiaircraft guns opened up on them, but at point-blank range the panzers smashed every position at almost no loss. The antiaircraft batteries had been manned by female volunteers from the Red Barricade gun factory in Stalingrad. The women had not been able to fire an effective shot in return, so poorly trained were they in the antitank capabilities of their guns.

In the late afternoon:

> The first German tank drove past the northern suburb of Rynok onto the elevated western bank of the Volga. The bank towered almost 300 feet above the mile-wide stream. The water was dark. A chain of tugs and steamers sailed up and down the river. The Asiatic steppe glistened across from the other side: a melancholy greeting from the infinite space.[3]

That afternoon two German Messerschmitt Me 109 fighters flew over the division and were so overjoyed to see the advance made by their comrades on the ground that they did victory rolls over the tanks.

The White House, 23 August 1942

Roosevelt was not happy with the way the meeting was going. Stalin's message had brought them all together to discuss its requests. The last sentence was the controversial one.

> With reference to what you say about the despatch of tanks and other strategic materials from the United States in August, I should like to emphasise our special interest in receiving US aircraft and other weapons, as well as trucks in the greatest numbers possible. It is my hope that every step will be taken to ensure early delivery of the cargoes to the Soviet Union, particularly over the northern sea route.[4]

The President's special assistant and trusted confidant, Harry Hopkins, was there as the administrator of Lend-Lease. Hopkins was so close to FDR that he lived in the White House. Assistant Secretary of the Treasury Harry Dexter White was present because all monetary Lend-Lease issues of coordination with the Soviets went through him. The State Department was represented by Alger Hiss. Admiral King was having a hard time not shaking the teeth out of the three of them. He would have done a lot more had he known that all three were communists and agents of the Soviet Union. Never before had treason wrapped its coils so closely around an American presidency. The chief NKVD officer in the United States described Hopkins as 'the most important of all Soviet wartime agents in the United States'.[5] Even Roosevelt had said, 'Harry and Uncle Joe got on like a house afire. They have become buddies.'[6] Hiss was actually using Lend-Lease transport to send highly classified US Government documents to the Soviet Union.[7]

White was adamant. 'Mr. President, we absolutely must, I repeat, must resume our convoys to the Soviet Union. If they go under, we cannot win the war against Germany.'

Hopkins added, 'There is a good chance, given the German drive towards the Volga, that Stalin might make a separate peace with Hitler if he thinks we are stinting on aid.'

Roosevelt looked closely at him. 'Did he ever mention that to you, Harry?'

'Not in so many words, but some of his closest advisors were a lot more explicit.'

Turning to King, Roosevelt said, 'Now just when can we resume the Arctic convoys, Admiral?'

King had had enough. 'You will have to ask my successor, Mr President, because if you order the resumption of the convoys I will offer you my resignation.'

Roosevelt straightened up in his wheelchair he was so surprised. He knew King was as blunt and salty a sea dog as ever ran the US Navy, but he was not used to such an ultimatum, anyway not since Douglas MacArthur had issued a similar threat back in 1934 over cutting the training budget for the National Guard. He had caved then, just as he was going to do now.[8]

Stalingrad, 23–25 August 1942

Units falling back into Stalingrad were amazed to find a veneer of normality after the relentless German pounding and constant retreating. The novelist Victor Nekrasov recorded his impressions:

> Shabby old trams clattered along towards us. There were lines of snub-nosed Studebakers. On them were long boxes – shells for the 'Katyusha'. On the empty squares, crossed with trenches, there were antiaircraft guns pointing upwards, and ready for action. In the market were great piles of tomatoes and cucumbers and huge bottles of amber-coloured baked milk. Here and there could be seen people in jackets, caps and even ties. It was a long time since I'd seen that. The women still wore lipstick.[9]

It was not to stay that way for long.

During their afternoon dash to the Volga the men of XIV Panzer Corps saw the massed might of Luftflotte 4 flying towards Stalingrad and greeted it with cheers and sirens. They were witnessing the preamble to one of the great aerial terror raids of the war. Its aim was to break the will of the population and defenders and it was directed against the dense downtown residential areas, factories and utilities. The antiaircraft batteries quickly ran out of ammunition because some officious fool had concentrated all their ammunition in one place. The Germans had identified it and specifically targeted it.

Nekrasov and his companions watched transfixed from a balcony. 'From behind the station the planes came in a steady stream, just as they do in a fly-

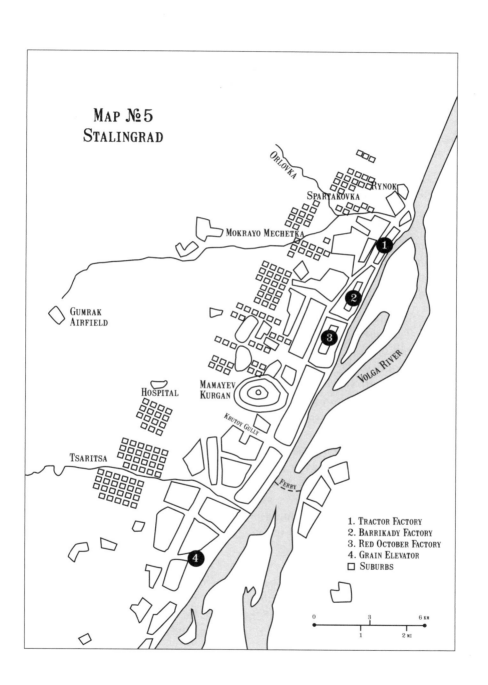

MAP № 5
STALINGRAD

ORLOVKA
RYNOK
SPARTAKOVKA
MOKRAYO MECHETKA
GUMRAK AIRFIELD
VOLGA RIVER
HOSPITAL
MAMAYEV KURGAN
KRUTOY GULLY
TSARITSA
FERRY

1. TRACTOR FACTORY
2. BARRIKADY FACTORY
3. RED OCTOBER FACTORY
4. GRAIN ELEVATOR
☐ SUBURBS

0   3   6 KM
      1   2 MI

past. I had never seen so many of them. They flew in flocks, black, repulsive, unperturbed, at various levels.'[10] These flocks were all part of a 1,600-sortie sequence of raids. Incendiaries ignited the wooden housing in the southwest of the city. Closer to the river, the tall white blocks of apartments were reduced to shells. A ball of flame 1,500 feet high erupted from the exploding oil tanks along the Volga, spewing burning oil across the broad river. The huge cloud of oily smoke would be seen 200 miles away. The telephone exchange and the waterworks were destroyed, the main hospital bombed, and even the bakeries had been targeted. The dead were everywhere.[11]

General Yeremenko wrote:

> We'd been through a lot in the war up to that time, but what we saw in Stalingrad on 23 August was something completely different. Bombs were exploding all around us and the sky was filled with columns of fiery smoke . . . Asphalt on the street emitted choking fumes and telegraph poles flared up like matches. The earth of Stalingrad was crumpled and blackened. The city seemed to have been struck by a terrible hurricane, which whirled in the air, showering the streets and squares with rubble.[12]

The city had been stunned. The raids would continue for the next few days killing at least 40,000 people. Luftflotte 4 lost only three aircraft. It was the largest raid on the Ostfront since the beginning of the war. Appropriately it was the apogee of the career of Luftflotte 4's commander, Generalfeldmarschall Wolfram Freiherr von Richthofen, who had first made his name in the terror bombing of Guernica in the Spanish Civil War. The close German ground–air coordination that Chuikov found so admirable was due to Richthofen's innovations.[13]

On 25 August, two days after the German panzers had reached the Volga north of the city, the Stavka declared a state of siege. The terror bombing continued to smash the city into rubble. Everything now rode on the city's defence. If it fell the rail links and the equally valuable river links to the Caucasus and Caspian Sea would be lost, slamming shut another funnel of Allied aid and cutting off 70 per cent of the Soviet Union's oil. The result would be systemic collapse of the war effort and the Soviet state. Stalin realized that he himself would be consumed by this scenario. He had consigned too many people to oblivion to believe he would escape. The Germans had a word for what was looming he thought. They called it *Götterdämmerung*, the death of the gods and the end of the world. He could taste the irony. Only briefly. Philosophy was of no use in this crisis. Sheer will was, and Stalin had that iron trait as few men had.

Stalin had defended this city on the Volga in the civil war. Then it had been named Tsaritsyn. In his honour it had been renamed Stalingrad, Stalin's city. Rebuilt as a communist industrial showplace it now boasted a population of half a million. It was a significant arms producer with four huge factories. The new Dzerzhinsky Tractor Factory had been converted to tank production when the war started. One of the oldest artillery makers in the country had been refurbished and named Barrikady Gun Factory. Other important factories were the Krasny Oktyabr (Red October) Iron Works and the Lazur Chemical Factory. There were oil refineries as well, with oil tanks along the river.[14] Volunteer factory workers were pressed into defence units and teenage girls and young women from the Komsomol were encouraged 'strongly' to join air defence batteries, such as the ones destroyed by XIV Panzer Corps. Evacuation of the population had begun, but factory workers remained behind to keep turning out war material, especially the T-34s from the Tractor Factory. They were given rudimentary military training.

The city stretched for 20 miles along the Volga and nowhere was more than 2 miles deep. A grid of straight streets ran perpendicular to the river as did a number of deep gullies, both of which offered quick routes of penetration to an attacker. The western approaches were high ground that dominated the city, and the defenders would have the broad Volga at their backs, a barrier to retreat as well as a barrier to be crossed by any reinforcements and supplies. On military grounds it was a wretched place to try to defend.[15]

The Stalingrad Defence Committee ruthlessly stripped nearby collective farms of their grain reserves and hunted down anyone guilty of defeatism or disloyalty. On the collective farms,

> thousands of Stalingrad's citizens were finishing the job of snatching a bumper wheat harvest from the invaders. The arms crews out there had been straining under the brutal sun while the Stuka dive-bombers machine-gunned them and set fire to trains filled with grain. Nevertheless, nearly 27,000 fully loaded freight cars had already rolled away to safety in the east. Behind them came 9,000 tractors, threshers, and combines along with two million head of cattle, bawling plaintively as they pounded towards the Volga and a swim to the safety of the far shore.[16]

With the start of the war Stalin had ordered rings of defences to be built around the city, but spring floods had washed them out. Some 200,000 men and women in the region were mobilized to rebuild them.

> As in Moscow the year before, women in kerchiefs and older children were marched out and given long-handled shovels and baskets to dig antitank ditches over six feet deep in the sandy earth. While the women dug, army sappers laid heavy antitank mines on the western side.

Most of it was too little too late; the defences were only 30 per cent complete when the Germans came charging right through them.[17]

Spartakovka, 24 August 1942

The 16th Panzer Division had found itself alone on the banks of the Volga just north of Stalingrad. The rest of 6th Army and its own XIV Panzer Corps had not caught up with it. The division went into a hedgehog formation to be able to defend itself from any direction. The next morning it attacked due south into Spartakovka, the northernmost suburb of Stalingrad. They met such a storm of steel from the well-entrenched defenders, both men of the 62nd Army and factory workers, that they recoiled. The Soviets counterattacked. Many of their T-34s were unpainted and even without gun sights, fresh from the assembly lines of the Tractor Factory and manned by the workers who had forged them. So determined were they that some of the tanks penetrated to the headquarters of the 68th Panzer Regiment and had to be destroyed at point-blank range. At the same time, another strong Soviet force attacked from the north.

The only success the Germans had was to take the landing stage of the big railway ferry on the river, severing communications from Kazakhstan to both Stalingrad and Moscow. Nevertheless, 16th Panzer was so closely pressed by the Soviets that only the determined support of the Luftwaffe kept the attackers from overrunning it. Its only hope lay in a link-up with the rest of the panzer corps.

The 'rest of the panzer corps', 3rd Motorized Infantry Division, was having considerable problems of its own. It had turned north and away from 16th Panzer after they had both broken out of the bridgehead to take up positions along the Tatar Ditch and bar any Soviet forces from descending into the narrow neck between the Don and Volga. The Tatar Ditch was an ancient trench and parapet designed to keep raiding Tatar armies from mounting slave and plunder raids into the Russian lands. It was still a formidable barrier that the Soviets had been trying to turn into an antitank obstacle.

On the way the division ran into a train which was being hurriedly unloaded. The Germans overran it and sent the Russians flying with a few well-placed shells. They found a treasure in the waiting boxcars. It was packed with American Lend-Lease supplies – 'magnificent brand-new Ford lorries, crawler tractors, jeeps, workshop equipment, mines, and supplies for engineering troops'. The officers especially liked the American jeep, freshly painted in Russian colours. They uniformly agreed that it was much superior to its German equivalent, the Kübelwagen.[18]

While the Germans were marvelling at their war booty, the Soviet 35th Rifle Division, reinforced with tanks, cut across the rear echelons of both German divisions, rushing to seal off the bridgeheads over the Don. It placed itself firmly between the German VIII Corps holding the bridgehead and the XIV Panzer Corps whose divisions had now finally linked up. Sixth Army was prevented from quickly joining up with the isolated mobile divisions.

Stalingrad, 28 August 1942

Four days after the 16th Panzer had reached the Volga and been joined by the 3rd Motorized Infantry, Colonel A. A. Sarayev, commander of the 10th NKVD Division, thought he had a chance to isolate them completely. He stripped Stalingrad of almost all of his units and city militia and threw them into the fighting in the northern suburbs. The panzer corps was now commanded by General Hans Hube who had come up from 16th Panzer after Paulus sacked his predecessor. Hube was a one-armed veteran of the First World War and about as aggressive and feisty a man as ever commanded armour.

His men and he were daily witnesses to the air battles above as the enemy repeatedly bombed them. Their own Me 109s fell on the Russian bombers like hawks among pigeons. He did not know that three Soviet armies were marching down towards him from where they had de-trained to the north. By now the Luftwaffe had achieved such air superiority over the Red Air Force that the German troops below looked up at the aerial battles as a show put on for them, applauding when aircraft after Soviet aircraft spiralled burning to the ground. To the west the Red Air Force made an attempt to attack Luftflotte 4's airbases in the Don bridgehead, but its planes were swatted out of the sky by Me 109s.

The next day Zhukov arrived in Stalingrad. Stalin had just appointed him as Deputy Supreme Commander. Zhukov had become a junior member of Stalin's 'Cavalry clique' during the Russian Civil War which later, no doubt, spared him in the purge of the officer corps. In 1939 he had defeated the Japanese Kwantung Army in the battle of Khalkin Gol, dropping bundles of samurai swords at the feet of a delighted Stalin. In no other man did Stalin repose such confidence to be able to retrieve a hopeless situation. After all, he had saved Leningrad and Moscow when they were on the brink of falling. Stalin had used him as a one-man fire brigade to retrieve hopeless situations in that first terrible part of the war. He was also the only man who could shout back at Stalin and live to tell about it, so valued had he become. So now he must accomplish the same miracle for Stalingrad.[19]

Zhukov did not like what he saw. He rang Stalin and told him the counter-attack must be put off for a week; the armies involved were simply too inexperienced, made up of older reservists and short of ammunition. The *Vozhd* had no choice but to agree. They both had to watch as the Germans blocked the northern end of the narrow neck between the Don and the Volga, cutting off Stalingrad from that direction.

What happened next alarmed even a man of Zhukov's fortitude. The sudden disappearance of the visible NKVD units in the city to reinforce the fighting in the northern suburbs took a while to be noticed, but when it was, the inescapable conclusion was that the city was being abandoned. Mass panic convulsed the population. No steps had been taken to evacuate them. Stalin had not wanted to show any alarm, and the local NKVD commander had not wanted to waste Volga river transport in moving civilians when he desperately needed it to move the wounded to the east bank and supplies and reinforcements to the west bank.

One woman remembered. 'Shops were simply left open – abandoned – as thousands of people tried to flee in any direction, to go wherever they could.' A wounded soldier in the city hospital noticed the sudden disappearance of the hospital staff; the administrator wandered through the wards apologizing that his staff had simply fled. The patients looked out the windows:

> We saw a scene of indescribable chaos – everyone out of their minds with panic – it looked as if the whole city was in the grip of some kind of collective hysteria. People were looting shops and buildings. Everybody was shouting: 'What's the news?' then there was a growing refrain: 'There's nobody in the city', 'The civil authorities have vanished!', and finally, and most ominously, 'The Germans are coming!'[20]

Amid the chaos, the workers at the Tractor Factory met. They decided to stay. From this assertion of will, calm eventually spread through the remaining population. Determination replaced the panic. There was also a deep, abiding hatred. The city would not be given up.

Somewhere amid the endless defeats and retreats, amid the terror from the skies, the soldiers at the front and the civilians in Stalingrad hardened. Stalin's 'not one step back' order had been the beginning. The introduction of a merciless ruthlessness to those who ran away or failed in their duty was part of it. Blocking units of the NKVD regularly shot men drifting back from the fighting without authorization. Penal battalions were established at division and higher levels; these were sent into suicidal attacks in order, as Stalin himself dictated, 'to redeem themselves with their blood for the crimes against the Homeland'. It was as if 'Order No. 227 became the ultimate expression of fear as a motivational tool.'[21]

It was more than that though. The Russians were reaching deep into their sense of themselves. Despite the 'union' aspect of the Soviet Union and the presence of numerous non-Russians, it was a Russian experience.

Lieutenant Colonel Andrei Mereshko put his finger on what caused the Russians to stiffen their backs and snarl at the Germans. 'Some officers and soldiers had believed that they could retreat all the way to the Ural Mountains but [in fact] any further retreat would lead to the death of the Motherland. There was nowhere left to retreat.'

Order 227 had been a slap in the face to the Red Army and the people. Mereshko went on, 'It opened the eyes of the army and the people, showed them the truth of the situation facing the country.' It led to the slogan, 'There is no land beyond the Volga.' Firing squads and penal battalions did not make Order 227 effective, one veteran said. 'The motivation had to be within us.'[22]

For some Red Army soldiers there was a different motivation. The men of the 64th Rifle Division (66th Army) were from an older age group only recently called to the colours. Their training had been minimal, their equipment incomplete, and their leadership brutal to the point of idiocy. They were also desperately hungry. Thrown unprepared into an attack, they lost thousands of men. The result was a serious mutiny, immediately brought to heel by the NKVD. Three hundred men were shot and another thousand sent to the penal battalions.[23]

Don Bridgehead, 30 August 1942

Seydlitz was straining at the leash to follow the XIV Panzer Corps to Stalingrad. Instead he had to wait until the huge column of Ford trucks had dropped off their supplies in the bridgehead for his corps. Everyone was impressed with the hardy American vehicles now painted in German grey. They were the booty from the captured ships of Convoy PQ-17, a gift from the Führer himself who had regretted the necessity earlier to divert most of that army group's transport to supply the attack into the Caucasus.

It occurred to Seydlitz that here was an opportunity. To the dumbstruck shock of the transport officer, Seydlitz, on his own authority, simply seized his trucks as soon as they were unloaded. Then he loaded the infantry of his two lead divisions on them. The men were tired, and if he could save them another 30-mile road march in this brutal heat, so much the better. He laughed to himself that he now commanded the LI 'Motorized' Corps. He carefully neglected to tell Paulus of his 'requisition' of all the Fords. You could say his family motto was coined by St Francis of Assisi: 'It is easier to beg forgiveness than seek permission.' Paulus was not a man to think outside of regulations.[24]

It did not take long for Seydlitz's two advance divisions to trample the Soviet 35th Rifle Division into the scorched steppe grass and motor towards Stalingrad, barely 45 miles away, three hours or so by truck if the columns kept moving. Seydlitz put his mobile elements, reconnaissance units and some truck-towed 88mm antitank and antiaircraft batteries up front to keep the retreating Soviets on the run as the Luftwaffe's Stukas and Ju 88s harried them from the sky. The outer layers of the defence of Stalingrad were overrun with hardly any fight. Then the Germans came to an abrupt halt at the inner defence along the steep banks of the Rossoshka River manned by remnants of the 62nd Army. Those much abused troops now fought back from good positions and stopped Seydlitz's infantry cold. The truck ride was over almost before it had started. Nevertheless, Seydlitz would hold on to the trucks as if they were an inheritance.

Paulus said nothing about the trucks when he joined Seydlitz at the head-quarters of the 76th Infantry Division. His new chief of staff, newly promoted Generalmajor Henning von Tresckow, did his best to justify Seydlitz's action.

To his relief Paulus had more to worry about than trucks. His old chief of staff, upon whom he had become too dependent many had said, had been wounded. His replacement would take time to get his hands around the situation and get to know the army. Tresckow had been quickly sent from Army Group Centre headquarters; his excellent record made him an obvious choice.

Paulus and Seydlitz were joined by Richthofen, who noticed how nervous the 6th Army commander was and how the tic on the left side of his face had become more pronounced. Paulus was also suffering from recurrent dysentery, the same disease that had sapped Lee at Gettysburg of his driving will and keen judgement, and Paulus was no Lee. Richthofen had none of his cousin's famous chivalry. He had a contempt for the weak. So a man like Paulus, nervous tic and all, took him aback. After all, the man wore gloves in this heat because he abhorred dirt, and he took a bath twice a day and changed into a fresh uniform each time. During active operations! What to make of such a man?[25]

Well, that was neither here nor there at the moment. They had more pressing problems. Richthofen, like Hitler, was an advocate of a swift victory that would solve the problem of overextension. That was little comfort to Paulus who was fully aware of how overstretched his resources were. His losses in infantry and panzergrenadiers had been grievous. Hence the worsening tic.[26] He was obviously without the reserves of will and boldness that would have buoyed a tougher, more experienced man. The difference between a creature of the staff and an instinctive and pugnacious fighting man was starkly apparent. What his training and his own eyes told him was a highly dangerous situation was subsumed in his robot-like obedience to Hitler's will. Blind faith had indeed supplanted reason. When the commander of XIV Panzer Corps suggested a withdrawal because his corps was almost out of fuel and badly overextended, Paulus had relieved him because it bespoke a lack of that same blind faith and replaced him with Hube.

One of the reasons for Paulus's nervous tic was the stout Soviet resistance in the inner defence belt, but that was deceiving. Had Seydlitz only known of the panic in the city, he would have thrown away the scabbard to blast through and dragged his fastidious and nervous army commander with him.

Stalingrad–Morozovsk Railway Line, 31 August 1942

The advance elements of Hoth's 4th Panzer Army reached the Stalingrad–Morozovsk Railway Line in the evening. A great opportunity now presented itself. A good part of both 62nd and 64th Armies could be cut off in Stalingrad's inner defence belt by an encirclement of the panzer corps of the two German armies. Army Group B headquarters quickly endorsed the plan as did Tresckow.

At this point Paulus took counsel of his fears. It would be far too risky to have his XIV Panzer Corps make such a manoeuvre while it was already heavily engaged with the defenders of Stalingrad's suburbs, threatened by heavy Soviet forces from the north, and cut off from 6th Army's main body and supplies. Paulus declined to make the attempt. The two Soviet armies had time to escape into the city. The last chance to destroy the enemy in the field was lost. The 6th Army was now committed to grinding urban combat. Paulus, who had been so apprehensive of his infantry losses, had thrown his army into the very situation that devoured men.

Chapter 10

New Commanders All Round

Soviet–Turkish Border, 2 September 1942

Disaster in the Western Desert had brought Rommel to the gates of Egypt just as the British were trying to come to grips with the impending Turkish entry into the war. That would threaten the vast oil resources at Baku but also those at Mosul in northern Iraq and at Abadan on the Persian Gulf, both sources vital to the British war effort. If successful, the Turks and Germans would not only have stripped the Soviets and Western Allies of crucial sources of oil but also have cut the Persian Corridor through which most aid now reached the Russians. The British scraped together six divisions for their 10th Army based in Baghdad; there would have been more, but two had already been rushed off to help stop Rommel. They also set up a largely paper 9th Army in Syria and used deception to inflate its very weak forces into divisions. The Americans had been persuaded to redirect several air squadrons to bolster 10th Army. The British had offered to deploy a corps of three divisions for the defence of Baku, but Stalin had categorically refused to allow even friendly foreign troops on Soviet soil.[1]

Stalin nonetheless was particularly worried about keeping the Persian Corridor open now that the Arctic route was temporarily stopped. The main route ran by rail and road from northern Iran to the rail centre at Dzhulfa in Soviet Azerbaijan, and then north through Yerevan, the capital of Armenia, and Tiflis (modern Tbilisi), capital of Georgia, where it picked up the Georgian Military Highway that took it over the high passes to Ordzhonikidze (former Vladikavkaz) in North Ossetia. Ordzhonikidze was the main sorting and transshipment station for all the supplies and equipment coming through Iran. From Ordzhonikidze it was sent by rail straight up to Astrakhan where much of it was then fed directly into the defence of Stalingrad as well as equipping the growing Stavka reserve accumulating east of the Volga and north of the Don.

The Dzhulfa rail centre was also the main junction with Baku and the shipments of aid coming by sea from the Persian port of Noushahr. From that port aid was also sent to the Caspian port of Makhachkala just north of the Caucasus range. From there it was transported to Ordzhonikidze. Two alternative routes ran from Tehran through Soviet Turkmenistan to Krasnovodsk on the Caspian and from there by sea to Baku. Dzhulfa, though, was the critical junction. If it failed, the only way British and American aid could get through was to reroute it across the Caspian from Noushahr directly to the ports of Makhachkala and Astrakhan at the mouth of the Volga. Given the lack of shipping, that would amount to only a trickle. If the terminus of Ordzhonikidze fell, only the unused sea route to Astrakhan would remain.

Stalin and the Stavka had also long been aware of Turkey's imminent entry into the war, even the codename, Operation Dessau. A casual observer could have seen what was coming as the Turkish Army massed on the border to be joined by a German expeditionary corps. If that were not enough, their agent within the Wehrmacht's general staff fed them the organization and date of the invasion. That had given Stavka time to alert the Transcaucasian Front's five armies to dig in and prepare. Stalin also ordered two more armies from Stavka reserve to reinforce them. Their commitment soon proved prescient.

On 2 September the Turkish ambassador handed Foreign Minister Molotov a declaration, just as Turkish armies were crossing the border into the Soviet Socialist Republics of Georgia and Armenia. The twenty-one divisions of the Turkish 2nd and 3rd Armies led the invasion. Eight divisions of former Soviet Muslim POWs were attached in separate corps to each army. Another fifteen Turkish divisions were assembling along the country's eastern and southern borders to threaten the British in Persia, Iraq and Syria. The Turkish chief of staff, however, was reluctant to engage the British fully. Turkey needed a way out of the war if something were to go wrong. He issued confidential instructions to those armies to restrain their aggressiveness.

The German Jäger troops were under no such restraint and flowed like water seeking its own level through the difficult terrain of the border area in 3rd Army's sector. They had to admit that the Turks might not be the brightest warriors ever to tread the earth, but they were always up for a fight, especially against a traditional enemy like the Russians. Third Army's objective was the Georgian capital of Tiflis, 130 miles from the border, with a secondary mission to threaten Batumi on the Black Sea Coast just beyond the border. After taking Tiflis 3rd Army would then cooperate with 1st Panzer Army's drive through Chechnya to Baku and the oilfields.

The mission of the 2nd Army was to strike through Soviet Armenia and into Azerbaijan. Its primary immediate mission was to seize the rail centre at Dzhulfa. The 2nd Army's attack also put the Armenians at the mercy of the Turks, who were determined to finish their genocide of 1915–22. It was almost as if they were responding to Hitler's question of 1922, 'Who remembers the Armenians?' They were going to ensure that no one did. The Final Solution of the Armenians was at hand.[2]

Stavka, Moscow, 3 September 1942

Stalin was impatient for an attack from north of Stalingrad on the encircling German troops north of the city. Zhukov had flown to the front to see to it. He found the armies available unready for such an offensive operation and informed Stalin over the scrambler phone. Stalin then called Marshal Alexander Vasilevsky, the Chief of the General Staff, whom he had also sent to the area to observe what was going on. He admitted the Germans had reached the northern suburbs. Stalin exploded over the phone:

> What's the matter with them, don't they understand that if we surrender Stalingrad, the south of the country will be cut off from the centre and will probably not be able to defend itself? Don't they realize that this is not only a catastrophe for Stalingrad? We would lose our main waterway and soon our oil, too!

Vasilevsky replied as calmly as he could, 'We are putting everything that can fight into the places under threat. I think there's still a chance that we won't lose the city.' Stalin rang him back shortly and ordered an immediate attack, regardless of the condition of the troops. The attack on the 5th failed for exactly the reasons that Zhukov had anticipated – the inexperience of the divisions and their lack of ammunition. It did one thing of great value, however.[3] When Zhukov explained that the attack had failed but that it had diverted 6th Army reserves outside Stalingrad to contain it. Stalin replied, 'That's very good. It is of great help to the city.' Zhukov tried to tell him that the attack had served no purpose, but the *Vozhd* said, 'Just continue the attack. Your job is to divert as many of the enemy forces as possible from Stalingrad.'[4]

The build-up for the attack had been clear to the Germans, and Paulus's concentration of effort to stop it gave 62nd and 64th Armies a breathing space. At the same time, Chuikov alerted Yeremenko of the threat from 4th Panzer Army coming from the south, threatening to get behind the two Soviet armies. He drew the proper conclusions. On the night of 2–3 September the two armies withdrew into the inner Stalingrad defence ring. On the 3rd, Seydlitz's LI Corps linked up with Hoth's panzer spearheads to find only an empty pocket.

Seydlitz continued his two-division attack and tore through the repositioned elements of 62nd Army. Unit after unit was driven back with heavy losses or simply collapsed as the Germans approached the western outskirts of Stalingrad. Two rifle divisions completely disappeared from 62nd Army's order of battle in this fighting. The German attack was concentric with LI Corps driving from the west, XIV Panzer Corps from the north, and XLVIII Panzer Corps (4th Panzer Army) from the southwest. Zhukov's continued attacks from the north, however, drew most of the combat power out of XIV Panzer Corps' attack against 62nd Army. More importantly, Paulus diverted his air support from the attack on Stalingrad to contain Zhukov's attacks. Renewed Soviet attacks on 5 September caused Paulus to order Seydlitz to suspend his attack in order to commit all German air support in that direction. Hoth's panzers also found stiffening resistance slowing their progress against 64th Army. Crushing Soviet artillery and rocket-launcher fire and infantry counterattacks eventually brought them to a halt.

Werewolf, Vinnitsa, 4 September 1942

Chief of the Army General Staff Halder was presenting a major appraisal of the deteriorating condition of the fighting forces on the Eastern Front when Hitler savagely interrupted him. 'Who are you to say this, Herr Halder, you who in the First World War occupied the same revolving stool, and now lecture me on the fighting man, you who have never been awarded the black Wounds Badge?'[5] There was a stunned silence among all the officers in the briefing room. Hitler had flung at the Army's Chief of Staff the ultimate insult.

One too many times Halder had argued with Hitler's wishful thinking. He may have been sitting on the same revolving staff stool, but that had not prevented him from gaining a clear understanding of the exhaustion of the German forces on the Eastern Front as well as the inadequacy of resources deployed along two divergent directions across vast distances.

Three days later the tension came to a head. Jodl had enraged Hitler with his reports of his visits to the front. He had reported that List had stated he did not have the resources to complete his mission. Jodl had not spent his career on the revolving staff stool and had seen as much combat as Hitler had in the First War and was twice wounded. Hitler screamed at him. 'Your orders were to drive the commanders and troops forward, not to tell me that this is impossible.'[6] Jodl in turn lost his temper and screamed right back that List had followed Hitler's orders. Again Hitler screamed. 'You're lying. I never issued such orders – never!' He stormed out into the black of the Ukrainian night. 'It was an hour before he came back – pale, shrunken, with feverish eyes.'[7]

That night he ordered stenographers from the Reichstag to report to head-quarters in order to take verbatim notes of his deliberations. From then on, the rift between him and his Wehrmacht generals widened. Hitler sulked, even refused to shake hands with his generals and thereafter took all his meals alone. On the 9th, he relieved List and announced that he would now personally command Army Group A. The commanders of 17th and 1st Panzer Armies would report directly to him. In reality, because Hitler took no direct interest in the details of command, the army group's chief of staff functioned as its commander.

One general, who had just returned after a week away, 'was so shocked by Hitler's "long stare of burning hate" that he thought: "This man has lost face; he has realized that his fatal gamble is over, that Soviet Russia is not going to be beaten in this second attempt."'[8]

Stalingrad, 7 September 1942

Now confident that the threat to his northern flank had been stabilized, Paulus order Seydlitz back into the attack in what he hoped would be the final push that would take the city. Supported by assault guns and groups of 40–50 Stukas, the lethal German combined-arms machine ground steadily towards the bank of the Volga.

However, Stalin's instinct that continuous attacks by Stalingrad Front from the north would give the defenders of the city vital breathing room was again proved correct. Seydlitz and his chief of staff visited Paulus at 6th Army headquarters that night and found him on the horns of a dilemma. He was still worried about his northern flank, and Zhukov's attacks gave him every reason for it. Should he continue to attack due east into the city or north to contain Zhukov? In the end, he ordered Seydlitz to wheel the flank of his corps north to support XIV Panzer Corps on the 9th. At the same time, he ordered Hoth's XLVIII Panzer Corps (resubordinated to 6th Army) to attack southeast to break through to the Volga and split the 62nd and 64th Armies.

Sukhumi, Black Sea Coast, 8 September 1942

With the fall of the main passes, the Vikings and Slovaks fell like an avalanche on the rear areas of the Soviet 46th Army. Most of its main units had been scattered in regiments and battalions fighting in the mountains and passes. As the Germans burst through from the Klukhor Pass, overwhelming the final reserves of the 394th Rifle Division, all these detachments in the mountains were suddenly isolated and out of the fight. The Soviets had not one tank to contest the advance.

The only force standing in the Germans' way was the 7th NKVD Division which was just then experiencing a visit from Beria himself at its headquarters at Zakharovka a few miles north of Sukhumi. Despite Beria's interference, they held out for two days, displaying a determination to fight to the death. On the third day, they collapsed under the weight of the enemy's combined arms attack. Rudel's Stukas first destroyed the division headquarters. Then, one by one, they took out each of the antitank guns into the depth of the enemy defences. The panzers and their grenadiers burst through the broken lines and shot anyone in blue trousers. They would take no NKVD prisoners.[9]

Beria himself waited too long to escape the chaos. His staff car was intercepted by a German tank lurching onto the road to cut off the NKVD. The collision did the car no good as the tank crunched right over it turning the second most feared man in the Soviet Union into bloody jam.[10]

Following the tanks, the mountain corps marched. To the east the Alpini were also heading to Sukhumi. They had only half the distance to go. Ahead of them were only elements of the shrunken 351st Rifle Division.

The 46th Army's headquarters had just transferred to Sukhumi when the

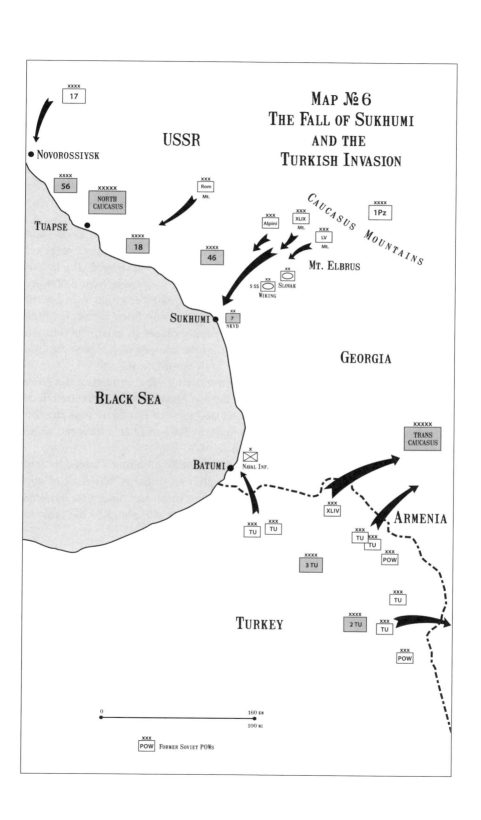

XXXX
17

USSR

MAP № 6
THE FALL OF SUKHUMI
AND THE
TURKISH INVASION

● NOVOROSSIYSK

XXXX
56

XXXXX
NORTH
CAUCASUS

XXX
Rom
Mt.

C A U C A S U S

XXXX
1Pz

TUAPSE ●

XXXX
18

XXXX
46

XXX
Alpini

XXX
XLIX
Mt.

XXX
LV
Mt.

M O U N T A I N S

MT. ELBRUS

XX
5 SS
WIKING

XX
Slovak

SUKHUMI ●

XX
7
NKVD

GEORGIA

BLACK SEA

XXXXX
TRANS
CAUCASUS

BATUMI ●

X
Naval Inf.

XXX
XLIV

ARMENIA

XXX
TU

XXX
TU

XXX
TU

XXX
TU

XXX
POW

XXXX
3 TU

XXX
TU

XXXX
2 TU

XXX
TU

XXX
POW

TURKEY

0   160 KM
                     100 MI

XXX
POW FORMER SOVIET POWs

Vikings and Slovaks blew into the city. Besides its naval personnel, there was only one rifle regiment in the city. Since there were no prepared defences, the Soviets fell back into the ruins of the 14th-century Genoese fort and the 18th-century Ottoman fortress. The Soviet sailors either defended their own facilities or powered up what ships they had to escape. The German corps commander directed his men from the Kaman Cathedral where tradition said that the bones of St John Crysostom were buried. All this time Rudel's Stukas played the vital role of heavy artillery, blasting away the enemy holed up in the ruins. The Alpini streamed into the city before their German counterparts late that day and were thrown into the final assault on the ruins.

By the next day, this beautiful Georgian city with its palm trees, spas and botanical garden was fully under German control and largely intact except for the port facilities which the Soviet naval personnel had destroyed. The last of the defenders were dead or prisoners. Of the latter, there were over 8,000. By this one victory, the entire coast north to the Taman Peninsula was cut off including 12th, 18th, 47th and 56th Armies and the surviving elements of the Black Sea Fleet. The North Caucasus Front simply ceased to exist. The German mountain corps commander commented that the victory had come none too soon for the first snow was falling in the high mountain passes.[11]

One flinty sailor had no intention of surrendering. He commanded the Azov Sea Flotilla which had initially found refuge in Novorossiysk after the fall of its own bases earlier. Vice-Admiral Sergei Georgievich Gorshkov took the last of his ships to sea, crammed with refugees, to Batumi over a hundred miles down the coast on the Turkish border.[12]

Hitler received the news with a righteous tirade. 'All along I knew,' he told the staff, 'that my will would triumph,' he pointed to them, 'when all of you doubted. When I convinced the Turks to come in on our side, you doubted still. Now we are crushing the Russians between us.' He pounded the table in a triumphal rage that approached a wolf's howl.[13]

London, 8 September 1942

Churchill read Stalin's message to the cabinet. 'I received your message on 7 September. I realise the importance of the safe arrival in the Soviet Union of convoy PQ-18 and the need for measures to protect it. Difficult though we find it at present to assign extra long-range bombers for the purpose, we have decided to do so.'[14]

Convoy PQ-18 had been in the planning stage before the destruction of PQ-17. The Soviets had provided a long list of desperately needed supplies and equipment. The Anglo-American losses with PQ-17 and from the Home Fleet had not deterred Stalin at all from acting as if PQ-18 was inevitable. By finally agreeing to an earlier Allied planning proposal to provide long-range bomber support, he hoped to encourage them to push forward with the convoy.

Churchill announced:

> I have spoken to President Roosevelt about the convoys. We are in
> agreement that, at this time, it is not possible to resume them. The First
> Sea Lord has made it clear that it would be suicide to run another convoy
> until the late autumn when the long Arctic winter nights will make them
> much less vulnerable.

He did not say that Roosevelt had told him that there was growing
opposition, especially from the US Navy, to resuming the convoys. He had
enough reasons of his own to avoid sending another convoy. Politically it
would be impossible. The country had been stunned by the tragedy of the
convoy and then the drubbing given to the Home Fleet. He would meet intense
resistance across the political spectrum if they were resumed so soon.

In any case, Stalin would have to be satisfied with the excuse of the danger
of continuous daylight of the Arctic summer. That would give them perhaps
three months more before they had again to grasp that painful nettle.

The Volga River, 8–10 September 1942

Corporal Werner Halle, 71st Motorized Regiment (29th Motorized Division),
and the rest of his battalion got their first hot meal in a long time. They had
seen hard fighting and even harder losses. Halle recorded in his diary that 'we
were frequently without company or even platoon leaders . . . each one of us,
this may sound hard but this was the way it was, could easily guess that he
might be the next to go . . .'

They had been fighting in the southern suburban towns of Krasnoarmeisk
and Kuperosnoye, attacking along the seam between 62nd and 64th Armies.
The 14th and 24th Panzer and 29th Motorized Divisions of XLVIII Panzer Corps
attacked straight towards the southern suburbs of Stalingrad in order to split
the two Soviet armies and cut the city off from the south in accordance with
Paulus's decision of the 7th. The attack had slowed to a crawl in the narrow
streets, where:

> Russian soldiers doused them with Molotov cocktails. From windows,
> enemy snipers picked off whole squads of unwary foot soldiers. Artillery,
> once used to decimate unseen targets miles away, was now employed to
> rip the guts out of buildings just fifty yards in front of the stalled German
> divisions.

Nevertheless, the Germans fought on. They had not far to go. The next
morning Halle and his comrades broke through the rest of the way to the Volga
at Kuperosnoye. Stalingrad was now cut off from the south, and all river traffic
stopped below the German foothold on the bank. Now 62nd Army would be
defending the city alone.[15]

By now 62nd Army's commander, Anton Lopatin, had given up all hope of holding the city and decided to abandon it. He gave the order but was defied by his chief of staff, General N. I. Krylov, who then notified Khrushchev and Yeremenko. They immediately relieved Lopatin and put Krylov in temporary command. Now they had to find a new commander.

Bakumi to Dzhulfa, 10 September 1942

The attack of the Turkish 8th Division along Georgia's Black Sea coast towards the port of Batumi was more a victory parade than a battle. The native Georgians in the province of Adjara had converted to Islam when conquered by the Ottoman Empire in 1613 and joyously welcomed the Turks. The Soviet 47th Mountain Division guarding the port murdered their Russian officers and commissars and went over en masse to the Turks. The division had recently been re-raised after being destroyed in 1941. It had been filled mostly with ethnic Turks from Azerbaijan. As a result the Turkish 8th Division's entry into the outskirts of Batumi triggered joyous celebrations in Istanbul and Ankara and not a few very discreet ones in Baku.

Things suddenly got deadly serious for the 8th Division as it found the Soviet Black Sea Fleet naval personnel in the port of much sterner stuff. They got even sterner when Gorshkov's flotilla escaping from Sukhumi arrived to add more troops to the battle as well as a determined new commander in the vice admiral. He could only hold on and resist to the end, hoping against hope that the sudden collapse of the North Caucasus Front could be repaired in time to relieve the garrison. Against the Russian sailors, the Turks threw some of the finest battalions in their army in tactics reminiscent of the First War. Gradually, the once beautiful city of Batumi was reduced to a stinking, corpse-filled rubble.[16]

Turkish 3rd Army's main attack towards the Tiflis valley ground forward 'despite the frustrations of the difficult terrain, bad weather, and inadequate air support'. General de Angelis was in his element though. This Austrian officer was a brilliant tactician and under his command XLIV Corps, Turkish III Corps, and the legions of former Red Army POWs outmanoeuvred the exhausted Soviet 45th Army and trapped large numbers of its men who promptly surrendered. Many of them were Muslim natives of the Transcaucasus, not overly fond of Russians. Only the Georgians fought on tenaciously, though they had no love for the Russians. The Turks were the enemy of their blood, who had tormented them for 500 years. They tolerated the Russians because they had saved Georgia from extinction by the Ottomans and Persians at the beginning of the 19th century and been its protective big brother ever since. In that part of the world what happened hundreds of years before was like yesterday.

De Angelis had forcibly to protect his Russian and Georgian prisoners from the troops of his Chechen-Ingush Legion. They could have taught the Einsatzgruppen a lot, and it was only the armed intervention of the Jägers that saved the POWs from torture and mass murder.[17]

To the east, the Soviet 71st Army defending the approaches to Yerevan had stopped the Turkish 2nd Army cold just within the border in bitter and costly fighting. Further to the southeast, however, native Azeri Turks provided vital intelligence and outright assistance to the invading Turks, and Soviet 72nd Army crumbled as its Azeri conscripts threw up their hands and surrendered by the thousands to their countrymen in the Azeri Legion. The stouter units were swamped with massed infantry attacks. By the 10th, the Turks were crossing the Arak River above and below Dzhulfa. The town fell almost without a fight.

Stavka, Moscow, 11 September 1942

You could almost hear in the General Staff building the loud crack all the way from the Caucasus. It was the deep, grinding snap of collapse. With the fall of Sukhumi and Dzhulfa, the Soviet control of the vast region of mountains, exotic peoples, and oil suddenly had been fatally wounded. With Dzhulfa, the main route to the Persian Corridor and the last major source of Allied aid was severed. There were over a half million Soviet troops in the region and no way to sustain them if the Germans and Turks eventually linked up at Baku.

Less than two weeks before, the situation seemed to have passed beyond the danger stage as the Germans were clearly exhausting themselves. The land was too vast, their forces too few, and the Soviet defenders too stubborn. It helped the defenders too that a major reorganization on the 1st had rationalized their forces. All forces had been put under the single command of General I. V. Tiulenev's Transcaucasian Front. The North Caucasus Front had been downgraded to a group while the strong Northern Group had been created to block Kleist's 1st Panzer Army from crossing the Terek River and overrunning the Grozny oilfields and taking Ordzhonikidze and its vast stocks of Allied supplies and equipment.

The Northern Group's four armies with eighteen rifle and two cavalry divisions, two rifle corps, and seven brigades had been slowing Kleist to a snail's pace. Its persistent counterattacks had driven the Germans back to their foothold on the eastern side of the Terek at Mozdok. A good part of its tank force was made up of British Valentines and American M3 Stuart light tanks. The Valentines tended to burst into flames, a matter that Stalin brought up with Churchill, suggesting that the Soviet use of diesel in their T-34s was superior.

Kleist resumed his attacks on the 11th and met the same determined resistance, but by the next day the Soviets seemed to be in much weaker strength. In the night two of their armies had begun withdrawing. One was being sent to staunch the open wound left by the encirclement of the Northern Group due to the fall of Sukhumi and the other to retake Dzhulfa.

Breaking contact with half your force and reshuffling the rest of it to cover the same front is one of the most difficult manoeuvres any army can make. It can succeed, though, if the enemy does not interfere. That was a break that Kleist was not about to give. Luftwaffe reconnaissance reported the roads leading south filled with Soviet troops. General Traugott Herr's 3rd Panzer Division was Kleist's spearhead. He divided his command into combined arms battlegroups (*Kampfgruppen*) and drove his panzers right into the confusion of the Soviet passage of lines and transformed it into a bloody rout.

At this point Kleist was presented with an operational dilemma. He had multiple missions: to seize the oilfields at Grozny and to take Ordzhonikidze and the high mountain passes of the eastern Caucasus to open the road to Baku. He had reached that point where all three of these locations were within his grasp. His 3rd Panzer was within 36 miles of Ordzhonikidze and 13th Panzer about the half that distance from Grozny. It was time he asked army group headquarters to put on alert the parachute battalion that had been prepared for just this moment. Upon the approach of German forces, the Soviet garrison of Grozny was under Stalin's orders to destroy the oilfields. Only a surprise descent gave a chance of saving them for the fuel-thirsty German armies fighting from Voronezh to Mozdok.

For Stalin the loss of Sukhumi entailed another and perhaps even more serious loss – Beria. He needed a replacement. For that he reached into the second tier of the NKVD chiefs and plucked out Victor Abakumov. He had survived the purge of the NKVD in 1937–8 because he had been single-mindedly ruthless in carrying it out. Single-minded and ruthless were just the qualities Stalin was looking for.

With Stalin's approval, Abakumov liquidated Beria's senior lieutenants and replaced them with his own. When he personally cleaned out Beria's safe, he found a document that really caught his attention. It was a file, and not just any file but Stalin's, prepared by the tsar's secret police, the Okrana. It was not the file of a suspect or revolutionary. It was that of an informer. From Beria's notes, it became clear that this file in the hands of the NKVD and the senior staff of the Red Army had prompted preparations for a coup that Stalin preempted with the purges that had decapitated both organizations.[18] For Abakumov, whether Stalin had been a traitor to the communist party was a matter of indifference. He would have served the tsar as diligently had he provided a ladder to power. Still, this poisonous document could prove useful. Who knew what course the war would take, and betting men were putting their money on the Germans.

Krasnofimsk, 11 September 1942

'Everybody off!' men were shouting at the Pacific Fleet sailors in the railcars that had just pulled into a siding at the town's rail yard. The men were all volunteers for the front and were to join the 2nd Battalion, 1047th Regiment of the 284th Rifle Division stationed there, 139 miles west of Sverdlovsk in the Urals.[19] They got a hearty welcome from the Red Army soldiers who were amused by the sailor's blue and white striped collarless shirt, the Navy's emblematic *telnyashka*, under their pea jackets.

It was something that 27-year old Warrant Officer Vassili Grigorievich Zaitsev had come to take great pride in ever since he had been conscripted into the Red Navy in 1937. He had worked as a payroll clerk for the last four years, earning a promotion for his diligence and reliability. Like so many of his comrades he had volunteered for the front as soon as the war had started, but only recently had his request and that of so many others in the Pacific Fleet been approved to join the fighting at Stalingrad.

Zaitsev had grown up in the foothills of the Ural Mountains where his grandfather had taught him to shoot and hunt. The old man came from a long line of hunters and was devoted to Vassili, his favourite grandson, to whom he passed his vast experience of stalking and marksmanship. Bullets were expensive and had to be used with care. One shot, one kill, was the old man's method. Young Vassili became an expert shot, never wasting a bullet and became so good at building hides that even his grandfather could not find them. To him tracking an animal was like reading a book. Like all bureaucracies the Red Navy failed to exploit this talent. Instead, because Vassili had taken accounting courses, they thought him a perfect payroll clerk. Some things never change.

However, anyone who got to know the payroll clerk would be struck by several things: 'his modesty, the slow grace of his movements, his exceptionally calm character, and his attentive gaze. His handshake was firm, and he pressed your palm with a pincer-like grip.'[20]

Southeastern Front Headquarters, 12 September 1942

Chuikov had been ordered by the Front military council to report immediately to its headquarters on the east bank of the Volga. It took him hours to find one of the irregular transports coming from the other side. He had time to walk through the field hospitals huddled along the bank in dugouts and tents, crowded with wounded and overworked and overwhelmed staff. It was a depressing sight.

The next morning he reported and was briefed by Khrushchev while Yeremenko listened. 'The conversation was brief,' he wrote. 'I had been appointed Commander of the 62nd Army.' They told him Lopatin had been removed for defeatism. Khrushchev pointedly stated that his selection was based on Chuikov's beating the enemy on the Aksay while in command of the Southern Group. Then Khrushchev asked him, 'Comrade Chuikov, how do you interpret your task?'

Chuikov had not been prepared for such a question, but the answer quickly came from deep within.

> We cannot surrender the city to the enemy because it is extremely valuable to us, to the whole Soviet people. The loss of it would undermine the nation's morale. All possible measures will be taken to prevent the city from falling. I don't ask for anything now, but I would ask the Military Council not to refuse me help when I ask for it, and I swear I shall stand firm. We will defend the city or die in the attempt.[21]

They replied that he understood his mission completely.

Chuikov set out immediately to find his headquarters. As his ferry approached the right bank, he could see,

> the landing stages filled with people. They are bringing the wounded out of the trenches, craters and dugouts, and people are crowding round with bundles and cases . . . all these people have stern faces, black with dust and streaked with tears. Children, racked with thirst and hunger, no longer cry, but merely whimper, trailing their little hands in the water . . . One's heart contracts and a lump comes to one's throat.[22]

He found his headquarters on Mamayev Hill (or Kurgan), a vast artificial mound built ages ago by steppe nomads as a burial site and located in the centre of the city. He found the dugout and Krylov, yelling over the phone as shells hitting outside drizzled dirt from the rafters overhead on everyone. Here was a man that he might work with, just as tough and decisive as himself. That night he discovered what a hollow shell 62nd Army was. In his three armoured brigades there was only one tank left. One division had been reduced to a composite 'regiment' of 100 infantry, less than a company. The next division had only enough infantry left to amount to a battalion. His motorized brigade had barely 200 infantry. A division on the left bank had only 250 infantry. Only Colonel Sarayev's NKVD division and two other brigades were more or less up to strength.

Worse yet was the sense of hopelessness that was spreading like the pox among the men, accelerated by Lopatin's despair. Men were drifting back to the Volga to find a way across. Even senior staff officers were trying to get across, feigning illness. Nevertheless, he determined to attack on the 14th.

Stalingrad, 13–15 September 1942

Chuikov's first full day of command was welcomed by a German attack on the Kurgan itself. His command post bunker was struck so often that the telephone wires were cut again and again. He asked Yeremenko for several divisions to reinforce his disintegrating lines. Then he moved from the Kurgan, when the Germans had fought their way to within 800 yards of his command post, to a command bunker dug in the side of the Tsaritsyn gorge.

In the short time since he had arrived, he had observed that the German tactics were consistent with what he had experienced at Kalach and on the Aksay.

> Watching the Luftwaffe in action, we noticed that accurate bombing was not a distinguishing feature of the German airmen: they bombed our forward positions only when there was a broad expanse of no-man's land between our forward positions and those of the enemy.

The solution seemed to be to reduce that expanse to no more than a grenade's throw, to grasp the enemy by the buckle. 'We must gain time. Time to bring in reserves, time to wear out the Germans,' Chuikov told his assembled commanders. He pointed to the map of Stalingrad on the wall. 'The scale was no longer the kilometre, rather it was the metre. The battle was for street corners, blocks of houses, individual houses.' Krylov drew the enemy positions with a blue pencil (Soviet units in red, of course).[23]

Chuikov knew he did not have a large force to throw at the enemy, and the enemy knew it, too. He recalled that the great Suvorov had said that 'to surprise is to conquer'. Although his infantry were weak, he was able to call on strong artillery support. The guns thundered at 03.30 in the morning of the 14th. He spoke to Yeremenko who promised him that at sunrise the Red Air Force would be in the sky over the city to disrupt the inevitable Luftwaffe appearance. He also said that the 13th Guards Rifle Division had been released from Stavka reserve and would begin crossing the river that evening.

The attack achieved some success in the centre, but at dawn the Luftwaffe arrived in strength and defeated Chuikov's air support. Units of 50–60 aircraft then bombed and strafed his attacking units, 'pinning them to the ground. The counter-attack petered out.'

The Soviet troops in the centre of 62nd Army's line had been all but wiped out. Chuikov looked about for any reserve. He faced down NKVD Colonel Sarayev who finally accepted that he was a soldier of the 62nd Army. His own lines were stretched thin, but he had 1,500 worker militia, and these Chuikov used to garrison a number of large buildings in the path of the Germans, each under the command of a reliable communist. It was not enough.

At noon the Germans struck back in great strength, overran the Kurgan, and despite heavy loss seemed on their way to break through to the river landing stage where the 13th Guards were scheduled to land. Already some of their heavy machine guns were raking the landing stage. The Germans thought they had won the battle and many were cheering and dancing for joy. News of the loss of the Kurgan spread through the Soviet defenders and came close to breaking their nerve. They had already seen all the artillery returned to the eastern bank and interpreted it as the first stage in the abandonment of the city. Rather it was a clever decision on Chuikov's part to mass his artillery where it could be easily deployed and controlled. It was far easier to feed the guns their ammunition on that side rather than haul it across the river.

Chuikov now threw in his last reserve – nine tanks, his own staff officers and political section, almost all of them communists, and the headquarters guard company. Major General A. I. Rodimtsev, commander of the 13th Guards, arrived to see Chuikov. He reported that he had a full division of 10,000 men, but a thousand lacked arms. Chuikov stripped all but his infantry of their small arms to make up the shortfall.

Still it seemed the Germans would win the race to the landing stages. Chuikov then made a crucial decision. Rodimtsev's regiments would have to begin crossing now, in broad daylight. The Germans would reach the Volga and overrun the landing stages if they waited for dusk. Already the Germans had reached the embankment north of the landing stages and occupied a number of buildings. At this desperate moment a member of Chuikov's staff recalled the scene as Rodimtsev was about to take his leave, Chuikov embraced him and said, 'I can't see either of us surviving this. We're going to die, so let's die bravely, fighting for our country.'

The Germans had already occupied buildings near the ferry, and their machine guns swept over the landing stages, killing the ferry commander and then his commissar who took his place:

> The harbour was in flames and the heat reached such intensity that the Katyusha rockets unloaded and stacked by the quayside, suddenly ignited. They were flying out of their boxes, exploding everywhere like ghastly fireworks. We were desperately running about, trying to separate the ammunition boxes, with German snipers picking us off.

Groups of German infantry were approaching the landing stages. All seemed lost, the city fallen, when the defenders were suddenly seized with a great rage and everywhere flung themselves at the Germans. 'We stood together, firing and firing – until our guns were almost melting from the heat.'

Now, on the east bank, Rodimtsev addressed the men of the first regiment to cross. They were terrified of the swarming Stukas and knew it was a death sentence to attempt to cross in daylight. Even if a man fell into the water alive, the weight of his equipment would carry him to the bottom. He reminded them of who they were and what they had already gone through. He calmed the recruits by telling them that battle would make them veterans. Then he pointed to the dying city and told them that the fate of their Motherland now hung in the balance. It would be a determined body of men that marched down to the landing stages to fill the boats clustered there.

Many died on the way across the river either from direct hits on their boats or sinking beneath the water. The others did not even wait for the boats to reach the landing stages but leapt into the water and raced ashore to close with the enemy as German machine guns winnowed their ranks. The ferocity of their attack stunned the Germans. One unarmed and bleeding soldier was seen to throw himself at a German soldier, snap his neck, and throw the corpse over his shoulder before moving on to the next one. They cleared the Germans from the embankment and pushed them back. Half the men who had crowded aboard those boats had died by the time the Germans had been thrown out of their lodgement. That night most of the rest of 13th Guards got across the river shepherded at the landing stages and into the city by Chuikov's surviving staff.[24]

With the day the Luftwaffe showed up in massive force to hammer the 13th Guards who were trying to orient themselves as they moved through the streets. Seydlitz's LI Corps resumed the attack as XLVIII Panzer Corps fought its way along the Volga shore. The arrival of the 13th Guards threw a rock into the gears of the German attack. The railway station changed hands four times, but by nightfall was still held by Rodimtsev's men. That night they retook the Kurgan. They had been the margin that kept the Germans at bay.

As hard had been the blows of Seydlitz's corps, the greatest damage done to 62nd Army was by XLVIII Panzer Corps attacking from the southeast. The 24th Panzer Division's two *Kampfgruppen* struck deep into the city and by midmorning had taken the rail junction barely a mile from the Volga. The Soviet infantry fought for every building and 'had to be individually thrown out of every street in hard hand-to-hand and close combat'. The 29th Motorized Division fought its way north along the Volga bank with the massive grain elevator looming ahead of them to the north:

> By the day's end, with their defences shattered and in shambles, all of the forces defending 62nd Army's left wing conducted a disorganized fighting withdrawal eastward into the southern section of Stalingrad and the narrow strip of land on the Volga's western bank south of the Tsaritsa and El'shanka Rivers.[25]

Symptomatic of the day's setbacks was a report by the NKVD that pointed to instances of outright collaboration with the Germans and a disintegration of morale. The 62nd Army's NKVD blocking detachment had arrested 1,218 men drifting to the rear and the Volga bank. They shot twenty-one and detained another ten. The rest were sent back to their units. Worse yet was the arrest of the commander and commissar of a regiment who had deserted their unit:

> For displayed cowardice – fleeing from the field of battle and abandoning units to the mercy of their fate – the commander of the associated regiment of 399th Rifle Division, Major Zhukov, and the commissar, Senior Politruk Raspopov, have been shot in front of the ranks.[26]

Chapter 11

Der Rattenkrieg

Grozny, 16 September 1942

Again the Israilov brothers, Khasan and Hussein, watched German parachutes flittering down through the night sky. This time there were hundreds. They were the men of 4th Battalion, Luftlande-Sturmregiment 1 (Parachute Assault Regiment 1), Flieger Division 7 (7th Airborne Division). Many of the men, including their commander Major Walter Gericke, wore the cuff band 'Kreta' in honour of their desperate air assault on the island of Crete in May 1941.

They were Hermann Göring's pride and joy. Their losses on Crete had been so high that Hitler refused to conduct another large-scale airborne landing. It then took an appeal to Göring by Army Group A for just one battalion to be used in a night air drop. He had asked Hitler, who relented as long as it was only one battalion. The Luftwaffe was, in any case, hard put to divert enough Ju 52 transports for the drop of even one battalion.

As he came down in his chute, Gericke could see the lines of bonfires that had guided the transports to their drop zone. The Chechens had done just what they said they would do. Let's hope, he thought, they would have the promised number of men on the ground to assist in his mission. He was determined to go on no matter what,

Within half an hour he was conferring with Khasan. To enormous relief, he could tell by moonlight that the woods were filled with well-armed men. He shuddered for a moment. They reminded him of the natives of Crete who had come out of their homes with scythes and pruning hooks, kitchen knives and old swords, to fall on his paratroopers with a fury they had never expected. Mountain peoples are tough and unforgiving. An even greater surprise were the twenty-two Studebaker trucks waiting to move the extra ammunition and equipment that had been dropped with them. Israilov laughed as he pointed to them, 'Gift of the American people! We snatched them off the Georgian Military Highway for you. Just dressed as NKVD men and pulled them off the road.'

Their move through the countryside was mercifully uneventful. By dawn their objective was in sight, the vast Grozny oilfields, a forest of derricks and the cracking and refining plants that left a haze in the air. Now it all depended on the element of surprise. The German armies in the south needed not merely oil but refined petroleum products, and those were made by the cracking and refining plants. The oil by itself was of little immediate use. Gericke's mission was to take those plants. His problem was that there was a garrison in Grozny to protect the fields and, on Stalin's orders, the plants had been set for demolition if the Germans seemed about to overrun them. Gericke considered that even a surprise attack would not be quick enough to forestall the destruction of the plants.

The Studebakers were a godsend. He gathered his company commanders and quickly revised their plans. He turned to Israilov, 'You still have those NKVD uniforms?'[1]

'Of course, my friend.'

Within an hour the truck convoy entered the main road to the fields with Chechen drivers dressed in NKVD uniforms, a surefire unquestioned pass to anywhere they wanted to go. The Chechens spoke fluent Russian and had that cold self-confidence that could bluff through anything. Israilov slipped his men between Grozny and the fields waiting to ambush the garrison when it sallied out.

The few guards at the main cracking plant were overpowered almost without a shot, but it was too good to be true that everything would fall to Gericke's *coup de main*. The chief engineer at the plant was shot just as he set off the demolitions that sent the facility up in a ball of fire.

Stalingrad, 16–17 September 1942

Already that morning Chuikov had reported to the front military council that he was completely without reserves while the enemy continued to commit fresh forces. '[A]nother few days of such bloody fighting and the Army would disintegrate, would be bled to death. I asked for the Army to be immediately reinforced by three fresh divisions.'

That night a near full-strength 92nd Naval Infantry Brigade from the North Sea Fleet crossed the Volga as did a tank brigade. The sailors had not been incorporated into the Red Army but fought in their own uniforms, bell-bottom trousers, sailor caps with the ribbon hanging from the back, and their *telnyashka* shirts. They were as tough as the frozen sea they had sailed. With them was the 137th Tank Brigade with light tanks to help stop the Germans from getting to the Volga east of Mamayev Kurgan.[2]

That day's fighting raged along almost the entire perimeter of 62nd Army's front from the Red October complex in the north past the Kurgan and through downtown Stalingrad to the El'shanka River. Seydlitz's 295th Infantry Division stormed the hill only to be thrown off by battalions of the 13th Guards and 112th Rifle Divisions. That afternoon the Germans counterattacked and took the summit. They now had the perfect observation post to see everything within Chuikov's lines, the ferries and the opposite shore of the Volga, and to call down accurate artillery fire. They did not have, however, undisputed control of the hill. Chuikov's men were still in possession of significant parts of it which prevented the Germans fully exploiting its potential.

On Chuikov's southern perimeter, XLVIII Panzer Corps drove the fragments of Soviet units back and crossed the El'shanka River near its confluence with the Volga. Chuikov then consolidated these fragments under the 35th Guards Division which finally brought the Germans up short.

The high tempo of fighting continued on the 17th. Now the grain elevator on the bank of the Volga became the focus of both armies. This huge structure still filled with grain dominated the skyline of the city. So important was it that Paulus chose its likeness to adorn the Stalingrad victory medal he designed. Chuikov had to defend it because it anchored his line on the Volga. Guardsmen and naval infantry were infiltrated to garrison it through a network of tunnels. They held out until the 20th when the Germans finally stormed it. One German soldier wrote:

> Fighting is going on inside the elevator. It is occupied not by men but devils, whom no flames or bullets can destroy. If all the buildings of Stalingrad are defended like this, then none of our soldiers will get back to Germany.[3]

Already the Germans were referring to this brutal city fighting as *Der Rattenkrieg*, the rats' war.

Those 'devils' were suffering their own hell. One naval infantryman wrote:

> In the elevator the grain was on fire, the water in the machine guns evaporated, the wounded were thirsty, but there was no water nearby. This was how we defended ourselves twenty-four hours a day for three days. Heat, smoke, thirst – all our lips were cracked. During the day many of us climbed up to the highest points in the elevator and from there fired on the Germans; at night we came down and made a defensive ring around the building. Our radio equipment had been put out of action on the very first day. We had no contact with our units.[4]

East of the Volga, 17 September 1942

Warrant Officer Zaitsev was marching with his regiment at night to avoid air attack. Ahead of them on the horizon was a ghastly sight.

> The reference point visible to all, the hellish fires at the edge of the steppe, gave us the sensation of walking towards the end of the world. But those were the fires of Stalingrad!
>
> As morning approached the sun obscured the red of the flames on the horizon, but the dark crimson clouds became thicker. It was as if a huge

volcano was erupting, spitting forth smoke and lava. And when the sun's rays lit up between the clouds, we could see things circling, like a swarm of flies . . . it looked like the entire German air force – were flying over the city in formations, stacked three or four layers thick. They were unleashing their explosive payloads on the city below. The dive-bombers dipped down into the heart of this conflagration, and from the ground below them columns of red brick dust would shoot up hundreds of metres into the air.

Zaitsev's company commander announced, 'That's where we're headed, but right now, sailors, we have to prepare you for action.'[5] For the next three days the regiment received intensive training in street fighting, grenades, and close combat with bayonets, knives, and shovels. At the end, they traded in their Navy uniforms for ill-fighting Red Army brown, but they kept their striped Navy *telnyashki* underneath.

Grozny, 18 September 1942

It was a sight that few men of the 23rd Panzer would ever forget as they closed on Grozny and its oilfields. South of the city stretched a forest of derricks, here and there some of them were spouting fire like giant flamethrowers. Nearer the city a huge fire burned in the centre of the complex of cracking plants and refineries. The panzers were like the cavalry coming to the rescue, a theme so many of them had picked up from American movies before the war and in reading the Western adventures written by Carl May and so beloved of German schoolboys. Only this time, the cavalry rode in on steel steeds, and the settlers were the besieged battalion of Flieger Division 7.

They bypassed the city to ensure the capture of that part of the fields and their facilities that had not been destroyed. Smoke rose from the city, courtesy of the Israilov brothers and their bands of Chechen rebels who had attacked as the garrison had rushed out to secure the oilfields. The Germans would later blanch at the atrocities the Chechens had committed on the Russian population of the city. If any ethnic group was atrocity-prone, it was the Chechens. They were already hated in the rest of the Soviet Union as the cruellest of the underworld mafias. Now they were sating their revenge on the Russian civilian population. The communists went first, then they worked their way down.[6]

Fifty miles away to the west, 3rd Panzer was chasing the retreating Russians down the Georgian Military Highway. They bounced into Beslan and secured the road east to Grozny and then pressed on south. Outside Ordzhonikidze, the Soviet 9th Army gathered the fragments of units coming south and made its last stand. Strong tank attacks suddenly drove north out of the town. The British Valentines and American M3s, however, were very badly handled as if by amateurs who had never been in a tank before. Over a hundred tanks were left burning or abandoned when the survivors fled back into the city. Only later did the Germans learn that the Soviets had been using the stocks of Allied tanks from the parks outside the city, crewing them with infantry, truck drivers and whoever else could be scraped up. It would take the arrival of two of Kleist's infantry divisions to break the defence on 20 September and capture the vast sorting fields of British and American supplies and equipment.

Kleist's men had been at the end of a fraying logistics pipeline. Now they had everything. Food of all descriptions, boots, medical equipment and supplies, fuel, and above all fields full of American Studebaker and Ford trucks and jeeps. So many, in fact, that the Germans were able to refit XL Panzer Corps completely with more than its establishment of transport. There was enough left over to re-form two infantry divisions as motorized units. The Germans had got used to incorporating captured enemy equipment into their units, but they had never seen war support war in such a lavish style.[7]

Werewolf, Vinnitsa, 18 September 1942

Late than night Major Engel was writing in his diary of the day's events at the Führer Headquarters:

> F. seems determined to get rid of Keitel [Chief of OKW] and Jodl . . . asked what successor he was thinking of. He mentioned Kesselring or Paulus . . . the chief of staff [Halder] would have to go beforehand, there was simply nothing more there. At the moment he trusted nobody among his generals, and he would promote a major to general and appoint him Chief of the General Staff if only he knew a good one . . . Basically he hates everything in field grey, irrespective of where it comes from, for today I heard again the oft-repeated expression that he longed 'for the day when he could cast off this jacket and ride roughshod'.

Hitler had made it clear that the General Staff officers were out of touch. '"Same old song: too old, too little experience at the front." Chief said he had a better impression from younger General Staff officers,' such as Major von Stauffenberg, who often made statements before Hitler that affected operational decisions.[8]

Werewolf, Vinnitsa, 20 September 1942

Hitler had not been happy with Colonel Gehlen's report:

> I have told you, Gehlen, that the Russian is *kaput*, finished. And now you give me a report that says they have a million and a quarter men in reserve. What do take me for, a fool? After their losses, such a thing is impossible!

Gehlen's Foreign Armies East had, in fact, done a superlative piece of order-of-battle analysis. If anything, they underestimated Soviet numbers.

Hitler's reasoning was confounded by the fact that, with almost the same number of men at the front as the Germans, Stalin had been able to amass 1,242,470 men in Stavka reserve while the Germans essentially had no strategic reserve. Gehlen's office estimated that the Soviet class of 1925 was providing Stalin with 1,400,000 more men. The German class was little more than one-third that number.[9]

Halder received another disquieting report that went into his next briefing for Hitler. The information was as of the 14th and rated the fighting strength of all the infantry battalions in 6th Army. Seydlitz's LI Corps, which had been in the hardest fighting, was bleeding away. Of its 21 infantry battalions, 12 were rated as weak, 6 as average, and 3 as medium-strong. The pioneer battalions were rated average.[10] Halder knew that Hitler would not want to hear this; his mind always needed to assume every division was at full strength. He then kept assigning missions that dead men could not fulfill.

Gehlen's statistics-laden briefing which Halder supplemented with LI Corps' waning strength had been the last straw. Hitler acted quickly to decapitate the General Staff that he so despised. He summoned Halder and told him, 'Herr Halder, we both need a rest. Our nerves are frayed to the point that we are of no use to each other.' Halder took the hint and resigned.

Halder went to his room to pack and pen a note to his protégé Paulus. 'A line to tell you that today I have resigned my appointment. Let me thank you, my dear Paulus, for your loyalty and friendship and wish you further success as the leader you have proved yourself to be.' Even before Halder's aide could drop the note off at the OKW dispatch office, Paulus was reading the message from Werewolf giving him his old boss's job. He was to report immediately and turn his army over to Seydlitz. He felt an immense sense of relief even though his men had just raised the swastika flag over the huge and now shattered Univermag department store in the city centre. He would no longer be responsible for bleeding 6th Army to death. Over the last six weeks, his army had suffered 7,700 dead and 31,000 wounded; fully 10 per cent of 6th Army had been lost. Every day the fighting got harder, the Russians more determined, and his losses were not replaced. He thought that now perhaps his near uncontrollable tic might go away.[11]

Next it was Jodl's turn to be humbled. Hitler assembled the OKW staff to announce the immediate promotion of Major von Stauffenberg to General-major (brigadier general) and his appointment as deputy chief of OKW's Operations Staff. He came over to shake the stunned Stauffenberg's hand. The new general noted that the Führer's hand was trembling. Stauffenberg's appointment was seen for what it was, a rebuke to Jodl. Hitler clearly thought he needed a minder.

Most angry was Bormann. Hitler apparently had not known that Stauffen-berg was a deeply religious Catholic. It was too late to get to Hitler to warn him off. The Führer would lose too much face. What Bormann did not know was that Stauffenberg had come to find Hitler and his Nazis repugnant and had been so alarmed at the treatment of the Jews and the assault on religion that he been drawn into the anti-Hitler plot by Tresckow.

Now that he had got their attention, Hitler had one more announcement. 'I have decided to replace Weichs as well. A man with more ruthlessness is required at this decisive stage in the struggle against Bolshevism. Manstein will now command Army Group B.'[12]

Sevastopol, Crimea, 21 September 1942

Within twenty-four hours of his appointment, Manstein ordered the siege train of heavy guns that had been left at the shattered Soviet fortress to be moved to Stalingrad. At the same time rail construction troops were set to work to strengthen the line from Kalach to Stalingrad and a subsidiary line from Rostov through Kotelnikovo to Stalingrad.

The most imposing of the guns were the two 600mm and one 800mm railway guns. The former were named *Thor* and *Odin*. The latter, named *Schwerer Gustav* (Heavy Gustav), weighed 1,350 tons and could throw a 7-ton shell as far as 23 miles that would destroy any fortification known at that time. Developed by Krupp in the 1930s specifically to destroy the fortifications of the Maginot Line, Gustav was not ready in time for that battle. It had been ready to crack open Sevastopol. It was the largest-calibre rifled weapon in the history of artillery to see combat, and fired the heaviest shells of any artillery piece.

A second 800mm gun named *Dora* had already arrived at Stalingrad in mid-August. A train with a total length of almost a mile was needed to transport it to its siding emplacement 9.3 miles west of the city. It had fired its first shell on 13 September.

Two 280mm rail guns as well as two 420mm and two 355mm howitzers were also sent north in addition to four 305mm mortars. Both of the 420mm guns were short-ranged and left over from First World War. Manstein could not give 6th Army more infantry, but he could give it crushing artillery.

Stalingrad, 22 September 1942

The sailors looked askance at the boat and barge that had come to pick them up to cross the Volga. It was badly holed and leaking energetically. The boat operator was throwing boxes of canned American meat into the hold to make room for the ammunition being loaded. Zaitsev joked, 'What are you doing, Sarge? The Second Front is going to drown down there!' Leaks or no, the men crossed the Volga that night without incident. By five in the morning the entire 284th Division had made it across the river. They were part of what would be called 'feeding the fire', the constant stream of replacement formations slipped across the river to keep going the conflagration that was burning out 6th Army.

The Russians kept sending in new formations from the Stavka reserve while 6th Army received no reinforcements from outside its own army area except for half a dozen pioneer battalions.

Its only augmentation consisted of 70,000 Soviet citizens. These were the *Hiwis* (*Hilfswillige* or volunteer helpers). Some were anti-Soviet volunteers, including many Cossacks, and others were recruited out of POW camps. They wore German uniforms and performed credibly, usually well treated by the Germans but sure to be shot on the spot if captured. Some German divisions had as many *Hiwis* as Germans. Among the many non-Slavic nationalities, there were six battalions of Turkmen alone in 6th Army, as well as Balts, Armenians, Georgians, Azeris, Kazakhs, Uzbeks, Khirgiz, Tatars and many more. Hatred of communism also drove large numbers of Slavs including Russians into German uniform. The Ukrainians were especially well-represented, steeped in hatred for the seven to ten million of their people purposely starved to death by Stalin in the evil winter of 1932–3, the murder by hunger, they called it. Without their willing support, 6th Army would have been an empty shell by the time it reached the Don.[13]

As a counterweight to German air superiority, the massed guns on the east bank of the Volga smashed German communications and battalions massing for attack. Vassily Grossman, the Soviet war correspondent, wrote, 'On the other side of the Volga, it seemed as if the whole universe shook with the mighty roaring of the heavy guns. The ground trembled.'[14]

As Zaitsev and his sailor buddies were climbing into their barge, an anonymous figure was being driven along the northern flank of the German salient, sometimes within 200 yards of the German lines. It was the Deputy Supreme Commander himself. Zhukov. The next night he made a similar inspection to the south of Stalingrad. The genesis of the visit was when Zhukov had been summoned to Stalin to explain the failure of his offensive against the northern German salient. He told Stalin that he needed more reserves. Stalin picked up the map showing the location of all Stavka reserves. While he was studying it, Zhukov mentioned to Vasilevsky that they needed to find another solution.

Stalin's acute hearing picked it up, and he asked, 'And what does "another solution" mean?' The generals were surprised, and Stalin told them to go back to the General Staff and come back with something.

The next morning they presented an audacious plan. The German salient with its head at Stalingrad offered an enormous opportunity. Its flanks were increasingly being held by the Germans' Romanian allies, not the best of troops, to be charitable. Keep Stalingrad alive, they argued, feed just enough troops to keep the fire hot and the Germans' attention there. At the same time assemble the mass of the Stavka reserves on either flank. Then conduct a deep encirclement on both flanks, deep enough so that 6th Army's mobile divisions could not intervene. Late on the night of the 13th Stalin gave the plan his full backing. 'No one, beyond the three of us, is to know about it for the time being.' They assigned the codename Uranus to it.[15]

Now Zhukov and Vasilevsky were conducting an inspection of the forces north and south of Stalingrad, the jumping-off points for the planned offensive.

Stalingrad, 22 September 1942

Manstein did not prowl the front lines like Zhukov. He was close enough, as far as he was concerned, at 6th Army headquarters. He had flown in almost immediately after his appointment to command Army Group B. Perhaps no senior officer on either side had as keen a grasp of battle at the operational–strategic level of war. He said to Seydlitz and Tresckow, 'Anyone who can read a map should be horrified at the opportunity we are providing the enemy.' He traced with his finger the salient's long flanks.

> The enemy is not stupid. Presumably, his maps show the same things. We are spread thin and not strong anywhere. Only half of 6th Army has been engaged in the fighting for the city. The other half is spread out on the northern arm of the salient against the enemy's constant attacks. Our allies . . .

He hesitated and looked amused at the term:

> Our allies are also spread thin on both arms of the salient. Thus our salient consumes most of the fighting power that should have been directed at Stalingrad. And Ivan keeps feeding just enough men across the river to keep the objective out of our grasp.

Seydlitz spoke up. 'My old corps is about burnt out; we just keep getting weaker and weaker, suspended in this endless *Rattenkrieg* as my men call it now.' Manstein could see that the man was as exhausted as his old corps. The experience of throwing away lives for this pile of rubble and twisted steel had shaken him.

> Why, in God's name, we didn't manoeuvre around this damned place in the first instance, I don't know. All Paulus ever said was 'Führer's orders'. Führer's orders! I told the man to object in the most forceful terms, but he seemed to think that Hitler was an infallible genius who shit Knight's Crosses with Oak Leaves and Diamonds for those who followed his orders to the letter.

Months of inadequate sleep showed in him. He was made of far sterner stuff than Paulus, but the campaign was hollowing even him out. Of this Manstein took careful note. 'I tell you, *Herr Feldmarschall*, that we are like a candle that is about to sputter out. We need reinforcements immediately. The army is eating itself alive.'

The field marshal said, 'There are no reserves left on the Eastern Front that can be released.'

'No reserves? You have seven divisions of your old 11th Army sitting around. We need them here. And *Grossdeutschland* is in reserve as well.'

'They are the small change in my account. I must save them for a crisis.'

Tresckow could see that his boss was becoming distraught and changed the subject. He asked, 'What is the situation at OKW, *Herr Feldmarschall*?' He did not mention his clandestine communication with Stauffenberg who had kept him abreast of every one of Hitler's increasingly histrionic departures from reality.

'Well, *meine Herren*, it all comes down to my little bank account.' They looked puzzled, as Manstein half smiled:

> You see, when I got my marshal's baton for taking Sevastopol, a small deposit was made to my credit in the bank of the Führer's trust. A very small amount, I can assure you. Almost every other account has been cancelled. You see, our Führer no longer trusts any general in *Feldgrau*.[16] You and I, Seydlitz, are in our new commands because the Führer fired the whole lot of our predecessors because they could not transmute his will into miracles. Believe me, that can happen again. In any case, that small account of mine must be husbanded until the right time. I can draw on it only once, and then if I fail, I join the rest of the *Feldgrau* crowd.
>
> That means, gentlemen, that I have for a short time more operational discretion than any other German commander. That is until I stop pulling rabbits out of hats, turning water into wine, changing the laws of physics, human and mechanical endurance. And understanding women.

Werewolf, Vinnitsa, 24 September 1942

Manstein had been summoned back to the Werewolf by Hitler to report on his findings at Stalingrad. Stauffenberg joined the meeting. The field marshal was shocked by Hitler's condition. He had not seen him since their meeting in July. 'Well, well, Manstein. What have you found out? When will the city fall now?'

'It's not going to fall, *mein Führer*.' Hitler jerked as it struck. His face started to redden as rage rippled through his body. 'It's not going to fall unless we act more boldly than we have.' He laid it on thick. 'We are beating our heads against a stone wall at Stalingrad. The Russians just keep feeding men into the city. It's become another Verdun.'

Hitler stood up and began to pace. He screamed, 'I will never give up Stalingrad! Do you hear me, Manstein. *Niemals!* Never! It is a battle of prestige between Stalin and myself.'

'*Mein Führer*, there is another way to win this battle.' He then laid out his plan. Hitler focused intently on it. Stauffenberg made a few positive and insightful comments. As Manstein finished he said, '*Mein Führer*, I will present you Stalingrad as an early Christmas present, a very early present.'[17]

That night Stauffenberg invited the field marshal to dine with him alone to discuss details of the plan. It became clear that he had something else to discuss.

> You have seen the Führer. I tell you frankly, he cannot continue to exercise the high command in his present physical condition. He is near a complete breakdown. *Herr Feldmarschall*, you are the one who is pre-destined, through talent and rank, to take the military command.

Since that was Manstein's goal, he could only have been flattered that the man who had been described by everyone as the most brilliant officer on the General Staff had come to the same conclusion.[18] His brief time with Stauffenberg convinced him that the man more than lived up to his reputation; he had breathed new life into OKW and was bringing very able men with front experience onto the staff. Hitler clearly favoured him. His unheard-of promotion had surprised but not alarmed Manstein. War requires fresh, young talent.

Manstein could take a hint. 'I will be quite willing to discuss the matter of the high command with Hitler, but let me make this clear, Stauffenberg. I will not be a party directly or indirectly to any illegal undertaking.'

Stauffenberg replied,

> While the operational solution you have discussed is brilliant, and no one but you could execute it, Germany is at the end of its resources. There are no reserves on the Eastern Front. Every army group is under pressure and is becoming weaker by the day. It is not every day that we will capture an Allied convoy to live off its booty. If no one takes the initiative, everything will continue on like before, which signifies that we will eventually slide into a major catastrophe.[19]

'You could not be more mistaken,' Manstein replied with some heat. 'It is the course that you suggest that will lead to the collapse of the fronts and even civil war. A war is not truly lost as long as it is not considered as being lost,' he stated firmly. 'The Reich has not yet met that crisis you speak of, but if and when it comes I am positive the Führer will recognize it and turn over the high command to someone qualified.'[20]

> You clearly have not been around him these last months, *Herr Feld-marschall*. I do not think he is capable of such a decision because it would be a repudiation of his leadership. Consider what title we call him by? The Leader! Leadership is the essence of his power. To turn over the high command to someone else would be like committing suicide.

'Stauffenberg, you will not discuss this matter with me again.'[21]

The younger man said only one word. 'Tauroggen.'

Manstein reddened in the face and struck the table with his fist. 'Tauroggen has nothing to do with it.' Tauroggen was where the Prussian General Yorck von Wartenburg had defied the orders of his king and taken his army over to the Russian emperor in the struggle against Napoleon. His was an honoured place in German military history where his disobedience was the supreme act of patriotism for he had disobeyed his king to serve the higher needs of the nation.

Stauffenberg would not give up. 'Tauroggen also entails an extreme loyalty.'

The field marshal drank it in and suddenly became affable. 'What good would a staff be if the staff officers could no longer speak with complete freedom?' He then recited a famous quotation. 'Criticism is the salt of obedience.' They finished their meal in near silence.[22]

Tiflis, 27 September 1942

Panic ran through Tiflis like the plague. People remembered that Ordzhonikidze had once been named Vladikavkaz – Master of the Caucasus – by its Russian founders as they spread their rule over the mountains. Now a new master was spreading his power over the mountains, coming down the Georgian Military Highway that had not seen a foreign boot since it had been built a hundred years before. The Germans were coming. Every possible soldier in the city, to include its military school students, had been sent north to hold the descents from the passes through the mountains, but the 3rd and 5th Gebirgsjäger Divisions had swept around them and taken them from the rear one by one, making way for the panzers and motorized infantry.

The news from Tiflis spread south and panicked the 46th Army which fell back precipitately and began to melt away as the natives of the region deserted. The Turkish 3rd Army and the Jägers overran the weak rearguards and pressed on, taking the city with little resistance just as the panzers arrived from the north. With Tiflis in German control, all the Soviet armies to the east, the remnants of the Northern Group and others, were trapped.

At the same time, 17th Army, having consolidated its victories on the Black Sea coast, began the march to Tiflis with 5th SS Division *Wiking* and the Slovaks (LVII Panzer Corps) in the lead with orders to press on regardless of the slow pace of the following infantry corps. It was 214 miles from Sukhumi to Tiflis, and it would take the panzers less than a week to reach it. The Romanian divisions were left behind to garrison the coast and western Georgia.

The Turkish 2nd Army found itself stopped cold in the Armenian mountains outside Yerevan. The Armenians fought with the same ferocity as the Soviet defenders of the grain elevator. Although Dzhulfa had fallen with a great deal of railway rolling stock and mountains of Allied aid, the Turks there could not use the railway to move through Armenia. Although the Azeri Turks welcomed them as liberators, that area was a poor one from which to base a drive to Baku, 248 miles away over poor roads and no railway connections. Yet, when they had taken Dzhulfa, they had set in train the decisions that would lead to the collapse of the Soviet grip on this vast, rich region.

Kleist had his hands full in Tiflis trying to sort out control of the city. The Georgians were terrified of the Turks whose Ottoman masters had massacred the inhabitants in the late 18th century. Kleist put his foot down and ordered the Turks out of the city where they had already begun to loot and murder. Then there were so-called Knights of Queen Tamara, a proto-fascist group that had sprung up as the communists fled the city. Those Reds foolish enough to stay behind had met rough justice at the hands of the Knights. They were quickly enrolled as a German army auxiliary unit. With supervision they would be useful.

Most of all, Kleist needed to give his men rest, and what better place than this charming green ancient city built on the hillsides above a rushing river. He allowed the churches to reopen and was blessed by the Georgian Orthodox bishop. Luckily for the Georgians and the security of 1st Panzer Army's line of communications, the German political administration of conquered territories had not yet caught up with 1st Panzer Army.

The Germans got on well with the Georgians whom they respected as tough fighters in the Red Army. Now, with Soviet power crushed, they threw flowers in the streets as the mountain troops and tanks had entered their city. After almost 150 years, they would finally be free of the Russians and especially the brutality of the communists. It was a case of being careful of what you wish for. The Germans were particularly taken with the blond Georgians from the province of Mingrelia, the descendants of the Colchians of the legend of Jason and the Golden Fleece. The blond South Ossetians also amazed them. Their province lay north of Tiflis along the Georgian Military Highway as it descended from the mountains. They claimed to be the descendants of the ancient Aryan Alans, the steppe nomads who had terrorized the late Roman Empire in the wake of the Huns. Then there was the intoxicating Georgian wine and good food. Tiflis seemed like a lush paradise after the scorched steppes they had crossed north of the mountains.

For soldiers nothing this good can last as long as there is a higher head-quarters. The calls from the Werewolf were insistent. 'Move on, move on to Baku!' The oilfields and the Caspian Sea beckoned, only 280 miles away.

By the time 1st Panzer Army headed east, XL Panzer Corps had caught up with it, the men wistfully imagining what fun might there have been in Tiflis as they passed through. After them trudged the Jägers of XLIV Corps, now attached to Kleist, and the Turkish 3rd Army. It had been agreed that the Turks would garrison the regions of Azerbaijan along the path of the German advance and keep communications open. The Turkish commander was not happy that they would not be in for the kill at Baku. Blood on their bayonets would give Turkey a strong claim to at least part of the oilfields. As it was, they would have to be satisfied with the rest of Azerbaijan as their spoils.

Brother Turks the Azeris might have been, but they were also despised Shiias. The world was so complicated.

The Soviet collapse in the Caucasus was the trigger for the entry into Soviet Azerbaijan of the Indian XXI Corps (British 5th, Indian 5th and 8th Infantry Divisions). Stalin had been so frightened of the German advance that he desperately accepted the British proposal to reinforce his 53rd Army guarding Baku. Flying air support for the British and Indians were half a dozen American Air Corps squadrons. Flying ahead of the 1st Panzer Army to offer its own air support was, among others, the squadron of Hans Ulrich Rudel.

Tankograd, 29 September 1942

This vast tank factory just to the west of the Urals at Chelyabinsk had been nicknamed Tankograd (Tank City) by the tens of thousands of people who worked there pouring out the T-34 tank in increasing numbers. The factory complex, based on the already existing Chelyabinsk Tractor Factory, had sprung up almost overnight, assembled from dismantled factories and equipment moved ahead of the oncoming Germans in the autumn of 1941. It had been the unsung valour of the Russian people under brutal conditions that had caused it to appear seemingly out of nowhere and become the largest industrial enterprise in the Soviet Union. In a space of thirty-three days from when the order was given, it had begun production of the T-34. In addition to the tanks themselves, the complex produced their aluminium engines, Katyusha rocket launchers, and a great deal of ammunition.

The assembly lines continued to work at a high tempo, turning out hundreds of tanks a week as September came to a close. Yet the railroad spur that carried them away to the fighting forces had slowed its work. Now they loaded only half the tanks that came off the assembly lines. The rest began to fill up huge lots for the simple reason that they had no engines.

The destruction of PQ-17 had sent thousands of tons of aluminium from North America to the bottom of the Norwegian Sea or to German smelters for use in their own war industries. These shipments were nearly half of the aluminium used by Soviet war industry, vital for tank and aircraft engines. And it was not just at Chelyabinsk that production had slowed. The other great tank plants at Nizhny Tagil, Nizhny Novgorod and Sverdlovsk were also hobbled.

As well as aluminium, other raw materials such as copper were lacking. The steady stream of American trucks and jeeps, so favoured by the Red Army, had stopped too, now that the Georgian Military Highway had been cut. A thousand other things in the way of supplies and equipment were cut off, including food. Zaitsev and the defenders of Stalingrad would have no more Second Front spam, or boots, or powdered eggs and milk, no more chemicals for munitions to feed the artillery and the Katyushas, and the list went on and on. Of course, the Soviet Union had its own sources for most of these items, but it could not build tanks and planes in huge numbers and produce these other things as well. It was one or the other. Allied aid had meant it could concentrate on the weapons of war while the Allies provided the logistics of war. No longer.

This meant that the Stavka reserve armies training in their hundreds of thousands to the east of the Volga and north of the Don were not as quickly equipped as if the Allied aid had continued and, without equipment, training lagged. Everything slowed.

Kharkov Training Centre, 30 September 1942

As soon as 6th Panzer Division closed on the training centre, Erhard Raus paid a call on *Grossdeutschland*'s commander. The 49-year old Walter 'Papa' Hörnlein as he was known by his troops, was a spare Prussian with a good deal of nerve. It was rumoured that he had sent Hitler's headquarters a signal asking if *Grossdeutschland* was the only German division on the Eastern Front after it had been in continuous action from one crisis to another. He had a solid reputation as a reliable commander who always had time for his men.

Hörnlein was delighted to see Raus, whose own reputation had preceded him. 'How was the trip from that hellhole in France you all suffered at?'

'Ah, Brittany, I tell you the men couldn't wait to leave,' he said with a laugh. 'They were anxious to experience the good weather and famous food here in Russia!' He went on.

> In truth the men were eager to come. After returning from Russia in the spring we were brought up to strength and reequipped and trained hard. They were not happy about turning over all our tanks to *Leibstandarte*, though, and picking up the T-34s in Kharkov. That is until they got to play with them.

Hörnlein smiled in response:

> Well, Raus, I tell you, your men got the better end of the deal. This Russian tank is superb. It is a dream to maintain compared to our tanks, can go places ours can't, is better armoured, and its gun is better than anything but our long-barrelled 75mm. Now that we've put a radio in each and the electrically powered turret, we can do things with them in battle the Russians can't. Here, I will send over our mechanics and company commanders to help your men break in the new equipment.

'That will be a great help, but is there any word on when we move out and where?'

> Nothing, but God knows there is no shortage of crises. Stalingrad. The Caucasus. Who knows? I can tell you that Manstein has been here to see how well we are doing with the T-34s. He seemed pleased that the men were so enthusiastic. We've been ready to go for over a week now, but he said we had to wait for your lot.

Chapter 12

'Danke Sehr, Herr Roosevelt!'

Metal-Working Factory, Stalingrad, 1 October 1942

Zaitsev snatched a pistol from a wounded soldier and took cover behind a smashed locomotive's wheelhouse. In the building just ahead the Germans were firing from a second storey window and had just wounded his friend Misha. He took aim and dropped one of the Germans with a single shot. In the window above was another German rifleman. Zaitsev checked his pistol – only one round left. Wounded, he dragged himself through the rubble to underneath the window. The Russian's injured leg would not support his weight so he rolled onto his back to aim the pistol:

> I could see the arms of the enemy rifleman jerking with every shot, and he was cursing as he missed. Then he leaned forward to get a better angle. That was when I pointed the pistol at the base of his chin and pulled the trigger . . . The slug went through the top of his skull and hit his helmet with a clang. The Fritz tumbled out of the window, his nose smashing against the concrete.[1]

A few days later, Zaitsev and his friends were pinned down in a bomb crater by a German heavy machine gun firing from 600 yards. One friend spotted the gun with a trench periscope and handed it to Zaitsev who also spotted it. Then he jumped up and almost without aiming fired his rifle. The German machine-gunner dropped. Another man took his place, and another quick shot killed him, followed by a third. The machine gun ceased to torment the Russians.

Zaitsev's regimental commander, 'Bulletproof Batyuk', happened to be watching through his binoculars. He asked and was told it was Vassili Zaitsev. Batyuk grunted and said, 'Get him a sniper's rifle.'[2]

Werewolf, Vinnitsa, 4 October 1942

Stauffenberg took his visitor for an after-dinner stroll through the towering pinewoods outside the Führer Headquarters. Their aides followed respectfully out of earshot:

> I tell you, Tresckow, I am in the very good graces of the *GroFaZ* [*Grosster Feldheer aller Zeit* – the greatest warlord of all time]. I have replaced a number of our more stodgy staff with 'young fire eaters from the front', as he calls them. 'Just what I wanted! *Front Soldaten* [front soldiers].' You can't swing a cat without hitting a Knight's Cross, a German Cross in Gold, and a wounds badge. And they have breathed a new energy and inventive positive attitude. He has come out of his seclusion to dine with the new crew. Your recommendations have been very helpful in my selection of new men.

Standing there in the moonlight, his handsome features were eerily silhouetted – clean, honest, and determined. Tresckow commented, 'Every one of them vetted on his honour to end this regime.'

Stauffenberg said, 'Kluge is with us. But Manstein continues to deflect my appeals.'

Tresckow kicked some of the old pine needles aside with his boot. Their breath was already frosting in the air. You could feel the autumn coming and the Russian winter behind it, a thought that made every veteran of the war on the Ostfront shudder. 'You know, Stauffenberg, there is an old saying that if you strike at a king, you must kill him. We cannot risk merely arresting Hitler as some of our more foolish generals and those civilians in Berlin advise. They want to put him on trial.'

'No!' hissed Stauffenberg. 'One does not put the Devil through the criminal justice system. Then we would have civil war as the Nazis and the SS rallied to free him.'

'What then of Göring and Himmler? Both of them are salivating to be his successor.'

The other man said, 'We must decapitate the entire hydra or set them upon each other. It is the Army that must come out of this as the saviour of Germany.'

Tresckow took him by the hand, gripped it hard as he looked him full in the face. 'Then we must be sure to place our trust in the true Saviour.'

Baku, 8 October 1942

Like raptors, Rudel's Stukas fell screaming on the attacking line of Soviet tanks outside Baku. They were American M4 Shermans fresh out of the Baku Tank Training School, manned by the instructors and students. They died just like T-34s when a Stuka dropped its bomb with pinpoint accuracy. In fact, they died faster because the petrol engine ignited quickly.

The tank attack fell apart as the survivors tried to flee. Kleist had fixed the Soviet 53rd Army and the Indian XXI Corps in the plain outside Baku with his infantry now fairly mobile with all the American trucks captured at Ordzhonikidze. The Soviet tank attack had come close to breaking through when Rudel's Stukas responded to the call for air support. With the Soviet and British attention on their front, Kleist enveloped the Soviets from the north with 3rd Panzer Division slicing down the coast. At the same time, 13th Panzer attacked along the join between the Soviets and British. Fierce counterattacks by the Indian 5th Division cut them off. They formed a hedgehog formation fighting off Soviet and Indian attacks.

At this moment, Kleist unleashed LVII Panzer Corps against the Indian left flank. The British 5th Division found 5th SS *Wiking*'s tanks in its rear as the Slovaks cut the road to Persia.

It was an awesome sight for the men of 3rd Panzer to be driving through a forest of oil derricks that extended out into the Caspian Sea. Many of the derricks were on fire, like immense trees in the agony of a fiery death. Thick black smoke darkened the sky. Though it was a scene from hell, the Germans saw it in Wagnerian terms as the fiery death of Siegfried's dragon.[3]

The White House, 9 October 1942

Roosevelt and the chiefs had studied Stalin's letter carefully. After the loss of the Persian Corridor, Stalin was begging for a resumption of the convoys and an increased effort through Vladivostok. The tone of desperation was palpable.

The difficulties of delivery are reported to be due primarily to shortage of shipping. To remedy the shipping situation the Soviet Government would be prepared to agree to a certain curtailment of US arms deliveries to the Soviet Union. We should be prepared temporarily fully to renounce deliveries of tanks, guns, ammunition, pistols, etc. At the same time, however, we are badly in need of increased deliveries of modern fighter aircraft – such as Airacobras – and certain other supplies. It should be borne in mind that the Kittyhawk is no match for the modern German fighter.

It would be very good if the USA could ensure the monthly delivery of at least the following items: 500 fighters, 8,000 to 10,000 trucks, 5,000 tons of aluminium, and 4,000 to 5,000 tons of explosives. Besides, we need, within 12 months, two million tons of grain (wheat) and as much as we can have of fats, concentrated foods and canned meat. We could bring in a considerable part of the food supplies in Soviet ships via Vladivostok if the USA consented to turn over to the USSR twenty to thirty ships at the least to replenish our fleet.

As regards the situation at the front, you are undoubtedly aware that in recent months our position in the south, particularly in the Stalingrad area, has deteriorated due to shortage of aircraft, mostly fighters. The Germans have bigger stocks of aircraft than we anticipated. In the south they have at least a twofold superiority in the air, which makes it impossible for us to protect our troops. War experience has shown that the bravest troops are helpless unless protected against air attack.[4]

Admiral King was adamant against the resumption of the convoys:

Even if we wanted to, the disaster of PQ-17 has made it impossible for us to recruit the merchant seamen for the convoy, here or in Britain. Face it, Mr President, the only route left is across the Pacific in Soviet-flagged ships. And even that is in doubt. Our cipher boys have been picking up from the Jap diplomatic code that the Germans are twisting their arms to renounce their non-aggression treaty with the Russians and declare war.

Roosevelt and Churchill had been desperate to keep the Soviet Union in the war, but their ability to do so seemed to be slipping away. It was General George Marshall, Chief of Staff of the Army, who said what everyone had been thinking. For once, King was in full agreement with the Army:

Mr President, with the loss of the Persian Corridor, our last serious means to deliver decisive aid is gone. Add to that the loss to the Soviets of most of their oil production. The handwriting on the wall is clear. The Russians must sink or swim on their own. I recommend that all aid intended for the Persian Corridor be suspended and diverted instead to the build-up in Britain for the assault on Europe.

Roosevelt seemed to sag in his wheelchair:

We will honour our commitment to the Soviets by continuing to provide as much aid as we can across the Pacific. I just don't see how we can do more. If the Japanese attack the Russians, there is not much we can do about it.

King had the last brutal word. 'The diversion of Japanese naval and army forces in such an attack would only make our job in the Pacific that much easier.'[5]

Kotelnikovo, Army Group B Headquarters, 11 October 1942

This Russian rail station, 73 miles southwest of Stalingrad, was throbbing with activity as one train after another delivered the seven infantry divisions of Manstein's old 11th Army, veterans of Sevastopol. Interspersed among the troop trains, supply trains were feeding a number of growing depots. Railway engineers were busily extending spurs. Next to arrive were *Grossdeutschland* and 6th Panzer Divisions (LX Corps) with their 400 T-34s, an amazing sight to the infantry. Eleventh Army now numbered close to 200,000 men. Marching out of the Caucasus to join the army were the four infantry divisions of 17th Army's V Corps.

Manstein had prevailed upon Hitler to leave the cleaning up of the Caucasus and Transcaucasus to one German corps and the Romanians and Turks. The victories at Sukhumi and Ordzhonikidze had revitalized the Führer, who claimed the credit for the Soviet collapse since it had happened after he had relieved List and assumed personal command. Then Kleist's brilliant crushing of the Soviet–British force at Baku had even prompted him to dine with his generals again. Though much of the vast oilfield had been sabotaged, Hitler practically wallowed in the self-justification. He gladly tossed a field marshal's baton to Kleist.

The credit line he had promised Manstein seemed to shrink in inverse proportion to the good news he was receiving. At Hitler's order to throw 11th Army into the Stalingrad fighting, Manstein flew directly to Werewolf and flatly refused the order. 'What are you worried about? Reichsmarschall Göring is supplying a reinforcement to the front as great as 11th Army. The sheet balances.' He was referring to the establishment of twenty-two Luftwaffe field divisions, Göring's brainchild to transform surplus personnel into his own ground army; if Himmler could have one in the Waffen SS, so could Göring.

Manstein's response was 'Sheer nonsense! Where is the Luftwaffe going to find the necessary division, regimental, and battalion commanders?' For once Hitler had met someone with a personality as forceful and unyielding as his own and one that was immune to his charismatic power. More than one observer noted that Manstein's ego equalled Hitler's, but without the irrationality. This battle had already been fought. Against the entire weight of his General Staff and even his favoured Stauffenberg, Hitler had declined to deny Göring, who had proclaimed that he was not going 'to hand over "his" soldiers, reared in the spirit of National Socialism, to an Army which still had chaplains and was led by officers steeped in the traditions of the Kaiser'.[6]

Hitler was clearly on the defensive but for once did not slip into a rage at being countered. Instead, he said, 'There is Kleist's 1st Panzer Army that will become available in a few weeks as well.' It was all Manstein could do not to lecture the Führer of the German Reich like a green lieutenant. He summarized the deployment of forces:

> Protecting most of the long northern arm of our salient from the Don to the Volga are the Romanian 3rd, Hungarian, and 8th Italian Armies. If the Soviets attack in great strength, these forces will collapse. On the southern arm of the salient is the Romanian 4th Army which will do exactly the same thing. None of these allies are reliable in such situations unless they are closely corseted with Germans, which they are not.

At the apex of the salient 6th Army is slowly wasting away. It has no more reserves while the Soviets keep feeding replacements into the battle. We merely play into his hands by sending more troops into that sausage grinder.

He said nothing about his secret order to Seydlitz to pull back from close contact with Chuikov's troops once the inevitable Soviet offensive kicked off. The order, codenamed Operation Quicksilver, was to disengage 6th Army and pull its left flank all the way back to Kalach should the Soviets attack the Romanian 3rd Army in strength. At the same time Hoth's 4th Panzer Army was also to pull back immediately to reinforce the Romanian 4th Army should the Soviets attack there in strength. 6th Army's right flank would hook up with 4th Panzer Army's left flank thus reestablishing a strong front to serve as a springboard for a counterattack once the Soviets had overextended themselves. It was the perfect example of an elastic strategy. Sadly, the panzer corps of both armies had been wasted away in the city fighting for which they had never been intended, and each was lucky to muster the strength of one panzer division.

The field marshal had also left Seydlitz broad initiative in interpreting orders coming out of OKW. For example, Hitler had ordered all of the horses of 6th Army to be sent westward to cut down on the logistics burden of their support which in bulk exceeded the requirements of the troops by several times. Seydlitz realized that if he was to have any ability to manoeuvre, he would need those horses, for much of the German artillery and logistics services still relied on them. Hitler had also ordered him to employ as infantry any tank troops without tanks. When he received that order, he leapt to his feet and shouted, '*Wanzig, heller Wanzig!* [Madness, sheer madness!] Where does that man think I will find skilled *Panzertruppen* if and when new tanks arrive?' The tankers were not used as infantry.

Manstein went on:

> Across the Volga and north of the Don, the enemy keeps accumulating reserves for the very reason that he recognizes the vulnerability of our salient. If we continue to feed the Stalingrad battle, we do nothing but dissipate our own reserves and lay ourselves open to the obvious counterstroke that will trap everything in the salient in one great pocket.
>
> We must retain a powerful operational reserve to throw into the battle once the enemy plays his hand. That is why I insist that 11th Army's strength not be dissipated to deal with local emergencies but that it must be strengthened. And to it must be added 1st Panzer Army as part of the front's strategic reserve. *Mein Fuhrer*, you can never be too strong at the decisive point.

Hitler responded, 'But I tell you, Manstein, that the Russians are beaten already. The loss of the oilfields at Baku has doomed them. One more push and the whole rotten structure will collapse. Bolshevism is as good as dead.'

'Then, *mein Führer*, let us make sure and drive a great stake through its heart.'[7]

Stavka, 13 October 1942

The catastrophe in the Caucasus actually accelerated the plan that Zhukov and Vasilevsky had presented to Stalin. The news of the fall of the Caucasus and the Transcaucasian republics had shaken Soviet morale to the core. Time was rapidly slipping away, and with each day, the oil reserves drained away as well. Hitler's famous intuition had once again proven uncannily prescient. But he had not counted on Stalin's determination to roll the dice one last time. Only Operation Uranus had a chance of reversing the inevitable.

The problem was that Uranus had been planned for the end of November. Now it would have to be executed far sooner. Manstein had been correct. Zhukov and Vasilevsky had read the same map, and their eyes had been drawn to the weakness of the flanks at Stalingrad. From the flanks their eyes had moved east to the Don crossing at Kalach. Six weeks more and the armies they would unleash would have been strong enough, but that would have depended on the flood of supplies and equipment, especially the trucks and other logistical means, especially plentiful oil from the south, they would need for the rapid thrust from the Volga to the Don. Now they must make do with what they already had and with what could be stripped from the other fronts to the north, immobilizing the northern forces to a degree that they could not put pressure on the Germans.

Zhukov was a hard man to beat, but even he knew how their chances of success were dwindling. All the odds seemed to be stacking up in the Germans' favour. Now even the weather that had so often saved Russia seemed to support the Germans. The torrential rains of the autumn *rasputitsa* would be falling just as their armies needed firmly frozen ground for their success.

Now Stalin was truly afraid. He had more to worry about than the Germans. For the first time even those dogs who had licked his boots had cause to believe they had more to fear with Stalin than without. The loss of the Caucasus had done more than stagger the morale of the country. It had cracked the façade of his leadership as no other defeat had. Whispers compared it to the evaporation of the deep-seated faith in the tsar as benevolent ruler anointed by God after his Cossacks had sabred hundreds of peaceful petitioners in the Bloody Sunday Massacre of 1905.[8]

There were more than whispers. Abakumov was more than aware of this; he was behind it. In greatest secrecy he was showing Stalin's Okrana file to members of the Politburo and to senior officers of the Red Army. He had never seen so many shaken men.[9]

Stalingrad, 14 October 1942

Manstein threw the paper down on the floor. Hitler had gone back on his word to keep 11th Army as a front reserve. The order commanding its commitment to the renewed offensive at Stalingrad now lay at the field marshal's feet.

Led by four specialized combat engineer battalions especially flown into the city, 90,000 Germans attacked on a 3-mile front to smash their way to the Volga and finally to destroy 62nd Army. Chuikov had thrown a small spanner into the works two days before by launching his own morning counterattack. It had gained 300 yards, but the German counterpunch was near mortal. Everywhere the Germans ground forward, consuming one Soviet division after another. By the end of the day 14th Panzer Division had cut through to the Volga, splitting Chuikov's army in two.

Despite this success, Manstein's attention was still drawn to the flanks where Soviet forces continued to build up like black thunderclouds. He obeyed Hitler's order only so far as slowly redeploying 11th Army as far forward as the rail hub at Zhutovo station, 55 miles north of Kotelnikovo.

Stalingrad, 17 October 1942

Already it was growing cold. The freezing rains had soaked the ruins of the city making life even more miserable for both sides. They continued to fall day after day. The nights now brought frost. Chuikov had more to concern him than a natural phenomenon that apportioned its misery impartially. The huge German guns from Sevastopol had been devastating. They were unlike the German's aerial bombardment or even their normal artillery fire that simply transformed the urban architecture into a rubble-strewn fortress maze. Seven-ton shells reduced the ruins to mounds of shattered brick and concrete under which only the dead lay.

The Germans kept smashing their way forward, forcing Chuikov to move his headquarters behind the Red October factory. The one division he received as reinforcement was quickly burning out. The northern element of his command had been reduced to a small cut-off pocket. Sixty-Second Army had been pushed so far back that its heels were almost on the Volga's edge.

> Alarming information was coming in. Many units were asking for help, wanting to know what to do, and how. It is probable that divisional and regimental commanders were making these approaches in order to find out whether the 62nd Amy Command still existed. We gave a short, clear-cut answer to these questions: 'Fight with everything you've got, but stay put!'[10]

And they did. One German regimental commander talking on the field telephone with his forward elements could hear the Russians shouting, *'Urrah!'* A Soviet regimental commander when his command post was being overrun did not hesitate to call down a Katyusha strike on his own position. The German fighting men gave the Russians the ultimate soldier's salute when they said, 'the dogs fight like lions'.[11]

If there was a bright spot for Chuikov, it was that Vassily Zaitsev had been knocking off a half dozen fascists a day. The young sniper's kill score had already reached forty; he had become the darling of the war correspondents and the pride of the 62nd Army. The sniper team he had trained was killing another dozen or so Germans every day. Although the Germans would lose far more men in the course of the *Rattenkrieg*, the nature of sniper kills, coming out of nowhere to strike down men who thought they were safe, was far more unnerving to German morale.

Chuikov would have been immensely relieved to know that the build-up for Operation Uranus was steadily progressing, but even he had not been informed of it for security reasons. The Red Army was making such good use of concealment and deception measures that Gehlen's Foreign Armies East seriously underestimated its scale. It was paying far more attention to the build-up in front of Army Group Centre. This was Operation Mars, designed to encircle a German army on that front at the same time as Uranus was to encircle 6th Army. Nor did Gehlen detect that the forces assembled for Mars were now being bled away to support Uranus. Stavka had no choice. There were just not enough resources to support two major operations. There was no question as to which was more important – Stalingrad. Operation Mars was cancelled.

Ironically, Hitler had come to the same conclusion three days before when he issued Operations Order No. 1, suspending all offensive action on the Eastern Front outside of the fighting for Stalingrad. All the resources of the front were to be directed to the city on the Volga.[12]

Makhachkala, 17 October 1942

The lead elements of 1st Panzer Army had already passed this town on the Caspian just north of the Caucasus. The highway and parallel railroad from Baku had been too far inland to see the sea, but they now turned east to Makhachkala and the Caspian. Suddenly the men could see the blue waters disappearing into the horizon. It was a grand sight that few of them would forget, and it lifted their spirits.

Kleist's objective was Astrakhan at the mouth of the Volga 240 miles away. After what they had been through, 240 miles was nothing, especially since many of them rode in the backs of American trucks, ate American canned food, and wore excellent American boots captured in the dumps at Baku. Most remarkable, though, was that Kleist was able to reequip all his panzer shortfalls with American and British tanks from the same depots. The men had even composed a ditty of appreciation for all their comforts, ending with a resounding refrain, '*Danke sehr, Herr Roosevelt!*'[13]

Stavka, Moscow, 18 October 1942

Stalin raged, banged the table. He had just received the joint cable from Roosevelt and Churchill that the resumption of the Arctic convoys was impossible. The excuse was the collapse of morale among the merchant seamen of both countries. 'Put a few hundred up against the wall, if you want to improve the morale of the rest!' he shouted.

Gumrak Airfield, Stalingrad, 20 October 1942

Oberjäger Friedrich Pohl was a very calm man as befitted a successful sniper.[14] His arrival at the airfield southwest of Stalingrad had tested this self-possession as his Ju 52 transport had weaved and dodged repeated attacks by Soviet aircraft from the moment it crossed the lower Don. Had it not been for the daring Me 109 pilots escorting his transport, he would be dead. As deadly a shot as he was, his Kar 98k rifle with a 5x scope remained useless in its leather case.

The talents of this 27-year old Austrian had become in great demand as the Soviet snipers had been exacting a greater and greater toll on German lives and morale in the fighting for the city. Like every other German soldier on the Eastern Front, he had heard of the desperate fighting for the city. It was a sniper's happy hunting ground. Obviously they had need of his skill. That's all his company commander could tell him as he departed his Gebirgsjäger regiment. Waiting for him was a young General Staff officer who introduced himself as Captain von Boeselager, aide to 6th Army Chief of Staff Tresckow. German privates were not used to being greeted by officers upon arrival in a new assignment, especially such exalted ones.

He was even more surprised when the captain escorted him into a tent. Pointing to a major's uniform, he ordered Pohl to put it on. During the ride into the city, smoking and rumbling with the ongoing German assault, they had the most interesting conversation.

'Pohl, you have been temporarily promoted to major for a special mission. Henceforth, you are Major Werner König.'

'Who is that, *Herr Hauptmann*?'

'He's head of the sniper school at Zossen. That will be your cover. You are not to associate closely with anyone not in the line of duty. I will have a sergeant as an escort and spotter for you.'

'If I may ask, sir, what is the reason for all this acting?'

'As well you might, *Oberjäger*, or I should say, "*Herr Major!*"'

Staying calm while stalking Russians was one thing, but to be addressed as an officer completely flustered Pohl.

Boeselager had personally selected Pohl; it had been a difficult search to find an expert sniper and someone with a burning grievance. In Pohl he had found both. His combat record was clear, but the grievance was buried deep and took some finding: Pohl's childhood sweetheart had been declared a *Mischling* and disappeared into the hands of the Gestapo.

In response to Pohl's question, Boeselager explained, 'We want you to hunt down and kill Vassili Zaitsev. He is the best of the enemy snipers. The Russians have made a great propaganda story about him. We will build a similar story around you as Major König.' Then he turned an intently focused face on Pohl. 'You must kill this Russian.'

The captain then thought to himself, 'And then we will want you do something else for us.'[15]

Beketovka Bulge, 22 October 1942

Here and there the surviving men of artillery and antitank units among others were withdrawn from the death machine of Stalingrad. Taken to the east bank of the Volga, they were fed and deloused, given hot baths and rest. Then their shrunken ranks were filled with replacements. The reconstructed units were sent back across the Volga to the Beketovka Bulge, the remaining Soviet lodgement, 5 miles south of the city, held by 64th Army. Into the bulge were carefully fed the new tank and mechanized corps of the 51st and 57th Armies where they were hidden in villages and gullies with great skill. Although strict operational security ensured that they were told nothing, the smell of an offensive was in the air. The Red Air Force was doing its best to make sure that any German reconnaissance flight over the build-up area was a death sentence.

Nevertheless, the loss of Western aid was having a rippling effect. The number and strength of units being deployed for Uranus was not what had been planned, and now the date of the attack had been advanced by almost three weeks. The cut-off of aluminium from the West reduced tank and aircraft engine production by half. Food was not as plentiful. Lieutenant Hersch Gurewicz was one of those men brought out of Stalingrad to take part in the offensive. Given his first can of spam, he thought that the bloodbath in the city had a reason if the Soviet Union was actually getting help. Then the mess sergeant told him, 'Enjoy it, lieutenant, that's the last of it.'

Kotelnikovo, 24 October 1942

Tresckow realized that he could have talked himself blue in the face and still would not have convinced the commander of Army Group B to commit himself to treason. His visit to army group headquarters had been ostensibly for operational discussions, but the removal of Hitler was uppermost in his mind. Stauffenberg had been pressing him to continue to work for the field marshal's support. The two young officers had been unexpectedly successful in placing sympathizers in critical positions, but Manstein was the key. Without him, success was problematical.

Tresckow realized that despite Manstein's continuous expressions of contempt for the *GroFaZ* within his own small circle, he would not lift his hand against the man who was destroying Germany. The field marshal had taught his little dachshund to lift its tiny paw in a mockery of the Hitler salute, but that was about as far as he was willing to go. Tresckow had even recommended his nephew, Lieutenant Alexander von Stahlberg, to replace Manstein's wounded aide, hoping he might persuade him to come around, but although the two were to develop a mutual respect and devotion, the field marshal remained unconvinced.[16]

Still Tresckow persisted but only succeeded in making the field marshal more obdurate. 'Listen, Tresckow, Prussian field marshals do not mutiny. And do not bring up Tauroggen. Stauffenberg already tried that.'

'But, *Herr Feldmarschall . . .*'

'No, you listen. I am responsible for an army group in the field, and I do not feel I have the right to contemplate a coup d'état in wartime. It would lead to chaos inside Germany. I must also consider my oath and the admissibility of murder for political objectives.'[17]

Tresckow responded, 'Do you really think that you are bound by an oath to the anti-Christ? The Evil One is surely enjoying the trick we have played upon ourselves. Once our personal oath was given to the kings of Prussia and the German emperors, men of Christian honour. It has been perverted by Hitler and put at the service of unspeakable crimes.'[18]

Clearly Manstein did not want to hear this. He had his back up now. 'No senior military commander can for years on end expect his soldiers to lay down their lives for victory and then precipitate defeat by his own hand.' He looked pointedly at his guest. 'Besides, I do not think events have reached the stage where such action is necessary.'

He got up and went over to the map. 'Let's get to the business at hand.' He pointed to the 6th Army rear between Stalingrad and Kalach:

> I'm more and more worried about the Don flank to the north. If I leave the panzer corps in the city fighting, they will be ground to nothing and useless for manoeuvre on the flanks. Already they are badly under-strength. I want Seydlitz to pull out his XIV Panzer Corps [3rd and 60th Motorized, 16th Panzer] and place them in reserve near Kalach.[19] I want XLVIII Panzer Corps [14th and 24th Panzer Divisions] pulled out of the city as well.

The 29th Motorized Division had already been pulled out as an army group reserve, brought up to strength, and readied for an attack on Astrakhan, another one of Hitler's ideas. This was before Kleist's 1st Panzer Army began its drive on the city. Manstein smacked the map at a place called Yeriko-Krepinski, the rail station 25 miles southwest of the city. 'Concentrate them here.'[20]

Tresckow was taken aback. 'Hitler will immediately countermand the order.'

'Then we won't tell him – yet.' The younger man realized with a shock that this was the first time Manstein had actually disobeyed the Führer.

The rains had stopped. Outside it was snowing. The ground was freezing.

Astrakhan, 25 October 1942

Rudel's Stukas hung over the city, diving again and again to strike its oil tanks and shipping. Huge clouds of smoke from the burning oil roiled into the sky. The flames were consuming the last of the oil shipped by sea from the Baku fields. Kleist's panzers were fewer than 20 miles from the city. It was a rich prize, a combination of rail hub and river- and sea-port. Its loss would cripple much of the ability of the Soviets to draw on the resources of Central Asia and western Siberia. Yet nature had provided a defence for the city. It was not located on the Caspian shore but rather many miles inland amid the vast Volga delta, surrounded by the numerous channels of that mighty river. Defending the city was 28th Army with almost 35,000 men and 60 tanks. Originally scheduled to reinforce Stalingrad Front, this army was going to have its hands full defending Astrakhan.

Werewolf, Vinnitsa, 26 October 1942

Hitler had been beside himself with self-righteous delight at the fall of the Caucasus – a victory that his generals had done their best to persuade him not to attempt. Once again, he told the OKW staff, it was his understanding of the economic aspects of war that had guided the road to this splendid victory. Once again, his intuition and will had trumped all the arid professionalism of his generals. Now that Astrakhan was on the point of falling, he began to count all the economic resources and military booty.

Manstein encouraged him in this distraction because it gave him the cover to concentrate German theatre resources in the decisive battle. He shook his head when he thought how lucky Army Group A had been to subdue the Caucasus and Transcaucasus. He had certainly thought it would be a mountain pass too far. By all the rules of war, the campaign should have bogged down and thus dissipated German forces too much to concentrate decisively any-where. The field marshal had to conclude that it was only some sort of miracle of the sort the devil seemed to favour Hitler with that had brought such a victory. But just when he had thought that he could count on Kleist's 1st Panzer Army in the final showdown on the Volga, Hitler had insisted that it seize Astrakhan instead.

He would throw a sop to the Führer but still concentrate most of 1st Panzer Army for the counterstroke to the Soviet offensive he knew was coming. Gehlen kept insisting that the heavier blow was aimed at Army Group Centre. Be that as it may, Manstein was certain that Kluge was not nearly in so dangerous a situation as Army Group B.

He had sent a staff officer by aircraft with his oral order to Kleist to leave the Turkish corps of former Soviet POWs to invest Astrakhan. It was an act of supreme ruthlessness. He knew they stood little chance against the Soviet 28th Army, but all he needed them to do was divert the enemy and buy him time. The remaining panzer, infantry and Gebirgsjäger corps were to cross the Volga north of Astrakhan and strike northwest parallel to the river in the direction of Stalingrad.

Manstein knew that his callous treatment of the former Soviet POWs fighting for the Germans would appeal to Hitler and smooth the way for what he wanted to do in any case. He might not have been as forthcoming had he not needed Hitler's approval of supporting 1st Panzer Army by air in its long dash from Astrakhan to Stalingrad. He needed Göring's Ju 52 transports. To his relief, Hitler jumped at the idea of taking Stalingrad from the rear, and to his surprise Göring was eager to throw the resources of the Luftwaffe into the effort. He realized this was the opportunity for him to make a decisive contribution to the victory.

Stalingrad, 28 October 1942

The patrol dragged in the German prisoner with a potato sack over his head. He could not wait to talk. The news that had run through the 6th Army was that the greatest sniper in the Wehrmacht, Major König, head of the sniper school itself, had been summoned to kill the Soviet 'head rabbit', a play on Zaitsev's name, which meant hare. Colonel Batyuk took Zaitsev aside, 'So now you've got to eliminate this super-sniper. But be careful and use your head.'

It did not take Zaitsev long to realize he was, indeed, up against a super-sniper. Reports began to come in of one Soviet sniper after another being shot. These were experienced men, not beginners. The deaths surged along the entire front. This Major König was ranging wide, giving no indication of where he might show up. Zaitsev was truly puzzled:

> For a long time . . . the characteristics of this new super-sniper remained difficult for me to identify. Our daily observations provided us nothing useful, and we could not pinpoint what sector he was in. He must have been changing his position frequently, and searching me out as carefully as I was in searching for him.[21]

Ironically Pohl was thinking almost exactly the same thing about Zaitsev. The army's propaganda unit had begun to copy the Soviet practice of showing how many of the enemy the major had shot by prominently displaying a hammer and sickle with an x drawn over it for each kill. It had a great effect along the firing line. Germans were now shouting over to the Soviets about how long it would be before König bagged Zaitsev. That was punctuated by the four or five Red Army men that the major was picking off each day, usually officers and forward observers. Even Chuikov became concerned and urged Zaitsev on.

Kotelnikovo, Army Group B Headquarters, 30 October 1942

That morning Manstein received the news of the death in combat of his older son, Gero, who had fallen while assigned to his father's old division. It was as if someone had struck him in his soul. His grief was intense, of the kind that Herodotus had written of two and a half thousand years before. In peace sons bury their fathers, but in war it is the fathers who bury their sons.

As men stricken with such a numbing loss do, he spoke of Gero the boy in his sweet innocence. He spoke of how frail Gero had been as a child and the efforts his wife had made to build his strength. 'We made no attempt to influence his choice of profession, but he was drawn to the calling of his ancestors. It was simply in his blood to become a regular officer.' The most poignant lines of Manstein's later war memoirs were of his son.

> There was not a single flaw in this boy's make-up. Modest, kind, ever eager to help others, at once serious-minded and cheerful, he had no thought for himself, but knew only comradeship and charity. His mind and spirit were perpetually open to all that is fine and good. It was his heritage to come from a long line of soldiers; but by the very fact of being an ardent German soldier he was at once a gentleman in the truest sense of the word – a gentleman and a Christian.[22]

As soon as the word spread through the headquarters, Tresckow flew down from Stalingrad immediately and called on his old master to offer his condolences:

> I know that it may be of little comfort now, but Gero's life is an example to us all, especially we older men. I cannot but think that he would agree with me that when I go before God to account for what I have done and left undone, I know I will be able to justify what I did in the struggle against Hitler.

Manstein was shaken from his grief by Tresckow's linking of his son and Hitler. The younger man went on:

> God promised Abraham that He would not destroy Sodom if just ten Gerichten [righteous men] could be found in the city, and so I hope that for our sake God will not destroy Germany ... A man's moral worth is established only at the point where he is ready to give up his life in defence of his convictions.[23]

Manstein was getting angry, but Tresckow did not relent:

Tell me, *Herr Feldmarschall*, do you doubt that Gero would have been one of those ten righteous men? If so, then how could you not join him in that righteousness?[24]

It was a discouraged Tresckow who returned to 6th Army headquarters that night. The signals NCO brought him a message and said, 'This arrived from the army group commander while you were in the air, sir.'

Tresckow signed. What now, he thought? He read and at first could not believe. It said, 'Count me among the righteous. *Manstein.*'

Chapter 13

Der Totenritt bei Leninsk

Along the northern Don River, 1 November 1942

The Romanian 3rd Army was strung out thinly along the northern arm of the Don River and huddled in the morning cold. It was badly armed and worse commanded by officers who thought bullying and screaming were the sum of leadership. Then a short but crushing artillery strike hit them. Almost immediately 500 tanks of 5th Tank and 21st Armies of General N. F. Vatutin's Southwest Front hit. They came out of the morning mist followed by waves of infantry. The Romanians had already been half-beaten men. The first blow from Operation Uranus finished the job. Their army quickly came apart surviving as little more than a flag on a map at OKW. The Italian 8th Army to the west was being fixed in place by the 1st Guards Army. The Italians would be of no help to their fellow Latins.

To the east Colonel General K. K. Rokossovsky's 65th, 24th and 66th Armies of the Don Front attacked 6th Army's I and XI Corps. Understrength and spread thinly along terrain difficult to defend, they were soon fighting for their lives. Stalin had a special regard for this general of whom he said, 'I have no Suvorov, but Rokossovsky is my Bagration', alluding to one of the great Suvorov's exemplary disciples.

Zhukov was everywhere, urging the commanders forward. He was optimistic because there were no German units, especially panzers, to corset up the Romanians. That would have held things up, a special worry since the attack was not as strong as had been hoped. Zhukov would have given anything for another three weeks to prepare. Already the reequipment of Soviet tank units with T-34s had slowed because of the shortage of aluminium for their engines. The Red Air Force was also feeling the same problem. As it was, the ground forces employed for the overall operation included only 71 per cent of the men and 79 per cent of the tanks originally planned. Zhukov had also warned his commanders that fuel was in short supply and that enemy fuel dumps were critical objectives.[1]

As soon as the seriousness of the Soviet attack had been confirmed, Seydlitz ordered Operation Quicksilver executed. It would be the most difficult of all manoeuvres, to retreat while still in contact with the enemy. He thanked God that Manstein had ordered the concentration of his XIV Panzer Corps in his rear near Kalach.[2]

That was not doing the Germans west of the Don crossing at Kalach any good. Fifth Tank Army's spearheads knifed down through 6th Army's line of communications. T-34s surged over the tracks of the single rail line supporting 6th Army, savaged truck convoys and overran supply dumps and maintenance yards. The tank crews delighted in blowing up trains as they passed. For sheer spectacle, it is hard to beat an exploding locomotive and a long line of rail cars thundering off the tracks into wreckage and ruin. Nothing seemed able to stop the Red Army spearheads as they drove east towards Kalach. They came so fast that the panicked Germans made them a gift of the precious fuel dumps. The icy mists and snow were working for the Red Army as Richthofen's reconnaissance aircraft were kept grounded. He recorded in his diary then, 'Once again the Russians have masterfully exploited a bad weather situation. Rain, snow, ice and fog are preventing any action by the Luftwaffe at the Don.'[3]

Generalleutnant Karl Strecher's XI Corps with three divisions (44th, 376th, 384th Infantry) found itself attempting to disengage while being strongly assailed by Soviet 65th Army in its front even as it was struck in the rear by the 21st Army's 3rd Cavalry Corps. The 44th *Hoch- und Deutschmeister* Division, Seydlitz's old division of tough Austrians, led the way to the bridges over the Don that would unite them with the rest of 6th Army, wiping out the flank regiment of the enemy's cavalry corps. It was slow going because of a fuel shortage afflicting the entire army. They still had their horses, though, and that meant their artillery and wounded came out with them. Luckily they had been bypassed by the Soviet tank corps heading for Kalach. But the cavalry hung on to the German flank, striking suddenly and without warning out of the snow, while masses of infantry from 65th Army pressed hard on their heels. One officer opined it was like the Franco-Prussian War of 1870, the last time German soldiers were so threatened by cavalry in the open field. His companion replied, 'No, Heinz, Napoleon's retreat from Moscow in 1812 comes closer. Pray God we do not find our Beresina.'[4]

The Soviet attack had hit the 376th Division which had already been reduced to barely 4,200 men. Being farthest west it fought as the rearguard and quickly began to come apart. Its survivors, accompanied by terrified Romanian stragglers fleeing eastward, merged with the more resolute Austrians who pressed on through the blowing snow.

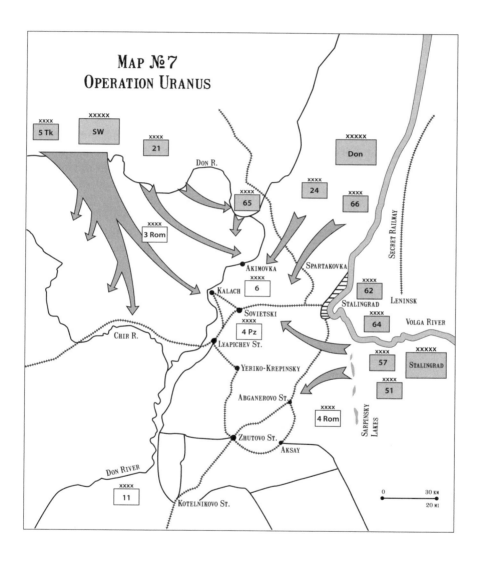

MAP № 7
OPERATION URANUS

5 Tk

SW

21

Don R.

24

Don

65

66

3 Rom

SECRET RAILWAY

AKIMOVKA

SPARTAKOVKA

6

KALACH

62

SOVIETSKI

STALINGRAD

LENINSK

4 Pz

64

VOLGA RIVER

CHIR R.

LYAPICHEV ST.

YERIKO-KREPINSKY

57

STALINGRAD

51

ABGANEROVO ST.

4 Rom

ZHUTOVO ST.

SARPINSKY LAKES

AKSAY

DON RIVER

11

KOTELNIKOVO ST.

0   30 KM

20 MI

Stalingrad, 1 November 1942

Chuikov had only been told of the offensive a few days before. For him it must have lifted an enormous burden. 'We all clambered out of our dugouts to listen for the sounds of our counter-attack. It wasn't possible – it was too far north.' one soldier wrote later.[5] It was not long before Chuikov's scouts were reporting that the Germans were breaking contact all along the fighting lines, slipping away like quicksilver disappearing through a crack in the floor.

Along with the scouts came the snipers desperate not to let their prey out of their sights. Those unwary enough to rush too far forward were dropped by a single sniper who seemed to be covering the German withdrawal from the area of the Barrikady Factory.

Chuikov quickly linked up his isolated elements and pushed them forward to keep after the Germans. In a matter of minutes, his men were passing the famous factories and other buildings that had become the graves of countless Russians and Germans, past ground over which the armies had shoved and pushed against each for the gain of blood-soaked yards. Only the cold had smothered the stench of countless rotting bodies as the snow blanketed their remains and softened the broken outlines of the city's buildings. By day's end they were on the outskirts of the city where the Germans had abandoned an endless number of derelict vehicles, tanks, guns, and every other assorted piece of equipment armies possess.

One of the last German soldiers out of the city turned to take one last look at the desolation. Then he spat in its direction, turned, and marched west.

Akhtubinsk, 1 November 1942

The small collection of villages known as Akhtubinsk served as a railway, road and river hub, 180 miles north of Astrakhan and 80 miles southeast of Stalingrad. Some thought had been given to its importance. At dawn the engines of the Soviet fighter-bomber squadrons were just being turned over when the Me 109s swooped out of the sky in their strafing runs. Hardly an aircraft got off the ground before it was shot up.

Within a few hours the small town fell to the 3rd Panzer Division. An hour later the first squadrons of Ju 52s began to arrive at the military airfield. It was a first-rate airfield as befitted the R&D Institute of the Air Force of the Workers' and Peasants' Red Army. It had also been the airfield from which Soviet fighters had been attacking 1st Panzer Army for days. Now Me 109 squadrons circled, flying top cover. On the runways tanks had pushed the blackened hulks of Soviet aircraft off into the grass to let the transports land.

They brought fuel, ammunition, and everything else. The fuel came directly from the refineries captured intact at Maikop. And they brought mail, to the joy of men who had not had a mail delivery since they had reached Tiflis weeks before. As important, they brought in Luftwaffe ground crews and their equipment to sustain the Stuka, Ju 88 and Me 109 squadrons supporting the panzer army's final drive on Stalingrad.

Kalach, 2 November 1942

By early morning three Soviet tank corps were converging from the west on the bridge over the Don at Kalach. On the east bank, XIV Panzer Corps was echeloned behind the town. Their arrival had stopped a panic that was spreading through the supply, maintenance and medical echelons. Seydlitz had placed them there to defend the major river crossing and to support his infantry divisions converging on the line Kalach–Sovietski–Verkhne-Tsaritsynski. Manstein had assured him that 11th Army would be committed to tie in to the right of 6th Army.

The Soviet 26th Tank Corps was winning the race to the river, running down and scattering the last of the frantic rear-echelon troops rushing to safety. Its commander, Major General Rodin, was determined to take the bridge by *coup de main*, a painful German speciality so far in the war, one that he hoped to turn on them. Lieutenant Colonel Grigor N. Filippov, commanding the lead 19th Tank Brigade, was just the man to administer the lesson.

At the head of his column were two captured German tanks and a reconnaissance vehicle, driving with their lights on to alleviate any suspicion. Incredibly they drove past hundreds of Germans in the dark who simply waved at them. It was six in the morning with just an edge of light on the horizon when Filippov came upon two Germans with an old Russian peasant. A word to his men, and the two Germans were shot dead. Filippov climbed down from his tank to talk to the trembling old man. 'Uncle Vanya, which way to the bridge?' As soon as he heard Russian, the man's shaking ceased. He immediately climbed into the first tank and pointed the way.

Not long afterwards his column reached the high west bank of the Don with Kalach at the other end of the bridge. They barrelled down the steep road and charged right onto the bridge, scattering the guards. From the bluff above sixteen T-34s fired down into the town in support. The head of the column broke into the town right into the guns of an understrength tank company of 16th Panzer Division.[6] The first Soviet tanks were quickly knocked out, but now the bridge was filled with Soviet tanks. Enough were getting across to widen the bridgehead.

On the bluffs above the river Soviet artillery had arrived and began to fire into the town to support Filippov's tanks. Motorized infantry were descending the road to the bridge and behind them more tanks. The German support troops were fleeing eastward from the town as more of 16th Panzer's weak units were thrown into the fight to retake the bridge. One by one the weakened units of XIV Panzer Corps were committed to eliminate the Soviet bridgehead over the river. But Soviet strength flowed in faster than German, and the corps was

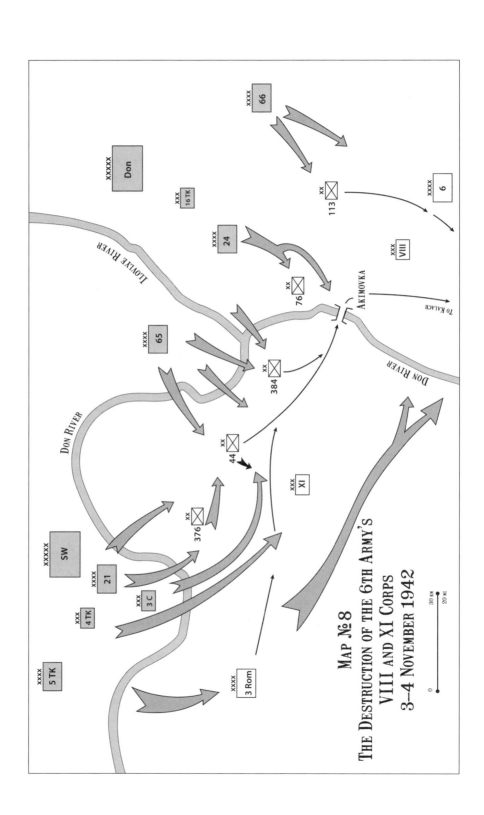

MAP № 8
THE DESTRUCTION OF THE 6TH ARMY'S
VIII AND XI CORPS
3–4 NOVEMBER 1942

slowly pushed back. A desperate call from Seydlitz to Hoth released most of XLVIII Panzer Corps, concentrated at Yeriko-Krepinski, to the battle for Kalach, but Hoth kept back the 29th Motorized Division as an operational reserve.

Zhutovo Station, 2 November 1942

Raus's aide woke him at two in the morning. '*Herr General*, Manstein orders us forward.' The Austrian was instantly awake. Within moments his orders went out to assemble the division and get it ready to move at first light. In ten minutes he was dressed and stepped out into the cold and was enveloped in the icy mist. He was still taken aback by the T-34s of his headquarters guard, despite the German cross and the months of training he had put the division through with these reconditioned Soviet tanks. The panzergrenadier guard at his tent was cradling his Stürmgewehr with more than a little affection. The men had taken so well to the new automatic assault rifle that he believed they would mutiny if ordered to turn them in for the old bolt-action Kar 98.

A similar order had also set *Grossdeutschland* into a frenzy of activity. Hörnlein was just as pleased as Raus with his new equipment. The morale of both divisions of LX Panzer Corps was high. As with all the divisions of 11th Army, Manstein had seen to it that they had winter clothing and rations.[7] These two panzer divisions were the newly forged spear-tip of the operational reserve that the field marshal so carefully amassed. He had by now disobeyed so many Führer orders that his head was in a noose. Only success would prevent the hangman from dropping the trap door. As the news of the Soviet offensive along the Don began to build a picture of the extent of the attack, he ordered 11th Army to move north to support Seydlitz's withdrawal. The orders went out at night for movement at first light the next day. Raus and Hörnlein had their reconnaissance battalions moving out by 03.00 and their panzers by 04.00.

Beketovka Bulge, 2 November 1942

South of Stalingrad Soviet engineers had carefully cleared the minefields in front of narrow sectors of the overstretched 4th Romanian Army. One day after the Don Front's attack to the north, Soviet guns roared in the early morning to smash into the defences of the 1st and 18th Romanian divisions guarding the southern flank of 6th Army. The targets of the guns shifted inland after only a few hours as the Stalingrad Front unleashed its 13th Tank Corps (57th Army) 4th Cavalry and 4th Mechanized Corps (51st Army) to overrun the thin Romanian positions and plunge deep into the enemy rear. With 350 tanks these three corps were the equivalent of a tank army. Their objective was Kalach towards which 5th Tank Army was aiming from the northwest. A German observer noted that the Soviet attack ground forward methodically 'as if on a training ground: fire – move – fire – move'.[8] In Stalingrad, the men of 62nd Army heard the noises of battle and realized that the offensive was true after all. 'It was an incredible feeling. We were no longer alone.'

By the end of the first day, 4th Mechanized Corps had advanced 27 miles to Verkhne-Tsaritsynski, half-way to their objective. The 13th Tank Corps had penetrated even closer to Kalach in a running battle with 6th Army's withdrawing divisions. The 4th Cavalry Corps, guarding 4th Mechanized Corps' southern flank, reached Abganerovo. Behind them came a wave of rifle divisions. The Soviet attack was aided just as that in the north by an icy mist that blinded the defenders and grounded German air reconnaissance.

The successes of the day hid a dangerous lack of supplies and trucks. The build-up for the attack had been grossly hindered by the difficulty of getting material and supplies over the ice-choked Volga. The river was not yet fully frozen over but filled with huge chunks of ice rushing downstream. Leading formations had only enough food for one more day. Nevertheless, the morale of the attacking troops was sky-high. They knew they were turning the tables on the ravagers of the Motherland. They shot hundreds of Romanian prisoners out of hand.

Raus and Hörnlein's reconnaissance battalions had heard the thunder of Yeremenko's attack to the north. It was not long before they encountered the fleeing rear-echelon troops of the 4th Romanian Army.[9]

Yeriko–Krepinski, 2 November 1942

Generalmajor Leyser, commanding 29th Motorized Division, had put his men on alert ready to move off at a moment's notice that morning as the rest of the XLVIII Panzer Corps took off for Kalach. He did not have long to wait as the radio filled with frantic calls from the Romanians holding the line to the east. Out of communication with army group, Hoth ordered Leyser east.

The 29th roared off to meet the enemy. Leading the way was the 129th Panzer Battalion, deployed in a wedge formation with fifty-five Panzer III and IV tanks in front. On the flanks were the self-propelled antitank guns. Behind in their half-tracked armoured personnel carriers came the grenadiers, followed by the artillery. The commanders stood in their open turret hatches. Visibility was less than 100 yards. Then the fog lifted.

At the same moment the tank commanders stood up straight: before them, not 400 yards away, approached the tank armada of the 13th Tank Corps. The cupola hatches slammed shut. The familiar commands rang out: 'Turret 12 o'clock!' – 'Armour-piercing' – Range 400' – 'Many enemy tanks' – 'Open fire!'[10]

It was the classic meeting engagement which goes to the side which reacts quickest and most aggressively. Today it was Leyser's panzers. To that response was added the advantage of more effective communication. Every German tank had a radio and could respond immediately to a changing situation. Only the company commander in Soviet tank units had a radio, which put a premium on follow the leader and preplanned actions. The difference was lethal. The panzers killed and killed. Tank after tank blew up or collided with others. Within half an hour the remnants of 13th Tank Corps were retreating eastward.

Amazingly a train suddenly appeared from the east and stopped to disgorge masses of Soviet infantry. The Soviets had actually driven a train full of troops into their breakthrough. The cleverness of the idea died right there as the 29th's artillery got the range and smashed one wagon after another.

Hardly had the 13th Tank Corps been routed than word came over the radio to Leyser that another Soviet corps had penetrated 24 miles south. This was 4th Mechanized Corps with about ninety tanks. Leyser's division had taken few casualties and now resumed its wedge formation driving south across the hard, snow-covered ground. The Soviet corps should have been much farther to the west when Leyser's panzers found it at a place called Verkhne-Tsaritsynski. Its commander, Major General Vassili Volsky, had handled his unit poorly during its advance causing so many delays that it brought the Stalingrad Front commander to a state of incandescent rage. Yeremenko was already in a foul mood because Volsky had had the unheard-of temerity to write to Stalin personally, stating that Uranus was too risky. Clearly his timidity was a direct response to his lack of faith in the operation. He had already morally defeated himself when Leyser caught up with him and finished the job. Dozens of burning pyres, the remnants of his tanks, sent their smoke into the air as the survivors fled eastward.

Abganerovo Station, 2 November 1942

The scouts of the Soviet 4th Cavalry Corps relayed the oddest reports to their commander, which he passed up the chain of command, sowing confusion at each level. Large columns of T-34s were coming north towards the corps' penetration at Abganerovo Station. The 61st, 63rd, and 81st Cavalry Divisions of the corps were all raised in Turkestan and had never seen combat. The Central Asian cavalrymen were mounted on hardy steppe ponies. One brigade was even mounted on camels.

By the time it was clear from their markings that these were not Soviet tanks, *Grossdeutschland* and 6th Panzer Divisions were closing on Abganerovo Station from both sides. By then the Russian corps commander, General Shapkin, realized he had to break out and threw an entire cavalry division at the closing arm of 6th Panzer while another tried to escape through a gap between two dry river beds.

The Turkmen cavalry swept forward, spurring their little steppe horses. With a resounding '*Urrah!*' thousands of sabres came out. The Germans were open-mouthed, amazed, at the spectacle of 5,000 horsemen surging towards them.

They thought they had slipped back in time to the wars of Frederick the Great or Napoleon. All it took was fingers depressing triggers to send streams of machine-gun bullets into the packed ranks for the spectacle to turn into carnage. Then the tanks and artillery fired high explosive and shrapnel. Whole ranks went down in the storm, those behind piling up on the dead and wounded heaps of men and screaming horses.

The Germans covering the gap between the dry riverbeds now noticed:

> . . . something that was neither men, horses, or tanks. It was only when it had surged over the crest of the range and was preparing to storm forward . . . that it was identified as a camel brigade. The enemy was received with such a burst of fire that his leading elements broke down at once and those following behind ran back wildly.

The German tanks pursued firing at the frenzied camel cavalry. The mass of surviving camel riders turned and ran through an area that was still marshy despite the snow. 'The camels proved quicker and better able to move across the country and consequently won the race.' Also in the race was Shapkin, lashing his horse to the rear while two of his division commanders lay dead among their men.[11]

As Raus's tanks stopped at the marshy ground, *Grossdeutschland* was chasing the surviving cavalry division in their direction. They came streaming into a trap as 6th Panzer's tanks turned about and its panzergrenadiers deployed on the flanks of the oncoming Turkmen horsemen. In moments the dense ranks of cavalry disintegrated into an abattoir of dying and wounded men and horses. Here and there groups of horsemen tried to break through only to be cut down. At last the survivors leapt off their horses to surrender.

Raus radioed Hörnlein thanking him for beating the enemy into the killing zone, 'just like a safari!' Hörnlein took it well, though it annoyed him that his fine division had only played the role of beaters for 6th Panzer. At this point LX Panzer Corps wheeled west followed by 11th Army's two corps, its new mission: destroy Soviet forces as far as the Volga.

The Bridge at Akimovka, 3 November 1942

In the darkness of the early morning, strong elements of 3rd Cavalry Corps crossed the Don just west of 6th Army's western flank and rode for the bridge at Akimovka over the Don, 20 miles north of Kalach. They were to slice right behind the German XI Corps. These were mostly Cossacks, raised to the saddle and combat-hardened, not unblooded Turkmen. Nine miles north of the bridge the Red Army's 16th Tank Corps (24th Army) was cutting through the 76th Division (VIII Corps) aiming to cut off any Germans west of the Don.

At the bridge there was chaos as mobs of Germans and Romanians fled the disasters to the west. Many of the Germans had been separated from their units

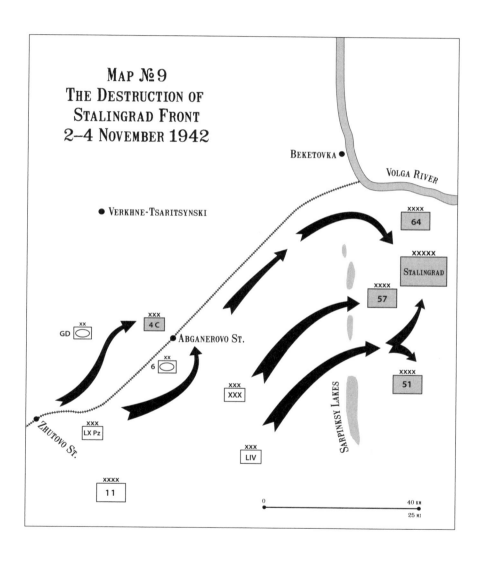

MAP № 9
THE DESTRUCTION OF
STALINGRAD FRONT
2–4 NOVEMBER 1942

BEKETOVKA ●

VOLGA RIVER

● VERKHNE-TSARITSYNSKI

XXXX
64

XXXXX
STALINGRAD

XXXX
57

GD | xx
○

XXX
4 C

ABGANEROVO ST.

6 | xx
○

XXX
XXX

XXXX
51

ZHUTOVO ST.

XXX
LX Pz

SARPINKSY LAKES

XXX
LIV

XXXX
11

0   40 KM

25 MI

or were the few survivors. Here and there small units and guncrews hung together during the unrolling disaster. Among them were Soviet prisoners harnessed to carts to replace fallen horses. Any man who dropped was shot.

> Some of the ugliest scenes developed at the approaches to the bridge . . . with soldiers shouting, jostling and even fighting to get across to the eastern bank. The weak and the wounded were trampled underfoot. Sometimes, officers threatened each other for not letting their men pass first. Event the Feldgendarmerie detachment with sub-machine guns was unable to restore a semblance of order.
>
> Men tried to cross the Don itself trusting to the ice which was strongest along the banks but treacherously thin in the centre where many fell through to their deaths. No one came to help. For a people steeped in war, comparisons to the Beresina were uppermost in most people's minds.[12]

Now the innate ability of the German Army to pull itself together appeared. Officers, pistol in hand, stopped the rout, sorted out the men, put them into *ad hoc* combat units to defend the crossing and wait for the Russians to attack. Through all of this the core of *Hoch- und Deutschmeister* hung together, crossed the bridge, and headed south. On its way it was joined by the retreating columns of the 113th Infantry Division, all that was left of VIII Corps since the Russians tank corps had rolled over 76th Infantry Division. Two weak divisions were now all that was left of two of 6th Army's corps.

Sovietski, 3 November 1942

Seydlitz felt as if a primeval force was blasting out of the radio at him. Hitler was in a rage, that state that had overawed and terrified countless men. He could picture Hitler frothing at the mouth that his orders had not been obeyed to the letter. 'What is going on? How dare you not obey your orders?' the voice demanded. He then looked at the radio operator, drew his finger across his throat. The sergeant's eyes dilated to saucer size as he realized the general had ordered him to cut off the Führer. The general just winked at the sergeant. 'Damned ionosphere.'[13]

The ionosphere was acting up all over the place from the perspective of OKW. It was amazing how a conspiracy could affect the weather so conveniently. The patient efforts of Stauffenberg and Tresckow to place reliable men in critical positions were paying off. However, the need to win the battle had subsumed but not replaced the plot against Hitler. The plotters were patriots who did not see a catastrophic German defeat on the edge of Asia to be a necessary precursor to removing Hitler. The hecatomb of disaster was a price they were not willing to pay. They would win the battle and get rid of Hitler, but winning the battle required disregarding the Führer orders.

Kalach, 3 November 1942

In truth Seydlitz did not need the distraction of a madman at that moment when the fate of a quarter of a million German soldiers hung in the balance. The corps attempting to withdraw from the northern Don had met with disaster. The Russians were pouring across the crossing at Kalach and pushing back his weak XIV Panzer Corps. Even the commitment of the two divisions of XLVIII Panzer Corps had not stemmed their advance. At the same time the divisions pulling out of Stalingrad were in danger of being cut off. Behind them Soviet rifle divisions were filling the roads to join the battle.

At last the weather had cleared enough for the Luftwaffe to support the fight. The Red Air Force filled the skies to contest every German air mission, especially over the fighting at Kalach. Soviet antiaircraft units lined both banks of the river. Both sides watched the air battles, with burning aircraft plummeting to the ground again and again. Richthofen's Stukas repeatedly struck at the bridge. The Soviet fighters were waiting in swarms and fought their way through the Me 109 escorts to down the dive-bombers. The Germans had never seen such suicidal determination on the part of the Russians to close for the kill. Although they lost two planes for every German, it was a price they willingly paid. The bridge remained intact and packed with units crossing to join the battle.

What struck both Seydlitz and Manstein was the size of the Soviet reserves, which the enemy had hidden so well. They would have been even more disconcerted had they known the size of the force that would have been available if the Soviet timetable had not been disrupted and advanced three weeks. It was not simply a question of numbers. The Soviet reserves were rested, well-fed, well-armed, and clothed for winter fighting. The men of 6th Army in contrast were exhausted after months of brutal fighting, their units shells of their former selves. Despite the horrific lessons of the previous winter, they had not even received their cold-weather clothing.

Manstein realized that the crisis of the battle was approaching. Sixth Army could shatter at any moment. Retreating while in contact with an aggressive enemy is probably the least attractive situation a soldier can find himself in. He's liable to be infected with panic and be cut down by the enemy on his heels. To pull off a successful retreat takes hardened men under tight control.

As bad as the situation was, Manstein took a moment to imagine what the situation looked like to the enemy. His perceptions were remarkably accurate. Stavka at that very moment was optimistic over the developing battle at Kalach. Stalin on the other hand was shrewdly concentrating on the defeat of Stalingrad Front's pincer by the LX Panzer Corps. That paled, however, at his apprehension over 1st Panzer Army's rapid drive up the Volga's eastern shore heading straight for Stalingrad. Powerful German forces were about to assail Yeremenko's armies from both sides of the Volga. He dispatched Vasilevsky to oversee the battle there. He also parted with the pearl of the Stavka reserve, the 2nd Guards Army, telling Yeremenko of this by phone. 'You will hold out – we are getting reserves down to you,' he commanded menacingly. 'I'm sending you the 2nd Guards Army – the best unit I have left.'[14]

Stalin was fulfilling the primary role of the commander – the allocation of the reserve. Manstein was about to do that same thing. His remaining front reserves were the four divisions of V Corps (9th, 73rd, 125th, 198th Infantry Divisions) that had been transferred from the semi-tropical coast of the Black Sea to the snowy steppe, and the four Gebirgsjäger divisions that had scaled the Caucasus. The mountain divisions had not even arrived yet and were still entraining at Rostov. 'Seydlitz, I'm sending you V Corps. It's my last reserve. But I intend to constitute a new reserve in a few days. You must contain the enemy at Kalach in the meantime.'[15]

The Sarpinsky Lakes, 3 November 1942

That reserve was 11th Army and its panzer corps, but now it had another vital mission – to destroy Stalingrad Front. With that mission accomplished and all threat from southeast of Stalingrad eliminated, the 11th Army would then be able to countermarch to be thrown into the battle for Kalach. It was a logical plan. It reminded the field marshal of the German victory at Tannenberg in August 1914. He was also reminded of the great Moltke's aphorism that no plan survives the first shot. The danger in his plan was that Southwest Front could be a tougher nut to crack than he anticipated. Timing here was everything. It did not matter if he destroyed Yeremenko's command if it took so long that 6th Army collapsed in the meantime. Everything now depended on the panzers and on the men of the army he had led to victory at Sevastopol. He had been able to ensure that they were rested and equipped to fight in the winter.

Yeremenko's front had just lost its first-echelon tank, mechanized and cavalry corps. Behind them were his rifle divisions pursuing the fleeing Romanians. They had emerged from their defences between the Sarpinsky Lakes, a chain of elongated lakes stretching for about 25 miles south of the Beketovka Bulge. The panzer corps now ploughed on northwest to round the northernmost Lake Sarpa. The two infantry corps were to penetrate the defences between the lakes as the whole 11th Army wheeled east. The speed of the two panzer divisions, however, would put them in combat again before the infantry could arrive along the line of lakes. Manstein calculated that this would work to his advantage. Yeremenko would concentrate on the threat from the panzers and commit his own tank reserves against them. He still had four tank brigades and the survivors of his decimated first-echelon corps. Russian tenacity would now be at a premium.

By the time *Grossdeutschland* was approaching the Beketovka Bulge, the short autumn night had come, but Hörnlein pressed his men on. The reconnaissance battalion was far ahead of his leading panzer battalion when, out of a side road, a Soviet tank column appeared heading west. The wind was blowing snow again, and the Soviet tank commanders were buttoned up. Soon both columns were on the same road but heading in opposite directions. One Soviet tank commander, though, did brave the elements to stand in his turret, the price of leadership. He could make out the T-34s heading east, but it was too dark to see their German markings. He yelled across to the men in the turrets and shouted with some annoyance, '*Na frontu, tovarishche! Na frontu!* [To the front, comrades! To the front!]' as he waved west, baffled that so many tanks could be leaving the battlefield.

He did not have time to wonder much more as he saw the turrets in the other column all turn simultaneously to face his tanks. With a boom, they fired almost all at once, and his brigade died at point-blank range. There were no misses, and every shot found a vital spot that ignited death by fire or explosion. The German tank commanders fell back into their turrets just as they fired to avoid the rain of exploding ammunition, flaming fuel, and jagged metal that flew between the columns. The burning column did wonders for the morale of the follow-on panzer grenadiers and artillery. That is what's called a bonus affect.

Leninsk, 3 November 1942

The end point of Stalin's secret railway supplying Stalingrad Front was boiling with activity as the advance elements of the 2nd Guards Army (two rifle corps and 2nd Mechanized Corps) began detraining and deploying to the east. At the same time artillery batteries that had been supporting 62nd Army just a short while before were arriving and also heading east. Overhead squadrons of the Red Air Force were also heading east. Stavka had directed that the 8th Air Army that had been supporting Yeremenko's westward thrust now be diverted to supporting the defence of Leninsk from Kleist's oncoming 1st Panzer Army.

Stalin had every right to fear Kleist. His four panzer divisions were flush with tanks – what was left of their original German panzers and hundreds of American Shermans and British Valentines. The excellent automotive characteristics of both tanks had resulted in relatively few breakdowns in the enormous distances covered from Baku and Ordzhonikidze. For the first time in the war, the Germans had a fully motorized field army – III Panzer Corps (3rd, 13th, 23rd Panzer Divisions), LVII Corps (5th SS *Wiking*, 50th, 111th, 370th Infantry Divisions), and XLIV Corps (97th and 101st Jäger Divisions) – every man and pound of equipment and supplies rode in a combat vehicle or a truck, almost all of which were the big, robust American Lend-Lease ones.

Stavka, Moscow, 3 November 1942

For the commander of the 384th *Rhinegold* Infantry Division, it was the ultimate humiliation. He stood in the snow with his aide holding a white flag. In front of him was a nameless Soviet division commander to whom he was surrendering. His division had been trapped by the onrushing tank spearheads of Don Front. He had lost contact with the rest of XI Corps which had disappeared to the south more as a rabble than an organized force.

The news was radioed to the Don Front commander, who was riding that indescribable high of pursuing a retreating enemy. Rokossovsky had the scent of a kill in his nose; the Germans had littered their path with discarded equipment of every kind, a sign that panic was turning into rout. His Don Front armies were pressing forward everywhere. Already his 16th Tank Corps had taken the Don bridge at Akimovka, trapping thousands of Germans and Romanians on the west bank. So he was shocked that night when Stalin himself had called to tell him of Yeremenko's defeat and to order him to redouble his efforts and link up with Southwest Front to crush the Germans between them.

He was even more shocked to hear a note of worry in Stalin's voice, something he had never heard before. He was so shocked that it took him a few minutes after he hung up to realize that the *Vozhd* had threatened to shoot him if he failed.

He instinctively felt his jaw as his tongue ran over his stainless steel teeth. As a disciple of Tukhachevsky he had been arrested in the great purge that decimated the senior officer corps in 1937–8; his NKVD interrogators had made much of his aristocratic Polish ancestry as they broke nine of his teeth, cracked three ribs, smashed his toes with hammers, and pulled out every one of his fingernails. He endured three mock executions when the men around him were all shot. He survived because he proved that the officer who was claimed to have denounced him had actually died in 1921. He was unexpectedly released in 1940 and reinstated because Marshal Timoshenko was in desperate need of good officers to command the growing Red Army. Yes, Rokossovsky took Stalin's threats seriously. Don Front would redouble its efforts. He had a trump that Stalin had given him. 'I assign Chuikov's army to you – 62nd Army is closer to the enemy than you are. Southwest Front's 1st Tank Corps will cross the Don south of Kalach and take Lyapichev Station, cutting off a major supply route. You will link up with them.' then Stalin hung up.

Chuikov was stunned when Rokossovsky gave him his new mission – attack 6th Army's flank. 'Comrade General, my army is not fit for manoeuvre in the open field. My divisions are mere skeletons. We have little ammunition and supplies; the floating ice in the river has nearly cut off our support from the east bank. All my artillery is on the east bank, and for the same reason can't be brought across.'

These are orders from the *Vozhd*, Chuikov. We have a priceless opportunity to encircle the fascists, and your army is the only one that can close the circle in time. Don't worry. I am sending 16th Tank Corps right after you. My 16th Tank Corps will then pass through your army and link up with 1st Tank Corps.

Chuikov gave his orders. Then he visited one of the cramped field hospitals in a basement. He found Zaitsev to his surprise on the floor on a thin pallet. 'What happened?' he asked.

'That damned German sniper nearly bagged this hare, Comrade General.' Zaitsev laughed through a painful wince. He described how König and he had danced around each other as the Russian had followed the withdrawing Germans. 'He got two of my team, and I forgot to be patient.'

'There will be more Germans.'

'But this one I especially wanted.'

Chuikov forced himself to smile. 'We've been ordered forward; maybe we'll get him for you.'

Rokossovsky's men would have to run hard to catch up with Vatutin's armies. Already most of 5th Tank and 21st Armies had crossed the Don and were pounding away at the increasingly fragile front that Seydlitz had thrown up. The 1st Tank Corps had crossed the Don just above its confluence with the Chir River, 25 miles southwest of Kalach, and cut the main rail line supporting 6th Army from the west. The Germans had only one more line: Rostov-Kotelnikovo–Zhutovo–Lyapichev. Unfortunately, Lyapichev was directly in the path of the oncoming 1st Tank Corps.

Kalach Front, 4 November 1942

The next morning 1st Tank Corps hit Lyapichev. They burst into the town in the early morning scattering the support units clustered there. Tanks crossed the tracks in a dozen places to fire into the wagons packed in the sidings. Some of them were still full of men, troops of V Corps, which Manstein had ordered north to support 6th Army. One division had already detrained and was marching north.

Now Germans boiled out of the cars only to be run down or machine-gunned by the tanks. Their antitank guns were tied down on flatcars, and the only weapons they had were small arms, entirely useless against tanks. The Soviet *tankisti* would call this day 'the German hunt' as they killed and killed. Germans ran across the snow in all directions away from the town. A Soviet motorized brigade arrived next to disgorge its infantry to sweep through the streets and yards. The corps commander, General V. V. Butkov, surveyed the slaughter and carnage. For him revenge for his Motherland was indeed sweet. 'Take no prisoners.'

The German 9th Division marching north from the station turned almost to a man to stare south at the sudden noise of battle. Within minutes commands were echoing up and down the column to about turn.

Another train with men of a third division was approaching the station from Zhutovo when the driver noticed smoke and fire ahead. He had just begun to slow the train down when a T-34 lumbered onto the track in front of him and turned to straddle the rails. The driver slammed on the brakes, and the wheels shot cascades of sparks as the brakes took hold and began slowing the train. Too late. The tank fired. The round struck the engine head-on, exploding the boiler and scalding to death the engine crew. As the shattered vehicle shrieked its death, it jumped the tracks, and careered over into the snow. Behind it car after car followed it off the tracks, to crash and splinter, spilling out hundreds of men.

Kotelnikovo, 4 November 1942

The elation in Stavka at the seizure of the enemy's main rail hub was matched by shock at Army Group B headquarters. Even Manstein's famous iron nerve wavered for a moment, then righted itself as more information came in. The rest of V Corps was detraining outside Lyapichev and throwing up defences to contain the enemy's tanks as was the 9th Infantry Division to the north. The problem was that the V Corps was meant to stabilize Seydlitz's and Hoth's hard-pressed armies. His counterstroke force was still engaged with Stalingrad Front. The race against time was on, and it looked like the crisis would burst before 11th Army could accomplish its mission and rescue 4th Panzer and 6th Armies.

As the Soviets were rampaging in the railyards, *Grossdeutschland* and 6th Panzer had penetrated past the northernmost of the Sarpinsky Lakes and struck deep into Stalingrad Front's assembly areas. Their black cross T-34s sowed endless confusion among the Russians. Unit after unit was taken unawares as the Soviet-made tanks approached only to discover that they were German-manned. One by one the second-echelon tank brigades of 65th and 57th Armies were encountered and destroyed before they could be properly deployed.

To the south, 11th Army's two infantry corps engaged the Soviet rifle divisions that had followed the initial breakthrough. Here the Germans had a clear advantage of seven fresh full-strength divisions against three Soviet rifle divisions. In three hours of intense fighting, the Germans drove the Russians back into their defences between the lakes. Continuing the attack, they broke through, taking thousands of prisoners, and pursued the enemy north where they expected to meet up with the two panzer divisions.

The infantry corps would soon have to finish off Southwest Front on their own. Manstein had been keeping a close watch on the progress of the two panzer divisions. They were desperately needed in the fighting to the west, but to pull them out too soon would allow Southwest Front to survive and threaten the German rear with another attempt at encirclement. Not yet. Not yet.

Leninsk, 4 November 1942

Major General Rodion Malinovsky was under the oppressive cloud of Stalin's suspicion. As with Rokossovsky, his future rode on the attack of 2nd Guards Army to stem Kleist's advance. His sin in Stalin's eyes was to have possible foreign connections, a fact that had already sent countless men to the *gulag*. At the age of fifteen the young Malinovsky had joined the Imperial Army to fight the Germans. His courage and stout heart earned him a St George Cross. Sent to France with the Russian expeditionary corps, he rose to sergeant and was badly wounded. When the corps was disbanded after the October Revolution, he stayed on to fight the Germans as a recruit of the French Foreign Legion with which he won the Croix de Guerre. In 1919 he returned home, joined the Red Army, and distinguished himself in the Civil War. In this current war, he had proved himself again and again to be a skilful and successful leader. He was so able that Stalin, despite his suspicions, gave him command of his finest army. Now that army was all that stood between Stalingrad and the enemy.

It was a formidable obstacle. Its 2nd Mechanized Corps held 17,000 men and was 220 tanks strong, almost all of them new-model T-34s. The armour of the German-manned Shermans was a bit thicker than the T-34's, and its turret basket allowed the crew to fight the tank more effectively. Balancing that was the fact that the T-34's high-velocity 76mm gun had a penetrating advantage over the Sherman's 75mm weapon. The corps' three infantry brigades were all motorized. Malinovsky's six infantry divisions were tough, experienced, and well-equipped. Every formation was commanded by a veteran officer who had done well in previous assignments. The oncoming battle would be for the first time between evenly matched mechanized forces, each with strong air support, and each commanded by a talented and tough commander.

Perhaps because they were so evenly matched they took the same mirror-imaging approach. Fix the enemy in the front with infantry and wheel a massive tank attack around a flank and into the rear. Ominously they both picked the same flank. Fifteen miles east of Leninsk, the infantry corps of both armies collided in a great bruising fight over the low mounds that were all that was left of the ruins of the 13th-century capital of the Golden Horde, Shed-Berke. Both wanted to use the mounds as a defensive line to hold the other until their tanks could fall on the enemy's rear. To the north over 600 tanks of both sides were converging on the same point – on the German right and the Soviet left – in the greatest meeting engagement in history.

It was a titanic crash of iron cavalry. There was no manoeuvre, no long-range duelling, as the masses of tanks flew at each other and fired at almost point-blank range. Tanks rammed each other like ancient galleys. The ranges were so close there were hardly any misses except where panic or excitement threw off the aim. Every hit at such ranges on hull or turret penetrated whether it was an American 75mm or Soviet 76mm gun. The Shermans lived up to their American nickname of Ronsons by lighting up after a single hit as their fuel caught fire, while the T-34s exploded because too much ammunition was vulnerably stored. Whether it was a Sherman gushing fire from its hatches or a T-34 with its turret twisting in the air, blown off by exploding ammunition, men died horribly. 'In modern mechanized war men do not die in fields of flowers with shouts of *Urrah* on their lips.'[16]

Imperceptibly the tide shifted in the German favour. The electrically powered turret baskets in the American and German tanks allowed each crew to fight more effectively even in the point-blank mêlée. Rudel's Stuka squadron more than did its part. Overcast skies with cloud at 300 to 600 feet, execrable flying weather, kept most of the Red Air Force and Luftwaffe grounded – except Rudel who only looked at it as a dare from the weather god. Rudel led his squadron in sortie after sortie that killed tank after tank.

On his seventh sortie as dusk was settling he flew over the fighting to the enemy's rear to find tempting fuel targets. He dropped down low and flew over a village into heavy flak, but flying just over rooftop level protected him. He looked down a long gulley behind the village and found Malinovsky's tank reserve.

> I see a mass of tanks, behind them a long convoy of lorries and motorized infantry. The tanks are, curiously, all carrying two or three drums of petrol. In a flash it dawns on me. They are taking advantage of the twilight and the darkness because by day they cannot move with my Stukas overhead. This accounts for the petrol drums on board the tanks.

He realized that the force was preparing to strike deep into the army's rear and did not want to be dependent on fuel convoys. He alerted the squadron.

> Attack of the most vital importance! You are to drop every bomb singly. Follow up with low level attack till you have fired every round. Gunners are also to fire at vehicles.

Rudel led the way, dropped his bombs, and then attacked with his 20mm cannon. Normally those guns would have been ineffective against tanks, but the fuel drums were another matter. With the first bombs, the column stopped abruptly and then in a few minutes resumed its orderly exit from the gulley. But by now Rudel's squadron was swarming over them, and the Russians scattered in panic out of the gulley and across the steppe.

Every time I fire I hit a drum with incendiary or explosive ammunition. Apparently the petrol leaks through some joint or other which causes a draught; some tanks . . . blow up with a blinding flash. If their ammunition is exploded into the air, the sky is criss-crossed with a perfect firework display, and if the tank happens to be carrying a quantity of Very lights they shoot all over the place in the craziest coloured pattern.[17]

Only night finally grounded the Stukas, which had accounted for almost forty tanks and dozens of trucks. By his quick thinking and aggressiveness, Rudel had wrecked Malinovsky's reserve tank brigade and his motorized brigade which he had been preparing for the killing stroke against 1st Panzer Army. Unknown to Rudel, there was a vital bonus amid the burning tanks and trucks scattered though the gulley and the surrounding steppe. Malinovsky was among the dead.

As night fell the loss of the army commander and much of his senior staff was not known yet. The great meeting engagement had cost them over a hundred tanks to the Germans' sixty. The fighting between the infantry of both armies flared and rumbled all day. As Rudel was riding the dusk into his last attack, SS *Wiking* broke through the Soviet 13th Rifle Corps and rampaged through the enemy's rear. Late that night, after the fighting had stopped, the Germans could hear the noise of tank engines revving up and stood to their own vehicles lest the Russians come in the night. It was only the remnants of 2nd Guards Army pulling out in defeat. The Germans would immortalize the tank battle as *Der Tottenritt bei Leninsk* ('The Death Ride of Leninsk').

Chapter 14

'Manstein is Coming!'

Kalach, 4 November 1942

The area around Vatutin's command post in the town was littered with shattered tanks, bodies, and the debris from the large number of German supply and maintenance units that 5th Tank Army had overrun. Hundreds of German prisoners were being escorted back across the bridge to the west bank of the Don. To the east was the smoke and noise of battle. As long as he held the Germans close they could not disengage and escape. Stalin had called him personally to congratulate him on the success of Southwest Front and to explain that it was still possible to trap the enemy between his own 1st Tank Corps at Lyapichev and Rokossovsky's 16th Tank Corps.

Chuikov was less sanguine, remembering an old Russian military proverb, 'It was all smooth on the map, but they forgot the ravines.' He had an army to command – officially – but he could scrape barely a division's worth with enough ammunition and equipment to accomplish his task. These were the survivors of dozens of divisions and brigades smashed, depleted, replaced, the lucky survivors of the months of the *Rattenkrieg*. Now they streamed out of the ruins of the outer suburbs of Stalingrad, denizens of cellars, broken buildings, all the dark and claustrophobic shelters of city fighting and into the open, snow-covered country. Chuikov himself did not realize what effect such a sudden change would have until it struck him himself. There was an unnerving feeling of vulnerability in the empty expanse of the fields, with barely a bit of stubble or steppe grass showing out of the thin layer of snow.

It was not quite empty. Hoth had placed his 29th Motorized Division to hold the wide-open right flank of the two German armies. Its victory over the 13th Tank Corps two days before had proved the wisdom of that move. Now it hovered over a broad stretch of open country as befitting its epithet, the Falcon Division. It did not take long for its reconnaissance elements to discover Chuikov's infantry trudging over the snow to the southwest. They would have been safer had they clung to their broken city. Leyser had taken the risk of pulling his division up to within 10 miles of Lyapichev in case 1st Tank Corps broke through. It would also allow him to counter any threat to 4th Panzer Army's flank.

Chuikov was just such a threat. Ever since his men had left the psychological protection of the last of the suburbs, he had wondered when the Germans would discover they were there. He had fought them too long to believe they would leave such a flank wide open. His question was answered all too soon as Leyser's artillery laced down his column, spewing men in every direction. Before they could recover from the shock, the panzers were cutting through them, followed by the German infantry firing from their halftracks. An hour later a German bayonet prodded Chuikov's chest. He groaned. 'Hey, *Herr Leutnant*, this one's alive, and he's a general!'[1]

Sarpinsky Lakes, 4 November 1942

Yeremenko did not have time to worry about the defeat of 2nd Guards Army. The Germans were outside his own bunker. Smoke from the burning head-quarters was drifting down into the small space, choking everyone. He spun the cylinder of his revolver. Wounded three times in the war so far, he concluded that he had already used up all his luck and more. He would not survive this defeat one way or another. Stalin would have less mercy than the Germans. No surrender.

The German 11th Army's infantry corps had broken through between the Sarpinsky Lakes the day before as its panzer corps had finished off the last of his tank brigades. Stalingrad Front had simply disintegrated. The Germans were rounding up 80,000 prisoners as their infantry columns were marching north through the night towards the city. At last Manstein ordered the panzer corps west. He now had his operational reserve. And not a moment too soon.

Verkhne–Tsaritsynski, 5 November 1942

At first light Butkov's 1st Tank Corps burst out of its concentration at Lyapichev and headed east. Behind it rifle divisions widened the breakthrough. The tanks swept over the thin German antitank defences of what was left of V Corps. Twenty-five miles in the other direction Rokossovky's 16th Tank Corps had skirted through the outer Stalingrad suburbs and was heading southwest. Each tank corps had only slightly more than 12 miles to go to trap both German armies to the north. All that stood between their 300 tanks and the objective was 29th Motorized Division.

Zhukov drew all the resources of the three northern fronts together to ensure that nothing would stand in the way of the union of the two tank corps. Wave after wave of Sturmoviks, the premier ground-attack aircraft of the Red Air Force, were concentrated from the 16th and 17th Air Armies. Low on fuel, outnumbered eight to one, and tormented from the sky by swarms of Red

Falcons,[2] the Falcon Division was broken and brushed aside as the two tank corps closed the distance between them. At 10.37, their lead elements met a few miles outside the little town of Verkhne-Tsaritsynski, the site of the mauling of the 13th Tank Corps three days before. The area was littered with wrecked Soviet tanks. That did not lessen the joy of the men in both corps. The Germans were surrounded! The commanders met and hugged, tears streaming down their faces as all along the front where the corps met, men climbed down from their tanks to embrace and celebrate. Vodka appeared everywhere. The closing of the ring happened so quickly that the propaganda units were not able to film it properly. So next day it was carefully restaged for them.

Behind the celebrations the rifle divisions of Rokossovky's 66th Army were force-marching south to strengthen the ring around the Germans. Vatutin's 8th Cavalry Corps had crossed the Don 20 miles south of Lyapichev and its units were fanning out in the German rear. Stalin was visibly relieved when the news arrived that the ring had been closed. That night every Soviet radio station interrupted its programming to announce to the Soviet peoples that their glorious sons in the Red Army had closed a death trap on the enemy who had strained and struggled for months to take Stalin's city on the Volga. Stalin was only momentarily relieved. After all, he could not conjure up the fuel that was running out for his tanks. Current operations, especially around Stalingrad, had badly depleted fuel stocks. The consequences of the loss of 90 per cent of the Soviet oilfields at Maikop, Grozny and Baku were finally being felt on the battlefield. Like a knife twisting in the Soviet belly, the refineries at Maikop were already producing refined fuels for the Germans. Fuel trains were already reaching Kotelnikovo and their loads were then immediately being hurried north by truck.[3]

Kalach Pocket, 5 November 1942

For Seydlitz the crisis of the battle was at hand. His army and Hoth's were now fully encircled. Manstein had just appointed him to command both armies in the pocket.[4] As well as enemies on the ground, the Red Air Force was savaging the overcrowded pocket, now called the Kalach *Kessel*. To the west Vatutin had pushed him away from the Don. To the north and east Rokossovsky's infantry were pressing. To the south the enemy's two tank corps had barred the way for relief. And those were only the problems caused directly by the enemy. His men had had no shelter since they had abandoned Stalingrad; fuel, food and ammunition were fast running out. The two panzer corps were down to fewer than fifty tanks each with almost no fuel to run them. The wounded were dying of exposure, and there was little the doctors could do without supplies and field hospitals.

From Werewolf came the stirring command:

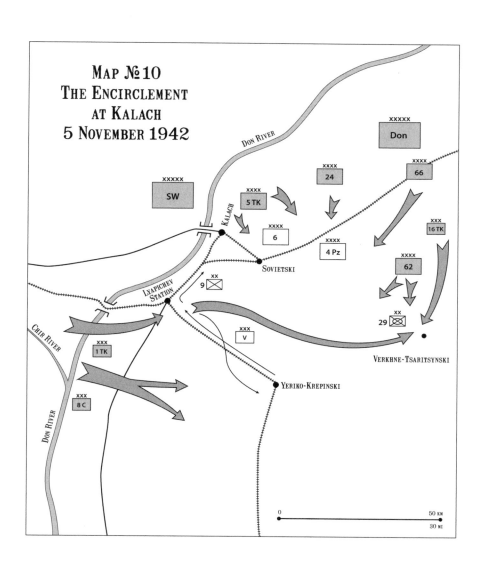

MAP № 10
THE ENCIRCLEMENT
AT KALACH
5 NOVEMBER 1942

DON RIVER

Don
XXXXX

SW
XXXXX

24
XXXX

66
XXXX

5 TK
XXXX

6
XXXX

4 Pz
XXXX

16 TK
XXX

62
XXXX

KALACH

SOVIETSKI

9
XX

LYAPICHEV
STATION

V
XXX

29
XX

VERKHNE-TSARITSYNSKI

CHIR RIVER

1 TK
XXX

DON RIVER

8 C
XXX

YERIKO-KREPINSKI

0   50 KM
           30 MI

Stand and fight it out; not one step back. The world will see the resolve
of the 4th Panzer and 6th Armies *wie hart wie Kruppstahl* [as hard as
Krupp steel]! Already vast resources are concentrating to break through
to you.

'How reassuring,' thought Seydlitz. 'If adamantine resolve were all it took,
then Hitler would already be ruling the world.' As it was, he would put his
faith in Manstein. The word quickly spread through the trapped armies.
'Manstein is coming!' It worked like a jolt of adrenalin to reanimate the
sagging morale of the troops.

The Soviets were rushing troops into the ring around the two trapped
armies. Manstein would have to come soon. Seydlitz would not have enough
strength to attempt to break out while Manstein was breaking in. He concentrated all his remaining panzer and motorized forces into a single battle
group, Kampfgruppe *Hoth*, putting that general in charge of the break-out.
With them were his veterans of the *Hoch- und Deutschmeister*. He mused
that having broken open the Demyansk Pocket earlier that year, they would
see the irony of breaking out of another pocket now. More than that, despite
what they had gone through, they were still tough veterans who got things
done.

Now Hitler actually came to his aid. Göring, elated with his success at
resupplying 1st Panzer Army by air, pledged to resupply the armies in the
Kalach Pocket to which Hitler assented. Unfortunately, there was no airfield
left in the pocket. Instead a steady stream of Ju 52s flew over the pocket
dropping supplies by parachute. The Red Falcons had a field day, falling on
them as if they were flocks of pigeons. To the horror of the Germans on the
ground, transport after transport blew up in the air or spiralled down in flames
to crash among them. Yet amid the carnage raining down on them, thousands
of parachutes also landed with desperately needed food, ammunition and
medical supplies. The men who rushed to retrieve one parachute were taken
aback, though, to discover that the entire canister was full of condoms.
Another group found a canister packed with Iron Crosses.

Richthofen's fighters flew escort but found they had their hands full as the
Red Air Force put everything it had into the air battle to keep the pocket from
being resupplied. In truth, Luftflotte 4, despite its high kill-ratio, was being
flown into the ground. Its losses were mounting with few replacements in
aircraft or pilots. The Red Air Force was also paying far too much attention to
its airfields. Richthofen urged Manstein, 'There are too many Russians, and
they keep getting better. Hurry, or I won't be able to support you.'

Leninsk, 6 November 1942

The remnants of 2nd Guards Army retreating into the town were given no rest
and less hope by Kleist's pursuing panzers. A German reconnaissance battalion

cut Stalin's secret railway a dozen miles to the north. Already artillery fire was falling amid the supply dumps and rail sidings. Fire and smoke seemed everywhere, as did large numbers of terror-stricken rear-echelon troops and deserters.

There was even more reason to panic had they known that SS *Wiking* had swung south to the Volga and raced up the river road to play havoc among the supply units and the masses of equipment, food, and ammunition that had built up as the floating river ice had cut off almost all traffic to the west. On the east bank were numerous boats and barges immobilized by the ice. Many of the Scandinavians in the *Nordland* Regiment had been fishermen and small-boat operators. Ice was nothing new to them, and a few managed to dodge the floes and get to the other side. The first soldier of the Wehrmacht to plant his boots on the landing zone in the city was a Norwegian. He looked around and walked up the beach past wrecked boats and equipment of every type. A few more followed him, spread out in a skirmish line. He was met by a man with a white flag and a red cross on his armband. Stalingrad had fallen to a squad.

Zaitsev was resting on a pallet in a basement hospital when the word spread that the Germans were back in the city. At first there was stunned silence, then men began to weep. All for nothing! Rumours are often just rumours, he thought. Then a silhouette filled the doorway, that same silhouette he had had scores of times in his sights. Instinctively, he grabbed his sniper's rifle from where it was propped up against the wall. One shot, and the German, or more accurately a Swede, fell forward onto the floor. As fast as a hunted hare, Zaitsev slipped out the door and up the basement steps. In moments he was lost to sight among the ruins.

LX Panzer Corps assembly area, north of Abganerovo, 6 November 1942

Raus could see the village of Verkhne-Tsaritsynski a few miles to the north. Here and there knocked-out tanks were the only bumps on the otherwise flat expanse of farmland beyond which were over 200,000 trapped German soldiers. To the west of the town, Hörnlein was also conducting his own personal reconnaissance. The corps' northward march had been rapid; they had arrived yesterday, but Manstein was determined not to dissipate their combat power with a hasty attack.

Instead ammunition, fuel and food had been funnelling into their assembly areas. The crews worked quickly to replenish their ammunition, top off their fuel and get as many hot meals as they could. Then, most importantly, they slept. Just as they were about to curl up in whatever shelter they could find, men began running from vehicle to vehicle with the news that Stalingrad had fallen to 1st Panzer Army. Of course, the announcement did not say that only a few hundred men had been able to cross the river. There were a few cheers for the victory that had been hanging in the balance for so long, but sleep was more alluring to bone-tired men than victory's sweet song.

As they slept, the two infantry corps of 11th Army marched to take up the right flank of the panzer corps. The infantry corps on the right would enter the city from the south while that on the left would prevent any Soviet counterthrust from striking the flank of the relief force.

Stavka, 6 November 1942

The Soviets picked up the news of the fall of the city from the German intercepts. Stalin was enraged. No one mentioned that he had personally directed that Chuikov's army join the encirclement of the Germans. Now he ordered that Rokossovsky's 66th Army be thrown into the city instead of strengthening the encircling ring. Zhukov called from the front to argue against it. 'Comrade Stalin, the 66th Army is vital to this operation. We can retake the city once we have destroyed the trapped enemy.'

But Stalin was having none of it. The impossible had happened. The city that bore his name had fallen after he had made its successful defence the pivot of the war for the Soviet peoples. 'You are thinking only in military terms, but I must balance that with the political cost. How will the morale of your armies be affected if they find out the city had fallen?'

Zhukov replied, 'They will simply get on with it.'

Stalin was getting angry. 'The will to fight will be gone. No, you must retake the city immediately, and no one will be the wiser. We can pass it off that the enemy just infiltrated a few saboteurs.'

One last time Zhukov tried to argue, but Stalin cut him off. 'Just do it.'

As he hung up the phone, he was thinking ahead. The battle could go either way. Should Zhukov win and destroy the trapped Germans, then it would be a disaster for Hitler. Would he sue for peace? Stalin thought, 'I certainly wouldn't. There is still a lot of war in the Germans even if they lose this battle.'

But if the battle went the other way, the game was up for the Soviet Union. Lenin's legacy would be in danger. His spies in OKW had told him that Hitler had talked of a negotiated peace in the spring. How attractive would that be if he were victorious? Stalin put himself in Hitler's place and knew that such a peace would be a punitive one. Yet what other choice was there? With the loss of the oilfields and Allied aid, there was not a lot of war left in the Russians. He expected that the Soviet Union's name would become inaccurate as such a peace was likely to shear it of almost all its non-Russian territories. It would be reduced to a Russian core with its centre of gravity moving east. The communist state could survive in this core. The Russians had proved to him that they were a state-minded people, willing to defend Lenin's legacy.

All well and good, in theory, he thought, but what is to happen to Stalin? He had left a blood-stained path to power. How the knives would sharpen. It would require the iron control of the NKVD if he were to survive. He was pleased in his appointment of Abakumov to replace Beria. The man was pitiless and relentless in his sniffing out of disloyalty, even before the thought had occurred.

Abakumov was indeed pitiless and relentless, but even he could smell a disaster in the wind. The existential question then became, 'How will Abakumov fare?' Already members of the Politburo were putting out certain feelers and if Stalin knew about them . . . Loyalty had its limits. Kill for Stalin? Of course. Die for Stalin? Now that was a different matter.[5]

Werewolf, 6 November 1942

'*Mein treuer Reinhard*,' Hitler exclaimed, as Heydrich entered and gave him the stiff-armed salute, the *Hitler Gruss*. He came over and took Heydrich's hands in his own he was so delighted to see him. 'I am surrounded by generals with their red-striped trousers. They always tell me what cannot be done. With you I know I have a man who just does the impossible. The only one here like you is this young Stauffenberg. You must meet him.'

'We have already met, *mein Führer*. He greeted me personally at the entrance to your compound.' Hitler was pleased. He had developed the utmost confidence in his new OKW Deputy Chief of Operations. Stauffenberg was not so pleased. He had already known enough of Heydrich to despise him before they had even met. But after shaking his damp, soft hand, he had viscerally recoiled from the man, though he had enough self-control not to show it.

That reaction only added urgency to his plan to pry military intelligence out of Heydrich's grasp. As they walked the long path through the pinewoods to Hitler's bunker, Stauffenberg commented that the SS Panzer Corps being created in France was a juicy plum for any able man willing to throw his fate onto the scales of the battlefield. 'You would understand, I am sure. The urge to test oneself in battle is irresistible, as you showed when you took part in the air battles against the English.'

Heydrich smiled a bit. It had been a delicious experience, and he chafed to do more than cow Czechs and kill Jews. Of course, getting control of all intelligence functions of the Reich was one thing, but his future would require more combat distinction than a few air brawls with the British.

Stauffenberg went on:

> The Führer has not transferred the SS back to the Eastern Front because he is convinced that the *Amis* will land shortly in France. We all bow, of course, to his strategic insight. Think what glory would shower down on the man who drove them into the sea. This time, I wager, they will not be allowed to get away. Ah, here we are!

He was not foolish enough actually to suggest to Hitler that he appoint Heydrich to command the SS Panzer Corps. He knew that Hitler would not take it well for an Army officer, even one as favoured as he was, to make any suggestions about command appointments within the SS. It was Hitler's private army aglow with a fire for National Socialism that he felt the Army did not show enough. He was confident that Heydrich would bring up the matter but only in private with Hitler.

And he was right. Hitler made the announcement at the next OKW staff meeting. 'I have decided to entrust command of the new SS panzer corps to my faithful Heydrich. Until the corps is deployed, he will retain control of all intelligence functions already under his purview.'

Stauffenberg was aghast. He had overplayed his hand badly. He had wanted to reassert Wehrmacht control of the Abwehr and had been willing to buy it with a potentially dangerous assignment. Stauffenberg had weighed the importance of the Abwehr against putting a very sharp sword in Heydrich's hand. The plotters needed the Abwehr to open channels for a negotiated peace after Hitler's removal. Now Heydrich had the sword and the Abwehr.

At least he would be in France and not on the Eastern Front when it came time to remove Hitler. Hopefully Canaris could continue to deceive Heydrich as to his feelers to the *Amis*. Suddenly things had become a lot more dicey.[6]

76/78 Tirpitzufer, Abwehr Headquarters, Berlin, 7 November 1942

Admiral Canaris had just returned from a clandestine meeting in Switzerland with a representative of the British MI6. The man had borne Churchill's answer to the admiral's question of what terms Germany could expect to end the war. 'His Majesty's Government will make no peace with Hitler or his regime.' What it left unsaid was even more important than what it did say. Churchill was implying that peace was possible if Hitler were removed and the Nazis suppressed.

He was interrupted by the arrival of a courier from Stauffenberg, a reliable young officer. The dispatch he delivered informed him of Hitler's decision to subordinate the Abwehr to the Sicherheitsdienst and Heydrich as well as the latter's appointment to command the SS Panzer Corps organizing around Toulon in southern France. It was clear that if Hitler and his entourage were eliminated it would leave enormous power in his former protégé's hands. If anyone could keep the Nazis in power after Hitler, it was Heydrich.

Canaris went over to the window to watch a cold rain beat down. Something would have to be done to make sure Heydrich did not step into Hitler's shoes. He called for his aide. 'Order Major von Fölkersam to report to me immediately.'

LX Panzer Corps assembly area, north of Abganerovo,
7 November 1942

Before dawn *Grossdeutschland* and 6th Panzer Division had assembled without incident. Raus observed that,

> The officers looked at their watches. They and their men were fully conscious of the significance of the approaching hour. Suddenly the silence was disrupted by the sounds of explosions. All the guns of the division fired, and it almost seemed as if the shells were going to hit the assembling German troops. Involuntarily, everyone flinched and stopped, but the first salvo had already screamed over the heads of the men and was coming down on the hastily prepared forward positions of the Soviet rifle division that had just arrived the day before. The earth quivered from the explosion of the heavy shells. Stones, planks and rails were hurled into the air. The salvo had hit the centre of the enemy's chief strongpoint. This was the signal for the Witches' Sabbath which followed.[7]

As the artillery kept up its rapid fire, the tank engines turned over. In a deep wedge formation Raus sent over a hundred tanks through the snowy steppe. The blow was so powerful that the Russians of the 343rd Rifle Division were stunned:

> His light and heavy batteries stood intact in their firing positions. They had been enveloped and caught in the rear by German tanks before they had been able to fire an accurate round. The limbers which the Russians had moved up quickly had not reached the guns. The horse teams drawing them had fallen under the machine-gun fire. Horse-drawn limbers and ammunition carriers, which had overturned, continued to lie about for hours afterward. Horses which had survived were nibbling at the frozen steppe grass while standing in teams together with the bodies of those which had bled to death in the fire. Here and there, horse teams dragged a dead horse along. Blood on the snow marked their paths. The remnants of the Russian infantry had been scattered and had disappeared in the tall steppe grass as if they had been whisked away by a gust of wind ... The numbers of captured Russian guns and other heavy weapons, as well as of horses and vehicles of all kinds, including field kitchens, increased by the hour.[8]

Raus was amazed that the Soviet 16th Tank Corps had not sought to counter his attack on the rifle division in the Soviet first-line defence. He had no idea that Stalin's order to redirect that division as part of the 66th Army to retake Stalingrad had sown confusion in the enemy command. The 66th Army had just begun moving its rifle divisions into the belt of encirclement to give defence in depth against any German attack so that the tank corps could mass to counterattack. The 343rd Rifle Division had just arrived when it received the order to move back to retake Stalingrad. It was preparing to move when Raus fell upon it.

As night fell, Raus saw to the resupply and refuelling of his division. LX Panzer Corps kept him informed of *Grossdeutschland*'s similar success. It too had gutted an enemy rifle division and not suffered any tank counterattacks. That luck could not last. Tomorrow the Soviet tank corps could be expected to come out fighting.[9]

His right flank would be secured by the 11th Army's XXX Corps' three divisions marching west after the defeat of Southwest Front. On its right LIV Corps's four divisions would drive up through Stalingrad, make contact with the SS *Wiking* elements in the city, and then strike west against Vatutin's armies.

That night, as the German panzer divisions rested, Zhukov was again on the phone to Stalin, begging him to rescind the order to redirect 66th Army east to drive the Germans out of Stalingrad. Reconnaissance stated that, because crossing the Volga in the face of so much floating ice was so dangerous, only a battalion or so of Germans had been able to cross, out of the entire 1st Panzer Army waiting on the east bank after its victory at Leninsk.[10]

This time Stalin relented. The loss of two rifle divisions to Raus and Hörnlein's panzers underlined how serious their threat was. But Stalin sought to have it both ways. Two of 66th Army's four rifle divisions could reinforce the two tank corps, but the other two would have to retake Stalingrad. The grand old man of the Prussian Army, the late Field Marshal Helmut von Moltke had had a phrase for this back and forthing: 'Order, counterorder, disorder.'[11]

Verkhne–Tsaritsynski, 8 November 1942

After night had fallen Raus's and Hörnlein's divisions stopped only long enough to resupply their ammunition and top off their fuel. After midnight they moved out. 'Only the pale light of the stars made it possible to identify, at very close range, the dim outlines of the tanks and their dark trail in the thin layer of snow.' Raus knew that he was going to engage the 16th Tank Corps some time that day. It would be far better if he could arrange the terms rather than let the enemy commander have a say. The way to do that was to take something that would attract the enemy to him like iron filings to a magnet. The village of Verkhne-Tsaritsynski answered perfectly. Roads led out of it in all four directions, and although the Soviets were smart enough not to garrison it and make it a target, in German hands it would be like a bone in the throat.

The outlines of the village were just becoming visible as the morning mist, which had cloaked the German advance, lifted. A reconnaissance detachment

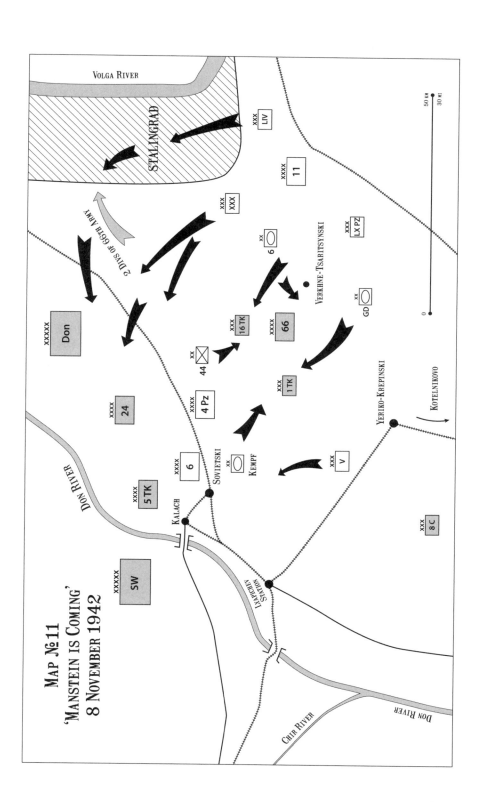

Map № 11
'Manstein is Coming'
8 November 1942

found it empty, and the reinforced 11th Panzer Regiment and attached units forming a *Kampfgruppe* rolled forward, commanded by the redoubtable Colonel Walther von Hünersdorff, one of the most talented and aggressive officers of the panzer corps. Then suddenly the scouts at another point reported, 'There is a heavy concentration of hostile tanks in a broad depression south of here. More tanks are following.' The Soviet tanks started to emerge from the depression but were immediately knocked out by panzers that had lined some low hills surrounding it. The Soviet tanks withdrew. Then the panzers sprang forward to line the depression and fire down into the enemy tank concentration. The Soviets assumed an all-around defence and fired back. Within half an hour it was over and nothing remained of the Soviet brigade but a tank graveyard for seventy burning vehicles.

As the battle in the depression raged, another Soviet tank brigade coming from the north attempted to come to the rescue just as the tail of 11th Panzer Regiment entered the village. The attached panzergrenadiers, antitank units, and engineers were able to take over the defence of the village, leaving the panzers for mobile defence. A third enemy tank brigade was seen coming from the west to join the battle. Both the German and Russian commanders were broadcasting in the clear because of the need for quick action. But it was the Germans who were faster off the mark and more tactically nimble. The German radio intercept reported to Hünersdorff the Russian message, 'Motorized brigade on the way; hold out, hold out!' He attacked the brigade coming from the east and sought to turn its flanks. The Russian commander kept lengthening his own front, but kept suffering heavy losses from the accurate German crossfire. Finally, he withdrew down a sunken road, sacrificing his rearguard and leaving forty tanks on the field.

Part of what the Germans were intercepting were the frantic conversations between the commanders of the two tank corps. Major General Maslov, commanding 16th Tank Corps, was begging Butkov for help. Butkov whose 1st Tank Corps was now sparring with *Grossdeutschland*, was reluctant. Maslov pleaded, 'I've lost two tank brigades already. The enemy will break through if I don't get any reinforcements.' Maslov was running up against a divided command. He reported to Rokossovsky while Butkov reported to Vatutin. By the time that got sorted out, 6th Panzer was burning out the last elements of Maslov's corps. Into that battle Butkov now sent two of his four brigades.[12]

The Soviets were committing numerically superior forces to the battle but piecemeal. Using his panzergrenadiers, engineers and antitank units to hold the village, the German colonel manoeuvred his tanks to strike one enemy brigade after another with superior numbers. From radio intercepts and air reconnaissance he knew the tank brigade from the west would take an hour to reach the field while the mechanized brigade was approaching the village. He directed the main body of his panzers through a depression that brought them onto the Russian rear. The tank battalion of the brigade was quickly shot up, causing the motorized battalions to veer off and escape to the northwest. The last Soviet brigade, arriving after the defeat of the mechanized brigade, ran straight into the reconcentrated panzers. A bitter duel took place in which the Russian tanks, which had advanced without cover, suffered brutal losses.

Still another mechanized brigade was attacking, but Hünersdorff struck it in the flank so quickly it could not change front. The tank battalion of thirty tanks was destroyed, and the motorized infantry fled. From the west, the tank brigade finally arrived and with motorized infantry broke into the village, overrunning a 105mm gun battery and a number of antitank guns. German engineers with antitank mines rushed the T-34s and took them out one at a time.

> Now the Soviets were attacking from the southeast hoping to cut off the *Kampfgruppe*. Finally, the Soviet commander staked everything on one card. Heavily concentrated and echeloned in depth, all his tanks rolled forward like a huge wave about to swallow up the German forces. This mass attack, too, was stopped in the hail of fire of more than 100 German tank guns.

Now Hünersdorff played his trump. He threw in his panzer reserve to counterattack the enemy's flank, which quickly folded. Then those panzers that had been in the defence also went over into the attack, closing to very short range. The Soviets fought hard but all of a sudden, like a receding tide, they flooded back, leaving a mass of wrecked and burning tanks in their wake. The 16th Tank Brigade had been burned out. Maslov did not live to report his failure, but Butkov's brigades were still on the way, and Rokossovsky had thrown in the 66th Army's separate tank brigade as well.[13]

Hünersdorff's victory had come at the cost of leaving his panzergrenadiers and others to hold off more attacks on the village by tanks and motorized infantry. He was shocked to get a message from an officer in the village asking permission to abandon it. The reply was an emphatic no, but the situation had reached a crisis point. The troops in the village were almost out of ammunition. For hours as Hünersdorff's panzers had parried one tank attack after another, the Soviets had been attacking the village. German antitank gunners and engineers with shaped charges had knocked out tank after tank that had barged into the village. Again and again, the Germans had thrown back each infantry assault, but now they were at the end of their resources, and there seemed no end of Russians.

The *Kampfgruppe* commander looked at his exhausted *Panzertruppen*. The men had been in constant and desperate action for many hours. He leaned out of his tank turret and screamed in rage at the men, 'You want to be my regiment? Is this what you call an attack? I am ashamed of this day!'

That provoked just the response he had intended. The panzer crews were so infuriated at the colonel's insult that it was like a shot of adrenalin for each man. He ordered that they break into the village, 'at maximum speed whatever the losses'. They attacked with such fury, spraying their machine-gun fire in every direction, that the Russians were unnerved and fled across the steppe.[14]

Even now the Germans could not rest. Butkov's and Rokossovky's brigades were converging on them. Out of ammunition and with very many wounded loaded onto the tanks, Hünersdorff withdrew his *Kampfgruppe*. The Russians converged on the village in triumph, their tanks wending their way through scores of other burning Soviet tanks and over the bodies of their own motorized infantry. It was a Pyrrhic victory. They held a meaningless village, but it had cost them most of a tank corps. The Germans had thirty tanks knocked out but were able to recover almost every one before they withdrew. Panzergruppe *Hünersdorff* and the rest of 6th Panzer had lived to fight another day. That was the essence of Manstein's elastic concept of battle on a tactical level. Holding terrain is not important; killing the enemy in large numbers is. Trading one to achieve the other was the essence of the art of war. As such it earned the ultimate accolade of the army group commander for 6th Panzer.

> The very versatility of our armour and the superiority of our tank crews was brilliantly demonstrated . . . as were the bravery of the panzer-grenadiers and the skill of our antitank units. At the same time it was seen what an experienced old armoured division like 6 Panzer could achieve under its admirable commander General Rauss [*sic*] . . .'[15]

To the west Hörnlein was making easier progress against 1st Tank Corps, weakened as it was by sending two of its four brigades to help Maslov. Infantry were streaming in from Lyapichev; Butkov fed them into the fight, holding his own tanks back for counterattack. To his distress, *Grossdeutschland* was crushing them in its advance. Butkov commented bitterly to his deputy, 'the Germans are spitting out our infantry like sunflower seed shells', referring to the way Russians would eat a mouthful of seeds and be able to spit out a stream of shells.

On the ground it was less colourful and more brutal. German Private Alfred Novotny found himself in his baptism of combat, a recent replacement. He watched in stunned amazement as the artillery roared its preparation for the assault. Stukas followed to dive into the attack. Panzers were arriving adding to 'the smoke, the noise, and the confusion'. He could think only of school and old friends as fear seeped through him.

Then the signal for the attack was given:

> We got up from our foxholes and started running towards the Russian lines, screaming '*Hurra*' as loudly as we could. The moment this happened, all fears and thoughts of being wounded disappeared. We were all on our feet, screaming and running, as one, green replacement beside old hares.

The Russians opened fire and its noise mixed with the screams of the wounded, and the suddenly still bodies of men with whom we had spoken just moments before. We hit the first positions of the Russians and I jumped into a hole to escape the artillery barrage. I could not understand that I was still alive with so many of my comrades already dead.

The fighting was fierce. A small unit which was equipped with flame-throwers was attached to us. On our flanks and ahead of us, they burned everything in sight. The smell of burning flesh, cloth and wood became unbearable. With the screaming of the Russian soldiers, the whole scene was like something out of a horror movie.

Novotny felt something shift under him. It was not the dirt but the face of a young, dead Russian soldier:

I will never forget his face, which seemed to be looking directly at me. It was my first hour of combat.[16]

Through the back door, 8 November 1942

Just as Butkov was preparing his counterattack against Hörnlein's penetration, Hoth unleashed the last of his panzers to break out of the encirclement. General der Panzertruppen Werner Kempf, commander of XLVIII Panzer Corps, was in overall command of the breakout effort. His force was such an amalgam of survivors that it was called Kampfgruppe *Kempf* rather than by any unit name. It included barely fifty operational tanks, a regiment's worth of panzer-grenadiers (out of the six that had belonged to the XIV and XLVIII Panzer Corps), engineers, flak and antitank elements. Attached also was the *Hoch-und Deutschmeister*, in the strength of a weak regiment, all that was left of the 44th Infantry Division. Every gun within range fired as part of an intense barrage, most using up what little ammunition they had left.

The artillery fell on the 14th Guards Rifle Division defending the inner side of the encirclement. The division had only arrived the day before in a special convoy of American trucks stripped from the supply services to exploit 1st Tank Army's crossing of the Don and seizure of Lyapichev. The Soviet Guards were frantically trying to turn every ripple or depression in the ground into a defence position when the artillery struck them. Bodies flew into the air or were torn apart like rag dolls, antitank guns were broken and twisted, and the Russian batteries were decimated. Yet the surviving Soviets hung on and waited for the Germans.

As the German panzers had ground through the outer encirclement belt, frantic calls up the chain of command had led to Vatutin going over into an all-out attack to break into the pocket before the Germans could break out. Such an attack would prevent the encircled Germans from concentrating enough force to break out. He had not reckoned enough on Seydlitz's single-minded determination not to remain passive about his own fate.

Nevertheless, Vatutin's attacks were wearing down 6th Army's exhausted divisions. With its artillery concentrated on supporting the break-out, 6th Army had little with which to oppose 21st and 5th Tank Armies' attacks. Only the Luftwaffe could fill the gap, but every aircraft was committed to supporting the breakthrough. At that moment when Vatutin's armies were cracking open the pocket in the north, Kampfgruppe *Kempf* flung itself south at the 14th Guards.

The soldiers of the 14th Guards were veterans, and their political officers had been hammering home that they were the only thing standing between the German 6th Army and escape. Now was the time to hold firm and extract a bloody vengeance for the sufferings of the Motherland. Their comrades dead about them, half their antitank guns destroyed, and their artillery shattered, they hung on. Rolling towards them were men motivated by a similar determination, but this one was fuelled by desperation. Every weapon the Soviets had left opened up as the panzers flew at them in a wedge formation. To their right came the *Hoch- und Deutschmeister*, men even more desperate and determined than the panzer crews. They had been through one harrowing retreat and were fed up with being hounded by the Russians. This time Ivan was on the receiving end.

Stalingrad, 8 November 1942

The East Saxons of the 24th Infantry Division were simply not prepared for what they encountered as they entered Stalingrad from the south. They and the other divisions of 11th Army's LIV Corps thought they knew what the siege and destruction of a fortress city looked like. The men of the 24th Division were, after all, veterans of the epic siege of Sevastopol. Had they not finally broken the formidable Fort Stalin?

Sevastopol had fallen in the bright July sunshine of the Crimea framed by the blue water of the Black Sea. Stalingrad was not like that at all. Winter had left the blackened ruins sprinkled with filthy snow under dull, leaden skies. The destruction was far more thorough, and everywhere among the broken brick and concrete were the bodies, frozen excrement, and the detritus of countless used-up divisions. The few people they saw were civilians scavenging through the ruins. They fled as soon as they saw Germans. The East Saxon regiments filed up in awe past the grain elevator, all scorched and with huge, jagged holes.

Eventually, they met a patrol in SS uniform whose men spoke with a thick Danish accent and claimed to be from SS *Wiking*. They guided them to an outpost of that division. The commander of the lead regiment was put in touch with the senior SS officer, who excitedly told him that air reconnaissance just reported large numbers of Soviet troops marching back up the west end of the pocket towards the city. On his own authority the commander changed the direction of march to the northwest. His decision was immediately confirmed by his division, corps and army commanders. The rest of the corps was turned in that direction as well.

They were in a race to intercept the enemy's 64th and 299th Rifle Divisions of 66th Army, directed by Stalin himself to retake the city from the German contingent that had occupied it. Stalin would have been far less satisfied with this action had he known that the army commander had selected the 64th Rifle Division for the mission. Given Stalin's obsession with treason, the knowledge that this division was being trusted to retake the city that bore his name would have enraged him. As well it should: the men of the 64th were still disaffected from their suppressed mutiny in August and now bore a deep and abiding hatred for the 'justice' meted out to so many comrades.

Werewolf, 8 November 1942

Hitler's face turned red. His eyes glowed with rage. His staff knew the signs of an impending tirade. In his hand was the message from Manstein that finally had answered his constant stream of precise orders, every one of which had been disobeyed.

> *Mein Führer,*
>
>   There are . . . cases where a senior commander cannot reconcile it with his responsibilities to carry out an order he has been given. Then, like Seydlitz at the Battle of Zorndorf, he has to say: 'After the battle the King may dispose of my head as he will, but during the battle he will kindly allow me to make use of it.' No general can vindicate his loss of a battle by claiming that he was compelled – against his better judgement – to execute an order that led to defeat. In this case the only course open to him is that of disobedience, for which he is answerable with his head. Success will usually decide whether he was right or not.[17]
>
>   I have disobeyed your specific orders in order to fulfill the greater strategic goal of destroying the Red Army which you yourself have stated repeatedly. We have reached the crisis. Now let me finish this battle, and I will lay before you a great victory.
>
>   *Manstein*

Stauffenberg was ready. An aide hustled in a young soldier dressed in the black uniform of the *Panzertruppen*, his arm in a sling. At his throat hung a Knight's Cross. '*Mein Führer*, allow me to introduce a front soldier straight from the Kalach pocket, Hauptmann Bruno Detweiler. He has a message for you from the men of the 6th Army.'

If there was anything that tempered Hitler's conduct it was a front soldier – he imagined he had a bond with the combat veterans dating to his own service in the trenches of the First War. Here was one who had been wounded in battle and wore the Knight's Cross, proof of his valour. The fires in Hitler's eyes banked, and he suddenly looked kindly.

The young man was plainly awestruck. He pulled himself together, saluted, and began his report. He described the conditions of the fighting, the state of the men and their morale. Then he said,

> *Mein Führer*, the men have great faith in you. You have promised them that you will rescue them from the encirclement, and the men say repeatedly that their *Führer* has never broken his word to them.

Hitler was greatly affected by the speech. He took the Hauptmann's hand in both of his and warmly shook it. When the man had departed, he grumbled to Stauffenberg, 'I will give Manstein enough rope to hang himself.'[18]

Kotelnikovo, Army Group B Headquarters, 9 November 1942

Manstein had no intention of measuring himself for a noose. He was preparing one for Zhukov. He had also had one in mind for the *GröFaZ* himself with the help of the other *Gerichten*. But the battle was reaching that point when all the previous actions, both German and Russian, suddenly presented opportunities. Most of those opportunities were now tumbling into the hands of the Germans.

The 11th Army was wheeling in on the Soviet flank and rear as well as breaking into the Kalach Pocket. It was for this reason that he had fought Hitler tooth and nail to retain it as a powerful operational reserve. Now his Sevastopol veterans were flooding through the ruins of Stalingrad. The reports kept streaming in:

> *09.30, 11th Army HQ.* Two enemy divisions defeated on the outskirts of the city. The lead rifle division collapsed at first contact. Thousands of men have just shot their political officers and surrendered.

> *09.52, LX Panzer Corps HQ.* Panzer Corps destroyed two remaining tank brigades; linked up with Panzergruppe *Kempf*. Resupply convoys are flowing into the pocket.

Manstein did not know that the men of 6th Panzer as they broke into the pocket were shouting their division motto to the benumbed survivors of Seydlitz's army, '*Raus zieht heraus!*'

> *10.25, 6th Army HQ.* Northern front of pocket holding. Directing LX Panzer Corps to attack enemy in direction of Kalach.

> *12.10, LX Panzer Corps HQ.* Panzer Corps passing through 6th Army to continue attack against enemy 5th Tank Army.

> *14.44, 11th Army HQ.* XXX Corps attacking flank of enemy 24th Army. LIV Corps attacking enemy rear. Enemy appears to be panicking. Very few enemy tanks in this sector.

16.35, 6th Army HQ. Major tank battle in progress.

That tank battle was the epic clash between the panzers of Raus, Hörnlein and Kempf and those of Vatutin's 26th Tank Corps and 8th Cavalry Corps. Overhead the air forces filled the sky and rained down disintegrating or flaming aircraft as the struggle in the air was as intense as that on the ground. Zhukov took personal command of this battle and committed the Southwest Front reserve, 1st Mechanized Corps. Even that was not enough.

The German panzer commanders had thrust into the Soviet positions and then gone over to the defence. The enemy threw in wave after wave of tanks backed by entire rifle divisions. Raus never forgot the scene:

> Thousands of Russians filled the snowfields, slopes, and depressions of the endless steppe. No soldier had ever seen such multitudes advance on him. Their leading waves were thrown to the ground by a hail of high explosive shells, but more and more waves followed.[19]

Here the superior gunnery skills and optics as well as the powered turrets made the German T-34s such killing machines that they never were in Soviet hands. Artillery from 6th Army's replenished guns joined the fight as well while the war lover Rudel showed up with his squadron to join the battle as did other squadrons of Stukas and Ju 88s.

Sergeant Alexei Petrov was overwhelmed by the massive shelling and air attack:

> To Petrov it was worse than Stalingrad . . . On the flat plain were thousands of bodies, tossed like broken dolls onto the ground. Most were Russians . . . At the height of the bombardment Petrov saw a tiny figure no more than three feet high.

It was the upper torso of a body of a Red Army man. His hips and legs had been severed by a shell burst and lay beside him:

> The man was looking at Petrov and his mouth opened and closed, sucking air, trying to communicate one last time. Petrov just stared at the poor creature, until the arms stopped flailing, the mouth slackened and the eyes glazed. Somehow the soldier's torso remained upright and forlorn beside the rest of his body.[20]

Into this chaos 6th Panzer lurched forward with 150 tanks, cutting through the Russian masses. Raus's assault-gun battalion attacked on a parallel axis cutting off large numbers of the enemy between them:

> Even the strongest nerves were unequal to this eruption of fire and steel. The Russians threw their weapons away and tried like mad men to escape the infernal crossfire and the deadly armoured envelopment. This was a thing that rarely happened in World War II. In mobs of several hundreds,

shelled even by their own artillery and their own rocket launchers, they ran . . . towards the only open spot, only to find detachments of panzer-grenadiers in their way to whom they surrendered.[21]

As the panzers sliced through the collapsing Soviet forces, 11th Army was completing its wheel northwestward to cut the supply lines of Don Front and pushing its 65th and 24th Armies back towards the Don, joining the broken 5th Tank Army and 21st Army of Southwest Front.[22]

Kalach, 10 November 1942

By the next morning there was a massive traffic jam as the Soviet armies were feeding into the single bridge over the Don at Kalach, desperate to escape the Germans. German artillery and the Luftwaffe followed the horde, killing large numbers and sowing more panic. They were packed so tight that every shell and bomb found a target. NKVD troops trying to control the roads to the bridge were shot down as men rushed to cross. All this time the bridge received the unrelenting attention of the Luftwaffe's dive-bomber squadrons. Between their attacks, the Me 109s would make strafing runs, their bullets stitching a bloody trail through the crowds packing the bridge, exploding supply trucks, until no one could get through. But the mobs heaved and pushed their way over the dead, pushing burning vehicles over the side to crash through the ice in the Don with a loud crack and hiss as they sank. The end to escape came when finally a well-aimed bomb dropped a span. Still the crowds pushed forward spilling the men in front over the broken edge of the bridge to splatter on the ice below.

Along the banks thousands of men attempted to cross the ice. Hundreds fell through, but many more found ways across where the ice had frozen thickly enough to carry their weight. To the north more thousands followed the bank itself to find the bridge at Akimovka, where the German XI Corps had streamed across in the other direction in the same sort of panic flight.

But for the four armies packed into the approaches to Kalach, there was no escape. Over the next few days, the Germans would count over 200,000 prisoners.

The Kremlin, Office of the General Secretary of the Communist Party of the USSR, 11 November 1942

Stalin knew the game was up and sank into that same depression that had sent him to his *dacha* after the German invasion of 22 June the year before. Now he just sat in his Kremlin office and stared at the walls. Frantic calls from Zhukov and Rokossovsky went unanswered. Abakumov and the delegation from the Politburo found him there. He said, 'I did not summon you.'

Khrushchev answered, 'No, that is not the normal procedure when someone is about to be arrested.'

Stalin jerked upright. The old look of overwhelming malevolence filled his face, that look that had quailed so many others, that look that spoke death. Khrushchev's jaw dropped. Another man simply voided himself in terror. A shot made them all jump. Stalin flew backwards into his chair and fell like a rag doll onto the floor. Abakumov held a smoking pistol. 'I warned you all. A bullet is much safer than an arrest warrant.' He turned his own cruel face on them, then went over to Stalin's desk, kicked the body aside, righted the chair, and sat down.

Chapter 15

Coda

Brest-Litovsk, Ukraine, 22 November 1942

Vyacheslav Molotov's stony expression masked an acid hatred. That he, the Soviet Foreign Minister, had to come to beg terms from the fascists was enough to make him gag. But the Germans, being what they were, could not help but heap indignity on the Soviet delegation. The gloating expression of his counterpart, Joachim Ribbentrop, that loathsome bully, made him want to leap across the table and throttle him.

Ribbentrop greeted Molotov with a smirk, 'We meet again, Herr Molotov.' The Russian ground his teeth. Their last meeting had been to sign the notorious German–Soviet nonaggression treaty of 1939 that allowed Stalin to gobble up the Baltic republics and share in the conquest of Poland. Then they had been equals. Now, the Russians had come as supplicants.

The Germans could not help gloating, a national characteristic. They knew that the death of Stalin at the hands of the NKVD had cast the apple of discord among the Soviets, with Red Army and secret police units in open combat in Moscow itself. The war itself had ground to a halt as the Germans prepared to gather the fruits of victory from a broken foe and the Russians were consumed by a growing civil war. To stir the pot more they had released General Vlasov and his followers to wage his anticommunist crusade.[1]

Molotov was not even allowed to beg for terms. They were thrown in his face as the Celtic conqueror of Rome, Brennus, had thrown his sword on the tribute scales, saying '*Vae victis!*' ('Woe to the conquered'). Always one for cloaking an event in a precedent of the past, Hitler had chosen Brest-Litovsk as the site of the peace conference between Germany and the Soviet Union, or rather as the place where he would dictate terms. He had done the same at Compiègne in France, choosing the same railroad car in which the victorious allies of World War I had forced a humiliating armistice upon the Kaiser's army in November 1918. Brest-Litovsk had been the place the Imperial German Army had dictated peace to a broken, revolution-convulsed Russia in the winter of 1917–18. Hitler savoured the fact that the second treaty was an even twenty-five years after the first act and on the same stage.

As to the terms, they were worse than 1917–18. The Soviet Union would lose the Ukraine, Belarus, the three Baltic states, Moldova, the Caucasus, the three Transcaucasian Republics, the Kuban, and the vast area from Stalingrad to the Caspian Sea. The Finns would recover all the territory that they had lost in the Winter War of 1939–40 and more, and Romania would receive Moldova. Turkey's spoil would be large chunks of Georgia along the Black Sea coast, and all of Azerbaijan, but not the oilfields around Baku. Germany would keep the rest. Lithuania, Latvia and Estonia as well as the Crimea would be absorbed into the Reich proper. Belarus, the Ukraine, and the Kuban would be administered as conquered territories in accordance with Hitler's *Lebensraum* policy. Georgia and Armenia would become German client states. A special demand that heaped the bitterest humiliation on the Russians was the surrender of Leningrad. Hitler was determined to deny a broken Russia an outlet on the Baltic. In any case, there would soon be no city there. He was going to level this symbol of Russia's great power status established by Peter the Great when he built the city in 1712. More important by far was his vengeful will to smash utterly the cradle of Bolshevism.[2]

Evil had triumphed.

Toulon, 23 November 1942

Major Fölkersam enjoyed playing dress up. Perhaps it had something to do with the nature of the Brandenburgers' special operations mentality. He had earned a promotion and a Knight's Cross after the *coup de main* at Maikop for dressing up like an NKVD officer. For the Soviets it had been a very stylish uniform. But it did not hold a candle to the uniform of an SS officer that he now wore. He had to admit it was a splendid fashion statement. He actually preened himself in the mirror that morning, admiring himself in his black and silver.

Now he was standing by the roadside in the leafy outskirts of this French city looking every inch the SS Sturmbannführer. At least the Knight's Cross at his throat was real. His detachment of Baltic Germans, also dressing the part, manned the checkpoint. Every man had been with him at Maikop. He looked at his watch. It had been more than convenient that Heydrich was a man of rigid pattern. It had nearly cost him his life when the British had sent their assassination team to Prague. Like clockwork he left his residence at precisely the same hour every day and drove down precisely the same route without escort. He was telling the Czechs he despised them. Only he had the devil's own luck to be unexpectedly out of town that day they lay in wait for him. Heydrich was the living embodiment of the German saying, '*Ordnung muss herschen*' ('Order must rule').

That he would be travelling down this road today was something that had not been overlooked. Canaris had kept a finger on his every movement, something he kept Fölkersam constantly aware of. The major looked at his watch again just as the black car with its SS flags turned round a bend in the road. 'Just like clockwork, indeed.' he said to himself. The car was without escort, an act of bravado Heydrich had used as he had driven through the streets of Prague. 'You make this too easy.'

The car slowed as it approached the checkpoint. Fölkersam's men jumped to attention, as the major met the car just as it stopped. He gave a terrific *Hitler Gruss* stiff-armed salute. '*Herr Obergruppenführer*, my apologies ...'

The rear passenger window unrolled. Heydrich's long face coldly looked at him. Fölkersam never forgot the look he saw on that face in the moment before he shot it between the eyes.

Stalingrad, 23 November 1942

Evil now walked through the ruins of Stalingrad savouring his victory. Around him stretched a vast sea of broken brick and concrete, with only the department store shell in any recognizable form. From its balcony flew a huge swastika. The only thing to mar Hitler's triumph was the smell of rotting corpses, though the snow had done much to cover it. In an act of personal cruelty, he had ordered that the captured commander of the Soviet defence be there to watch him strut his triumph and rub it in the abject man's face. Manstein had been appalled and personally offered Chuikov his apologies.

Hitler motioned his SS bodyguard and the flock of sycophants to stand back as he walked into the square in front of the building. It was obvious that Göring, Himmler and Bormann were disappointed that they could not share this historic moment and be photographed at his side. It was not sentiment, but the opportunity to be seen as sharing in the victory and ultimately inheriting it.

It could have been lucky for them, though, if they had taken their chance to hang well back in the crowd. Oberjäger Pohl's instructions were to take out as many of these others as he could after killing Hitler. His presence had been passed off to the SS security detail as cover for any Soviet snipers who might have been left behind. He had a clean shot now from a rubble pile 300 yards away as Hitler conveniently stepped out from the crowd.[3]

That same thought occurred to Zaitsev. He was hiding in a large pipe about the same distance from Hitler but to the north. Now his sights centred on the forehead of the Fascist beast. He adjusted for the cold wind that was whipping through the ruins. The image of one of his mother's icons flashed through his mind. It was St George spearing the dragon.[4]

The cold wind, Russia's last desperate resistance, cut through Hitler's great-coat. But for Hitler it only served to excite the Wagnerian moment as it drove grey clouds through the sky. He could picture the Valkyries riding through the storm-tossed sky with the bodies of the new German heroes thrown over their saddles being borne to Valhalla. Again he had been right, and all his generals had been wrong. He could feel the power surge in him.

Then nothing. His head exploded. Two bullets were fired at the same instant. Pohl's hit him in the forehead, and Zaitsev's through the right temple. Blood and brains sprayed over the rubble.

The crowd heard the double crack and watched as Hitler's body twisted and jerked and then fell to the ground. For that stunned instant no one moved. In that suspended time Pohl's sight centred on Himmler, who stood out with his flock of retainers. He fired at the moment when the crowd surged forward. It was a hard shot as bodies flowed around him, but the Reichsführer threw his arms back as a bullet went through his right eye.[5]

Zaitsev, less familiar with the Nazi hierarchy, merely kept firing at the gaudiest of the uniforms milling around. Göring was conspicuous with his white overcoat and flashing baton; his peacock preening was his undoing. A Russian bullet struck him in the chest, and he fell with such a thud that he made the rubble bounce and brought down two of his aides. Manstein stepped aside as another Nazi party bigwig in his flashing uniform fell in front of him. He felt strong arms on him as Stauffenberg and his own aide pulled him back to the shelter of the building as the horde of courtiers fled for their cars. Major von Boeselager caught one of them by the arm, put a pistol to his stomach and fired. Martin Bormann screamed and careered off to stumble and fall amid the rubble.

Chuikov, with the instinct bred in the *Rattenkrieg*, bolted in the confusion. He paused at the corner of a ruined building, took a deep breath, and laughed. 'Zaitsev! God bless you, my boy!'[6]

Forces in the Battle of 20° East

Germans

German Fleet (Admiral Carls)

Battlegroup 1 (Admiral Schniewind)

Battleship	*Tirpitz*
Heavy Cruiser	*Admiral Hipper*
Destroyer Flotilla 5	*Friedrich Ihn, Friedrich Eckoldt, Karl Galster*
Destroyer Flotilla 6	*Theodor Riedel, Hans Lody, Erich Steinbrinck*

Battlegroup 2 (Admiral Kummetz)

Heavy cruisers	*Lützow, Admiral Scheer*
Destroyer Flotilla 8	*Richard Beitzen, Z-24, Z-27*

Battlegroup 3 (Admiral Ciliax)

Battlecruisers	*Scharnhorst, Gneisenau*
Heavy cruiser	*Prinz Eugen*
Light Cruiser Flotilla 1	*Leipzig, Nürnberg*
Destroyer Flotilla 8.1	*Z-28, Z-29, Z-30*

U-boat Flotillas 1, 7, 10, 11, 13, 14

Luftflotte 5

KG 26	42 He 111
KG 30	103 Ju 88
StG 5	30 Ju 87
KFlGr 906	15 He 115
JG 26	109 Fw 190

Allies

Home Fleet (Admiral Tovey)
Battleships	*Duke of York, King George V, Washington*
Cruisers	*Cumberland, Nigeria, Kent*
Destroyers	14 ships
Aircraft carriers	*Victorious* (42 aircraft), *Wasp* (75 aircraft)

1st Cruiser Squadron (Admiral Hamilton)
Heavy cruisers	*London, Norfolk, Wichita, Tuscaloosa*
6th Destroyer Flotilla	*Somali, Wainwright, Rowan*

Convoy PQ-17, Close Escort (Commander Broome)
Destroyers	*Fury, Keppel, Leamington, Ledbury, Offa, Wilton*
Corvettes	*Lotus, Poppy, La Malouine, Dianella*
Minesweepers	*Halcyon, Salamander, Britomart*
ASW trawlers	*Lord Middleton, Lord Austin, Ayrshire, Northern Gem*
AA ships	*Palomares, Pozarica*
Submarines	*P.614, P.615*

Soviet Forces in Operation Uranus

	Estimated 19 Nov		Actual 1 Nov	
	Troops	Tanks	Troops	Tanks
Southwest Front				
1st Guards Army	142,869	199	102,231	122
5th Tank Army	90,600	359	85,765	320
21st Army	92,056	199	82,911	111
Total	325,525	757	270,907	553
Don Front				
65th Army	63,187	49	50,121	49
24th Army	56,409	48	50,003	48
66th Army	39,457	5	33,764	5
Total	159,053	102	133,888	102
Stalingrad Front				
62nd Army	41,667	23	41,667	23
64th Army	40,490	40	35,439	20
57th Army	56,026	225	50,026	182
51st Army	44,720	207	39,224	175
28th Army	47,891	80	32,117	60
Total	230,794	575	166,356	400
Grand Total	715,372	1,434	603,268	1,115

Note: Manpower and equipment totals planned for the operation were at least 10–15 per cent higher than actual forces committed to battle because of the severing of Allied aid and the loss of the major oilfields to the south.

Notes

Introduction, 'The Dancing Floor of War'

1. Edward R. Stettinius, Jr., *Lend-Lease: Weapon for Victory* (New York: Macmillan, 1944), pp. 208, 215.
2. T. H. Vail Motter, *The Persian Corridor and Aid to Russia* (Washington, DC: Center for Military History, 2000), p. 4.
3. 'Khrushchev Remembers', The Glasnost Tapes, 1990.
4. Homer, *The Iliad*, tr. Robert Fagles (New York: Penguin, 1990) p. 16.1001–5.
5. William Craig, *Enemy at the Gates: The Battle for Stalingrad* (New York: Penguin, 2001), p. xi.

Chapter 1, Führer Directive 41

1. Paul Carell, *Hitler Moves East 1941–1943* (New York: Bantam Books, 1967), p. 479.
2. Joel Hayward, 'Too Little Too Late: An Analysis of Hitler's Failure in 1942 to Damage Soviet Oil Production', *Journal of Strategic Studies*, Vol. 18, No. 4, 1995, p. 2.
3. Carell, *Hitler Moves East*, pp. 479–80.
4. wikipedia.org/wiki/Stavka, accessed 7 June 2012. 'Stavka was the term used to refer to a command element of the armed forces from the time of the Kievan Rus.'
5. Geoffey Jukes, *Stalingrad to Kursk* (Barnsley: Pen & Sword, 2011), pp. 78–9.
6. Carell, *Hitler Moves East*, p. 480.
7. Anthony Beevor, *Stalingrad* (New York: Penguin, 1999), pp. 69–70.
8. 'Annex 5 to Report by the C-in-C, Navy, to the Führer, 13 April 1942', in *3 Fuehrer Conferences on Matters Dealing with the German Navy 1942*, Office of Naval Intelligence, Washington, DC, 1946, pp. 65–6.
9. *Aaron T. Davis, *Hitler and Directive 41: Decisive Decisions of World War II* (Los Angeles: Ronald Reagan Center for Strategic Issues, 2004), p. 82.
10. Vail Motter, *The Persian Corridor and Aid to Russia*, Appendix, Tables 2, 7, 10.
11. Zehra Önder, *Die türkische Aussenpolitik im Zweiten Weltkrieg* (Munich, 1977) p. 150.
12. John Gill, 'Into the Caucasus: The Turkish Attack on Russia in 1942', in Peter G. Tsouras, ed., *Third Reich Victorious* (London: Greenhill, 2002), p. 149.
13. Gill, 'Into the Caucasus'. pp. 149–50.
14. *Franz Baron von Oldendorf, 'Hitler's Grand Turkish Gesture', *Journal of Second World War Studies*, Vol. XXII, p. 832.

15. Adolf Hitler, *Hitler's Table Talk, 1941–1944*, ed. H. R. Trevor-Roper (New York: Enigma Books, 2000), pp. 554–5.
16. Mathew Hughes & Chris Mann, *Inside Hitler's Germany: Life Under the Third Reich* (New York: MJF Books, 2000), p. 184.
17. *Ivan Chonkin, *The Life of Andrey Vlasov: Patriot and Liberator* (New York: Hudson Press, 1982), pp. 119–22.
18. *Ibrahim Sayyid, *Nazi Propaganda in the Muslim World* (New York: International Press, 1987), pp. 121-23. Nazi propaganda was finding a receptive audience, especially in the Arab world which was becoming more and more agitated by the increasing Jewish settlement in the British Mandate of Palestine.
19. Gill, 'Into the Caucasus', p. 149.
20. *Vozhd* is a Russian term that means great war leader. In the movie *Enemy at the Gates*, the English wording used by the character representing Khrushchev to convey the emotional meaning of the term is 'the boss', with all the connotations of a Mob boss.
21. This figure of 2.5 million irrecoverable losses was provided by Russian military historians to the author in a symposium at the Moscow Military History Institute in July 1992.
22. This statement was made by Russian military historians to the author in a symposium at the Moscow Military History Institute in July 1992.
23. Richard Woodman, *Arctic Convoys 1941–1945* (Barnsley: Pen & Sword, 2011), pp. 13–14.
24. Woodman, *Arctic Convoys*, p. 14.
25. Albert L. Weeks, *Russia's Life-Saver: Lend-Lease Aid to the USSR in World War II* (Lanham, MD: Lexington Books, 2010), p. 142.
26. Alyona Sokolova, 'American Aid to the Soviet Union', *Vladivostok News*, 17 April 2005, www.freerepublic.com/focus/f-news/1385548/posts, accessed 15 February 2012.
27. Beevor, *Stalingrad*, p. 223.
28. Weeks, *Russia's Life-Saver*, p. 122.
29. Weeks, *Russia's Life-Saver*, p. 43.
30. Woodman, *Arctic Convoys*, p. 345.

Chapter 2, **A Timely Death**

1. Grossadmiral (Grand Admiral) was the German naval rank equivalent of a British admiral of the fleet or a United States fleet admiral.
2. Under the Weimar Republic, the German Navy was called the Reichsmarine; Hitler renamed it the Kriegsmarine.
3. Peter G. Tsouras, *The Book of Military Quotations* (St Paul: Zenith, 2005), p. 396.
4. German Naval History, www.german-navy.de, accessed 17 April 2012.
5. Erich Raeder, *Grand Admiral* (New York: Da Capo, 2001), p. 374.
6. David Irving, *The Destruction of Convoy PQ-17* (New York: Simon & Schuster, 1968), pp. 4, 10.
7. Woodman, *Arctic Convoys*, p. 65.
8. Alan E. Steinweiss and Daniel E. Rogers, *The Impact of Nazism: New Perspectives on the Third Reich and its Legacy* (Lincoln: University of Nebraska, 2003), pp. 186–8.
9. Raeder, *Grand Admiral*, pp. 255–65.
10. Jägers were elite light infantry trained to operate in difficult terrain.

11. Tsouras, *Book of Military Quotations*, p. 229.
12. Vasili Ivanovich Chuikov, *The Battle for Stalingrad* (New York: Holt, Rinehart and Winston, 1964), p. 14.
13. Michael K. Jones, *Stalingrad* (Barnsley: Pen & Sword, 2007), p. 76.
14. http://en.wikipedia.org/wiki/Henning_von_Tresckow.
15. Peter Hoffmann, *The History of German Resistance 1933–1945* (Macdonald and Janes, 1977), p. 265
16. Peter Hoffmann, *Stauffenberg: A Family History 1905–1944* (Montreal: McGill-Queen's University, 2008), pp. 163, 168.
17. Peter Hoffmann, *Carl Goerdeler and the Jewish Question, 1933–1942* (Cambridge: Cambridge University Press, 2011), p. 115.
18. *Friedrich von Heinzen, *Hoch! Hoch! Dreimal Hoch! Ludwig I, Ein Leben* (Frankfurt: Rolf Martin, 1996), p. 109.
19. Hugh Sebag-Montefiore, *Enigma: The Battle for the Code* (New York: John Wiley, 2000), p. 218.
20. wikipedia.org/wiki/Enigma_machine, accessed 18 February 2012. 'Enigma was the codename for a system of electro-mechanical rotor cipher machines used for the encryption and decryption of secret messages. Although Enigma had some cryptographic weaknesses, in practice it was only in combination with procedural flaws, operator mistakes, captured key tables and hardware, that Allied cryptanalysts were able to be so successful.'
21. Sebag-Montefiore, *Enigma*, p. 218.
22. Irving, *The Destruction of PQ-17*, p. 1.
23. Winston Churchill, *The Second World War* (New York: Penguin, 1985), Vol. IV, p. 98.
24. Raeder, *Grand Admiral*, p. 359.
25. www.german-navy.de/kriegsmarine/ships/destroyer/zerstorer1936a/z24/history.html, accessed 21 Feb 2012. Destroyer Flotilla 8 consisted of *Z-24*, *Z-25* and *Hermann Schoemann*.
26. Horvitz, Leslie Alan; Catherwood, Christopher, *Encyclopedia of War Crimes and Genocide* (New York: Facts On File, 2006), p. 200; Bryant, Chad Carl, *Prague in Black: Nazi Rule and Czech Nationalism* (Cambridge, MA: Harvard University, 2007), p. 140.

Chapter 3, The Second Wannsee Conference

1. Chuikov, *The Battle for Stalingrad*, p. 14.
2. Carell, *Hitler Moves East*, p. 483.
3. With the annexation of Austria to the Reich, its army of eight divisions was incorporated directly into the German Army bringing with them the lineages and traditions of the old Imperial Austrian Army.
4. Peter G. Tsouras, *The Great Patriotic War : An Illustrated History of Total War: Soviet Union and Germany, 1941–1945* (London: Greenhill, 1992), p. 79.
5. David Glantz, *Armageddon in Stalingrad, September–November 1942, The Stalingrad Trilogy*, Vol. 2 (Lawrence, KS: University of Kansas, 2009), p. 14.
6. Friedrich Paulus, wikipedia.org/wiki/Friedrich_Paulus, accessed 18 February 2012.
7. *Edward M. Williams, 'Soviet Equipment Employed by the Germans in WWII', *US Army Magazine*, Vol. XX, No. 3, 25 February 1966.
8. Paul Carell, *Stalingrad: The Defeat of the German 6th Army* (Atglen, PA: Schiffer, 1993), p. 36.

9. Beevor, *Stalingrad*, pp. 67–8.
10. Jukes, *Stalingrad to Kursk*, p. 81.
11. Sebag-Montefiore, *Enigma*, pp. 269–70.
12. Robert Gerwarth, *Hitler's Hangman: The Life of Heydrich* (New Haven, CT: Yale University Press, 2011), p. 50. Heydrich and Himmler's 'relationship was one of deep trust, complementary talents and shared political convictions'. Heydrich was fundamentally loyal to Himmler.
13. British television documentary, *Edward VIII: The Traitor King*, first aired by Channel 4 in 1995.
14. 1940-1944 insurgency in Chechnya, wikipedia.org/wiki/1940-1944_Chechnya_ insurgency#cite_note-history.neu.edu-4, accessed 13 March 2012.

Chapter 4, **Race to the Don**

1. *Henning von Tresckow, *Manstein und Hitler: Entscheidung 1942* (Frankfurt: Ernst Janning, 1962), p. 87.
2. Beevor, *Stalingrad*, pp. 69–70.
3. wikipedia.org/wiki/List_of_U-boat_flotillas, accessed 20 Feb 2011. The German U-boat flotillas in France were: Brest: 1st and 9th; Lorient: 2nd and 10th; St-Nazaire: 7th and 6th; La Rochelle: 3rd Flotilla; Bordeaux: 12th (+ Italian submarines). The German U-boat flotillas in Norway were: Bergen: 11th; Trondheim: 13th; Narvik: 14th.
4. Dudley Pope, *73 North: The Defeat of Hitler's Navy* (New York: Berkeley Books, 1958), pp. 98–9.
5. *Jason Colletti, *The Führer Naval Conferences* (Annapolis, MD: Naval Association Press, 1988), p. 199.
6. Irving, *Destruction of Convoy PQ-17*, pp. 24–31.
7. *Albert Adlinger, *The Devil's Twins: Heydrich and Dönitz* (London: Mayfair & Sons, 1973), p. 121.
8. Irving, *Destruction of Convoy PQ-17*, p. 24.
9. Irving, *Destruction of Convoy PQ-17*, p. 31.
10. Sebag-Montefiore, *Enigma*, pp. 203–4.
11. *Alistair Williams, *Former Naval Person: Churchill and the Naval War* (London: Blackstone, 1955), p. 129
12. *Desmond Richardson, *Decision of Ill-Omen: The Wasp in the Battle for the Arctic Convoy* (New York: D. H. Dutton Press, 1949), p. 32.
13. Irving, *Destruction of Convoy PQ-17*, p. 300.
14. Signal from C-in-C Home Fleet to Admiralty and Rear-Admiral Hamilton, originating at 11:55 a.m. GMT, 22 June 1942, cited in Irving, *Destruction of Convoy PQ-17*, p. 35.
15. Irving, *Destruction of Convoy PQ-17*, pp. 31–2.
16. David Wraag, *Sacrifice for Stalin: The Cost and Value of the Artic Convoys Re-Assessed* (Barnsley: Pen & Sword, 2005), p. 216.
17. Carell, *Stalingrad*, pp. 58–9.
18. Vail Motter, *The Persian Corridor and Aid to Russia*, Appendix, Tables 4, 7, 10.
19. wikipedia.org/wiki/Knight's_Cross_of_the_Iron_Cross, accessed 1 Mar 2012. 'The Knight's Cross of the Iron Cross (*Ritterkreuz des Eisernen Kreuzes*, often simply *Ritterkreuz*) was a grade of the 1939 version of the 1813-created Iron Cross (*Eisernes Kreuz*). The Knight's Cross of the Iron Cross was the highest award of Germany to recognize extreme battlefield bravery or successful military

leadership during World War II. It was second only to the Grand Cross of the Iron Cross (*Großkreuz des Eisernen Kreuzes*) in the military order of the Third Reich.'

20. Adolf Galland, wikipedia.org/wiki/Adolf_Galland#High_command_.281941.E2. 80.931945.29, accessed 1 March 2012.

Chapter 5, The Battle of Bear Island

1. Woodman, *Arctic Convoys*, p. 200.
2. Woodman, *Arctic Convoys*, pp. 200–1.
3. Irving, *Destruction of Convoy PQ-17*, pp. 37–8.
4. Irving, *Destruction of Convoy PQ-17*, pp. 50–1, taken from Lieutenant Douglas Fairbanks, Jr., USNR: 'Cruiser Covering Force June 25 to July 8, 1942'.
5. Douglas TBD Devastator, wikipedia.org/wiki/TBD_Devastator, accessed 6 March 2012.
6. Characteristics of aircraft aboard HMS *Victorious* and USS *Wasp*:

Aircraft	Speed	Range	Armament
Sea Hurricane	340mph/547km/h	600mi/965km	4 x 20mm cannon
Albacore	140mph/225km/h	930mi/1,497km	2–3 x .303in. MG, 1 x 1,670lb torpedo
F4F Wildcat	331mph/531km/h	845mi/1,360km	4 x .5in. MG
Vindicator	251mph/404km/h	630mi/1,014km	2 x .3in. MG, 1 x 1,000lb bomb
Devastator	206mph/331km/h	435mi/700km	2 x .3in. MG, 1 x 1,250lb torpedo

7. Irving, *Destruction of Convoy PQ-17*, p. 19.
8. Woodman, *Arctic Convoys*, p. 201.
9. Irving, *Destruction of PQ-17*, pp. 65–6.
10. The caution of *P.614*'s captain may have due to the fact that his boat was one of four built for the Turkish Navy but retained by the Royal Navy when the war started.
11. Wragg, *Sacrifice for Stalin*, p. 144.
12. *Joseph P. Hartwell, *Aerial Predator: The Life of Josef 'Pips' Priller* (Boulder, CO: Air Force Academy Press, 1992), p. 129.
13. Woodman, *Arctic Convoys*, pp. 204–5.
14. Irving, *Destruction of Convoy PQ-17*, p. 105; Woodman, *Arctic Convoys*, p. 207.
15. Woodman, *Arctic Convoys*, pp. 208–9.
16. Irving, *Destruction of Convoy PQ-17*, p. 107.
17. *William H. Crowdon, *Brave Cruisers: The Cruiser Covering Force at the Battle of Bear Island* (London: Collins, 1958), p. 90.
18. *Franklin R. Miller, *Treason on the Troubador: Mutiny in the Face of the Enemy* (Annapolis: Naval Society Press, 1980), p. 138. The mutineers were returned to the United States at the conclusion of the Treaty of Dublin and the American citizens among them successfully prosecuted for treasonously aiding and abetting an enemy in wartime.
19. *Alexander Stuart, *Convoy Disaster* (Aberdeen: Highland University, 1963), p. 221.
20. Irving, *Destruction of Convoy PQ-17*, p. 214.
21. Irving, *Destruction of Convoy PQ-17*, pp. 184–6.
22. Wragg, *Sacrifice for Stalin*, pp. 148–9.

23. Tsouras, *Book of Military Quotations*, p. 27.
24. A comparison of armour on the German and American cruisers at the Battle of Bear Island:

	Belt	Turret	Deck
Lützow/Scheer	3.1in. (80mm)	5.5in. (140mm)	1.8in. (45mm)
Wichita	6.4in. (160mm)	8.0in. (200mm)	2.25in. (57mm)
Tuscaloosa	5.0in. (130mm)	5–6.0in. (130–150mm)	3.0in. (76mm)

25. *Crowdon, *Brave Cruisers*, pp. 83–4.
26. wikipedia.org 'Battle of Drøbak Sound', accessed 3 March 2012.
27. *Edwin Markham, *On HMS London at the Battle of Bear Island* (London: Charing Cross Publishers, 1983), p. 93.
28. *Hartwell, *Aerial Predator*, pp. 153–6.

Chapter 6, **The Battle of 20° East**

1. *Rudolf Schumdt, *In the Wolfsschanze with Hitler: As Told by his Chief Adjutant* (New York: Harper & Doubleday, 1956), p. 232.
2. *Yelena Markova, *Hard as Men: Soviet Women in the War with Germany* (Moscow: Progress, 1978), p. 265.
3. *Schumdt, *Wolfsschanze*, p. 233.
4. 10th U-Boat Flotilla, wikipedia.org/wiki/10th_U-boat_Flotilla, accessed 5 March 2012.
5. *Samuel Morison, *The Battle That Won the War for Germany* (Annapolis: Naval Society Press, 1955), p. 299.
6. *Morison, *The Battle That Won the War for Germany*, p. 370.
7. *Richard Sullivan, *USS Wainwright: Hero of the Battle of Bear Island* (Annapolis: Naval Association Press, 1963), p. 189.
8. *Steven J. Yablonsky, *The Cruiser Action at The Battle of 20° East* (Philadelphia: Appleton, 1986), p. 157.
9. *James R. Edison, *Rolf Carls: The Knightly Admiral* (London: Castlemere Publishers Ltd), p. 311. Carls's rescue of so many British and American sailors made him the object of professional admiration in both countries to which he was welcomed after the war as a guest of their naval societies.
10. *Bruce W. Watson, *The Intelligence Duel at the Battles of Bear Island and Twenty East* (Washington, DC: Defence Intelligence University Press, 2010), p. 245.
11. *Robert C. Giffen, *The Battle of 20° East* (Boston: Liber Scriptus, 1952), p. 233.
12. Pope, *73 North*, p. 184.
13. *Dudley Patterson, *The Big George: The Story of the Battleship, USS Washington* (Norfolk, VA: Warships Press, 1955), p. 93. The *Washington* was the only battleship in WWII to sink two enemy battleships, one in each theatre of war. Off Guadalcanal in 1943 it sank the IJN *Kirishima* without taking a single hit.
14. *Hartwell, *Aerial Predator*, p. 142.
15. *Morison, *The Battle That Won the War for Germany*, p. 290.
16. Lieutenant David McCampbell would go on to become the US Navy's top-scoring ace of World War II.
17. *Wilson J. Johnson, *Duel of the Titans: Washington versus Tirpitz* (New York: Gotham Publishers, 1960), p. 322.
18. *Morison, *The Battle That Won the War for Germany*, p. 376.
19. *Gerhardt von Kitzengen, *Der Schalcht bei 20° Ost* (Frankurt: Markbreit, 1976), p. 299.

20. *Harrison Kitteridge, *For Want of a Nail: The Closure of the Arctic Convoy Route to Russia* (New York: Mason & Chandler, 1995), pp. 322–34.
21. *Schumdt, *Wolfsschanze*, p. 287.

Chapter 7, **Counting the Victories**

1. *Kessel*, literally a kettle, but meaning in a military sense an encircled pocket of enemy forces.
2. Carell, *Stalingrad*, p. 63.
3. Carell, *Hitler Moves East*, p. 511.
4. Benôit Lemay, *Erich von Manstein: Hitler's Master Strategist* (Philadelphia: Casemate, 2011), pp. 250–66.
5. Lemay, *Manstein*, pp. 34–8. *Mischlinge* was the Nazi term for Germans with a Jewish parent or grandparent.
6. Carell, *Stalingrad*, pp. 64–5.
7. Horst Scheibert, *Panzer-Grenadier Division Grossdeutschland* (Warren, MI: Squadron/Signal, 1977), pp. 7, 39–41.
8. NKVD – Narodnyi Kommissariat Vnutrennikh Del – People's Commissariat for Internal Affairs – the Soviet secret police at the time of the Second World War.
9. Jones, *Stalingrad*, pp. 46–7.
10. Remaining at this point were USS *Ranger*, *Saratoga*, *Enterprise* and *Hornet*. The first of the Essex Class, the USS *Essex*, was commissioned in December 1942 and joined the fleet the next year. Also in 1943, the new USS *Yorktown*, *Intrepid* and *Hornet* joined the fleet in the Pacific. *Yorktown* and *Hornet* were named for the original ships lost at the battles of Midway and the Santa Cruz Islands.
11. *Edward W. Pruitt, *Strategic Command Decisions of World War II* (Washington, DC: Center for Military History, 1962), pp. 138–40.
12. Carell, *Stalingrad*, p. 63.
13. Jones, *Stalingrad*, pp. 23, 25.
14. Homer, tr. Robert Fagles, *The Iliad* (New York: Viking, 1990), 9.1–8.
15. Philipp von Boeselager, *Valkyrie: The Plot to Kill Hitler* (London: Phoenix, 2009), p. 72.
16. Matthew Hughes & Chris Mann, *Inside Hitler's Germany: Life Under the Third Reich* (New York: MJF Books, 2000), p. 80.
17. Boeselager, *Valkyrie*, p. 74.
18. Chuikov, *Battle for Stalingrad*, pp. 18–19.
19. Jones, *Stalingrad*, p. 39.
20. Not to be confused with Rostov Veliki (Rostov the Great), a medieval city north of Moscow.
21. Carell, *Stalingrad*, p. 74.
22. Carell, *Stalingrad*, p. 78.
23. *Franz Halder, *Decision at Werewolf* (Frankfurt: Schiller, 1960), pp. 35–9.
24. *Erich von Manstein, *Desperate Victories* (New York: Steindorf, 1963), p. 131.
25. Craig, *Enemy at the Gates*, pp. 19–20.
26. Carell, *Hitler Moves East*, pp. 583–4.
27. Earl E. Zeimke, *Stalingrad to Berlin* (New York: Barnes & Noble, 1996), pp. 34, 39. Tank armies were made up of tank and mechanized corps, equivalent to panzer and panzergrenadier divisions.
28. Chuikov, *Battle for Stalingrad*, p. 31.

29. Stalin to Churchill, 23 July 1942, *Works*, Vol. 17, 1942, www.revolutionary democracy.org/Stalin/v17_1942.htm; accessed 30 March 2012.
30. Carell, *Hitler Moves East*, p. 587.
31. Chuikov, *Battle for Stalingrad*, pp. 33–6.
32. Jones, *Stalingrad*, p. 41.
33. V. I. Stalin, *Sochineniia*, Vol. 15 (Moscow, 1977), pp. 110–11.
34. *Gill, 'Into the Caucasus', pp. 150–1.

Chapter 8, 'Those Crazy Mountain Climbers'

1. *Edwin R. Unger, *Admiral Canaris: Master of Military Intelligence* (London: Blackfriars, 1980), p. 211.
2. *Vernon T. Nelson, 'Betrayal of the German Navy', *Naval Society Journal*, Vol. XX, No. 3, June 1970.
3. A marcher land is a hostile border area between two states such as the border between England and Scotland, which was called the 'Disputed Land' for centuries as each side raided the other.
4. *Mehmet Iconoglu, *Turkey and the German Alliance* (Cambridge: Massachusetts University Press, 1972), pp. 83–5.
5. Chuikov, *Battle for Stalingrad*, pp. 42–3.
6. Chuikov, *Battle for Stalingrad*, pp. 38, 47.
7. Chuikov, *Battle for Stalingrad*, pp. 51–2.
8. Beevor, *Stalingrad*, pp. 99–100.
9. Jones, *Stalingrad*, p. 29.
10. Beevor, *Stalingrad*, p. 97.
11. 'A Hoax at the Soviet oilfields', www.germanmilitaryhistory.com/blog/51608-a-hoax-at-soviet-oil-fields, accessed 13 March 1942.
12. *Baron Adrian von Fölkersam, *Green Devils: The Brandenburg Regiment in the Second World War* (London: Greenhill, 1985), p. 93. This book is considered the authoritative account of the German special forces in World War II and was the type of military book gem that Greenhill Books editor/owner, Lionel Leventhal, the grand old man of British military publishing, was famous for bringing to the English-speaking readership.
13. Carell, *Hitler Moves East*, pp. 557–8.
14. David Glantz, *To the Gates of Stalingrad: Soviet–German Combat Operations, April–August 1942* (Lawrence, KS: University of Kansas, 2009), p. 419.
15. Glantz, *To the Gates of Stalingrad*, pp. 429–31.
16. *Boris Oblomov, *Monster: The Life of Lavrenti Beria* (Boulder, CO: Eastview Press, 1993), pp. 290–2.
17. Carell, *Hitler Moves East*, p. 559.
18. *William S. Johnson, *Hoist on Their Own Petard: The German Use of Soviet Equipment in World War II* (London: Charing Cross Road Publishers, 1966), pp. 153–66.
19. *Alfredo Coletti, *Soaring Roman Eagles: The Alpini in the Caucasus* (New York: Frederick, Bolton & Myers, 1966), p. 156. In appreciation of this assistance, the Germans emblazoned their Caucasus mountain fighting badge with the image of an Alpini mule.
20. *Manfried von Sulzbach, *Conquering the Caucasus: German Mountain Troops in Action* (Warren, MI: Squadron/Signal Publications, 1967), p. 122.
21. *Coletti, *Roman Eagles*, p. 157.

22. Hans Ulrich Rudel, *Stuka Pilot* (New York: Ballantine, 1958), p. 57.
23. Albert Speer http://forum.axishistory.com/viewtopic.php?f=50&tt=28721&start=0, accessed 17 March 2012.

Chapter 9, **The Terror Raid**

1. Chuikov, *The Battle for Stalingrad*, p. 43.
2. Herbert Selle, 'The German Sixth Army on the Road to Catastrophe', *Military Review*, Volume XXXVII, September 1957, No. 6.
3. Carell, *Stalingrad*, pp. 124–5.
4. Stalin, Works, Vol. 17, 1942, to Roosevelt, 22 August 1942. www.revolutionary democracy.org/Stalin/v17_1942.htm; accessed 30 March 2012.
5. 'Alger Hiss', www.conservapedia.com/Alger_Hiss#cite_note-237, accessed 30 March 2012.
6. Herbert Romerstein and Eric Breindel, *'Reds in the White House'*, A review of *The Venona Secrets: Exposing Soviet Espionage and America's Traitors*, Claremont Institute, Summer 2001.
7. Racey Jordan with Richard L. Stokes, *From Major Jordan's Diaries* (New York: Harcourt Brace, 1952), p. 42.
8. *Aaron C. Davis, 'The Convoy Decision', *Journal of Civil–Military Relations*, Vol. XXXI, No. 12, June 1977, p. 1101.
9. Victor Nekrasov, *Front-Line Stalingrad* (New York: Fontana/Collins, 1964), p. 43.
10. Nekrasov, *Front-Line Stalingrad*, pp. 61–2.
11. Beevor, *Stalingrad*, pp. 104–5.
12. Jones, *Stalingrad*, p. 57.
13. Wolfram von Richthofen's cousin was the famous Manfred von Richthofen, the greatest German ace of the First World War.
14. David Glantz, *Armageddon in Stalingrad, September-November 1942*, *The Stalingrad Trilogy*, Volume 2 (Lawrence, KS: University of Kansas, 2009), p. 25.
15. Beevor, *Stalingrad*, p. 97.
16. Craig, *Enemy at the Gates*, p. 32.
17. Beevor, *Stalingrad*, pp. 97–8.
18. Carell, *Hitler Moves East*, p. 594.
19. Glantz, *Armageddon in Stalingrad*, p. 17.
20. Jones, *Stalingrad*, pp. 59–61.
21. Glantz, *To the Gates of Stalingrad*, p. 264.
22. Jones, *Stalingrad*, pp. 42–4.
23. *Alexei Suvorov, 'Red Army Mutiny at Stalingrad', *Military Review*, Vol. XXX, No. 12, Dec 1956, p. 55.
24. *Karl Schmidt, 'How Henry Ford won the Battle of Stalingrad', *Military History Review*, Vol. XXX, No. 12, 1957, pp. 199–202,
25. Craig, *Enemy at the Gates*, p. 10.
26. Beevor, *Stalingrad*, p. 113.

Chapter 10, **New Commanders All Round**

1. *Gill, 'Into the Caucasus', p. 154.
2. *Gill, 'Into the Caucasus', p. 153.
3. Beevor, *Stalingrad*, p. 117.

4. Craig, *Enemy at the Gates*, p. 78.
5. Gerhard Engel, *At the Heart of the Reich: The Secret Diary of Hitler's Army Adjutant* (London: Greenhill, 2005), p. 131.
6. Glantz, *Armageddon in Stalingrad*, p. 545.
7. Carell, *Hitler Moves East*, p. 577.
8. Beevor, *Stalingrad*, pp. 123–4.
9. *Bennett C. Archer, *The Battle for Sukhumi 1942*, Battle Study No. 137 (London: Peregrine, 2012), p. 77.
10. *Boris Oblomov, *Monster: The Life of Lavrenti Beria* (Boulder, CO: Eastview Press, 1993), p. 321.
11. *Archer, *Sukhumi*, pp. 94–6.
12. *Samuel Morison, *Gallant Sailor: The Life of Admiral Sergei Gorshkov* (Annapolis: Naval Society Press, 1955), p. 198.
13. *Gerhard Engel, *The Hitler I Served: The Story of Hitler's Army Adjutant* (London: Greenhill, 1993), p. 121.
14. Stalin, *Works*, Vol. 17, 1942, to Churchill, 7 September 1942. www.revolutionary democracy.org/Stalin/v17_1942.htm; accessed 30 March 2012.
15. Craig, *Enemy at the Gates*, pp. 79–80.
16. *Gill, 'Into the Caucasus', pp. 156–7.
17. *John R. Wilson, *The Wehrmacht's Foreign Legion* (London: Greenhill, 1985), p. 211.
18. *Peter G. Tsouras, 'Killing the Red Tsar'.
19. Sverdlovsk's name before the Revolution was Yekaterinburg, named after its founder, Catherine the Great. It was here that the Bolsheviks murdered the Romanov Imperial family. Its name was changed to Sverdlovsk after the name of a prominent Bolshevik.
20. Vassili Zaitsev, *Notes of a Russian Sniper* (London: Frontline, 2009), pp. 1–2, 9, 12.
21. Chuikov, *The Battle for Stalingrad*, pp. 74–6.
22. Chuikov, *The Battle for Stalingrad*, p. 78.
23. Carell, *Stalingrad*, p. 138.
24. Jones, *Stalingrad*, pp. 107–15.
25. Glantz, *Armageddon in Stalingrad*, pp. 125–9.
26. Glantz, *Armageddon in Stalingrad*, p. 134.

Chapter 11, **Der Rattenkrieg**

1. *Stephen J. Haithwaite, *German Airborne Operations in the Caucasus: The Battle for Grozny*, Battle Study No. 144 (London: Peregrine, 2001) p. 34.
2. Chuikov, *The Battle for Stalingrad*, p. 99.
3. Jones, *Stalingrad*, pp. 118–19.
4. Chuikov, *The Battle for Stalingrad*, p.101.
5. Zaitsev, *Notes of a Russian Sniper*, pp. 12–13.
6. *Archibald Perry, *Treason & Atrocities: Germany's Collaborators in World War II* (London: Blackheath Publishers, 1966), pp. 233–4.
7. *Ewald von Kleist, *Caucasus Victory* (Frankfurt: Sandvoss, 1955), pp. 239–42.
8. Engel, *At the Heart of the Reich*, pp. 133–4.
9. Earl E. Ziemcke, *Stalingrad to Berlin: The German Defeat in the East* (New York: Barnes & Noble, 1996), pp. 32–3.
10. Glantz, *Armageddon in Stalingrad*, p. 137.

11. Craig, *Enemy at the Gates*, p. 111.
12. *Guy R. Williams, *Hitler and His Generals* (New York: Veni, Vidi, Vici, 1976), p. 199.
13. Jonathan Trigg, *Hitler's Jihadis: Muslim Volunteers of the Waffen-SS* (Stroud: History Press, 2008), p. 47.
14. Beevor, *Stalingrad*, p. 152.
15. Beevor, *Stalingrad*, pp. 221–3.
16. *Feldgrau* (field grey) was the colour of the German uniform. It was actually adopted in 1954 by the East German People's Army (Volksarmee) which was at pains to explain that it was not really *Feldgrau* but *Steingrau* (stone grey), a case of 'What's in a name?'
17. *Rupert Graf von Hentzau, *Hitler, Manstein, and the High Command: Decision on the Volga* (London: Greenhill, 1992), pp. 239–41.
18. Benoît Lemay, *Erich von Manstein: Hitler's Master Strategist* (Philadelphia: Casemate, 2011), p. 392.
19. *Albert Tomlinson, *The Stalingrad Plot Against Hitler* (New York: Veni, Vidi, Vici, 1977), p. 290.
20. Lemay, *Manstein*, p. 292.
21. *Alexander Stahlberg, *Serving with Manstein on the Volga: The Memoirs of his Military Assistant* (London: Greenhill, 1985), p. 193.
22. Lemay, *Manstein*, p. 293.

Chapter 12, 'Danke Sehr, Herr Roosevelt!'

1. Zaitsev, *Notes of a Russian Sniper*, p. 54.
2. Zaitsev, *Notes of a Russian Sniper*, p. 59.
3. *Ranjit Singh, *The Indian Corps in the Battle of Baku* (New Dehli: Armed Forces Publishers, 1975), pp. 155–60.
4. Stalin, *Works*, Vol. 17, 1942, to Roosevelt, 7 October 1942. www.revolutionary democracy.org/Stalin/v17_1942.htm; accessed 30 March 2012.
5. *Mason C. Wilkenson, *Roosevelt and Soviet Aid: The Art of the Possible* (New York: Stafford & Sons, 1962), pp. 233–4.
6. Erich von Manstein, *Lost Victories* (London: Collins, 1958), pp 268–9.
7. *Helmut Graf von Kitzingen und Langheim, *Hitler und Manstein* (Frankurt: Ritterlich, 1977), pp. 339–41.
8. Bloody Sunday, 22 January 1905, a squadron of Cossack cavalry was ordered by a local official to charge and disperse a peaceful march on the Winter Palace in St Petersburg to present a petition to Tsar Nicholas II. The tsar was not even present in the city and had no hand in the tragedy at all. Nevertheless, it sparked the 1905 Revolution that was only barely suppressed but which served in effect as a rehearsal for the 1917 Revolution.
9. *Dale M. Patterson, *The Stalingrad Plot Against Stalin* (Boulder, CO: Eastview Press, 1999), p. 146.
10. Chuikov, *The Battle for Stalingrad*, p. 185.
11. Beevor, *Stalingrad*, p. 206.
12. *Jason R. Smith, 'A Masterpiece of Deception and Logistics: The Counter-Offensive Build-up for Operation Uranus', *Military Review*, June 1976,
13. *Helmut Ratzinger, *The Road to Astrakhan: A Soldier with 1st Panzer Army* (New York: Kingston, 1988), pp. 188–9.

14. The rank of *Oberjäger* was a variation of the rank *Oberschutze*, equivalent to private first class and awarded to a soldier who had distinguished himself but was not thought suitable for the first NCO grade of *Gefreiter* (corporal). For Pohl the rank was recognition of his deadly efficiency as a sniper.

15. *Friedrich Pohl, *A Sniper at Stalingrad* (London: Greenhill, 1980), p. 23.

16. Mungo Melvin, *Manstein: Hitler's Greatest General* (New York: Thomas Dunne, 2010), p. 289.

17. Manstein, *Lost Victories*, p. 287.

18. *Henning von Tresckow, *Desperate Days* (London: Greenhill, 1988), p. 211.

19. Melvin, *Manstein*, p. 289,

20. *Paul H. Vivian, '4th Panzer Army in the Battle of Stalingrad', *Military History Review*, July 1992, p. 32. Both the XIV and XLVIII Panzer Corps had participated in the late October assaults in Stalingrad; at that time they had about 300 tanks. By the time each had been redeployed on the flanks, each had fewer than 100 tanks, putting them at the normal strength of a panzer division.

21. Zaitsev, *Notes of a Russian Sniper*, pp. 157–8.

22. Manstein, *Lost Victories*, p. 271.

23. Joachim Fest, *Plotting Hitler's Death*, 289–90.

24. *Werner Maria Pohl, *Ten Righteous Men of Germany* (Berlin: Sandvoss, 1997), p. 310.

Chapter 13, **Der Totenritt bei Leninsk**

1. *Ivan I. Chonkin, *The Life and Extraordinary Adventures of Georgi Zhukov* (New York: Paladin, 1978), pp. 331–2.

2. *Walther von Seydlitz-Kurzbach, *Command Decisions in the Stalingrad Campaign* (Potsdam: Wehrmacht Press, 1955), p. 199.

3. Carell, *Stalingrad*, p. 158.

4. In Napoleon's retreat from Moscow in 1812 his starving, freezing army attempted to cross the Beresina River over a few makeshift bridges. Discipline broke down as a mass of stragglers jammed onto the last bridge as the Russians poured artillery into them. The French lost as many as 20,000 men and a large number of camp followers. To this day Beresina is a French term for military disaster.

5. Jones, *Stalingrad*, p. 241.

6. Craig, *Enemy at the Gates*, pp. 194–5.

7. *Christopher Reese, *The Cavalry to the Rescue: The LX Panzer Corps in the Battle for Stalingrad*, Great Fighting Forces Series (London: Peregrine, 2002), p. 77.

8. Beevor, *Stalingrad*, p. 249.

9. *Georgi Zhukov, *Operation Uranus and the Battle for Stalingrad* (Moscow: Russian Armed Forces Press, 1966), p. 221. The RAFP had an active English-language publishing division that earned it considerable profits in the West by offering excellent translations of major works by senior officers. The works were highly respected since by that time there was no official editing of the author's words.

10. Carell, *Stalingrad*, p. 161.

11. Erhard Raus, ed. Peter G. Tsouras, *Panzers on the Eastern Front: General Erhard Raus and his Panzer Divisions in Russia 1941–1945* (London: Greenhill, 2002), p. 121.

12. Beevor, *Stalingrad*, p. 259.

13. *Ernst Thalmann, *I served with von Seydlitz: The Account of a Signal Soldier in 6th Army Headquarters* (London: Charing Cross, 1961), p. 177.
14. Carell, *Stalingrad*, pp. 604–5.
15. *Erich von Manstein, *Decision on the Volga* (New York; World, 1955), p. 322.
16. Carell, *Hitler Moves East*.
17. Rudel, *Stuka Pilot*, pp. 131–2.

Chapter 14, 'Manstein is Coming!'

1. *Valentin V. Petrochenkov, *The Tragic Hero: Chuikov at Stalingrad* (London: Coopersmith, 1977), pp. 311–14.
2. Combat pilots of the Red Air Force were often referred to as Red Falcons.
3. *Albert Speer, *Making War Feed War* (Frankfurt: Sandvoss, 1966), pp. 339–42.
4. *Manstein, *Decision on the Volga*, p. 388. Since Hoth commanded only one panzer and one infantry corps in 4th Panzer Army, Seydlitz with the far larger force was put in command of both armies despite his being junior to Hoth.
5. *Nikita S. Khrushchev, *The Crimes of Stalin: His Rise and Fall* (Moscow: Progress, 1965), p. 304,
6. *Carl F. Goerdeler, *To Remove a Tyrant* (London: Greenhill, 1985), 316–18.
7. Raus, *Panzers on the Eastern Front*, p. 127.
8. Raus, *Panzers on the Eastern Front*, p. 128.
9. *Mason N. Dixon, *The German LX Panzer Corps at Stalingrad*, Elite Formations 98 (London: Peregrine, 2005), pp. 77–9.
10. *Nigel R. Nicholson, *Stalin and Zhukov: A Study in Command Relationship* (London: Collins, 1966), p. 332.
11. Tsouras, *Book of Military Quotations*, p. 314.
12. *Walther von Hünersdorff, *Panzer Battle* (Frankfurt: Altstein, 1965), p. 211.
13. Raus, *Panzers on the Eastern Front*, p. 128
14. Craig, *Enemy at the Gates*, p. 241.
15. Peter G. Tsouras, ed., *Fighting in Hell: The German Ordeal on the Eastern Front*, (London: Greenhill, 1995), pp. 78–82.
16. Alfred Novotny, *The Good Soldier: From Austrian Social Democracy to Communist Captivity with a Soldier of Panzer-Grenadier Division 'Grossdeutschland'* (Bedford, PA: Aberjona Press, 2003), pp. 44–7.
17. Erich von Manstein, *Lost Victories* (St Paul, MN: Zenith Press, 2004), pp. 361–2.
18. *Gerhard Engel, *Scenes from the Werewolf* (London: Greenhill, 1992), pp. 220–1.
19. Raus, *Panzers on the Eastern Front*, p. 168.
20. Craig, *Enemy at the Gates*, p. 241.
21. Raus, *Panzers on the Eastern Front*, p. 169.
22. *Eugene R. Wilson, *Disaster at Kalach* (New York: Hudson Publishers, 1977), pp. 321–2. The 66th Army had already been largely destroyed when the Germans had broken through the pocket and by 11th Army.

Chapter 15, Coda

1. *Paul McClellan, *Molotov: The Life of the Red Diplomat* (Vancouver: King's College British Columbia, 1988), p. 332.
2. *Sergei A. Alexandrov, *They Met at Brest-Litovsk* (Moscow: Voenizdat Press, 1968), pp. 92–6.
3. *Pohl, *A Sniper at Stalingrad*, p. 177.

4. *Vassili Zaitsev, *The Last Bullet was for the Motherland* (London: Greenhill, 1980), p. 238. This book and Pohl's above were issued by Greenhill at the same time, a coup for the publisher who was actually able to host both Zaitsev and Pohl at the same London reception. It was harder to get Pohl to come out of his self-imposed anonymity in the mountains of Southern Argentina where he settled after the war to escape the vengeance of die-hard Nazis.

5. *Tom Rafferty, *Double Shot: The Perfect Kill* (New York: Soldier Press, 1988), p. 239.

6. *Zaitsev, *Last Bullet*, p. 240.

Bibliography

Bekker, Cajus, *Hitler's Naval War* (New York: Zebra Books, 1977)

Beevor, Anthony, *Stalingrad: The Fateful Siege 1942–1943* (New York: Penguin, 1999)

Boeselager, Phillip von, *Valkyrie: The Plot to Kill Hitler* (London: Phoenix, 2009)

Carell, Paul, *Hitler Moves East 1941–1943* (New York: Bantam, 1967)

——, *Stalingrad: The Defeat of the German 6th Army* (Atlglen, PA: Schiffer, 1993)

Chuikov, Vasili Ivanovich, *The Battle for Stalingrad* (New York: Holt, Rinehart and Winston, 1964)

Craig, William, *Enemy at the Gates: The Battle for Stalingrad* (New York: Penguin, 2001)

Doenitz, Karl, *Ten Years and Twenty Days* (New York: Leisure Books, 1959)

Dunn, Walter S., *Hitler's Nemesis: The Red Army 1930–1945* (Mechanicsburg, PA: Stackpole, 1994)

Engel, Gerhard, *At the Heart of the Reich: The Secret Diary of Hitler's Adjutant* (London: Greenhill, 2005)

Galland, Adolf, *The First and the Last: The Rise and Fall of the Luftwaffe: 1939–1945* (New York: Ballantine, 1965)

Gewarth, Robert, *Hitler's Hangman: The Life of Heydrich* (New Haven, CT: Yale University Press, 2011)

Gill, John H., 'Into the Caucasus: The Turkish Attack on Russia, 1942', in Peter G. Tsouras, ed. *Third Reich Victorious: Alternate Decisions of World War II* (London: Greenhill, 2002)

Glantz, David, *Armageddon in Stalingrad, September–November 1942* (Lawrence, KS: Kansas University Press, 2009)

——, *To the Gates of Stalingrad: Soviet–German Combat Operations, April–August 1942* (Lawrence, KS: Kansas University Press, 2009)

Hoffmann, Peter. *Stauffenberg: A Family History, 1905–1944* (Montreal: McGill-Queen's University Press, 2003)

Hughes, Matthew and Mann, Chris, *Inside Hitler's Germany: Life Under the Third Reich* (New York: MJF Books, 2000)

Irving, David, *The Destruction of Convoy PQ-17* (New York: Simon & Schuster, 1968)

Jones, Michael K., *Stalingrad: How the Red Army Triumphed* (Barnsley, South Yorkshire: Pen & Sword, 2007)

Jukes, Geoffrey, *Stalingrad to Kursk: Triumph of the Red Army* (Barnsley, South Yorkshire, Pen & Sword, 2011)

Klapdor, Ewald, *Viking Panzers: The 5th SS Tank Regiment in the East in World War II* (Mechanicsburg, PA: Stackpole, 2011)

Lemay, Benoît, *Erich von Manstein: Hitler's Master Strategist* (Philadelphia, PA: Casemate, 2010)

Manstein, Erich von, *Lost Victories: The War Memoirs of Hitler's Most Brilliant General* (New York: Zenith Press, 2004)

Melvin, Mungo, *Manstein: Hitler's Greatest General* (New York: Thomas Dunne, 2010)

Merridale, Catherine, *Ivan's War: Life and Death in the Red Army, 1939–1945* (New York: Metropolitan, 2006)

Nekrasov, Victor, *Front-Line Stalingrad* (New York: Fontana/Collins, 1964)

Probert, H. A., *The Rise and Fall of the German Air Force* (New York: St. Martin's Press, 1983)

Raeder, Erich, *Grand Admiral: The Personal Memoir of the Commander in Chief of the German Navy from 1935 Until His Final Break with Hitler in 1943* (New York: Da Capo Press, 2001)

Rudel, Hans Ulrich, *Stuka Pilot* (New York: Ballantine Books, 1958)

Sebag-Montefiore, Hugh, *Enigma: The Battle for the Code* (New York: John Wiley & Sons, 2000)

Trevor-Roper, Hugh, ed., *Hitler's Table Talk, 1941–1944* (New York: Engima Books, 2003)

Trigg, Jonathan, *Hitler's Jihadis: Muslim Volunteers of the Waffen-SS* (Stroud: History Press, 2008)

Tsouras, Peter G., *The Great Patriotic War: An Illustrated History of Total War: The Soviet Union and Germany, 1941–1945* (London: Greenhill Books, 1992)

——, ed., *Fighting in Hell: The German Ordeal on the Eastern Front* (London: Greenhill Books, 1995)

——, ed. *Panzers on the Eastern Front: General Erhard Raus and his Panzer Divisions in Russia 1941–1945* (London: Greenhill Books, 2002)

Weeks, Albert L., *Russia's Life-Saver: Lend-Lease Aid to the USSR in World War II* (Lanham, MD: Lexington Books, 2010)

Woodman, Richard, *Arctic Convoys 1941–1945* (Barnsley, South Yorkshire: Pen & Sword, 2011)

Woodward, David, *The Tirpitz and the Battle for the North Atlantic* (New York: Berkley Publishing, 1953)

Wragg, David, *Sacrifice for Stalin: The Cost and Value of the Arctic Convoys Re-Assessed* (Barnsley, South Yorkshire: Pen & Sword, 2005)

Zaitsev, Vassili, *Notes of a Russian Sniper* (London: Frontline Books, 2009)

Ziemke, Earl F., *Stalingrad to Berlin: The German Defeat in the East* (New York: Barnes & Noble, 1996)